PENGUIN CLASSICS

WILLEHALM

FOUNDER EDITOR (1944–64): E. V. RIEU

WOLFRAM VON ESCHENBACH was the greatest of the medieval German narrative poets. Very little is known about his life, but it is generally accepted that he belonged to a Bavarian family of the lower nobility, that he may have served a Franconian lord and that for the better part of his creative period he enjoyed the patronage of the great medieval German maecenas Hermann, Landgrave of Thuringia. He probably died between 1220 and 1230.

Although Wolfram left some brilliant lyric poems, chiefly dawn songs of his youth, it is in his narrative poems, – Parzival, the unfinished Willehalm and so-called Titurel fragments – that his claim to be a poet of world stature lies. Parzival, on which Richard Wagner based his music-drama Parsifal, is a romance of self-perfection in knighthood, in which both the chivalric and the spiritual receive their due; Titurel narrates in an elegiac measure the story of Sigune and Schionatulander prior to their appearances in Parzival; Willehalm is a crusading poem with epic qualities which tells the story of the famous William of Toulouse.

DR MARION GIBBS was born in 1940 in Essex. She graduated with an Honours Degree in German from the University of London (Bedford College) in 1961 and subsequently wrote theses for the degrees of M.A. and Ph.D. of the same university. In 1964 she was appointed to the staff of Royal Holloway College, University of London, where she is now Reader in German. Her research is primarily in the medieval field, although her teaching also covers broader areas of German language and literature. Her published works are Wiplichez Wibes Reht, A Study of the Women Characters in the Works of Walfram von Eschenbach and Narrative Art in Wolfram's 'Willehalm', as well as a number of articles on Wolfram von Eschenbach. She was married to the late Ralph Tymms, Professor Emeritus of German in the University of London.

Professor Sidney M. Johnson was born in New Haven, Connecticut, in 1924. He did both his undergraduate work (B.A. 1944) and his graduate work (M.A. 1948, Ph.D. 1953) at Yale University, finishing with a dissertation on Wolfram von Eschenbach's *Willehalm*. He taught, first as an Instructor, later a full Professor, at the University of Kansas in Lawrence from 1951 to 1965. From 1965 to 1972 he was Professor and Chairman of German at Emory University in Atlanta. Since then he has been at Indiana University in Bloomington, first as Professor and Chairman of Germanic Languages (1972–8) and now as Professor of Germanic Studies. In 1978–9 he directed a study programme at the University of Hamburg and he has held visiting summer appointments at the universities of Colorado and Georgia. He has published a number of articles, primarily on Wolfram von Eschenbach, in professional journals. He is married with three sons.

In addition to *Willehalm*, Marion Gibbs and Sidney Johnson have collaborated on a translation with notes and commentary of Wolfram's *Titurel* and *Songs* (published in one volume in 1988) and of the medieval German *Kudrun* (1992).

WOLFRAM
VON ESCHENBACH

WILLEHALM

TRANSLATED BY
MARION E. GIBBS
AND
SIDNEY M. JOHNSON

PENGUIN BOOKS

PENGUIN BOOKS

Published by the Penguin Group
Penguin Books Ltd, 27 Wrights Lane, London W8 5TZ, England
Penguin Books USA Inc., 375 Hudson Street, New York, New York 10014, USA
Penguin Books Australia Ltd, Ringwood, Victoria, Australia
Penguin Books Canada Ltd, 10 Alcorn Avenue, Toronto, Ontario, Canada M4V 3B2
Penguin Books (NZ) Ltd, 182–190 Wairau Road, Auckland 10, New Zealand

Penguin Books Ltd, Registered Offices: Harmondsworth, Middlesex, England

This translation first published 1984

Translation, Introduction and Notes
Copyright © Marion E. Gibbs and Sidney M. Johnson, 1984
All rights reserved

Printed in England by Clays Ltd, St Ives plc
Set in Aldus (Linotron 202)

CONTENTS

INTRODUCTION

Those who know the name of Wolfram von Eschenbach undoubtedly think first, when it is mentioned, of his *Parzival*,[1] that magnificent early-thirteenth-century courtly epic in which the hero eventually attains the kingship of the fabulous Grail Castle after years of persistent searching. Of course, Parzival's search is not simply for a geographical location, however 'real' the Grail Castle may be. It is also a search for man's proper relationship to God, beginning in ignorance, and passing through disappointment, even antagonism, to the ultimate realization of Divine Love. It is one of the great quests of world literature, acted out in the idealized world of the courtly romance, but unlike its Old French source, the unfinished *Conte du Graal* of Chrétien de Troyes, it is crowned with joyous success.

If one then turns from *Parzival* to *Willehalm*, Wolfram's other major work, and expects to find the same atmosphere or tone, there is bound to be disappointment because *Willehalm* is quite different. To be sure, the same author or narrator is recognizable, interacting with his listeners, commenting on his story with asides (sometimes humorous ones), assuring one and all of the truth of his tale. But the tone is not the same as it is in *Parzival*. The different subject matter, this time the anonymous Old French *chanson de geste*, *La Bataille d'Aliscans*, demands a different tone. *Willehalm* concerns people of steadfast faith in God, not a God-seeker, and it is the tragic consequences of their faith in God and their love for each other that are of prime concern to Wolfram. In *Willehalm* he deals with the harsh realities of knightly life and religious war, and the somewhat more sombre tone of the mature poet is very much in evidence. Not that the picture is completely bleak: there are, after all, lighter moments of comic relief, tender moments of conjugal love and dramatic moments of high tension. Nevertheless, Wolfram himself states:

'There is not much joy in this tale. I should need to be very clever to discover any joy in it . . .' (p. 143). It *is* a serious tale, but as if in compensation, it has a dimension of realism and depth of emotion that go beyond the courtly romance. 'This story is true, though it may be amazing,' Wolfram assures us (p. 19).

THE LANGUAGE AND STYLE OF 'WILLEHALM':
PROBLEMS OF THE TRANSLATOR

There can be little doubt that, even to his contemporaries, Wolfram's language was complex and often elusive. In his literary excursus in *Tristan*,[2] Gottfried von Strassburg referred to 'some friend of the hare' who might come skipping along to lay claim to the laurel wreath of poetry, and he was almost certainly speaking of Wolfram (*Tristan* 4638ff.). When he went on to speak contemptuously of the narrative of 'inventors of wild tales, hired hunters after stories', he was no doubt betraying both his fear of his rival and his personal distaste for a wayward style so different from his own. He may not, however, have been alone in finding Wolfram's work so inaccessible as to require a special commentary to accompany it. That Wolfram was little moved by such criticism is apparent from the lines in *Parzival* which are usually believed to contain his retort. He opens that work with a powerful and complicated image which, he acknowledges, will be too difficult for foolish people to grasp, for they will find it eluding them 'like a startled hare'. Neither in those books of *Parzival* which were probably composed later rather than earlier, nor in his *Willehalm*, does Wolfram seem to be making concessions to his audience. His narrative remains complicated and often idiosyncratic, with a vividness all its own.

The story of Parzival, a tale on an enormous scale, is aptly told in often extravagant language, but *Willehalm* is no less striking, although its tone and message are, as we have said, so different from that of *Parzival*. *Willehalm*, too, is remarkable for its contrasting moods and the way in which Wolfram adapts his narrative style to his material. He is a master of the art of story-telling. He tells of the two mighty battles of Alischanz and describes both the beauty and the horror of the clash of knights in the reality of mortal combat, brave and noble men motivated by love and faith.

Action and movement are juxtaposed to periods of contemplation, when Wolfram speaks of the source of the conflict, the deep personal love of Willehalm and Giburc, and describes it with tenderness and sympathy. A different mood prevails in the episodes which have Rennewart as their central figure, yet there too there is variety, with the near-comedy of this strange young man and his often exaggerated behaviour only a very thin veneer upon a moving history, which reveals itself gradually and never fully. The whole poem, from the prologue on, is imbued with the deeply spiritual awareness which is one of Wolfram's major contributions to the substance of his source (see pp. 233ff. and 273ff.).

For all these moods Wolfram found the language, and one of the chief concerns of the translators has been to attempt to convey the range of his expression and to preserve, as far as possible, something of the vividness of the original. Unless one is much mistaken, Wolfram delighted in language and seems to have revelled in opportunities to demonstrate his mastery of it. For this reason we have not resisted the temptation to employ modern and colloquial vocabulary and expressions where they seem to correspond to the tone of the original. At the other end of the scale, Wolfram almost certainly liked to show his learning by his use of unusual words, technical terms, for example, or foreign phrases. We have tried to match him sometimes in language which may well have sounded pompous, even ludicrously so, to his audience. Where Wolfram peppers his narrative with foreign phrases we have often felt justified in retaining them, for Wolfram is almost certainly wishing to impress his hearers with his knowledge, and delight them with a certain foreign flavour.

His French may not have been particularly good, but he tosses in occasional phrases which we have retained in a modern French form, hoping thus to have captured the slightly nonchalant tone of the original. Sometimes, however, he uses foreign words to designate people and things for which he knows no German term, and we should not wish to apologize for retaining such words as *eskelir*, *amazur* and *emeral*, which Wolfram uses consistently to designate the heathen princes, nor for our adoption of the title *Baruc* for the spiritual leader of the Saracens and *Admirat* as the title for Terramer. Similarly, we have felt that his use of words like *sarjant* and *turkopel* was sufficiently specific for us to retain it, though in some such cases we have added an explanation of the word at its first occurrence, very much as Wolfram himself does on occasions when he knows that his audience may not be familiar with a word or concept. Thus he tells us: 'Setting up camp is called *loger* in French' (p. 123), and he supplies a translation for the French expression he uses on pp. 89–90. 'She was afraid of that *mal voisin*, the wicked neighbour, her brother.' Where he is denoting something quite specific and using a name which he may even have made up or adapted for the purpose, we have kept that name in its original form: thus *achmardi* (p. 208), *pofuz* (p. 181). On the other hand, it would have been impossible to suggest the extent of the influence of Old French on Middle High German as far as the language of chivalry is concerned, and in most cases we have found an English equivalent for the terms relating to fighting and equipment.

Place names presented a particular problem. In *Willehalm*, as in *Parzival*, Wolfram enjoys using exotic names of distant places, but, again, one feels that his geography is decidedly hazy. When he speaks of 'Grikulane' or 'Skandinavia', of 'Kaukasas' or the 'Ganjas', he seems to be groping in his mind for foreign-sounding names with which to designate the distant lands of the heathens and perhaps to mystify his audience. We have retained the spelling of the German text throughout for heathen cities and lands, even where the name seems to be identifying a recognizable location. It is impossible to say with any certainty whether Arabia, Persia and India meant the same to Wolfram and his audience as they do to us, but one would guess that they probably did not. Since names like 'Marroch' and 'Arabi' exist side by side with some less easily identifiable names and others apparently invented by Wolfram, we hope by our consistent decision to have preserved two features of his narrative in this respect: the possibly deliberate vagueness of geography which gives the impression of the vast reaches of heathendom, and the appealing quality of the exotic. In contrast, when Wolfram is speaking of places nearer at hand, one may surely assume that he knows what he is talking about.

Thus we have, for example, identified Wissant and Milan, Laon and Anjou. In this way we have tried to retain what must have been the distinction between the unfamiliar lands of the heathens, and the places associated with the Christians and familiar to Wolfram's audience.

The close relationship between poet and audience – a feature, of course, of narrative composed for oral transmission – is evident in such matters, and it also affects other essential features of Wolfram's style in communicating with his listeners and contributes to the vividness of the poem. From time to time he addresses his audience, demanding a response which may indeed have been forthcoming. Thus, for example, he appeals to them, often at moments of high drama: 'What could the Margrave do when, as if he did not have sorrow enough already, the young man, his sister's son, mentioned such trifling sins and spoke of them in his confession?' (p. 47); 'Would you like to hear now how things are going with that anger you heard about before? Do you want to know who calmed it, how help and high spirits were at hand for the Margrave and how the Roman Queen, loyally and after much heart-searching, placed at his disposal herself and her worldly goods and her favour?' (p. 89); 'Let's see whether mighty Aropatin can find combat there' (p. 189). The poem is full of such examples which imply the dependence of the narrator upon an audience which was listening to his tale and reacting as he went along.

For the sake of this audience, Wolfram sometimes adds familiar details, small touches which perhaps show him making concessions to them, putting this story of strangers in distant times into the terms his listeners would understand. Thus he refers to places near at hand: Nördlingen (p. 150), the Sand in Nuremberg (p. 209) or Beratzhausen (p. 195). On such occasions he is making a comparison with something almost certainly familiar to his listeners. When he makes comparisons which refer to Walther von der Vogelweide (p. 146) or the Emperor Otto (p. 194), for example, he is showing his awareness that his story will be all the more vivid if his audience can relate it to something which they know about.

'Have you ever seen the sun cutting through a foggy day?' he asks (p. 34) and so relies on a familiar experience to express with great vividness the movement of Willehalm as he breaks through the enemy ranks. To describe the splendid appearance of the heathen knights he uses a startling comparison: 'My daughter's doll is not so beautiful,' he says (p. 31), and in using a homely and seemingly incongruous point of reference he achieves a remarkable effect, linking himself as a father with the members of his audience and, with them, conjuring up this vision of these shimmering strangers equipped for battle, a far cry surely from the small girl's toy, which, even so, within its own proportions, may well be splendidly dressed. In somewhat the same manner he describes how the heathen kings Tenebruns and Arofel hammered away at Willehalm like smiths at an anvil (p. 51) or, in a prolonged image, he describes Gorhant's men in terms of house-building (p. 195) and concludes: 'I should not like to have carpenters like that today: I should not be able to pay their wages!'

There are many such instances of Wolfram's vivid, very personal style, and, happily, they do not elude translation. More difficult to handle are other features of his language. The complicated syntax has often proved a problem to the translators, and our intention has been to render the original as faithfully as possible, occasionally inserting words and supplying punctuation – sometimes against the principal editions of the text – where it seemed advisable in order to make the narrative clear to the modern English reader, as opposed to Wolfram's contemporaries, listening to the spoken word and used to doing so. Without doubt, Wolfram von Eschenbach was a master of his art and knew well how to engage the attention of his audience and hold it. He does this, for example, by placing a new noun, a new concept, in isolation, ahead of a statement, as an apostrophe to his hearers, making them sit up perhaps, and wait for what will come. An effective example of this technique occurs on pp. 181–2, where, describing Tibalt's equipment, he introduces the concept of 'salamander'. Following Wolfram's word order, we might have translated: 'Salamander: if I had ever heard that anything was whiter than snow, I could have compared with it all that Tibalt was wearing.' In modern English, however, the effect is lost and the word order awkward, so we hope to have found another, more acceptable way of achieving Wolfram's effect.

Such decisions have to be made again and again, of course, in translating, and one can only hope that one has been true to the whole achievement. In translating a poem composed over seven hundred years ago, one must also frequently admit that one cannot be sure exactly what is meant or what effect is intended. Here, too, one has to be guided by the sense of the whole and of what is most likely in the poet concerned. Thus we were not absolutely certain that on p. 25 Wolfram was thinking of the moulting process – one possible meaning of the noun used there – yet it is so much the kind of image he might have used that we felt justified in using it ourselves here. Similarly, it can only be instinct and a close acquaintance with Wolfram's work that made us feel that, on occasions, Wolfram is using some kind of proverb, or perhaps making up a generalized saying of his own which amounts to a kind of proverb. We have taken the liberty of placing such lines in inverted commas, or of inventing a rhyme to suggest what we believe to have been their function.

Clearly Wolfram himself had one limitation which, happily, we did not share, for it *must* be easier to write in continuous prose than to compose in rhyming couplets. On the other hand, when Wolfram occasionally inserts a filler to complete a rhyme, the resulting prose translation may seem repetitive or awkward, but this is probably inevitable in any attempt at a precise rendering. If it is possible to forget that one is *reading* and imagine that one is *listening* to an oral presentation, one will perhaps grasp those aspects of this great poem which cannot be expressed in our rendering. In embarking on such a translation we were motivated by the wish to make this work available to a wider audience as well as by the hope that, though sacrifices would have to be made, the overall achievement would remain intact.

There are three editions of the Middle High German text:

1. Karl Lachmann, *Wolfram von Eschenbach*, Berlin, 1833; 6th edition, Berlin/Leipzig, 1926, reprinted 1965, pp. 421–640.
2. Albert Leitzmann, *Wolfram von Eschenbach*, Halle, 1905–6, 2 vols. (= *Altdeutsche Textbibliothek*, Nos. 15 and 16); 5th edition, Tübingen, 1963.

3. Wolfram von Eschenbach, *Willehalm*, nach der gesamten Überlieferung kritisch herausgegeben von Werner Schröder, Berlin/New York, 1978.

We have used the Lachmann text as the basis for our translation but have occasionally followed the Leitzmann text where it seemed to make better sense. We have also consulted Schröder's text since its appearance and have occasionally referred to it in connection with passages that we found problematical earlier. In a very few instances we have retained in the translation what appeared to be an ambiguity in the text.

Despite the fact that Lachmann's was our basic text, we have followed the spelling of names used by Leitzmann, who is generally consistent in normalizing the spelling. We have used the form of the nominative case consistently, hence 'Giburc', instead of 'Giburg' or 'Gyburg', etc.

Schröder's edition provides an excellent list of all foreign and loan words in *Willehalm*, with their meanings. In addition, there is a list of all proper names and their probable sources and/or equivalents based on the most recent research. These are valuable aids for the interested reader, but since Schröder's edition is probably not readily available, we have appended two lists of names, at least identifying the place or person in respect to function in the poem and noting the first occurrence in each instance.

Feeling that more detailed introductory information to *Willehalm* might be desirable, but perhaps not of immediate interest to every reader, we have placed such an introduction *after* the translation. It may well be more meaningful if it is read after the translation, but we leave that to the reader's discretion.

We have also appended a short list of suggestions for further reading on Wolfram but have confined ourselves to works in English, which are more likely to be accessible to our readers. A more ambitious bibliography on Wolfram and his *Willehalm* could have been very long indeed, and in producing our translation, and for much of the material in the introductions, we are indebted to the many scholars who have written on the subject over the years. It would have been impossible and inappropriate to acknowledge our individual debts on each occasion, but those familiar with the scholarship will readily recognize what we owe to Ludwig Wolff, Bodo Mergell, Joachim Bumke, Werner Schröder and Carl Lofmark among others. There are, of course, other translations of *Willehalm* – notably the recent ones into German by Dieter Kartschoke and Otto Unger, and into English by Charles Passage – and we have consulted them on occasions.

At the same time as making these acknowledgements to scholars with published views on *Willehalm*, we should like to express our thanks to the many friends who, believing that they were invited for a social evening, have found themselves the guinea-pigs for our translation and have often made valuable contributions.

BOOK I

Thou Purity immaculate,
Thou Three yet One,
Creator over all creation,
Thy constant Power is without beginning and endures
without end.
If that Power banishes from my mind thoughts which
lead to the death of my soul, then art Thou my
Father and I Thy child.
Thou who art supremely noble beyond all nobility,
have compassion in Thy Goodness and turn Thy
Pity towards me,
Lord,
no matter how I sin against Thee.
Let me be mindful,
Lord,
of whatever blessings and infinite joy
have fallen to my lot.
I am assuredly Thy child and of Thy lineage,
poor as I am and mighty as Thou art.
Thine own Humanity grants me that kinship.
The Paternoster does indeed call me a
child of Thy Divinity
and acknowledges me as such.
Likewise does Holy Baptism give me an assurance that
has freed me from despair, for I have the certainty
that I am Thy namesake:
Wisdom above all knowledge,
Thou art Christ,
Thus I am a Christian.

No one has ever fathomed the ordering of
Thy Height, Thy Breadth, Thy Depth.
The course of the seven planets, too, is in Thy Hand,
so that they counteract the movement of the heavens.
Air, water, fire and earth are all in Thy Power.
All that surrounds the creatures wild and tame
stands at Thy Command.
Moreover, Thy divine Power has separated the bright day
and the dark night, and has set limits on each of them
through the course of the sun.
There never was Thine equal, nor will there ever be.
The power of all stones, the scent of all herb ,
Thou knowest in every detail.
Thy Spirit has informed the sound and the words of
Holy Scriptures.
My mind feels the force of Thy Presence.
I have remained ignorant of what is written in books
and I am tutored in this way alone: if I have any skill,
it comes from my mind.

May the help of Thy loving Kindness inspire my heart and mind aright and grant me skill enough to praise in Thy Name a knight who never forgot Thee. Even if he merited Thy displeasure by sinful action, Thy Mercy knew how to guide him to works of such a kind that, with manly courage at his disposal and by means of Thy Grace, he was capable of making amends. Thy Help often saved him from peril. He risked a twofold death, of the soul and of the body too, and frequently suffered anguish through the love of a woman.

Landgrave Hermann of Thuringia made this story about him known to me. He is called *en français* Comte Guillaume d'Orange. Let every knight who calls for his aid in time of trouble be assured that he will never be denied it, but that Guillaume will declare that same distress before God.

That doughty, noble intercessor knows every sorrow which can befall a knight. He was often stained with armour himself. His hand was well acquainted with the thong which binds the helmet to the head to keep a knight from paying with his life. Many a lance was broken on his shield, and he was often to be seen in the throng of the enemy. He was born to carry a shield. In France one hears it said that whoever knew how to identify his family maintained that it was equal to the power of any princes throughout the realm. His kinsmen were always the noblest. Apart from the Emperor Charles himself no such noble Frenchman was ever born. Thus his fame was and is outstanding.

You had and still have nobility, O helper,
when in your purity and humility you fought before the
Hand of the Almighty, so that It extended help to you.
O helper, help me and all those who trust in you for help,
since the tales tell us truly that you were
a prince here on earth, as you are in the next world, too.

St Willehalm, my lord, hear my words in your goodness.
My sinful lips cry out to you as a saint.
Since you yourself are freed from all the bonds of hell,
protect me, too, from perdition.

Some people have praised that which I, Wolfram von Eschenbach, have told about Parzival, according to the guidance which I received from his story. There were also many who criticized what I wrote and framed their own words more elegantly.

If God will grant me days enough, I shall tell of love and other grief which in consequence of their devotion men and women have been suffering, since Jesus was plunged into the River Jordan to be baptized. No tale in German tongue can easily match this whole work which I now have in mind. Let him who holds nobility in high esteem invite this tale to his own fireside; it is current among foreigners here. The best Frenchmen are agreed that no sweeter poem was ever composed in dignity and in truth. No interruption or interpolation ever distorted this tale. They told it there: now listen to it here. This story is true, though it may be amazing.

Count Heimrich of Narbonne disinherited all his sons, leaving them neither castles nor estates, nor any of his worldly goods. One of his vassals fought so often for him, that, when that man died in his service, Heimrich adopted his son. Out of affection for the father he had already acted as godfather to that boy. He told his own sons to go out and increase their wealth in whatever lands they might. If they were fit for the service of chivalry, and if Fortune provided them with their proper goals, they would reap many rich rewards.

'If you are prepared to exert yourselves, noble ladies will have rich rewards for you. You will also find a lord somewhere who knows how to reward service with fiefs and other chattels. You should turn your thoughts to ladies to attain high spirits, and involve yourselves in their service. The Emperor Charles is a man of excellence. Put your strong bodies and your handsome youthfulness at his disposal. Unless some grave trouble prevents him, he will heap riches upon you, and his court will gain honour through you. He is the man you should be ready to serve. He will recognize your nobility.' This was his will and his recommendation, and thus they parted from their father.

Now, if you please, let me tell you the names of the heroes, so that you will know them. One was Guillaume, another Bertram, while the third of his sons was called Buov, a handsome and charming man. Heimrich was the fourth, and his excellence adorned many a land. Arnalt and Bernart had to go on this journey, too. The seventh was Gibert, who was likewise courtly and noble.

How many troubles they endured and what joys they derived, and how their manly skill pursued with chivalry the love of women and the favour of their hearts, and how they often spent their time in ways that earned them high renown! Seldom ease, but great discomfort, was the heroes' later lot. They had been sent forth to achieve fame.

I shall save my breath and not tell you about the service of the other brothers, and of how they fared, but shall seize upon the one to whom this story is devoted. This was the man called Willehalm. Alas, that he was not allowed to stay on his father's lands! If he should now come to grief, then the sin would be greater than the credit achieved by Heimrich for his charity towards his godchild. I think it does not balance properly.

You have surely heard before – you do not need to hear that tale again – how such a situation was brought about through chivalry that joy was banished from many a noble heart. Willehalm won the love of Arabel, and because of this innocent people died. She who gave him her love and pledged herself to him in marriage was baptized and took the name of Giburc. What a host of men paid for that with their lives! Her husband, King Tibalt, lamented the loss of her love. His heart plunged violently from joy into sorrow. He mourned his honour and his wife, his cities and his lands as well. His agonized lamentation echoed to the far ends of India: his misery was later made known over there, as well as here in Provence. The waters of the sea cannot contain so many waves as there were people slain because of this. Now a rich crop of sorrow grew up in the field where joy had been cultivated previously. This joy was so flattened and trampled down in truly wretched fashion that it was sheer luck if the Frenchmen have even the seeds of it left today. The buoyant spirits of the heathens sank in the face of overwhelming sorrow.

Margrave Willehalm gained what he thought to be a great blessing. What happened in the meantime, what befell the Christians and the heathens, I shall not mention but shall tell instead of how the army crossed the sea. King Terramer brought it all at the same time across the water, in sailing ships and galleys, in transports and in boats. Any man who wants to boast that he has seen a larger army cannot have done so since that one occasion.

Terramer had summoned his kinsmen and his vassals. To Mahmete, his favourite god, and to his other gods, he often had many honours paid by means of sacrifices, and to them, too, he raised anguished lamentations about Arabel, who named herself Giburc and who, for the sake of the Christian faith, had become the focal point for many eyes through baptism. The noble Queen assumed the Christian way of life, for love of her dear friend and for love of the Almighty.

Terramer, her father, summoned his brother Arofel and the mighty Halzebier, and these two men brought many warships to his aid. They were sincere in their intention. The power of Terramer was immense and extended far and wide, and other kings received their crowns in fief and fealty from him and performed their services to him. The princes of his realm whom he chose to summon came in strength, and many a doughty man came running for his pay. How many thousands of noble Saracens did he enlist! Of those who could be called his men let me indicate the number thus: when that noble King was seen coming ashore from the ships for the sake of King Tibalt, he covered hills and valleys with his men. For this many a Christian paid on the field of Alischanz. Such chivalry was performed there that if one were to give it its proper name it could only be called 'slaughter'.

Whatever I recounted earlier about fighting with sword or spear, of hacking and thrusting, ended in some way other than in death. *This* fighting will settle for nothing less than death and loss of joy. No one was released on his word of honour when one man defeated another for whom high ransom might otherwise have been paid. There was only one hope on either side, and that was manly self-defence. The army of King Terramer and Willehalm's kinsmen resolutely took a chance on gain or loss. Manly desire urged King Tibalt to ride out in strength to recover his love and his lands, for he longed to avenge his loss and his shame. What more can I say, but that his father-in-law Terramer brought to join him many a high-born king, powerful and known for his courage? Mahmete and Tervigant were called upon many times before the battle commenced.

(Terramer was foolish to disdain the man whom his daughter prized so highly. Let me tell you one thing: I would not want to lose as a friend the one whom my daughter had chosen as her beloved.) Willehalm *au court nez*[1] was such a noble Frenchman that, if today a lady were to acquire an equally distinguished knight to serve her for love, it would have to be Willehalm and no other. His father-in-law had no reason to hate him.

Let things now roll on as they must, yet since then days of happiness have dawned from time to time and brought joy with them. Terramer had resolved to move towards Alischanz, where the fighting taught his army such a lesson that he was never happy again. How could such a wise and experienced man behave like that? They were both equally related to him, the renowned Willehalm and Tibalt, Arabel's husband, because of whom he endured heartache through grief for his brother and surrendered many a noble Saracen in tribute to death. A heart turned to flint by a clap of thunder would be moved by this tale.

On to the field of Alischanz came many a new shield, still quite intact but later to be pierced with many holes in battle. Terramer's army needed the length and the breadth of the field when, having disembarked, each man rode to join his unit which he identified by its chivalry. Before a blow was struck or a thrust delivered, there came the noise of trumpets and of many drums.

The sweetness of Giburc turned sour for them, heathens and Christians alike. Now I must tell you with true words of the suffering of good people on that fateful day.

The army of Margrave Willehalm, that handful of men which he was able to muster, could be seen fighting manfully on Alischanz to counter Terramer's invasion. They would not have wanted to miss it. Some of his kinsmen had come to join him, and they too had pledged themselves to serve him through thick and thin; in them he found nothing but loyalty. Thus Witschart and Gerart of Blayes rode beneath his banner, and the Count Palatine Berhtram,[2] who never admitted cowardice into the heart beneath his breast, as was indeed evident on Alischanz. There, too, was the radiant Vivianz, and to the end of my days I should be a stupid ass with regard to my understanding of loyalty if I were not to mourn for him. Alas, that his tender years should have ended in death before he had time to grow a beard! Because of this his whole family became strangers to joy, and with good reason.

Alas, Heimrich of Narbonne, your son's service for the sake of Giburc's love has been rewarded with misery! Such favour as she bestowed on him was paid for dearly, so that the gentle lady had her own share of sorrow.

On earth there occurred a day of loss, and in heaven one of new and special brilliance, when many noble guests flew up to the skies with the angels. They were not deceived in their hope of salvation, those who fought for Willehalm and had come forward with such bold bearing. Let me name more of them. If nobility is glorified by renown and if renown is indicative of nobility, then either one is broad enough to make good fortune complete. Gwigrimanz the Burgundian, and Mile, the Margrave's sister's child, both these princes have come to Orange. There shall be even more noblemen there. I am thinking of the splendid Jozeranz and Huwes of Milan. These four achieved renown here on earth and are now in paradise. Alas, Giburc, you sweet woman, you were purchased at great cost!

The brown-haired Gaudin arrived, too, and Kibelin with the flaxen hair, as well as Gaudiers of Toulouse and Hunas of Saintes. (If you will allow me to do so, I shall adorn this tale with these four men.) They were tremendously renowned, beyond anything one might wish for, so that the fame of the least among them would nevertheless be sufficient for all the people of three lands. This day spelt the end of joy for those women who knew what love was. I am referring to the women who had sent there the menfolk who shielded their joy from grief. If love is true devotion, then the death of many a hero brought misery and suffering to the women at home. I cannot name all those who came to fight for the Margrave, but, counting rich and poor, one can put the number at twenty thousand, when they were all gathered there. The bold Margrave would have liked to have had more of those who gave little quarter to the heathens – men from Provence and Burgundy, and from the actual kingdom of France – when he took the road undauntedly in the direction of destruction. This is how he saw the heathens encamped, so I was told: under many a velvet roof, under many a beautifully coloured silk, and their huts and their tents were lined with taffeta and pitched with silken ropes on the field of Alischanz. Their banners gleamed in costly and exotic stripes, just as the agate does. So many of these banners shone forth that I cannot, alas, tell exactly how many there were. If I want to estimate the heathen tents on the broad reaches of the field, I shall have to tell you that one cannot discern so many stars in the sky. (I am not exaggerating any more than my source directs me to.) Now the heathens realized that the Christians were coming, those men who were purchasing a place in heaven.

The Margrave with his wealth of courage urged his kinsmen to manly bravery, for the sake of God and of justice, to a warlike frame of mind, for the twofold love, for the reward of ladies here on earth and for the song of the angels in heaven.

'Brave men,' he said, 'you should be mindful and not let the heathens revile our faith, for they would rob us of our baptism if they could. Just think what use we should be, if we were to abandon the blessing which we have through the Cross. For, since Thy death was offered on the Cross, Jesus of Nazareth, the evil spirits have fled for ever more. Comrades, you should bear in mind that you are wearing the symbol of Him who saved us from hell. That symbol comes to us as a consolation indeed. Now defend your honour and your land, so that Apolle and Tervigant and the deceitful Mahmete do not trample your baptism underfoot.'

Margrave Willehalm and the Christians heard the sound of many trumpets. And now, however things might turn out, powerful, bold Halzebier, King of Falfunde, had arrived on horseback with all his men. He was riding at the head of many proud soldiers and many a noble amazur.[3] Since they bore the name of prince, it seemed to them a matter of little consequence that renown should come to them in advance of the mass of the army. Many a high-spirited prince came riding up with his men to fight in the service of Halzebier. Thirty thousand doughty foot-soldiers and knights on horseback were numbered among those who supported him. Halzebier came in force. At the same time, those of his troops who bore light arms – the turkopels as they were called – and who were encamped round about, initiated the first action of the battle. No matter how skilfully they pulled many mighty bows, they were thoroughly paid back for their shooting and their drawing, their feinting and their fleeing, when later the Christians had to offer resistance, and it was right that they should do so. The heathens held a council of war and decided on their battle-cry. They all cried 'Tervigant!' That was one of their esteemed gods, and they were glad to follow his commandments. 'Monjoie!' was the cry of the Christians whom God had sent there to serve Him.

Here a thrust, there a blow; this one kept his mount, the other fell to the ground. The fighting men on both sides were closely interwoven with one another, as knights began to fall to the ground from their horses, like feathers from a moulting bird. Many hundreds of noble heathens lay dead there. The Christians suffered hardship before they broke through the enemy ranks, and the heathens took revenge for that, manfully and undauntedly, so that the soldiers of God had reason for lamentation. If with my words I were to equip them and describe the splendid attire of the heathens riding there, then I would have to name many lands from which costly silks had been sent forth by ladies of discernment, out of love for their knights. The heathen knights were wearing fur-lined cloaks, such as even today a lady may give to her beloved to adorn him.

The Christians were striving for the eternal reward. As long as they were alive, the heathens endured destruction, and the Christians, too, reaped misery and losses. Never did you see the radiant summer in so many colours, no matter how variegated a spread of exotic flowers the month of May ever brought to us. Many a detachment rode there decked out like a meadow. (It grieves me to think that their god Tervigant may have destined them for hell.) Among a hundred men there was hardly one in armour, and so their beautiful appearance was dreadfully mutilated. They were generous with their lives. Whenever a blow fell where there was no shield, the touch of the sword meant that many a noble heathen became a carpet for the horses. The swords of the Christians did not spare their tall, snow-white turbans, and beneath them many noble heads were benumbed by death. The heathens, too, delivered such blows with their cudgels through the helmets that many of the Christians perished.

Pinel, *fils de* Kator, who was always in the front line when the onslaught was met, could be heard dealing many a mighty stroke, before this hero lay dead at the hand of Willehalm and all heathendom was plunged into sorrow as a result. He was indeed a noble heathen. The combat was bitter on both sides. The Margrave also slew a very powerful amazur.

Suddenly and chivalrously, not wishing to fight with his troops just yet, Terramer came riding up on a horse called Brahane and headed towards the battlefield. He feared that he would bring disgrace upon himself if he were to turn from the battle. His courage urged him to engage in mortal combat, in which the noble Mile lay dead at his hand and, until the end of their days, was greatly mourned by the Frenchmen who had tracked down many sorrows there. Terramer himself rode back into the midst of his great ring of men.

The ranks of the heathens were in shreds. Forward and back, this way and that, the army of Halzebier, the bold and mighty warrior, was ridden through in courageous actions. One could not have loaded on a barge so many banners as the Christians saw wafting towards them. Knights who had been resting came riding back to join the battle with many large units. Leading them was a man who never tired of fighting, nor of knightly deeds. People are still in agreement about his excellence: he strove for knightly fame. Noupatris was his name and he had youth and radiant good looks. In his land, Oraste Gentesin, he wore the crown. The love of women had driven him forth and sent him yonder in the world. His heart and all its sensibilities strove after the reward of women. On his bright helmet was a ruby crown and the helmet itself shone without blemish, shiny as a looking-glass. Riding towards him came Vivianz, the son of the Margrave's sister. He knew how to acquit himself with honour too. His pure youth was preserved in such a way that his virtue was not the least little bit blotched or blighted, for Queen Giburc had brought him up from childhood and had given him her counsel in such a way that his heart never turned away from resplendent fame. The young but prudent man saw coming towards him proudly one whose jousting had brought about grief and heartache. Both men were duelling to the death.

I am one of those who still mourn their deaths sincerely, whenever this tale is told, the one because of his renown and because he was a Christian, and the other because of his constant striving. His youthful nature craved for fame, since his heart afforded him many a knightly goal. The shaft of his lance was made of bamboo with an iron tip which was broad and sharp. The heathen came riding at full tilt at the head of his men. Among the Saracens there was no banner so fine as that which the high-spirited King carried in his hand. He touched the horse with his spurs, as though he were going into a joust. Expense was of no account, where costly jewels and gold were concerned. His banner was adorned with a precious spear in honour of Amor, the god of Love, for this knight was fighting in the service of Love. The horse leapt from its charge towards the young Frenchman who was likewise brave and chivalrous and high-spirited, as to this day is any man who hungers after fame.

Giburc the Queen, out of love for him as her kinsman, had equipped him lavishly. They came clashing together, driven by their swift charge. Did their lances remain whole? No: their joust penetrated the shields and both the men. Each one was pierced by the hand of the other, right through his armour and his body, and both lances were broken in the charge. The strength of each man was so weakened that death became his surety. Vivianz, sorely wounded though he was, struck King Noupatris through his crowned helmet, so that both the grass and the dust beneath him became moist with blood. That was when the heathen gave up the ghost, and there occurred for those of his men who witnessed this a pitiful experience and a wretched sight. They wanted to rush to his aid, but their help came too late. His death went unseen and unheard by many heathens there, who were themselves risking their lives for glory and the favour of ladies.

Witschart and Samson of the house of Blayes rushed up to Vivianz to help him, but he suffered grievously in spite of this. Amor, the god of Love, and his salve-jar and his spear[4] on the banner of Noupatris, had taken a penetrating route straight through him and could be seen protruding from his back, guided by the hand of the king who had thrust them through the body of Vivianz, so that his entrails were hanging out over his saddle as a result of the joust. This brought profound grief to many a man and woman. The hero jerked out the banner and bound his entrails back in place as if he had not felt a bit of pain from the battle anywhere in his body. The illustrious young knight launched into the fray once more. Tibalt's revenge and hatred have cast the very first die. Anyone who thinks the damage not yet great enough can come to hear of more, even though virtuous ladies will not find tales of dying pleasing when they concern those who serve them. They were predominantly knights in the service of Love, those jousters who had been summoned there and boldly risked their lives. Many a splendid heathen made his way to the head of the army. You will not hear the names of all of them – Noupatris had brought these men – but those who had the greatest reputations and demonstrated supreme skill in the attack I shall name without fail, kings and dukes and several amazurs. (I have a neighbour or two who would not remember them even if I were to mention their names twice over!)

There was Eskelabon of Seres who often received reward secretly from a noble lady-friend. If a woman once granted him her favour she agonized for his love for ever after. His brother, Galafre, was whiter than a swan, and, if my story leads me to praise him, people in the know will not contradict me. Both of them wore crowns. And along with them we should name Glorion, and the haughty Faussabre, and King Tampaste and Duke Morant, and say that all six of them rode many knightly jousts. The mighty Rubiun fought there, and King Sinagun, the son of Halzebier's sister too, and they did so in a manner which brought honour upon all heathens. No other heathen princes had closed with the Christian knights yet. Now Halzebier, too, had suffered casualties in the battle. Of his thirty thousand men a good two thirds lay dead. The Christians had to see to it that they formed a new defence against the army of Noupatris, who had five kings with him. Fighting though he was for Love, he was cast to the ground unlovingly. One thrust, one blow, and he lay dead at the hand of the young Frenchman, Vivianz.

Then the army spread out, but not in flight. Two men who had been sent out to reconnoitre brought Terramer the news that Halzebier had been defeated in the battle and that the generous Noupatris lay slain. They told him further that the battle was heading, by means of frequent onslaughts, towards the main body of the army, and that the Margrave had so few men that they could be covered with a hat.

'We should surround them with one tenth of our archers,' they said. 'They cannot hold out long against our army.' The word was passed to eskelirs and amazurs, and to those kings who were commanding the forces there, and to all men, young and old alike, that the enraged Terramer himself was proposing to enter into battle. At that, the lines of the heathen army began to move like flood water.

The Kings of Arabi and of Todjerne, Tibalt and his son Ehmereiz, came forward eagerly, and King Turpiun, whose land was called Falturmie. They reached the Christian knights sooner than King Poufameiz or Josweiz of Amatiste, or Arfiklant and his brother Turkant, whose land was called Turkanie. Their arrival caused tears for many lady-friends in France, who demonstrated their loyalty in their lament. While one king was preparing himself, the other was fighting. Many large divisions of the great army were waiting at the ready, as well as those whose names I have just told you. Now let me return to telling you their names. Arofel of Persia had been accorded fame in many lands, for multiple and single combat. Moreover, he was best provided of all those present with soldiers and kinsmen. In his camp were ten kings, his brother's children. Indeed, the heathen army was a mere nothing without those whom he was leading.

How the drums rolled there, and how the trumpets sounded! Arofel, the brother of Terramer, moved forward with many bands of men, pressed on by the desire for battle. On the plain of Alischanz could be seen many strange helmet decorations, devised by the knights whom Arofel had brought with him. That was his obligation and he was able to fulfil it. Terramer had made bequests to the high-spirited young men. I mean that he had designated certain portions to them; particular lands were assigned to his ten sons, where each reigned in splendour over his princes, according to his power and innate skill. Each one was riding into battle in company with other wealthy kings. Just see how vast the army was of those who had ridden in their service, and they themselves were serving their uncle with appropriate good manners and fulfilling his commands. Arofel of Persia, in whose service they were and who in turn served them, lay slain in that service. A generous man never lacked such aid.

Arabel-Giburc, one woman with two names, love and you have become intertwined with sorrow. You have pledged yourself to misfortune. Your love strikes at baptism, but those who are fighting for Christianity do not refrain from striking at the race of your birth either. Many of them will perish too, unless He who sees into the hearts of men prevents it. My heart accuses you. But why? I should first say what grudge I bear her, or what am I thinking of? The Queen was innocent, she who once was called Arabel and who abandoned that name in favour of baptism for the sake of Him who was born of the Word. The Word entered with tremendous power into the Virgin, who remains a Virgin and who gave birth to Him who, undismayed, died for our sakes. Any man who is found in dire distress for His sake will receive everlasting reward. He is favoured by the singers whose tones ring out so clearly. Happy is he who gains a place so close that he does not miss the melody! I mean the sound of the angels in heaven, and that is sweeter than sweet song.

Great sorrow was evident among Willehalm's troops. His men had not neglected to have the symbol of the death of Christ cut out and fixed on their armour, and this the heathens slashed to pieces, those faithless people. His death has granted us the Cross. It is His very Life and a blessing to us. We should cherish it with our faith, just as those Christians did there. The heathens swamped them on all sides. Many a band of heathens brought such suffering upon them that they could have done with new limbs. In that very place the Frenchmen achieved the death of the body but the peace of the soul. The sons of Arofel's brother are still unnamed, but they were approaching now at a gallop. They were Fabors and Passigweiz, Malarz and Malatras and Karriax was the fifth, then Gloriax and Utreiz, Merabjax and Matreiz, while the tenth was Morgowanz, of unsullied manly reputation.

In the cloud of dust produced by the swiftness of the charge, they came riding into the throng and towards the fray, the individual armies of the kings from across the sea. The sons of Terramer fought in such a way that the Christians were hemmed in on all sides, yet they still fought on bravely. The Christians were outnumbered one hundred to one by the knights and archers of the illustrious heathens. Then, very soon after, came the King of Amatiste, the high-spirited Josweiz, whose army was dripping blood and sweat in combat with the Frenchmen. He entered the battle with four of his companions. His father Matusales had sent many large forces to join him, so that they might keep an eye on him when he was fighting for glory. Four kings, Pohereiz and Korsaz,[5] Talimon and Rubual, rendered homage and chivalrous conduct to him. Their horses were caparisoned in brightly coloured silks. In fact, precious silks were to be seen on men and horses alike. Never did any spark in the fire glow so brightly and many a suit of armour was like the reflection of the sun. (My daughter's doll is not half so beautiful, and I am not poking fun at her when I say this!)

At that time the Christians could not overcome the immense array of Josweiz, the knights of Arofel and Halzebier's regrouped forces. With many charges the battle made great cleavages in their ranks, while the heathen army was strengthened by emerals and amazurs. There was the noise of drums and tambours, of flutes and trumpets. Now Terramer was about to join the fray, to discomfort the Christians. After all, he had the wealth of nine kingdoms, and many noble princes served his hand. Not counting those lands which paid tribute to him, Happe and Suntin, Gorgozane and Lumpin all served him, too. His best land was Kordes, for there the amount of his wealth could not be expressed in writing; and he also had in his possession the lands of Poye and Tenabri, Sembli and Muntespir. Many amazurs and eskelirs had travelled from his nine lands, where, in the name of their gods, they had sworn to join Terramer's expedition. You ask how his army was composed? Let me tell you what forces he had. A company assembled from far and wide was riding in the army of Terramer, and many Moors, black but radiantly beautiful, who had decked themselves out splendidly before they commenced their charge. King Margot of Pozzidant was there. His other land was called Orkeise, and it is situated so close to the edge of the earth that there is no cultivated land beyond, and so close to where the morning star rises that anyone who stands there thinks that he could reach out and touch it.

This mighty man, King Margot, brought with him King Gorhant, whose land was near the Ganjas. His people were covered with a horny skin, in front and at the back, and they possessed no human voice. The sound which came forth from their mouths was like the noise of the hounds, or the lowing of a mother cow. The Christian army was sorely afflicted by their fighting. King Gorhant's army fought with steel maces and all on foot: not one of them was on horseback, yet even so they were so swift, these horny men, that they could easily keep up with horses and wild animals. If I may put it like this: nothing could escape them that did not fly. It was said that many of King Margot's troops fought well; on horseback and on foot, they strove for the favour of women and for other reward, just as the wise man does to this very day.

Even so this great army was as nothing compared with those whom Terramer's grandson, Poidjus of Griffane, led on to that plain. Triant and Kaukasas were under his rule, too. And now he led the mighty King Tesereiz into battle. This man, whose land was called

Collone, was held in high esteem. He it was who led the Araboises and the Seziljoises and the men of Grikulane through the wild mountains, and the men of Sotiers, as well as the Latrisetans. The thoughts of Tesereiz were directed towards the ladies, from whom he craved favour and noble love. Along with Terramer rode Poidwiz, too, he whose father Anki had sent him there in force. Poidwiz himself had such extensive lands at his command that many units accompanied him. However broad the field of Alischanz may have been, his men certainly needed the space: the close quarters caused them trouble.

Terramer arrived, then, with forces assembled from places far apart from one another. We hear it said of his charge that it could shake huge cliffs, and plants and forests with them. Many of his men were slain by the bold Margrave, whose helmet, hard and costly, had been wrought in Totel. His sword was called Schoiuse, and his horse, on whose back he performed many deeds of chivalry, was called Puzzat. This is how Terramer was welcomed by the Christians: they resisted his attack until they succumbed to his superior power. As a result, many a soul fared well, for the Christians died and gloriously secured the reward of eternal life. He still bestows such gifts, He who is both man and true God, and who gives and takes away both joy and sorrow. His aid is always there, unceasingly for those who, like these men, believe in Him.

Whoever died fighting for Willehalm gained victory for his soul on the field of Alischanz. Woe to you, Devil! How rarely does a guest keep clear of you! Wretched innkeeper that you are, even so you are always surrounded by visitors. If I were to find a landlord sitting there looking so grim, then, if I possibly could, I should be glad to continue my journey.

Let Him who was in the womb of the Virgin direct me to a better place, in order that I shall not need to tread too long the path that leads to hell. May He grant this to me in His goodness.

It was Terramer of Kordes who determined when pauses for rest should be taken and when troops should be replaced in the battle. Those who caused the heavens to resound with the sound of angels when their swords clashed piled up a vast hoard of remorse for their souls. On the other hand, the fighting of the Christians cut many paths as wide as streets, straight to hell. The heathens were made acutely aware of what causes hell to rejoice, for many thousands of them lay strewn about dead.

The Christians fought bravely until their strength began to fail, and they became scattered among many strange tongues by the overwhelming power of the heathens. The Margrave saw the great losses caused by Tibalt's revenge. Sorrowfully he spoke then: 'My kinsmen's strength is sinking, now that our cry "Monjoie!" has been silenced. Ah, Giburc, sweet love, how dearly have I paid for you! If Tibalt had come without Terramer's forces, our loving union might now well last still longer. As it is, I want to seek nothing but death, and leaving you in such need will be a second death for me.'

He lamented the loss of his lovely wife even more than the loss of his own life and the loss of his kinsmen. 'God, since Thou willst not let me continue to enjoy Giburc's love,' he spoke, 'take on Thyself this burden of consolation: that the Christians who fight here will avoid the miseries of the Last Judgement when their affairs are brought before Thee. This I beg, poor fool that I am.'

The clash of many charges and the sound of trumpets, the noise of drums and tambours and the yelling of the heathens resounded so loudly that it could awaken a lion's new-born whelps. (They are always born dead, as you know, and the roar of their father gives them life.)

Perhaps I can describe Margrave Willehalm like this: have you ever seen the sun cutting through a foggy day? He fought just as radiantly in search of his relatives. Wherever the fighting was thick, he made it thin, made room where there was a throng and whenever things closed in on him, he spread them out. With Schoiuse, the sword he carried, he hacked such passageways that many a detachment was dispersed.

Towards the River Larkant, Sir Vivianz was swept away from the field and into the water. The costly banner that he had tied over his wounds had slipped down. That weakened him severely, although he still fought valiantly for the sake of his honour and to kill many heathens. He did not stay there long, for the Larkant, which had many branches, was flowing swiftly at that spot. Vivianz heard a loud noise and saw Gorhant's army coming. Their voices produced such a sound as to make the waves in the sea shake. Margot, Terramer's kinsman, had brought his horny-skinned army. Vivianz, who had been brought up by Giburc at Termis and Orange, refused to flee. The Margrave's sister's child plunged, as if driven by a whirl-wind, into the army of King Gorhant, which had come all the way from India. The heathens were angry that both their horn and their own flesh were slashed by his sword.

The Count Palatine Berhtram came riding up, ready for combat, to where he heard that frightful noise. He wanted to turn back and would have done so, if he had not feared to disgrace all the French thereby. Then that chivalrous knight heard someone crying 'Monjoie!' from the direction of the river and saw Vivianz striving for death, as if he wanted to die. Berhtram summoned his courage for battle. Did the cry 'Monjoie!' urge him to do that? Or did a lady's love compel him? Or did Vivianz' predicament move him? Or did his manly nature order him to seek renown there? If my source has told me, then I shall tell you on whose account he endured fighting with Gorhant and rescued Vivianz.

Five other Frenchmen – wealthy counts they were – came riding up for combat. The seven had to suffer pain. The Count Palatine's well-armed charger, on whose back he had accomplished glorious deeds, was killed. Vivianz, shrewd as he was, brought him a Turkish horse. (I'm glad he thought of that, because Berhtram had never been more in need of a horse.) Kibelin and Witschart came rushing to their aid. At a ford in the Larkant there were now nine Frenchmen, and happy to see one another they were. The fighting moved back on to the plain, and there they all acquitted themselves well.

An emeral called to the heathens, as did King Rubual: 'Help our gods to achieve what is theirs by right, and see to it that Heimrich's family may never take root again. They thought to destroy our renown by force. Now King Tibalt can thank all his gods indeed, for the French will pay us a toll that they have no choice but to pay. If that which the Margrave has done with Arabel, the Queen, was a joyous gain for them, that could yet be mingled with grief. Now let us no longer spare that stubborn fruit of the house of Narbonne. Is our land to pay for the gift of Heimrich to his godson? So many a doughty hand has come here with Terramer that we would be dishonoured, if these Christians were to escape scot-free. No, they won't! They have been swept into the very heart of our forces. Now the French over there think that the Margrave is giving us a hard time here, as he was ever wont to do. But the "six" that he used to throw is hardly a "one" on the die now. We've come at the wrong time for him!'

Terramer spoke scornfully when he saw the men of France fighting bravely against many a troop: 'You heroes of heathendom, take revenge for our former power that we derived from our gods and for the fact that that damned Arabel has strayed so far from their commands. She whom I used to call my child has been stolen from me and from our gods, and by a tavern mob at that! Those soup-swillers have forced Tibalt to part from his wife, and all their children, too, who are here for just revenge, were parted from their mother. Just imagine those milksops daring to send us such disgrace-ful news! Men, take heart! Honour the gods and then me, so that Tibalt in his revenge will exact here this very day such a toll that – Tervigant willing – Arabel will have to bring shame upon her Christian ties and upon her baptism. She says that before she would turn away from Jesus I should see her burning at the stake. So be it!'

The weakened Vivianz and Count Joseranz, Samson and Gerart, Kibelin and Witschart, Berhtram, Gaudin and Gaudiers, these nine were fighting where Halzebier's army had gathered. This was the army that Willehalm *au court nez* had defeated earlier, when Pinel the *courtois*, the son of King Kator, had lost his life. He is held in higher regard even today than many a king still living. Except for Feirefiz Anschevin[6] and the Baruc Akerin,[7] if he were to bear arms, I have never heard tell of a heathen whose widespread reputation was so brilliant. Pinel would certainly rank third. The deeds of the three were so famous, recognized as surpassing the glory of other heathens.

Now the downfall of the Christians is drawing near. The heathens soon covered hill and valley with their forces. Whatever anyone else did, Halzebier could still be heard lamenting Pinel, who had been slain there. The King of Falfunde was grief-stricken at the death of his nephew. Halzebier was handsome, with curling brown hair and a span's breadth between his eyebrows. He had the strength of six men, this King of Falfunde. He was powerful of limb and bold of heart, equally adept at fighting with his right hand and with his left. His lofty reputation was protected from disgrace by his nobility. He was courageous in the service of women.

Now Pinel was avenged boldly after King Halzebier had seen Vivianz scattering the heathen troops by his charge and killing Libilun, Arofel's sister's son, as well as Eskelabon and Galafre, Rubiun and Tampaste, Glorion and Morant. These seven kings quickly lay dead, slain by the hand of Vivianz. Halzebier repaid these great losses with one stroke of his sword. Vivianz was felled from his horse to the ground. That gallant young man lay there unconscious, he who previously had been a veritable hailstorm to the heathens, as many an amazur could attest.

After that had happened to Vivianz, Halzebier captured these eight noblemen: Berhtram and Gaudin, Gaudiers and Kibelin, Hunas and Gerart, Samson and Witschart. Halzebier in his manly strength recognized them by their knightly prowess. Their bearing made him think that they were blood-relatives of the Margrave and that he would have valuable hostages for Queen Arabel, and so he had the eight men led away.

Many a troop of men who were sorely distressed by what had caused them to mount up came hastening there. Many men began to ask who had been making all this din. They did not know who had inflicted such losses on Terramer that his heart was bathed in sorrow.

As many a troop broke through the others, Vivianz, the handsome lad, got precious little rest from the thundering horses' hooves. After a while, when the men had all gone elsewhere, he regained his senses. The Margrave's sister's son saw a wounded horse standing there. Weakly he began to walk towards it and managed to mount the horse shakily. He did not forget his shield but carried it away with him.

If it would help at all, I would lament Heimrich's daughter's son. If I wish to do justice to loyalty and to knightly renown, and if my mouth is skilled enough, I'll tell you the tale plainly, of how the highly praised Vivianz sacrificed his life for our salvation, and how his hand now lies dead that defended our faith until he lost his life.

The name that was made available to us in baptism, when Jesus was named Christ at His blessed immersion in the Jordan, that name of Christian is still conferred on us who have received baptism. A sensible man never stops thinking of his Christianity. For this, Vivianz too fought so hard until death robbed him of his youth. His body was the very root of virtue. If his body had hovered as high as his reputation, no sword would have been able to reach him in any way. When I think of my own chances of salvation, I am anguished, and yet I rejoice at the way Vivianz died, he who surely gained distinction for his soul.

The young hero, recognized in the eyes of God, rode towards the River Larkant. He whose soul was not doomed to die rode exhausted from the battlefield towards a spring, following the directions of the angels. He saw a poplar grove, a linden and other trees there and turned to them for their shade. The Archangel Kerubin protected his soul from the devil. O Vivianz, every knight can call upon God in the name of your martyrdom when he finds himself in distress!

The young man spoke from his sweet mouth: 'All-virtuous God, may my suffering be given into Thy majestic power. Grant that I may live long enough to see my uncle and to confess to him whether I have ever gone against my upbringing in my behaviour towards him and whether I have committed such a misdeed.'

Kerubin, the radiant angel, spoke: 'Now rest assured that before your death your uncle will see you. Trust in me.'

Thereupon the angel disappeared from his sight, and immediately Vivianz lay stretched out as if he were dead. Exhaustion had overcome him.

Willehalm *au court nez*, the disconsolate Frenchman, can now count his losses and name himself as the man who has suffered the greatest losses of anyone who ever took up knighthood and practised the art of chivalry. His best help lay dead, except for the eight who had been captured. The battle had gone thus: the cry 'Monjoie!' was silenced, his twenty thousand men had been reduced to those fourteen who were still enduring the stresses of combat as they stood to their lord's defence and refused to leave him, except to offer up their lives for him. The heroes were simmering in blood and sweat from the terrible heat.

When new troops from the heathen army came riding to the attack, the Marquis hid himself in a cloud of dust, from which he and his fourteen men rode fighting, having hacked their way to fame with their swords. They looked at each other and began to count. Only then did they see how many of them were left there outside the heathen army on a grassy spot.

Willehalm, who had always been preserved from disgrace, spoke: 'Happiness and high spirits, you are both sinking away from me! How few in number are my men! If my kinsmen lie dead and likewise my brave vassals, with whom shall I then rejoice? No nobleman of my rank has ever experienced such losses. Here I stand, bereft of joy and help. Let me say one thing: these losses, coming all at once, would have been too much even for the Emperor Charles. Those that he sustained at Roncesvalles and in his other campaigns could not be compared with mine in severity. Because of this, I must always lament, if I am any kind of man.

'O Giburc, sweet Queen, how my heart is being taxed for your love now! I am completely overburdened with the weight of my grief, so that I must experience now through you the future pain of Purgatory. Let whoever is prepared to do so say that I have suffered even greater losses than any heart in human breast has ever borne at any time since Abel died through his brother's hatred.'

You should applaud his grief. He took counsel with his experienced and steadfast men, who mourned along with him, one lamenting the death of a father, another a brother. Their coats of mail had been tailored too wide for them with swords, and yet with manly courage, undaunted, the brave heroes advised their lord thus: 'You can see how much help you have at your command. Choose one of two alternatives now, neither of which will bring us any comfort: either we turn back to our death in battle, or we flee from our misery. Giburc, the Queen, has often enriched us with her loving generosity. Virtue like hers would be sufficient to bring honour to thirty lands. Now there is not one hand left at Orange to defend her. Your courage and your boundless generosity inspired us to follow you away from Orange. Continue now in that same spirit. No matter which path you wish to take, we are doomed to further losses. If the heathens overpower us, that won't make us happy at all.'

The thought of leaving his relatives and vassals who lay dead there began to grieve the noble Margrave greatly. Despite the bright sun and with no breeze in the cloudless sky, it began to rain – from his eyes, as if all the Christians were his own children and were plunging his heart into sorrow. If no one but Vivianz had fallen on the field of Alischanz, he would still have had reason to weep.

Then he turned away, as I heard tell, following his men's advice, and headed quickly towards Orange, skirting the heathen army. After what they had suffered, they were happy that no one was riding after them, nor were they attacked from the front.

Thus he thought that he had got away, but *le roi* Poufameiz of Ingulie had just come from the sea with a fresh army which had not even seen the enemy that day. They caused the Margrave immense suffering. Mounted on many fine Castilian chargers, they attacked him.

The Christians shouted 'Monjoie!' at once and turned to meet them. The intrepid Margrave determined where the King himself was riding; his troop was long and broad, riding in close formation. He found many other units there, none of which had felt the blow of a sword that day.

Charge! And how they did charge! the Margrave's comrades had to hack room for themselves with their hard, sharp swords, there were such close quarters there. The heathens could see the Christian troop breaking through. The Margrave was thus able to avenge his suffering. Many a heathen, emeral and amazur, lay dead at his feet. Just as the pickaxe breaks through thick walls and as the carpenter drives his wedge through the tough knot, so did Willehalm's sword Schoiuse, a scourge to the heathens, bite into the ranks of the infidel, all the way to King Poufameiz. His helmet decoration cost him his life. What Poufameiz had on his helmet was as expensive a decoration as a lady had ever laid on her knight, with the exception of Feirefiz Anschevin, of course, whom Queen Sekundille provided for,[8] and who had such helmet decoration that King Poufameiz could not equal it, nor Noupatris or Tesereiz, no matter how much wealth they had at their disposal. One of his lady-loves had sent the King of Ingulie to Alischanz – thank you for reminding me, Frau Aventiure[9] – so that Love should be enhanced. Nowadays neither Christian nor heathen ladies bestow such lavish gifts, however much service one sees performed for them.

The young, handsome, sweet stranger's helmet decoration gave off such brilliance that it pierced the eyes of the Margrave like the sun's rays, while he was fighting with him. His armour was resplendent with precious jewels. The lamenting of heathendom was increased at that time by their duel, for the Margrave killed Poufameiz. He knew how to avenge the losses he had suffered. In that fight, however, he lost all his remaining fourteen men. Then he was chased away, back among the first army, by those coming from the sea.

There Arfiklant of Turkanie and Turkant, the two brothers, confronted him. In fighting with them, the Margrave inflicted on heathendom suffering, with its accompanying sorrow, for he slew the two young kings. With wounds from many, his horse Puzzat bore him away from them. Meadows and planted fields were trampled under hoof indiscriminately by his pursuers. His horse waded through human blood, for there was much of that lying on his path. Thus he fought courageously here and there on the plain.

Le roi Talimon of Boctan and Turpiun, the mighty King of Falturmie, opposed him next. How did Turpiun fare? Like Pinel, fils de Kator, whom Willehalm had slain previously. Talimon came riding up on a horse named Marschibeiz, far from his eight battalions. Talimon broke a lance with a thrust from behind at the Margrave, who was still crying 'Monjoie!' bravely. He defended himself in similar fashion. He wheeled his horse around to face the charge and struck Talimon down dead. He took Marschibeiz, the horse, which was fitting for a king to ride, and led it away by its bridle.

Undismayed, he fled from many a large troop. Lances cracked loudly about him, from behind and in front. Thrusts and blows pounded in on him from all sides. That's how he had to fight. He was forced to abandon the captured horse and killed it with a thrust behind its shoulders. He did not want to leave it for the heathens, as happens in fighting even now. Thus did they rush headlong with him through a cloud of dust. His valour permitted him to escape from everyone who was pursuing him. He turned towards the mountains.

The wild dwarfs would have had trouble to climb where his horse took him. Look out! Did any of them get cut down? Then the Margrave has escaped!

BOOK II

He reined his horse and gazed back, up and down across the land.
Now valley and mountain and the whole of the plain of Alischanz
were covered with countless heathens, as though in a huge forest
there were nothing blossoming but banners. Bands of men were
getting in each other's way, as they rushed hither and thither on the
fields and at many fords on the River Larkant.

Now that Willehalm had a chance to see them properly, he saw
what an enormous force they were and spoke angrily: 'You
contemptible Saracens! If dogs and pigs as well as women had borne
so many battle-ready men, then indeed I should still say that there
were too many of you. Alas,' he said, 'Puzzat, if only you could
advise me which way to turn! How I could use your strength if we
were now fit and free from wounds! Then, if the heathens took it into
their heads to chase me, some of their kinsmen would have cause to
regret it. Now both of us are lame, and I am bereft of joy. You can be
sure of one thing: if we get back to Orange, provided that the
heathens have not taken it away from me, I shall make you happy
with vetch and oats, peas, barley and sweet hay. Now I have no solace
but you. May your speed bring me consolation.'

The horse's coat was brown, and covered all over with white foam,
as if it had a winter's snow upon it. The noble Willehalm took his
cloak, a piece of silk from Triant, and expertly he wiped all the sweat
from the horse's back. Then Puzzat's weariness began to leave him:
he snuffled and snorted, and thanks to Willehalm's care he recovered
from the tremendous weakness which had come over him.

Now they had tarried long enough, and so at once the Margrave
led the horse past many a cliff towards the River Larkant, into the
river-bed. He had ridden a very short distance through the under-
growth when he glimpsed, lying in front of him, the shield of the

43

noble Vivianz. On this the game of war had been played: axes and cudgels, bows and swords had been aimed at it in joust, and it had been hacked to pieces. Willehalm recognized the trimming round the edge of the straps inlaid with emeralds and diamonds, rubies and chrysolites, exactly as Giburc, who knew about such matters, had stipulated. She it was who had sent young Vivianz on to the field of Alischanz in costly splendour. His death was to bring grief into her heart. When the Margrave found Vivianz, he noticed a spring and a linden-tree above his sister's child. All the joy which he had ever known vanished from his heart, and, his eyes wet with tears, he spoke:

'Alas, pure child, of princely birth! My heart must bear its affliction of grief without the healing power of joy. If only I had been slain with you! Then I would turn towards repose. Sorrow: I must for ever more be numbered among your company! Why do you not swallow me up – it is you that I am talking to, broad Earth – so that I may soon become as one with you, for it is from you that I come? Death: now claim your share of me! No matter what grief I ever grappled with and whatsoever trouble oppressed me, I was only an apprentice in misery. Now I have more sorrows than ever grew within my heart before. If only I might now slink away like a fox, so that the light of day might never again shine upon me! Whatever joy I may once have had in my heart has been banished from it by Death. Death: how can you do without me? I am still alive and yet I am dead. Alas, that such immense grief can endure within my heart, and that the heathens have not slain me with their swords and their spears!' Because of his grief, all his strength deserted him, and he sank, unconscious, beneath his horse. That silenced his lament.

After a while he regained his senses and then new lamentation began, as he knelt over Vivianz. I could well believe that he was unhappy at the sight, and bereft of all joy. He unstrapped the battered helmet and, weeping, straightway took the wounded head upon his lap. Overwhelmed with grief, he began to speak:

'You and I are of one blood. No matter what they may say of that seed which came from Eve, the virtues of all those who have been born since the time when Adam's rib was made into a woman were conserved for you. Your noble, blessed heart was purer than sunshine. Lofty fame was never a stranger to you. There was such sweetness in your body that the salty taste of the broad sea would surely have become as sweet as sugar if just one of your toes had been thrown into it. It grieves me to think of it. Your sweet wounds exude the fragrance of spice and ambergris, filling my heart and making it swell with sorrow. My sighs of lamentation will remain unstilled until the end of my days. Alas, Vivianz!' he went on. 'What ceaseless misery you will now give to Giburc, the queen. As a bird broods over its young and tends it, so did she care for you and bring you up almost entirely in her own arms. Now that most devoted of women will be inconsolable because of you.

'You were born into this world to be my joy, full of virtue as you are, and now I have exchanged that joy for sighing. Alas, how my palace, Termis, was enhanced by your presence! I esteemed your fame so highly that for your sake I gave one hundred pages their swords, as everyone will concede. To your one hundred companions I gave two hundred Castilian steeds, in addition to their armour, and the Queen herself had two suits of clothing made for each of them from her own coffers, so that I never knew such generosity. Many rich silks were brought from Tasme and Triant and Ganfassasche and intended for your retinue. My beloved Giburc thought more of you than of her own children. For all of you she had made up fine brown wool from Ghent which is called "bridal cloth", and the third set of clothes was made of fine red wool. Now, in the midst of all this finery, you lie dead. How your shield was adorned, and how she who never concealed her devotion to you thereby contributed to the evidence of her generosity! That shield cost five hundred marks. Your helmet decoration was all so fine that if some rich Saracen might be compared with you in this respect, he would be worthy of a woman's reward. Alas, how much has Love lost in you, when such a high price must be paid for courtly love and the greeting of noble ladies! You were distinguished in France, for, if a woman's eye beheld you, her heart and her mouth declared that the sight of you was like springtime itself, and every woman might without question desire your beauty for herself. Nothing, either in the air, or on the dewy grass, or any being who once suckled at his mother's breast, has ever represented in his death so great a loss to Love. When my relatives, who hitherto had reason to rejoice, so great was our renown, hear these bitter tidings, they will be ushered into wretched suffering. This is what your untimely death will mean to them. What good is it that I am still alive? This sorrow inflicts upon me such an abundance of sadness that it will renew itself again and again, by night and by day, as long as my life may last.'

Thus he meditated in his misery until the battered body in his lap uttered a sob and began to stretch out. Vivianz' heart was throbbing wildly, struggling as he was with death: he opened his eyes then and saw his uncle, just as the Angel Kerubin had promised him he would, at that very place. The Margrave bade him speak and asked him:

'Have you partaken yet of that whereby your soul shall come joyfully into the presence of the Trinity? Have you made your confession? Has any baptized man given you his aid since I myself lost track of you?'

With little strength remaining to him now, Vivianz replied: 'Since I left the field of Alischanz, I neither heard nor saw anything, except that the Angel Kerubin spoke to me and told me that I should see you standing over me once more. My uncle and my lord, I wish to make my confession in preparation for the journey which I must take. Sinner though I am, I have received much acclaim and many high honours. It happened that the Queen demonstrated her renown through her treatment of me, and yet I never became so clever in my relationship to you both as to be able to ascertain any worthwhile service with which I might respond, nor could I have done so if there had been a thousand of me. In all my actions it was my intent to maintain towards you a loyalty which no fickleness could ever split away from me.

'When, at Termis, I rose to manhood with your support, and, together with my comrades, achieved my knighthood, what expense the Queen bore on my account! It would have been quite enough for all the emperors who ever reigned. The help which Queen Giburc gave to me was plain for everyone to see, and it was more fitting to her nobility than to my own meagre attainment. I know for sure that, if God is wise, He will graciously reward her for it, if He is as He has always been. Uncle, I depend on you, for the sake of our kinship, to cherish her all the more for my sake: never tire of doing so, and remember also what I said at Termis – when many hundreds of noble knights were there to hear and see, and I was prompted by my high spirits – that I would never flee from the Saracens. If I have repaid your support with wrongful deeds, if I have ever been cowardly in battle, then let my soul suffer for that.'[10]

What could the Margrave do when, as if he did not have sorrow enough already, the young man, his sister's son, mentioned such trifling sins and spoke of them in his confession? Full of sadness, he responded: 'Alas, for such a splendid creature! Why did I want to gird you with a sword, when you should hardly have been carrying a little sparrowhawk? The radiance of your youth was a mirror to all Frenchmen. Not a single whisker had so far grown on any part of your handsome face. Why did I call you a man? It would have been more appropriate for you to be found still at home with other children, than carrying a shield, beneath which you have been slain. I shall have to answer for your death when I come into the presence of God, for no one is more guilty of slaying you here than I. Your death will inflict such copious suffering for my foolishness that it will bring forth sorrow for all time until my life's end. The fault is rightly mine. Why did I lead a little child against the powerful warriors from all the heathen lands?'

As the Margrave's kinsman lay feeble like this in his lap, Willehalm spoke to him with heartfelt grief and asked: 'Have you that with you which is consecrated in France each Sunday, when no priest neglects to bless with the power of God a piece of bread which protects the soul from death? I received some from an abbot in front of Saint Germain, when the rite was conducted in Paris. I have it here in my pocket. Take it, for the sake of the salvation of your soul, which will rejoice to be thus accompanied when it must go forward in fear and stand before God's judgement.'

The young boy replied: 'I have none with me. If death brings me release, my innocent confession shall lead my soul out of these tribulations to where it shall find rest. Yet give me the Body of Him who, as a man, died by the lance of the blind man,[11] though as God he remained alive. Because he was the companion of Christ, Dismas never experienced hell, for Jesus heard indeed from his cry that he recognized Him and guided his soul away from damnation.[12] Now I too utter that same cry to Him who created me and provided me with an arm to fight in His service. Kiss me, and forgive me for whatever wrong I have ever done to you. My soul wishes to hasten away, so, if you desire to give it some means of support, let me receive it without more ado.'

When he had received it, the young boy died, having already made his confession. Such a fragrance was there when his body and his soul parted from one another, as though all lignum aloe trees had been set alight.[13] Thus did he make his journey thence. (What is the point of making a long story about it?) The Margrave bent over his sister's child and made his lamentation. His bridle had caught firmly on a stumpy branch of the linden tree when he had fallen from his horse. Now, for the time being, his eyes had poured forth all the tears which they could muster; his heart was quite dry and his eyes completely free from moisture. Then he was able to look about him and seek out the way to Orange, towards which his heart was still urging him. He did not tarry long.

He thought of the losses he had sustained and of what the day had cost him, and how disastrously it had turned out. Repeatedly he embraced the dead lad, his sister's son, and then the brave and powerful Margrave lifted him on to his steed in front of him. Avoiding the open highway altogether, he rode up-river, along the Larkant, and headed towards the mountain, in his anxiety to avoid the enemy. Yet, even so, he was accosted by people unknown to me; there were just too many of them for him, now that he was so close to his goal. Each one levelled his spear and spurred his mount to attack him. He did as anyone would who needed to defend himself: he threw Vivianz to the ground. And so the intrepid man fought until he had freed himself from them, for they lost track of him in the dense undergrowth. Then he turned back the way he had come and returned to where he had left Vivianz. Following the dictates of his loyalty, he watched over his nephew that night, though often his heart was breaking as he did so.

Thus did he struggle and agonize over him the whole night through. He was thinking hard about the next day, when the sun would begin to shine, and he was wondering whether he would be able to carry him away, and what he should do if he should happen to be attacked again. He would have to drop him again at once, and in that case the shouting and mockery of the heathens would be all the greater. It oppressed him beyond measure to anticipate such anguish, and he thought to himself: 'If I leave you behind out of fear, then it will be the greatest disgrace I have ever suffered. Yet I may not place too big a load on Puzzat, if I am to meet the onslaughts of the heathens, for then I shall be able to manoeuvre better in combat with them.'

Meanwhile, day was breaking. He kissed his nephew and rode into an encounter with fifteen kings. They, too, had stood watch that night, in a state of discomfort, in honour of their god Tervigant, and following the command of Terramer and the dictates of their own oath of allegiance. You see, a pause in the fighting had been ordered, but with no thought of aiding the Christians. Each king was riding alone. The others who had not been injured had enough to do to cope with the dead and wounded. All the low-born knights carried their lords and their kinsmen from the battlefield, over the length and breadth of which the kings had stood watch under arms the whole night through. Even eskelirs and amazurs – the captain of each battalion, many a bold, rich emeral – were keeping watch over the battlefield, from the mountains to the sea, lest there remained of the Christian army any man still alive who would have to be slain.

Early that morning, the Margrave rode towards the fifteen kings. Ehmereiz of Todjerne, the son of noble Giburc, recognized him: he was glad to see him and wanted to be the first to joust with him. I do not know whether that took place, for each of them soon afterwards broke the weapon which he had in his hand, when fifteen spears were levelled at the Margrave and each of them was broken into pieces. He hardly stayed put in his saddle in the face of their onslaught, but he did not forget his sword Schoiuse, for with it he rained many resounding blows on the kings' helmets. Let me tell you their names and the names of the places where these powerful kings held sway over princes. Since there are seventy-two languages, it seems to me that a man has the wits of a child if he does not accept that each tongue has its own land which gives its name to the language. If all these tongues are named, not twelve among them observe the rite of baptism: the others wield immense power across the vast lands of heathendom. Those who opposed the Margrave had some of this power, too. Ehmereiz, the renowned son of Tibalt, is called after the land of Todjerne. Similarly, Akerin may with all honour be called the lord of the princes of Marroch, of the race of the Baruc, who had Gahmuret buried at Baldac with Christian rites. People can still tell of these things: what a funeral he arranged for him when he died in his service! How eloquent was his epitaph, how magnificent his cata-falque, ornamented with emeralds and rubies, as the Baruc had himself ordained that it should be![14]

All this was appropriate to the display of grief, but let us not talk about that any more, for I propose to give you the names of all the kings. *Le roi* Mattahel of Tafar was there, and *le roi* Gastable of Komis. The shrewd Margrave saw that the battle was not going to proceed without them. There was *le roi* Tampaste of Tabrasten, and *le roi* Goriax of Kordubin, who was brave and wise; *le roi* Haukauus of Nubia fought very boldly there too, and *le roi* Kursaus of Barberie, that man devoid of any misdeed. There too were *le roi* Bur of Siglimessa and *le roi* Korsuble of Danjata; *le roi* Korsude of Saigastin did not have much success there, and the helmet of *le roi* Frabel of Korasen was pitted with scars. *Le roi* Haste of Alligues asked the Margrave why he was getting in his way. Finally, let me name *le roi* Embrons of Alimec and *le roi* Joswe of Alahoz.

The blood of all these kings flowed through their chain-mail, except for the son of Giburc: Willehalm did not wish to harm him, and yet he did not spare him on his own account. My story attributes his protection to Giburc: it was in her safe conduct that Ehmereiz rode away, for the Margrave did not fight with him. Immediately his stepson spoke to him:

'Alas,' he cried, 'what shame you have brought on the gods through my mother! Your magic lured her from their command-ments and from my father Tibalt. Because of this, Termis will be crushed and the whole of Christendom laid waste. You have tarried here too long. Now you will pay with your life because such a womanly woman betrayed our religion on your account. This injures all my kinsmen. If I hope to observe the dictates of decorum I may not revile the woman who bore me, yet I shall always hate her. My crown would sit better on my head if Arabel had not brought shame upon it. Since then my sense of propriety has often been filled with fear.'

When Ehmereiz, the child of Giburc, came riding up so chivalrously and his whole suit of armour showed no sign of poverty whatsoever, for it was expensive and brightly gleaming, the Margrave did not harm him; nor did he reply to what he had said. Whatever he said about Giburc, the Margrave put up with from him, but from him alone: the others were wounded or slain. Eight of them had to flee, but seven lay dead there. Leaving them, the Margrave rode on, towards two high-spirited kings, into fresh hostility. These were likewise brave knights and veritable rocks in time of battle, yet these two heroes who had gained much renown were heading for a heavy toll. The one was the noble King Tenebruns of Liwes Nugruns; the other was Arofel of Persia, Giburc's uncle. They were encamped alone, apart from their armies.

If the dewy grass in May-time is covered with blossoms brought forth by the sweet air, these two, because of their fame and buoyancy of spirits, were still more beautifully adorned and so decked out as to bring credit to Love. If I were to describe their helmet decorations fully, then I would have reason to mourn my master, Heinrich of Veldeke, for he would have been able to do it better: he would not have been so slow-witted but would have told you better than I am able to do how the ladies of these two knights had lavished riches upon them with subtlety and taste.[15] Now they swung themselves into their saddles to ride into combat.

When the Margrave rode towards them, they both lowered their lances for the assault and aimed straight at him, and he let them come charging at him. When the stalwart Margrave had countered this double attack, he did not conceal his destination. He was wanting to ride on towards Orange, where the Queen held his heart in her safe keeping. The two kings, however, hammered away at him, like smiths at the anvil, so his sword Schoiuse was unsheathed and bravely wielded, and both spurs were dug into Puzzat's flanks. They fought courageously, and King Tenebruns was slain. But then the Persan really caused the Frenchman trouble with his fighting. How they charged at one another! Fragments from their shields flew up into the air.

King Pantanor once gave a sword to Salatre, who gave it to King Antikote, who gave it to Essere, the emeral, who gave it – this beautifully decorated sword – to Arofel the bold, who was not given to relenting either. Thus the sword passed from hand to hand until it came to the Persan, Arofel, who bore it bravely and wielded it courageously, for he was skilled in fighting and never let anyone outstrip him in pursuing renown. I could tell you a great deal about his nobility, and about how he gained the reputation among the Saracens of venturing much in the service of ladies and for the sake of any friends in trouble and, of course, in order to defend himself. In the whole of Terramer's army there was no better knight than Arofel of Persia. Giburc's generosity came from the same family as his, and he himself had excelled to such an extent that no more generous hand was known anywhere so long as he was alive.

The mighty Arofel was fighting boldly now, and indeed he had already attained renown in full measure. His horse carried him forward with such force that the straps above his knee snapped in several places and came loose from his belt; in the sudden charge his chain-mail leg-covering slipped down to his spurs and this was how he lost his unprotected leg. The lower edge of his hauberk, his cloak and his shield had shifted upwards at the same time, so that his leg was exposed. The Margrave cut through his massive white thigh, and that rendered the king defenceless.

Now he who previously had fought courageously offered his oath of surrender, and untold treasures, too. He had been unhorsed and Willehalm dismounted also, rejoicing at this defeat. Without impairing his honour in doing so, Arofel made him an offer of thirty elephants which were in the harbour at Alexandria, with as much gold loaded on them as they could carry, together with safe passage as far as Paris for all this treasure.

'Noble hero,' he said, 'you will gain no honour if you kill me now that I am half dead, and you have already slain my joy.'

When the Margrave heard what he was saying and realized that he was offering him immense riches in exchange for his shattered life, he thought of the death of Vivianz and of how that might be avenged and his own burden of grief made a little lighter. He asked the king to tell him about his lineage, and from which land he had come to make this journey across the seas and to his doom.

The King replied: 'I come from Persia, where I ruled as king over princes and until this day possessed great power. Now I am brought to nothing. Alas, my brother's daughter, that I should pay for you with such a price of suffering! Arabel and Tibalt, if you both lay dead, here in my place, people should not mourn your death so much as mine.'

The King was speaking nothing but the truth, but Willehalm replied in a rage: 'You will pay for all my heartache, and for the fact that your brother Terramer has slain my dearest kinsmen, egged on by plenty of advice and help from you. If you had at your disposal the whole of the Kaukasas mountain, I would not accept the gold unless you were to pay for my kinsmen with the trials of death.'

Arofel replied: 'If anyone has anything in exchange for which you will let me remain alive, hacked down as I am and only half a man, then you will receive that for me in full. Look, there stands Volatin, my horse, who would be enough in himself to repay my debt to you completely. Out of loyalty I took into my care ten kings, my brother's sons, who are here with a vast retinue. It was for their sakes that I left Persia. If there is anything there in my kingdom which you desire more than my death, take it and let me go on living in my anguish.'

Why should I make a long story about it? Arofel was slain on the spot. With his own hands the Margrave pulled off all the armour and the trappings which he found on the corpse and then – I am telling you the truth – he struck off Arofel's head and so deprived the ladies of a servant who had been a fertile ground for their joy. Thus had dawned a day of loss for Love, and even today Christian ladies should still be mourning this heathen man. Willehalm did not take flight at all until he had removed the suit of armour which he had been wearing, for he had immediately thought of the better one worn by the dead man as he came into battle against him, and this he now put on, complete with all the helmet decoration. Thus later, when it was a matter of great urgency, his own wife did not recognize him, no matter what familiar words he addressed to her. The costly trappings gleamed as he swiftly mounted Volatin, as Arofel's horse was called.

He girded both swords about him and took the shield of Arofel as well, which was fit for a king to wear. His own horse Puzzat was badly wounded, and so he at once took off its harness, so that it might find food for itself, but it followed him away from there, and, wherever its master rode, it took the same path after him.

Thus the brave Margrave rode on with no one pursuing him until he glimpsed Orange and the brightly shining roof upon the palace. At this his joy soared, though previously it had fled precipitously from his heart. He heard the sound of trumpets and saw great clouds of dust stirred up by bands of riders. Terramer had given his daughter's son permission to go to Orange and kill Giburc. (Judge for yourselves if it was fitting that Poidjus of Griffane should reward his aunt in this way for their kinship. It would have been more appropriate for him to have protected her and all women.)

Now King Tesereiz came hastening to see to it that no harm came to Giburc. I know for a fact that any knight who possessed the qualities of Tesereiz would still receive the love of ladies. A man carries within his heart the love of a woman and this is how the ladies bestow high spirits. Whatever lofty deeds a man may perform, the legal title to them resides in a woman's hands. Noble love rates highly when it is put to the test.

The roads and pathways were crammed full of troops. On those that led towards Orange the Margrave made use of his mastery of heathen tongues. People could see that his shield was a heathen one and that the horse he was riding was heathen too, and that all his armour came from heathen lands. Willehalm, the fighting hero, rode towards all these troops and, courageous as he was, he knew how to ride calmly and at a steady pace through any gaps between detachments, whether over meadows or in cultivated fields. Many of the troops stood gaping at him.

Poidjus of Griffane was waiting on the plain until his army had all joined him there. He also had a large battalion of the men of Tesereiz. In his company, and summoned there from his own land, were the men from Sotiers and the Latrisetans, and those from Collone. Men from Palerne, too, were in the service of his crown, while the people of Grikulane, from the wild mountains, men who knew how to fight with bows and slings, were also glad to serve Tesereiz. The Margrave did not hesitate to ride through the army towards Orange, but this landed him in trouble. People began to scrutinize the saddling of the wounded horse, and the heathens recognized him from a peculiarity of his, namely that he put a small piece of fur – beautiful ermine it was – underneath his armour: the edging of this fur hung down behind, over the saddle-bow, so that, when Puzzat was following so faithfully in Willehalm's tracks, the heathens recognized him and said: 'That horse was ridden by the man who killed Pinel and also slew our comrades Arfiklant and Turkant. It was the same horse which carried the man who killed Turpiun, the mighty King of Falturmie. Whoever this knight may be, I am sure that it was he who inflicted these losses on us. This horse is following him so closely that he must surely be a Christian who is trying to get away from us by trickery. That ermine garment underneath has come here from the land of the French.'

With that they spurred their horses, and then there was nothing for it but to charge.

There were always twenty or more thrusting at him at a time, so that the lances were broken on him and shattered to pieces. He was tossed like a ball from hand to hand, between one battalion and the next. They chased him over hill and dale, and Arofel's horse Volatin and his own sword Schoiuse became the guardians of his life. The King of Collone, who had often received rewards from ladies, bade him ride at a pretty pace, as he came up very close to him.

'I must find out who this is,' said Tesereiz, the Garland of Love, his bright lance gleaming with its splendid colours. 'If you are a Christian,' he said, 'then joust with me for the sake of fame. If you really are the Margrave, if your Lord Christ once gave you his aid, so that out of love for you Arabel, the Araboise, gave up rich lands and a noble crown, to gain your love, then, for the sake of your nobility, I shall protect you from the heathens, indeed defend you for the sake of your love. For, if a Saracen had been so honoured as you, with your reputation, then all our gods would have rejoiced. No one can match me here in fighting power; my army rivals all others from Grikulane to the River Rhône. I intend to convert you to the worship of our illustrious gods; then you will be able to serve the ladies with your fighting and so win for yourself their greeting and their reward.

If I am obliged to fight with you, then I know very well that this will be damaging to Love. I was never so reluctant to fight with any man before, for I have no desire to harm you.'

Again and again he asked Willehalm to turn aside, telling him that he would bestow great riches upon him: he was wanting to get him to surrender. Then, in a thrust from the right a lance was aimed at the Margrave. He caught hold of it unbroken and jerked it out of the hand of the heathen, whose joust was thus foiled.

Meanwhile, Tesereiz cried out: 'Now turn aside, if you really are in the service of Queen Arabel!'

His request was granted very harshly, as Volatin was hurled round to face the King of Latriset. Then the horses were spurred, and Manliness came face to face with Courage, and Generosity with Goodness, and on each side were Purity and High Spirits, Loyalty and Good Breeding. The combat was a game of chance played by these eight. Love was the ninth player, but their gain proved to be her loss.

The two came charging at one another, and neither missed his target, so that both spears were snapped in two: this joust taught Tesereiz about death, this man who had increased his fame and helped to bring purity into the world.

Praise be to the field and the grass on which the Lover lay slain! The field must have been sweet as sugar within a radius of a day's ride from that spot. The brilliant, courtly knight could have supplied all the bees with nourishment. Since bees discover sweetness, then, if they were at all clever, they could derive their sustenance from the air which comes wafting from that land where Tesereiz now truly met his knightly end. He who was slain by the Margrave was a burgeoning branch of Love, and Love had sent Willehalm there, too.

The messenger of Giburc's love was in the thick of battle. The army was attacking from the rear and from the right, and many of the enemy declared: 'If Mahmete will grant it to me, I shall get you.' Many detachments, now refreshed, beset him on all sides: he escaped, but Puzzat, his horse, lay slain and for this he lamented. Then Schoiuse dealt many blows, to the discomfiture of the heathens.

There was a grove of chestnut trees, overhung with grape-vines, and into this cover he fled, away from the enemy. Volatin bore him swiftly to Orange, in front of his gates. Only now was he really overcome with grief and suffering from the death of his noble army, and his nephew Vivianz. An old chaplain, whose name was Steven, was standing at the defence-post above the gate, and Willehalm told him that it was really he who had come there, but Steven did not believe him, and the Queen herself came forward. She observed his helmet decoration and its costliness overwhelmed her. Moreover, she noticed from his shield that he could be a heathen, and Volatin, the horse of Arofel, did not look like Puzzat.

'You are a heathen,' she said. 'Whom do you think you can fool here by telling these stupid lies about the Margrave? His courage has always urged him to fight alongside his men and never flee from them on account of any trouble. Many a man would fight with you for venturing so close, if it were not for the fact that it is beneath the dignity of all my knights here.' Yet all the time her defence was reduced to the chaplain: there was no other man inside.

The Margrave spoke to the Queen: 'Sweet Giburc,' he said, 'let me in and give me that comfort which you know so well how to give. After all my sorrow you make me think of joy. I have been longing for you too much.'

She replied: 'I am not accustomed to seeing the Margrave return alone. You shall have a stone waved at you, so that you'll lie flat on the ground. I shall not let you stay here any longer.'

An advance party of the heathen army was coming past, herding along five hundred men; poor Christians they were, whom they were lashing with whips. Giburc, hearing and seeing this, was filled with pity. She turned to the Margrave and said: 'If you were the lord of this land you would be ashamed of the suffering which is being inflicted on your people there. If you fail to help them, then I shall know for sure that you are not the Margrave.'

There was a cry of 'Monjoie!', as Schoiuse, with its famous sharp edges, was brandished aloft. He charged and attacked with such force that anyone who got in his way was slain. The heathens fled in fright, leaving behind camels and dromedaries, laden with a variety of wines and foods. The shrewd Margrave benefited from wearing the suit of armour of Arofel, whose power over the entire army was so great that no one attempted to defend himself. They were afraid that it really was Arofel, and they were so shocked at the prospect that they left their loot behind. The Margrave cut all the bonds of the Christians and bade them round up the animals. He left behind nothing which could be of any use to him.

Thus he could honourably come before his gates, yet even now the Queen thought she was being deceived. Repeatedly the Margrave and the men who had been freed begged her to let them in. Fear made the Queen ask something of the Margrave which was little to his discredit:

'When, for the sake of adventure, you were striving after high renown in the service of Charles l'Empereur and oppressing the Romans, you received a scar on behalf of Pope Leo. Let me see this on your nose: then I shall be able to tell whether you are the Margrave. Only then shall I let you in. If I have delayed too long, then I shall in fear and trembling seek your favour – I shall not fail to do that – and purchase it with my devoted service.'

He unfastened his helmet and his coif, and pulled them off his head. The Queen had not been tricked, and she recognized the scar.

Joyfully she greeted him: 'Willehalm au court nez! Welcome, noble Frenchman!' She gave orders that the gate be opened, and now she lamented over and over again that he had not been able to gain access before, no matter what he had said.

When, tentatively, she gave him kiss after kiss, the Margrave spoke to her like this: 'Giburc, my sweet beloved, you are completely free from any hatred that I have ever had, for I cannot be angry with you. Now let us give each other consolation, for even then we shall not be released from sadness.'

Giburc was sorely afraid when she heard these words and thought to herself: 'Can I ask him to give me a true account of Alischanz, whether he and Vivianz held the field with their forces against King Tibalt, or how things turned out there?'

Weeping she asked for this news: 'Where is the radiant Vivianz? Where are Mile and Gwigrimanz? Alas, that you have come alone! Where are Witschart and Gerart, the brothers from Blayes, and your kinsmen from Commercey, Samson and Jozeranz and Huwes of Milan, and the Count Palatine Berhtram, who himself bore your standard, and Hunas of Saintes, to whom you never refused your service at all, nor he his to you? My lord, and my beloved, tell me, where are Gaudiers and Gaudin, and the fair-haired Kibelin?'

The Margrave began to lament: 'I cannot tell you the fate of each individual one of them. Enough that Vivianz is dead. I myself saw how death shattered his young heart as he lay in my lap. Your father Terramer has inflicted much heartache upon me and will continue to do so before he has finished. My loss cannot be measured.'

When Giburc heard from what he said that her father himself had come across the sea to Alischanz, she said: 'All the armies of Christendom cannot withstand him. He can summon aid from far and wide, from Orjente to Pozzidant, as well as all the lands of India; from Orkeise to Marroch, and from that wide area, too, which runs right from Griffane to Rankulat, he has mustered all the best men to come with him, his vassals and all my kinsmen. There is little joy ahead for us. If only we had enough forces, so that the heathens might be obliged to engage in hostilities on the city walls and at the gates, and come to grief in doing so! I know that they are presumptuous enough to besiege us. Now let every single person defend himself: this is the best advice I can offer. Our first concern is for our lives: we shall not be so quick to sacrifice these. The heathens can still come to grief before we die at their hands. Indeed, Orange is so well fortified that it can easily bring discomfort on all these foreigners.'

The woman spoke manfully, as if she were endowed with the body and heart of a man, and Willehalm himself made a fitting response, drawing her close to him, so that they kissed tenderly. Then he spoke undauntedly and said: 'Suffering and solace go hand in hand. Who might possess the advantage that I have, in that you have bestowed noble love upon me, and not risk his life, and everything he ever owned, for it? I can see some real hope in prospect if you can defend this city. Many princes whom I have never yet asked to do so will ride into this country for my sake. I shall loose your bonds with swords, no matter how they may besiege you. I am well acquainted with the loyalty of my kinsmen, and, what is more, the Roman King[16] is married to my sister and will not let me down now. My old father, Heimrich of Narbonne, will reward you with his service for bringing honour and renown upon himself and all his children. Now tell me on your honour as a woman: will it grieve you if I ride off, or please you if I stay behind? Whichever way your counsel sends me, that is the direction which I shall take, even unto death. Your love has commanded my service ever since, in your goodness, you received me.'

Now the heathen army came flooding along. Akerin, King of Marroch, arrived with his many troops. Terramer, the Protector of Baldac, came towards Orange under arms as fast as he could. Everyone connected with the army, whether on horseback or on foot, had to take up his place before Orange. There was such a procession of banners that it looked as if all the trees in the Spessart were hung with silks and satins, but the heathens did not encounter any resistance. The chivalrous Willehalm entrusted the gates and the battlements above to the troops which he had rescued in that attack upon the group of heathens with the baggage-train. He urged them to take heart and reminded them of how they had been freed, bidding them think of this if the heathens were to approach. Women and children carried many stones up to the fortifications, each one dragging as much as he could. They were wanting to exact a high price for their lives.

Terramer himself did not neglect to ride around Orange, eager for battle and contemplating his daughter's downfall. When the army had come to a standstill, each detachment in its full strength, and at the walls and gates neither saw nor heard any sign of knightly activity as might have been performed on horseback, Terramer's son Fabors assigned each king his siege position, as required by Terramer himself.

Then Terramer and King Tibalt, with all their forces, set up their camps in fine style before the gates, close to the great hall where Giburc herself was. Two powerful kings, Pohereiz and Korsant, lay encamped on the other side, with widely arrayed forces, and lodged with them were many princes decked out in costly armour, for the sake, I dare say, of their ladies at home. Thus two sides are covered by the enemy, but who is to guard the third gate which leads out towards the plain? The King of Griffane and *le roi* Margot of Pozzidant and the horny-skinned Gorhant controlled this one, while the fourth was assigned to Fabors and Ehmereiz, Morgowanz and Passigweiz,

Giburc's three brothers and one of her sons, and these high-spirited young kings were probably not very happy about this. You ask how the fifth gate was protected? King Halzebier was guarding it, and I have heard the names of still more: Amis and Kordeiz, King Matribleiz and the mighty Josweiz, who was encamped in a manner befitting the fact that Matusales was his father – he who weeded out the good from the bad, like thistles from among the seeds – and that his father's help had aided him, when he left his land and came in full honour across the sea, for Josweiz brought with him many heroes who had been selected for their skill in fighting. Thirty kings were assigned to him, and many powerful and illustrious eskelirs, amazurs and emerals. Without hesitation they swore now to besiege the city for a year, as the revengeful Tibalt bade them do.

Orange was surrounded, as though for a whole week it had rained nothing but knights. We have seldom heard it told since then that so many costly tents were pitched so magnificently on a field in front of any city. When the army outside had settled down, and the army inside was secure, so that there was no threat of attack and their troubles were eased, Giburc led the Margrave away, this battle-weary man, in order to attend to his comfort, and to make her own lament. She went into a chamber and proceeded to attend to her beloved skilfully, removing his armour and examining him at once to see if he were wounded. He had indeed some arrow wounds, so, with her white hands, the Queen took a mixture of vinegar and dittany, made bluish with lapis lazuli, and the flowers of beans which are also beneficial in such cases. If any arrow-head remained in the wound, it would be drawn out by this remedy. She bound his wounds with as much attention as Anfortas ever received,[17] and afterwards she embraced him tenderly.

Was that the time for pleasure? Well, what shall I say about it now? For, if they both wished to do that which they were free to do, then she did not offer resistance for long, for he was hers and she was his (and I have every right to claim what is mine!)

Lovingly they dropped on to a soft, silk mattress, and the Queen herself was just as soft – like a young gosling, gentle to the touch. A tender battle was being waged inside there against the child of Terramer, no matter how angry Terramer himself, or Tibalt, might be outside. I can imagine that no shot nor blow caused Willehalm pain any longer!

But afterwards the Queen was thinking of his trials, of his desperate suffering and his appalling losses. She laid his head upon her left breast and he fell asleep against her heart. Devoutly she called out then to her Creator: 'I know, Altissimus, that You are the Highest God, ever constant and free from falsity, and that Your true Trinity is full of virtue and compassion. Since we are in need of compassion, my beloved husband and I, now that we have lost our friends, whom You Yourself have elected to the company of the angels, it will bring shame upon Your divinity if we are not recompensed for those who, in Your name, fought for such a reward at Alischanz, and if instead we are to be deprived of all earthly joy, this man of his kinsmen and I of those who were my subjects. Now I am learning to do something which I have never done before: to beg for one small consolation. May You grant, in Your goodness, that my life may now come to an end, since my father has inflicted such terrible revenge upon me. The seventy-two tongues which, it is said, are spoken by the people of the world, would not adequately express my agonizing sense of loss, for I have lost much more than that.

'Alas, Vivianz, my beloved one, how all the world will mourn your radiance and your fame! How could death befall you? You are in truth the only one whom I love so especially that I can never experience a grief comparable to that which your death shall inflict upon me in all the years to come. If only I might die in your place! And in the place, too, of my other friends who have performed many deeds of chivalry in battle against the heathens! Alas, that my precious, sorrowful beloved has lost them and must do without them! Alas, what a great loss I have suffered in terms of the loyalty of many heroes which I came to know when I left the land of the Araboises, the King and his children, and when baptism thrust unbelief away from me, and I became a Christian! Now the pursuit by my father has inflicted grief upon me. Tibalt should not have done this.'

A flood of tears rose up in her heart and flowed from her eyes down over her breast, on to the cheek of the Margrave. It was not long before they woke him as he lay there, and the courtly Willehalm, naked of all dishonour and now a stranger to joy, comforted the Queen and promised that she would indeed be released: 'God's very nature is Helpfulness. He has often led me out of fear. If His safe conduct now leads me through the enemy ranks without trouble, I shall soon return to you. My lady, you must advise me now whether to remain here or to ride away. Your command is all I need, in either case.'

Giburc replied: 'You alone cannot fight against the army assembled from all the heathen lands. You must ride for help. *Le roi* Louis of Rome and your relatives will demonstrate their honour by aiding you now. I shall remain behind in these dire straits and defend Orange against the heathen army, until the French arrive, or, if the heathen power should prove still greater, until I die.'

Now the day had come to an end and it was night-time. Only now did the Margrave partake of a *petit repas*, brought to him by young girls, but his armour was lying by his side and swiftly he was helped into it. Then, fully equipped though he was, he was reluctant to leave before the Queen embraced him.

Giburc said to him: 'My lord Marquis, let your distinguished high renown be steadfast now towards me, so that no one can persuade you to be unfaithful to me, poor soul that I am, but take pity on me, and think of your own reputation. I know well enough that many women in France would be well-disposed towards you and, in their love, ready to offer their honour and their very selves to you. If then, lovingly, you were to remember what I have suffered for your sake, you would conserve that payment for me. If the beautiful French women offer you their love in exchange for your service and would like to comfort you into forgetting me, then think of your loyalty and, if anyone tries to discourage you by saying that I shall never be released, send him riding away from you, and fight instead at the head of those who dare to fight. Think what I have sacrificed for your sake, and remember that in Arabie people called me queen of all the princes. In those days I was considered beautiful, or so people said who saw me, friend and foe alike. You may still find me pleasing to you, if only we can get out of this trouble.'

He vowed that the lance of sorrow would always pierce his heart until he managed to release her with brave assistance, and he further promised her that, neither in joy nor in grief, would he consume any nourishment other than bread and water until his sword had lifted that suffering which he knew her to be enduring. Thus did Giburc send him away from her: Volatin was brought up to him and, weeping, the Queen let him out as the gate was softly opened.

Now there was uproar, with the guard riding round the army in many large divisions. Once more the Margrave benefited from wearing the armour of Arofel, as many of the enemy came riding towards him. 'That is the King of Persia,' they said, one to another.

It helped him, too, that he could speak the heathen tongue. Undismayed he looked and saw a road which he recognized, leading towards the land of the French.

BOOK III

The army kept moving into position around Orange for five days, and even then some continued to arrive. Many saddened troops, whose leaders and kinsmen had been slain, were disconsolate. They said that the divine renown of Apolle, Tervigant and Mahmete had been disgraced. Terramer, the wise and experienced man, kept asking for news of how things had turned out, for he could not tell by himself what astounding things had happened to his powerful, noble men. Such a destructive battle had never been fought on earth since the beginning of time.

There was great lamenting in languages of many tongues for Arofel of Persia, also for Tesereiz, Pinel and Poufameiz and generous Noupatris, for Eskelabon, who earned great fame for women's favour. *Le roi* Talimon of Boctan was mourned along with the others, and the death of Turpiun, the doughty King of Falturmie, was a severe blow to heathendom.

When they had ascertained their losses and realized indeed that they were missing twenty-three kings who had been killed there, Terramer's anguish knew no respite. Amazurs and eskelirs and countless emerals, so many of them had been felled that precise figures were completely impossible. The loss drove Terramer to such heart-felt lament that it would have killed a lesser man.

He spoke in sorrow: 'Whoever says that I am mighty, does not know me properly, even though all the lands of heathendom stand ready to serve at my command. I can only now ascribe a great miracle to the god of Christendom, for it is a miracle indeed which has befallen me, that a handful of knights almost destroyed me on account of my vengeance. What I wanted to do was to take revenge for the faithlessness of which people had accused Arabel, my daughter, who deserted Tibalt. I swore then by my gods that I would avenge their honour, so that never again would any children of mine think it fitting to accept baptism for the sake of Jesus, who carried the cross himself on which he was fixed with three nails through his flesh and blood. My faith would be all askew, if I believed that he died and yet in death gained life and that he were three, yet at the same time one. If my old faith is still with me, I don't believe that his Trinity will get my support. He may well have good knights. My uncle Baligan paid the price for that when he fought against the Emperor Charles, by whom all the power of heathendom was crushed.[18] To be sure, my army is more powerful and more broadly based. It is my firm intent to give Arabel unheard-of torment and a shameful death to disgrace Jesus. I cherish that desire in my heart.'

Those who came first and also later wanted to storm Orange and tear it down, to avenge their lords and kinsmen on Giburc, the Queen. Those who were inside the citadel were prepared to defend themselves no matter how hostilely those outside were acting. The Margrave got through them without harm. Now you will hear what loyalty is really like. Good Fortune had protected him, and the Grace of Giburc, too. He both stayed and rode away: Volatin bore his body away, but Giburc kept his heart there. Furthermore, her heart went with him on all the roads he travelled. Who will look after Orange? The exchange was accomplished properly, for *her* heart is heading towards friends, *his* heart shall fend off enemies and save Giburc from despair. Her heart ought to have respite now, but sorrow was left for the two of them.

Giburc did not want to give up Orange and her life as well to her father, so that he might kill her himself and thereupon force the Christians to join the ranks of the unbelievers. He offered her three 'honours' and told her to take her choice of one: that she fall to the depths of the sea with a heavy stone tied round her neck, or that her flesh and bones be burned to powdery ash, or that she be hanged from the branch of a tree by Tibalt himself. She said: 'The well-brought-up guest has always shown good manners to his hostess. What are you thinking of, father, by offering me such games that I neither can nor will play? I can make a better bet. The French shall play my hand for me, and they won't let me be overtrumped!'

Meanwhile day began to break. That conversation took place one night and was concluded differently later. The heathens asked: 'Where is the Marquis?'

She replied: 'He has arranged a tournament to win honour and will return for it soon for my sake. It shall take place before these gates. Then you can see who will carry the field for Love's reward. He has lost a few people now and is still mindful of the loss. You wretched Saracens, some of you relatives of mine, you are waiting here for great trouble. A twofold death will find you. Although you offer me three deaths, two are very close at hand for you: the end of this short life and the fettered bondage of your souls before your god Tervigant, who has made fools of you.'

When Terramer rightly saw that no threat of a frontal assault could subdue Orange and when the Christians did not want to negotiate, he ordered siege equipment to be made. On all sides, whether valley or mountain, he wanted to attack the city. However many siege weapons were made to attack Giburc – catapults and other stone throwers, movable towers on tall stilts, battering-rams, protective structures, ballistas – all that frightened her little. Now most of her army lay dead on the fortifications. However, she resorted to the stratagem of having helmets bound to each dead man's head, and she propped shields up on the battlements, using whatever she could find, new ones or old. These troops were not going to desert out of cowardice. Joy and sorrow were all the same to them.

No matter how quickly the sorrowful Margrave had left Giburc, his thoughts never budged from her. They were with her in Orange. Even if I am not so skilful in telling you her distress, take pity on her for God's sake at least.

I didn't hear how many days it took the doughty Margrave to get to Orleans. I was told about his lodgings, however, namely that he avoided the nice places and rode down a wretched alley to a small house in front of the moat, where his horse Volatin could scarcely stand upright. He had pledged himself to misery, and his high spirits were all subdued. He did not want to raise them by any means. He saw to the comfort of his horse and of his host, so that the host said that no guest had ever shown him such generosity. For food he ate nothing but water and bread. His joy was limping along.

Early in the morning he set out again. Now there was a powerful man in that town, well known because he had the right to collect tolls. The King had granted him that right. He decided to direct his anger at the Margrave without reason, and the latter offered him a proper reply, saying: 'I don't have to pay any toll. I am not transporting goods on pack-animals. I am a knight, as you can see. If you see any damage that I might have done to the countryside, you should let me pay for that. I avoided the sown fields by sticking to the roads, and I rode the well-trodden paths. They should be free for everyone. I have paid for the food for myself and my horse.'

The magistrate and his men had quickly surrounded him, for on all sides the town militiamen came trotting up, as the magistrate had requested. He said that Willehalm would have to pay a toll of such magnitude that he would feel the loss of it. However, it was a sinful shame that they did not let him ride on. The magistrate told his men to grab his bridle, but Willehalm said: 'This horse is carrying no baggage save me and this shield. I'd sooner fight than pay the toll.'

Out came his sword. I wouldn't want to collect the toll that the magistrate received then, even next door for anyone's sake, for he became shorter by a head. The Margrave's passage through the crowd was met with the slashing of many a sword, but he made room when pressed. He had to hack such a path through the town, the people and the horses, that his street became very wide. The fighting bore in on him, but many wounded men fled back away from him. The alarm was sounded by tolling the bell. The town should be disgraced because they raised the hue and cry against one solitary man. They arranged themselves in detachments, but now he had reached open country. I heard tell he inflicted damage later.

They followed in his wake, some here, the others there. He trotted easily in front of them, not fleeing, but his turning around chased them all the way back to the city gate. With that their troubles began to increase. Volatin was wheeled around, and 'Monjoie!', the Margrave's battle-cry, resounded loudly. Swiftly his charge covered the ground back towards the gates. The townspeople fled in all directions. If he had not feared to commit a sin, he would have wrought damage, as armed men are ever wont to do. He seized a lance from one, but they had had enough of the fighting, and he stuck his sword back into the sheath. All the militia trekked back into the town. Thereupon Willehalm set out for Laon.

Arnalt, *fils du comte de* Narbonne, heard the wretched cries resounding in all the streets. Up till then he had been lying asleep. He roused the many knights who had been lying around him taking their ease, every one of them. Now the magistrate's wife came. She fell down before him on the rug and complained to him of the disgrace to the King and of her own loss, saying that her husband had been killed 'by a man travelling alone. He has chased away all the people and has got clean away. Alas, it is a wretched profit that we have gained from the toll he paid for the use of the Roman King's roads!'

Count Arnalt spoke to the woman: 'Who can it be that he has harmed you so severely? Woman, if it is a merchant, then he might well ask for a convoy and pay his fee for it, for his goods are subject to a toll.'

Those accompanying the woman said that he was carrying a shield: 'His armour is rusty, yet in all the land of the French no one has ever seen such an expensive surcoat. It is as brilliant as the sun, as is his shield and cape of fur. He yelled "Monjoie!" as he made us flee back into town. That was his battle-cry.'

The Count spoke: 'All of you are contemptible who advocated taking a knight for a merchant! Why should a knight have to pay a toll? If he had killed all of you, I should not weep a bit. I must chase after him for the King, whose crown my sister shares.'

Quickly he was armed, and all his worthy men heard his orders to mount up. Knights and foot-soldiers alike wanted to capture the Margrave and hold him for ransom. If the wounded men were supposed to refresh themselves with what he gave them in return no one's thirst was quenched. Arnalt said: 'Gentlemen, whoever that be, he's using the King's battle-cry, the one Emperor Charles fought under, who bequeathed it to his son, who rules the Empire now and never allows anyone to use the cry except those who guard his marches against the forces of other kings. This tricky man whom we must catch is trying to get away by using the cry that he thinks should save him. If he thinks that he has gained honour at our expense by this stratagem here, just let him flee through field and wood, we'll be hot on his trail.'

Arnalt rode away ahead of his men. There were plenty of people on horse or on foot, whoever could carry a staff or a club, and all the militiamen. (It wouldn't take half so many bees to kill a strong bear.) The Marquis from Provence was not the man to show them his heels. Their pursuit could force him in no way into a headlong gallop. Now he heard the earth resounding. At that very moment the Margrave saw Arnalt of Gironde coming. In his heart he said then that the right ones had finally taken the field.

Arnalt had got ahead of his men by some forty lengths or more. Willehalm turned towards him with a deft gallop. Each man pressed his charge closer. Neither spear remained intact. Arnalt's saddle lay empty, because he had been felled behind his charger in the clash with his brother. That had never happened to him before. He could easily have done without it. The Margrave was so angry that he would gladly have killed him, and the pursuit of the others was still too far away to help Arnalt. He survived only by a question and by the fact that he gave his name, saying properly: 'I am Count Arnalt. Who is it who has unhorsed me? He can have a good deal of praise for that.'

'I am Willehalm, the Marquis,' he said. 'O my brother, let's have no more fighting here!'

He caught Arnalt's horse and led it to him. Arnalt recognized the Margrave by his voice. He pulled him down on to the grass and wanted to kiss him over and over again.

'Brother, I must do without that,' said the faithful Margrave. 'I live in such sorrow that death would be much kinder to me. I have left behind my only real kiss, with Giburc, who is in danger right now in Orange. So long as she is subjected to such perils, I shall never allow a man's or a woman's mouth to touch mine. I am bearing such a heavy load of troubles that my horse has had a difficult time of it carrying them this far. What amazing things God has bestowed on me! Here I have to defend myself against myself! When I jousted with you, I was really fighting with myself.'

Arnalt spoke, saying: 'You are telling the truth. Unwittingly my body performed hostile acts against my own body. You kept your arrival silent like a hunting-dog on the leash. Our two selves can be counted as one. If anyone wanted to distinguish two hearts, he would find only one here, for my heart was always yours, and your heart shall always be mine. Alas, my lord, my brother, let me hear and see what is troubling sweet Giburc, my sister, my lady? Can my help recompense her? She has well deserved to have every noble Frenchman's strength in service at her command. One can serve both God and the honour of our land in serving her, and this for the sake of her conversion to Christianity through baptism. You once paid dearly in gaining her love. My young kinsmen, whom she raised as fledgelings and who have now flown away from France, are they with her in her distress?'

The Margrave named Mile and Vivianz as dead and told Arnalt how the clash at Alischanz had both begun and ended, and how Terramer had come to surround Orange in siege and what anxious moments he had had before he succeeded in riding away through their ranks. At the news of this suffering and of these terrible things, the wellspring of Arnalt's heart rose and poured forth from his eyes. He said: 'Alas for my kinsmen who have been struck down by death! Who brought King Tibalt with such forces across the sea? Or what did you think we might do to help Giburc and, in view of the losses we have suffered, to keep our losses from even increasing? All those to whom I have ever rendered service will be reminded of their debt to me now. Our entire lineage would be disgraced, if Giburc were taken away from you. Tell me where you want to assemble your forces and ride with my assistance to get powerful help quickly. Lament your loss to the nobles of the realm. Three days from today a court will be held at Laon which will attract all the French. They will come from far and wide. Heimrich and Irmschart, our two parents, have been chosen by the King for honours at his festivities. Also, my four brothers are supposed to be coming with our mother. I think that Heimrich, my father, will bring the largest group of men. Count it as a great stroke of luck, for you will find all the nobles there. If you tell me your way, I shall ride ahead of you or after. Now don't be in such a hurry to leave that you can't ride back into town with me and take off your armour, have a bath and some fresh clothes.'

'We must part,' said the Margrave. 'If I could ever be happy again,

I would rejoice at the prospect of these festivities. Do you suppose that He who knows all suffering and is called the Highest will grant me release? May He look with favour upon me. If my Lady, the Queen, is there, it could help my cause. It should not displease her to plead my case with the King, and I would call that a sisterly deed. If any of my kinsmen come there, they will take pity on me for the loss I have suffered. And if my brothers who are there – I am also Heimrich's son – want to show their loyalty, they will feel pity for my sharp pain and for my arid grief of heart. My joy will never more turn green. To Heimrich and to Irmschart and to my other relatives I shall turn and ask for grace. May God see that I get help! Brother, let me urge you to act so that Giburc may be rescued. Admonish all your friends to help.'

With that the Margrave departed, and Arnalt rode back to town weeping, but not because he had been felled in the joust. Suffering began to consume his happiness at such great cost that even an emperor could not have withstood it. The death of his noble kinsmen caused him the heartfelt grief.

All those who had been riding after Arnalt came galloping up, here a troop, there a troop, and they gathered around him. He didn't let them go any further. But this one and that one still didn't know whom they had been pursuing, when they saw a spearhead in the Count's shield, brought back from the joust. They asked: 'What are you thinking of? That man will get away from us. If you don't want to fight with him, why don't you let us pursue him?'

Arnalt began to tell them the truth of the matter: 'It is Willehalm, the Marquis. I shall by no means allow him to be killed on French soil. He is not at all a stranger to us, even though the burghers of Orleans did not behave properly towards him. O Stupidity, what trouble you cause those who are at your beck and call! Why should my brother have to pay a toll like a merchant? If anyone knows anything about knighthood, he would let him pass free of toll.'

Those who were standing there with the Count noticed that he was crying. They asked him what he was thinking about that made him so unhappy. Arnalt then told them that the Saracens had captured and killed thirteen of his kinsmen: 'Now let me lament. Those noblemen were mostly all of such tender years that none had a beard yet. My brother has inherited enough trouble by himself without our adding to it. His men have perished, and in addition his wife is besieged. He doesn't know how long Orange can hold out, or with what help they will be saved. It is in God's Hand.'

He sent out many messengers who travelled night and day to those who were obligated to serve him. He called upon his men and his relatives.

The Margrave too was travelling on. Towards evening he found a monastery. The monks did not know him, yet they took care of him nicely. His shield had been wrought in Samargone, the capital of Persia, and its boss was very expensive. Even Adramahut and Arabi, the wealthy cities in Morlant, are unfamiliar with the silks out of which his surcoat was made, set here and there with beautiful jewels, so that one could see the expensive silks showing right through. His fur cloak was fashioned similarly. (Chrétien dressed him in old dimity at Laon, but whoever speaks such nonsense is only showing his ignorance.)[19] Willehalm had taken from Arofel the Persan, who lay dead before him, a more expensively and skilfully made outfit than had ever been offered by a lady to her knight, except for the one that King Feirefiz had received in love from Sekundille. That exceeded all others in sumptuousness.

Great fatigue had brought him to the point where he spent half the day and the entire night in the monastery. Then his impatience drove him on. It was too much for him to wait any longer. He entrusted his shield to the monastery and rode towards Laon.

Many a Frenchman and Breton and many Englishmen and noble Burgundians had come there for the celebration. (I can't name them all for you.) From German lands there were the Flemings and Brabanters and the Duke of Lorraine. The Margrave became convinced, since there was such a crowd of troops, that it would take a long time to find a good-hearted landlord who would put him up. He therefore stopped looking for lodgings and rode to the King's court. No one was fighting to get hold of his bridle, to take charge of his horse for him. While he was riding along or even once he had dismounted, no one, whether on horse or on foot, offered him any kind of greeting at all. He saw countless people there, short, tall, young and old, and they all treated him with hostility. He didn't want to go begging to any of them, young *or* old. Therefore he headed towards an olive and a linden tree. The people who were lying and sitting under the trees saw to it that they left him all the shade for himself. They didn't want to have anything to do with him. He was given so much room that there was a wide area around him. And he did not ask anyone to sit down. He took the bridle in one hand, unfastened the costly helmet from his head and dumped it on the grass at his feet.

All the people of the court began to look at him, the ladies in the windows as well, because he was wearing armour. They said it was a peculiar thing for him to be armed without their having previously heard that there was going to be a tournament. If a knight wanted to attend, he could at least bring his armour on a pack-animal. The Margrave was holding his bridle in his hands where he was sitting. Then he began to take his coif from his head, pulling it off quickly. His skin was grimy and his beard and hair all tangled.

It was announced to the King – something that he did not like – that a man had dismounted from a beautiful charger at the olive and the linden. 'None of us can imagine or find out who it is. He is wearing rusty armour, and he looks quite wild. What he is wearing over his chain-mail is expensive and splendid. No eye has ever seen such a beautiful knightly outfit. No one in all Christendom even knows the name of the silks. There is a heathen saddle and trappings on his horse. He would fit much better in battle than at a dance. Nor is his beard, his skin or his hair so gleaming that one could call him clean. He has come here from a battle. We are also curious to know what he wants, coming here so ready to fight. We would like to hear all about that knight, since we don't know him and have no information about him. His surcoat and fur cloak rival the sun. Each one competes with the other in costly splendour. He is a foreigner to the French. From whatever land he comes, he acts very much as if he were a stranger.'

Then the King and his wife said: 'Let's go and look at him from the windows and find out what he is seeking or what he has in mind, since he has come armed alone like this to the imperial court.'

A wolf peers into the sheep-pen with just such an innocent gaze as Willehalm had then, so the story tells me.

The Queen said to the King: 'That man sitting down there in front of us is, I think, Sire – I could almost swear – my brother Willehalm, who has caused the French all sorts of painful laments with his travelling about. Now he is probably wanting a new army again to fight against the heathens for the love of Queen Giburc. I should not like to know that he was in here. Don't any of you go outside. Lock the door securely. If he knocks on it, send him away.'

What she ordered was done. The Margrave, that sad man, was still holding his horse. Many of those who were there still did not recognize him. Furthermore, he was acting as if it were only right that he should have to put up with their refusal to offer him respect and hospitality. He saw many crowds of people coming to the court and then leaving. No one who might have shared in his troubles offered him any friendly consolation commensurate with his great discomfort.

Then a merchant of the city came and very politely asked him to come with him for the sake of the honour of all merchants: 'You have indeed suffered much, regardless of where you have come from. Knights should greet you better than this. Since everyone who has seen you, alone as you are, has forgotten to do that, allow me the pleasure of being able to render you service. Sir, let me respectfully request that you do me this honour in my old age.'

The merchant was called Wimar, and he was born of a noble family. He said: 'I do not think it a loss to offer you something in honour. If you will let me do this today, every one of my colleagues will say afterwards that my renown has become great.'

The Margrave spoke as follows, saying: 'I am very happy about your request, and I shall reward you, if I can, seeing that no one, neither marshal nor any other man of the court, has taken care of me. They have disgraced the court by letting me stay so unattended, before you in your kindness singled me out for greeting in front of all of them. I have good reason to be displeased, for I recognized many of them here who at one time were glad to bow over my hand for some gift of mine and who now have refused to greet me. You go ahead, and I'll walk behind.'

'I'll walk, but you shall ride,' said the merchant courteously, 'or I would rather stand here for weeks on end.'

Then the Margrave said: 'If I were to let you be my page, I should know nothing about good fellowship. Let me maintain proper etiquette: I can just as well follow you on foot. I must do as fellowship dictates.'

The merchant did not let him win the argument. Willehalm had to mount up and ride away, with the merchant walking along. The countless children on the street who were tagging along after the Margrave asked with whom he wanted to fight. Whoever saw him riding like this fled from him in the alley and evaded his wrath.

Wimar brought him to his house. There he was properly disarmed. But before that happened, his horse was given careful attention. Down pillows and rich quilts were ordered by the host to be placed on the rug, but the guest declined such a soft seat for himself. He was afraid that he would forget the dangerous situation Giburc was in. He asked to have some grass brought in, 'And let me wallow in it like a cow. If I was ever a mother's child, then the world was chock-full of sorrows when she gave birth to me. My host, I am not a lord. My loss tells me otherwise.'

Down pillows, quilts, mattresses, he would sit on none of them. His sadness troubled his host. Green grass and fresh clover were brought in abundantly and spread under him. His host complained sorely that Willehalm would not avail himself of greater comfort, as would be appropriate for a weary man, and such as he willingly offered him. But the host was still unaware of the troubles of his guest, which were told to him only later.

Now Wimar had ordered many new, fresh foods to be roasted and boiled, fish and meat as well, both game and domestic meat. He went to such expense that if that amount had been required as ransom for his life, he and his wife would not have needed any more. Then, with proper manners, a small table was set up for the Margrave alone. When Willehalm had washed his hands, his host brought before him politely, as merchants are renowned for doing, many kinds of boiled and roasted foods. If any poor man were so supplied, he would think it good. Drink such as that would be appropriate for the Emperor to offer, but the Margrave did not wish to enjoy any of it. He had promised not to. He thought that he would have been insane to eat anything more than bread or to drink anything but water. He wanted to suffer, you see, until the Hand of the Almighty redeemed the precious pledge he had left in Orange.

There was the roasted peacock before him, with salty broth, a delicacy of the host's. He had never eaten any better than that. He refused the capon, the pheasant, the lampreys in gelatine and the partridges. His host said: 'Sir, if better food were known in this land, I should be happy to provide it for you. Tell me, if you wish for something else. Let me have it prepared for you.'

The Margrave sighed and spoke: 'Kind Sir, my affairs are such that I shall never be happy until that fateful day when God's power can arrange for my oath to end. If His consolation will allow me the joy of receiving good fortune then, Sir, there will be time enough after that for me to enjoy good food. You must not give me anything but water and some bread to dunk in it. I ask neither you nor anyone else to make any improvements. Whatever lives from sea or land I shall avoid, for I must endure suffering until I have found better consolation.

'Kind Sir, I have lost noble kinsmen and worthy men. In addition, I have left in peril a woman who holds my heart there. My body here is bereft of joy. Now ask no more, just leave it at that. You have demonstrated your kindness in your treatment of me. As a result, your renown is enhanced. I am the Marquis of Provence, Willehalm by name. If I am ever in a position to be generous, you will be recompensed for this food, no matter how poor I am here and now.'

The host spoke: 'Sir, how lucky I am that your trip here has made you a guest in my house! Those nobles who refused to greet you here should be ashamed of themselves. Please be so gracious as to accept my poor service in good faith. If I have any Christian sense, I shall feel sorry for your suffering until such time as your joys increase.'

The host could easily hear and see that Willehalm had suffered, and was still suffering, discomfort from his grief. He did not want to ask him further to partake of any better food. Instead, he gave him hard bread and that drink by which the nightingale lives, as a result of which its sweet song is lovelier than if it had drunk all the wine there is in Bolzano. Some of this nourishment was consumed, but soft bedding was refused. The Margrave lay down on the grass that had been brought in for him earlier. The host took his leave and went away, leaving the sorrowful man lying disconsolately. If he had ever been happy before, that had all become only a dream to him now. His heart bore a full load of grief.

Then the Margrave thought: 'Since my affairs have come to such a pass that none of the best people here have deigned to speak to me and have thereby disgraced themselves, if I live until tomorrow morning, I shall give them such cause to lament, that children who are yet unborn will still have enough to tell about that day ever after.'

He lay in anger without sleeping until the daylight shone upon him. His armour was lying next to him, as was Arofel's brilliant sword. He put on his leg-coverings of mail. Then his host, the merchant, came and asked him what he intended to do. Heimrich's son answered: 'You can see, I'm putting armour on my legs. I have also decided to put on the rest of my armour, so that I can be better protected from thrusts and blows. I think I am too noble to be in such a disgraceful situation. This and any other sword would have been girded around me for nothing, if I were to continue to be an object of mockery to the French.'

He asked his host to see how his armour fitted at the back. (He could check on it in front himself.) The host said: 'Sir, it fits very well. I am sorry to see you sliding into such suffering. Your discomfort pains me. If you wish, I have clothing to give you better than any that all the lands of the French can produce.'

'I still say what I said last night,' the Margrave said to his host. 'You have shown me kindness. Unless I am doomed to die, my thanks will be unstinted. I'll part the King's hair all the way down to his beard with this sword, and I'll do it in front of all the nobles. I have suffered scorn and mockery from him after all my disastrous losses. I can say that only to you.'

The host became so terrified that he sank down next to him and said not a word in reply. The Margrave went to his horse. Volatin had been saddled and curried. 'I shall give proper thanks for these lodgings,' said the Margrave, 'if things turn out well.'

Then he mounted his horse and rode straight away back to where his host had found him the previous evening. By that time the sun had risen high in the sky. Many people were making their way towards the court, striding, ambling and trotting. Impatiently the

Margrave tied his horse's bridle fast to a branch of the olive tree. He wanted to follow the others, to stand before the King and shout. But then he thought to himself: 'If I see this coward, this King, and if I kill him, and if his people don't kill me, I shall still lose the nobles. What if all my efforts come to naught? Then the help will be lost that I promised to Giburc, whom I left in great peril. I shall wait for my father, with all the worry of uncertainty. That I must endure until he comes. If he has a father's mind, he will show it in his treatment of me. My brothers will help me too, as will my noble kinsmen.'

Now his host, the merchant, came and slipped past in front of where he was sitting and disappeared into the crowd. He told the people in the palace who the knight was. Then all the people, young and old, ran down the steps. Many noble men received the Margrave joyfully. He came towards them and said to all of them: 'Whoever has accepted gifts from me and who saw me sitting here last night was very ill-advised to leave me sitting here alone, when I had always given him my aid. If my pack-animals were carrying gold, velvet, silks and other cloth, you would all be nice to me. If you saw many of the horses that I have in my march walking along with me, then I would not be able to sit or stand anywhere without a crowd of people around me. Shame on the court, if a prince has to encounter such a despicable reception from the household! You think that I am ruined? No, I am of a different mind about that!'

On both his surcoat and his fur cloak you could see evidence of fighting, for they had been slashed, in places pierced. His sword, girded round him, had a golden hilt. His armour looked rusty. Since his retinue was so small, he soon stood alone without the knights. This was an unfamiliar experience for him.

The King, who had heard Mass sung, came to the great hall where many princes were present. The Queen had come there too. The Margrave, wearing his sword around his waist, followed the others until he saw the King and his sister, the King's wife. The King and the princes sitting there were not pleased to see him coming. None of them was so high-born that he did not fear his wrath.

The Margrave then moved his sword around and put it on his lap without having taken it off. I think all of them, the poor and rich alike, were not happy that he was sitting there among them. Some wished him far away in Kanach or Ahsim, in the heat of Alamansura, or contrarily in Skandinavia, frozen in the ice. There again, many a clever nobleman wished that Willehalm were at the Katus Erkules,[20] while yet another wished him off to the island called Palaker in the liver sea[21] – and defenceless at that, 'so that no Frenchman would ever hear of him again. The military campaigns and journeys to Orange that he has asked for have cleaned France out of good chivalry. Never did a man have so many relatives for whose sake we have to fight.'

'Now he doesn't even want to greet anyone,' said one man, but he didn't know what was going on.

'Quiet!' replied another to him then. 'You will see something today that will make many a prince unhappy. He has suffered losses again, and his sword will be bathed in blood before we leave here. Again the heathens have ridden all too close to him. Orange be damned, that stone was ever quarried for it! We shall have to swear or promise him an army this very day, or you'll see him go berserk!'

Then another Frenchman spoke and said: 'My lord, the King, should give him Vermandois and Arras in fief. Look at how strangely the bold, powerful man behaves! My lord should compensate him for the march in that way, if he wishes to have peace. His behaviour is uncouth.'

Now Irmschart and Heimrich came with a large retinue. Their four sons, princes all of them, and seven thousand knights or more had been brought there by the venerable old Prince. The chamberlains with their staffs of office could hardly make enough room for the old Princess Irmschart of Pavia to progress towards the great hall. Many noblemen followed her. When she came in, she was received with a kiss from the lips of the Roman King. At the same time her daughter kissed her joyfully, for she was delighted that she had come. After the King had greeted his mother-in-law she sat down next to her daughter. Now Heimrich came too, equal in power to any prince. A baron carried his sword before him, and many noble knights followed him.

The King acted properly. He stood up to receive Heimrich and led him by the hand to the Roman Queen, who gave him a gracious kiss in greeting. After that the King seated him close to his very side. At the same time, Heimrich's four sons were greeted with deference by all the princes present. Each prince had to take his place, as did all the others. Many carpets had been laid all around the great hall to muffle the noise of the celebration, and over these layers of dewy roses had been strewn, to a hand's depth. Their beautiful appearance was trampled underfoot, but that produced a sweet scent.

Still the Margrave sat there, as he had since he first arrived. Not a single one of those who could have greeted him had done so. In the face of that he behaved as you shall soon hear. He offended the sense of propriety of those who would listen to the words that he spoke in the King's presence. Silently he thought: 'Since Terramer caused me such heartfelt sorrow in my losses, I have not seen happiness any more, save that which I see here. I can say this of my good fortune: it has a way to go before it is dead and buried, even though I've lost so much in terms of joy. Almost all my kinsmen are sitting here, including the woman who bore me. I think *she* will not be silent. *She* will tell Heimrich that I am the child of both of them. My brothers who are present here will show their loyalty to me, if they hear of my painful loss.'

'Now I'll risk it,' he thought. Then he stood up to argue loudly. Striding past many, the angry man stood before the King and spoke: 'Your Majesty, you can be happy that my father is sitting next to you. I'll tell you one thing: even if you were three, I would have taken you hostage, but I shall refrain from doing that out of politeness. May He, whose Arm bears the Hand that passes in blessing over the angels, impart the sweep of His blessing to my father, white-haired with age, and to my noble mother. Your Majesty, you believe that you are powerful, but did I give you the Roman crown for such wretched reward as I have received from you? The realm was in my hand. You were the same man as you are now, when I took up arms against all the princes who knew you and were reluctant to recognize you, because they feared that they would lose honour and renown with you. I refused to allow that at all, and they had to accept you as their ruler. That was a mistake on my part. Alas, that I ever had the misfortune of placing my hands between yours! You had the advantage then of the many troubles that I had suffered for your father, of the many campaigns I had fought. I have also fought many for you. Now it has been seven years since I saw my father and mother or any of those brothers of mine. I could easily lodge a complaint against you, but for my mother's sake I won't.'

His four brothers leapt towards him. They received him warmly and embraced him again and again, although it was in the King's presence. Bertram and Buov of Commercey, Gibert and Bernart *le fleuri*, all admonished him to moderate his anger for the sake of his honour. They went back and sat down, but the Margrave remained standing.

Then the Roman King spoke, saying: 'Sir Willehalm, since it is you, I think it is high time for me to acknowledge your princely rights, for since I was a young page, I always lived according to your advice, nor did I ever want for your help. You have no cause to direct your anger towards me. You know that whatever you wish in all my lands will be done. I have grants and fiefs. Use them, as is fitting, to your advantage.'

Willehalm's sister, the Queen, said: 'Alas, how little will be left for us! I should be the first he would drive out. I would rather have him serve us than seek his favour myself.'

The Queen had to pay dearly for her words. Whatever blame he had heaped upon the King before, she now received ten times over, and he accused her of being much too arrogant. In front of all the princes he snatched the crown from her head and hurled it down, so that it shattered in pieces. Then the raging guest seized the Queen by her braids and would have sliced off her head with his sword, had not Irmschart, the mother of them both, come between them. Thus her life was spared. With difficulty the Queen wrested her braids from his strong hand and fled to her chamber. When she got inside, she ordered the door to be locked with an iron bar. Even then she hid herself in fear.

Outside, King Louis wished he were at Etampes or Paris or Orleans, or wherever he could be safe, rather than here with Willehalm. 'I am suffering this disgrace at the hands of the Margrave without reason,' said the King. 'He is my vassal. Whatever I might have done to him, he could have made a formal complaint before the princes. If my wife is to lie dead at his hand, then that is an unwarranted loss, in view of what I said to him and what I was prepared to do for him.'

From a sense of propriety, as well as out of fear, all were distressed by the outrage that had taken place. Inside, the King's daughter was speaking to her mother: 'Madam, what are you doing entering the room like this? When did a queen ever come rushing to someone in such a state? You are behaving in a manner that ill befits the illustrious name of my father, whom all the realm serves. You are leaping so wildly that the lame would not be able to follow you. Who is so angry with you out there?'

'That is your uncle,' replied her mother. 'Help me to gain his favour, my beloved daughter.'

The Prince of Narbonne approached his son and greeted him for the first time, but Willehalm asked for permission to refuse, when Heimrich, his father, wanted to welcome him with a kiss. Instead, he spoke as he properly should: 'My kiss has remained behind in Orange, the city from which Tibalt has driven me. I left my proper kiss in Orange when Terramer ordered his men to attack me. My losses to his forces are so great that I can never be recompensed, unless your manly courage and your supreme loyalty do it for me; otherwise I must carry my heartfelt sorrow very quickly to my death. I left Giburc in such distress. My despair tells me – shall I say it openly? – that my kinsmen are going to let me down. Now help me, for the sake of the constant power of the Threefold Fellowship. I mean that the Father accorded His very own place to the Son, and the Holy Spirit vouchsafed this for the two of them. For the sake of these three names, I ask you to show your knightly virtue and acknowledge me as your child. Then your help will stand by me steadfastly with comfort for my feeble joy. Don't be dismayed at the power of the heathens, for you have carried your renown into your old age.'

'It's not proper for you,' his father said, 'to have doubts about me. I want to share your suffering, unless I am prevented from doing so by some great overburdening distress or by that compelling command which separates the soul from the body. It ill befits your noble manliness to harbour doubts about me and to demean our loyalty. Tell me quickly all your loss and lament, confident in my help. How the swords shall resound for it! I trust implicitly that God's Hand will guide my arm. Many heathen hearts, still warm today, shall grow cold as a result. If noble King Tibalt is lying in your march with his army, I'll be at your side ready to fight. Where are those whom I have sired? Take this disgrace upon you, as I do. It is not my son who has been attacked, but I, who say it is *my* disgrace. Whatever losses he has suffered I'll share with him. Tell me, did you attack them with your knights? How large were the heathen forces? How did my young relatives perform?'

The Margrave told him the truth: 'Their army was too much for me. If one placed cardamon seeds on the squares of a chess-board and doubled their number each time on each square, counting all the way to the end, then Terramer and Tibalt had more knights than that, and Arofel of Persia and Tesereiz, whom I killed, also had many knights there. At Alischanz I lost young and handsome Vivianz and Mile, my sister's child. If the kinsmen of those two are happy, then they have chosen to be disloyal. I have had captured or otherwise lost eleven other princes. I had to yield victory to the heathens, when Gaudiers and Gaudin, Hunas and Kibelin, Berhtram and Gerart, Huwes and Witschart, and also my nephew Jozeranz, and Gwigrimanz, the Burgundian – the eleventh man was Samson – were taken from me in battle, with the resounding clash of many charges and with the arrival of many fresh detachments. I do not know the fate of the eleven. Mile and Vivianz are dead.'

Three strong carts and a waggon could not have carried the water that welled from the eyes of the knights. Heimrich could barely keep from falling. Then many pretty hands were wrung so hard that you could hear them crack. Joyful, hearty laughter was silenced by the news of Vivianz' death, and there was nothing but sorrow for his kin.

Then Irmschart of Pavia spoke: 'Is this the way you show your bravery? You still have strong limbs. If you are going to weep like women or like a child crying for the least little thing, how does such wailing befit heroes? If you wish to live bravely, you must offer loans and gifts and help him who has come to us, whose losses we have all heard. We have suffered these losses with him. If all of you of Heimrich's lineage will honour his kinship, then Willehalm, my son, will be recompensed for what he has suffered. Whoever is deterred by cowardice would be better off dead.'

Yet anger still caused the Margrave to rail against his sister, who, to a certain extent, was paying for crimes she had not committed. The Roman Queen was repeatedly called by the names of those women who have love for sale. (I would have said those names, if I had wanted to say them in your presence, but I must suppress them out of propriety.)[22] Still, he insulted her more than enough. If he had ever exhibited manliness, or if he had ever intended following his heart's desire, to put his service at the disposal of ladies, and if he had ever received joy or sorrow for the sake of a lady's love, then chaste propriety was done a disservice in his 'manly' behaviour now. Yet no knight had ever been raised better or so *courtois*, without flaw.

He charged that Tibalt, the Arabois, had been her knight for a long time, saying: 'She may well be honouring that noble king with love's reward. He has often embraced her tenderly with his arms. That has happened more as an insult to her husband than for her own sake. I never would have taken Giburc away from Tibalt, except that I was avenging what was happening here. Giburc has paid me back in love's coin for what Tibalt borrowed.'

Then Alize, the King's daughter, came up. Willehalm did not want to offend against propriety any more. Whatever he might have said in anger was suppressed for her sake. If he had not yet accused her mother as he had, he would not have done it afterwards. The pure, sweet, beautiful young maiden wore her hair in short locks, curled tightly against her head. Whoever looked at her properly saw that she was slim and supple as a tender branch, lovely in many ways. Every curly lock had its own tie, fastened not too tightly. The little ties were fashioned artistically and decorated with jewels. Altogether it looked as if she were wearing a crown. Alize was so beneficent that one could have used her purity as a poultice on a wound infected with some dread disease. If it did not heal then, the wound must have been in penance for something quite unheard of. Around her waist the girl wore a belt brought from London, nicely fashioned, long and narrow. Its end fell down to the floor, and its clasp was a precious ruby. (Think of her as being better dressed than I can imagine.) She had such a lovely appearance that a disconsolate man could easily have his spirits raised by looking at her. Her breast was neither too low nor too high. The whole world loved her. Her body was all that one could desire and a guarantor of that which brings joy. Anyone who received a greeting from her lips had happiness all his life long. Such a radiance emanated from the maiden that people who were at home there as well as strangers from afar agreed that they had never seen so beautiful a girl.

Quickly her uncle, Buov of Commercey, leapt towards her, as did three other princes, clearing a pathway for the lovely maiden. All who were there spoke with one accord, when they said that to receive one look from her would be to experience great good fortune. Sadness would disappear thereafter.

Wearing just a dress without a cloak, the young girl walked to her uncle, who received her courteously. When that was done, she knelt at his feet. His eyes began to fill with tears, when he saw her fall before him.

'May I not have to atone for this before God,' he said to her. 'Why are you coming to me like this, my niece? You are too noble to kneel even before King Terramer. You are the daughter of the Roman King. All the Roman princes here present will think even less of me for this. Niece, permit me now to live under your command, and may your kindness guide me. If you are not mocking me, stand up, and whatever you ask of me, I shall do out of respect for you. You are undermining my reputation.'

The girl stood up. He clasped her to himself, saying: 'With your permission I shall take your lovely face into my hands. I would kiss you straight away, but for the fact that I have forsworn kissing. The best gain I ever made in love has been surrounded by Terramer's forces with such knighthood that kissing has become alien to me. God has fashioned you so that a whole forest of spears will be used up, if a noble man ever gains your favour.'

As best she could, Alize began her speech, weeping as she spoke. The maiden, completely free of guile, said: 'Alas for your nobility, which has never suffered disgrace! What have you done with your chaste propriety? Where does woman's honour find refuge, if not in a man's kindness? Uncle, your mind has become all too twisted. Who has made you angry towards my foolish mother? If she, who is supposed to be your sister, makes a slip of the tongue, and if you want to take revenge for that, then our whole family will suffer, and that will jeopardize both her nobility and your renown. If you think that I am making sense, you should let her benefit from my words. Forgive whatever she did to you. Do this partly for my sake here and now, so that the princes will see it. I make the same request for the sake of your own mother, my grandmother, and for Giburc, my lady, who often took me into her arms, as if I were her own child. She is too far away from me, alas!'

The Margrave spoke, saying: 'Dear child, take charge of my body, which stands here before you and which will neither ride nor walk anywhere, until it does so with your favour. Are you really aware of how your mother treated me? She could have decided to treat me as the King did, who, however, still has never treated me as would befit the Empire. Even if she hates the sight of me, I might have gained assistance except for the fact that now, and often in the past, she has done me out of the King's help. It would have been no disgrace to her, if she had just said, "That is my brother." Not everyone can be King. She should treat the princes nicely. Still, I think that my name is closest to the Roman crown. If she is ashamed of me, then I brought that shame upon myself, when I lost Emperor Charles. If I had dared to address her as sister, then people would have seen her receive me more pleasantly. When I came before her, I did not acknowledge her greeting. That was because she withheld it. What should the others have done? Still, I am the son of him who raised her as his daughter. She may yet live to see an alliance. The King has gained all his power through my hand alone. If I alone had not supported him, he would not have obtained his power with the help of those who now must acknowledge him lord. I handed over the Empire to him when all the princes, the lesser and the greater, and all the landowners were allied with one another and were resisting him hostilely. Niece, I did that for her. Now I am standing here before you and forgive the offence of your mother for the sake of the virtue that you already have and that which you will acquire. I shall also cool my anger towards her. Ask her to come here, back to the princes. If anyone has heard anything from me that I should do penance for, then before I completely ruin the celebration for the King, I shall hand myself over willingly as a prisoner at your disposal. The key lies in your command.'

Old Irmschart then said to the girl Alize: 'Run quickly to your mother! If she will not now lament the searing heartfelt pain which Terramer has inflicted on your family for Tibalt's sake, then no man should ever trust her again. Go with her, Buov of Commercey and Scherins of Pontarlier. Tell her plainly of the store of unconsumed misery that lies on our family. If that weighs little in her heart, then she has lost her womanly honour for ever.'

Alize took leave and went away, with her the two men, Buov and Scherins.

'I shall render tribute in rich payment, even though I am not a vassal. What am I good for after all, old woman that I am?' said Irmschart of Pavia. 'I shall donate an army at my own expense, to go to Orange to help you, dear son. My wealth is untouched. Now much of it will be spent, and if anyone is prepared to accept gold and does not disdain it, I shall share with them for your sake, dear son, as many gold coins as eighteen water buffaloes can haul away. I shall not flee from you. I shall wear armour myself. I am a woman strong enough to bear arms at your side. The brave man, not the coward, will be able to see me with you. I shall strike blows with my swords.'

'My lady,' said the Marquis, 'since your loyalty and your renown are giving me such generous help, I think it is high time for you to hear my advice. I know indeed that you are loyal. Send my father to fight, for he can take command of an army, and he will fight where it is necessary. A helmet is not meant for you, nor other weapons, nor a shield. But if it is not asking too much, Madam, give your support as you have offered it.'

Then that remarkable woman promised him fine horses and shining weapons, purchased with silver and gold, saying: 'Son, I shall not deceive you. I shall hand over to you a great deal, much more than I have ever yet mentioned.'

BOOK IV

Would you like to hear now how things are going with that anger you heard about before? Do you want to know who calmed it, how help and high spirits were at hand for the Margrave, and how the Roman Queen, loyally and after much heart-searching, placed at his disposal herself and her worldly goods and her favour? It was the Margrave's earnest concern that things went well for Giburc, for love and sorrow were oppressing him. What a pledge had he left behind him there!

Consider, too, the carnage which had occurred at Alischanz, as well as the desperate state in which Giburc had been left, she who had sent him away from her in search of aid. Giburc was his dearest possession, and his joy and even his senses were lost to him on account of his longing for her. His life must needs be one of restless impatience. No one could beat him by a single point when it came to a game like this. He was deeply grieved by the loss of his kinsmen but still more by the peril of Giburc. Firmly established in the very depths of his heart lay the foundation of all sorrows. He would have roused pity even in those who do not have the true faith, in Jews and heathens and publicans.[23]

The grief of Willehalm moves me to this very day. If anyone considers me the more foolish because of that, then I'll gladly endure such contempt. If I ever learn to speak properly, I shall defend him better and explain why he so forgot his good breeding, when the Queen behaved in such an overbearing way, that he tugged at her like that. Love and other suffering, and the deaths of kinsmen and vassals, provoked him to this behaviour.

By now Alize had returned and her mother had heard for a fact that the anger of the Margrave had finally died down, yet still she was reluctant to let her daughter in. She was afraid of that *mal voisin*, the wicked neighbour, her brother. She feared that another hailstorm would come down upon her, and this was why she did not wish to unbolt the door.

'To be sure,' she said, 'I should not get any protection from the King, nor his princes, nor from my noble father. Daughter, be careful that this reconciliation of yours does not cost me my limbs.'

Alize replied: 'With me here are Scherins and Buov of Commercey, who have also been reconciled out there. His anger has completely vanished.'

The Queen let the lovely young girl into her room, and after that Scherins told her all about the great misery and how their kinsmen had paid with their lives at Alischanz. 'And,' he explained, 'when the King was so slow to greet the Margrave today when he came before him to make his lament, you, my lady, paid the price for that.'

'Alas!' she replied. 'If only he had struck off my head! Then I should not need to mourn any longer now. That would have been a quick death. As it is, if loyalty was ever in my nature, I must now endure from morning until evening, day and night, that fertile suffering and the harvest of sorrow on account of my kinsmen. If anyone wishes me well let him now desire that I may die before sorrow secures for me such heartfelt pain that crazed grief brings dishonour upon my womanhood. If, at the hand of Terramer, I have endured such heavy losses on the field of Alischanz, then, alas, *mon cher* Vivianz, how many women not related to us shall for Love's sake mourn your radiant self! If my brother had any sense, then he must have taken leave of it when you went into battle beneath a shield, for that was still a burden to you, young as you were. Now that you are dead, joy will be a stranger to me for ever.

'Let those who wish for material aid come to me now, for I shall give them so much that no other queens will be able to surpass me. If I could, I should soon avenge my great grief. Now where are the soldiers? Buov of Commercey, inform such of them as are in the Roman Empire of the payment offered by the Roman Queen. And, if they were friends of yours, then remember those of our kinsmen whom we have lost.

'If my brother was angry today because I received him so unen-thusiastically, it was nevertheless wise of him to let me escape with my life. I shall request aid and support from the King and his vassals. If they really are men, our misfortune will be avenged.'

She went out, and Margrave Willehalm spoke to her in a voice full of sadness: 'Now may He who wore thorns upon His head as a crown soothe your anger. Even if you do not wish to strive for His reward by any act of service now, then you should at least be able to assert your loyalty before Him on the Day of Judgement, by grieving here for those who were and are your blood relations, your brother and your sister's children, thirteen of your family taken from me by Terramer's crossing of the sea, even though he found us ready to defend ourselves. Units and detachments joined up with me, each one coming from his separate land, and all of these the powerful Terramer has taken from me. Now turn towards the Right Hand of Him who created Adam. Commend to the great mercy of God those fearless kinsmen of yours, the brave creatures of God slain by Terramer, and remind Him that for our sakes He shed upon the earth the blood from His wounds. If He can help us now, let Him take pity on me in His divinity. Madam, you too should grieve that I am unrelieved of sadness, and give me some small consolation.'

'Alas!' she replied. 'To whom shall I give consolation, and what use is my life? Such joy as I had found has vanished. My exaltation has been laid low. Growing within me now is an agony akin to that of Anfortas, that torment which, in spite of his great wealth, he often had to endure from his wound.[24] I was noble enough myself as a result of my husband's election to the throne of Rome, before at Alischanz I lost the support of my high status, which is now on the decline. Wretched woman that I am, how many heroes have I lost, men who were of my blood and I of theirs!

'Alas, Joy, in the end achieving you brings scant reward! Alas, Heimrich of Narbonne, how Purity and Generosity, Manliness and Good Breeding, all flourished from your seed! Too early have I known ill-fortune through the handsome youth whom Queen Giburc took away from me and brought up as was appropriate to her. The sweet sight of him shall often inflict heartfelt pain on many a woman. Alas, Vivianz! How did death ever dare to touch you, yet leave my own heart whole?

'My brother, Marquis, you poor man, I shall comfort you as well as I am able, according to my own state. Believe me when I say that the loss of our relatives weighs heavy on me. Come now, Irmschart of Pavia, remember that it was you who brought me into the world and help me to lament this trouble loyally.'

The Queen went on: 'My brothers who are present here, remember that we are one body. You are men: I am a woman. There is no other difference, for we are all of one flesh.'

Irmschart of Pavia replied: 'If we have loyalty in our breasts then we two, Heimrich and I, shall lament our common loss, along with my sons, whether they be here or elsewhere. You are my liege-lady, as well as my child, and we praise God and thank Him that now in all sincerity you are taking pity on our losses. Now for the first time we shall see whether you are the liege-lady of the princes. Make your lamentation, then, about the battle of Alischanz, to him who wears the Roman crown, if your service is really capable of moving him to action.'

'My lady,' said Heimrich. 'Your hand shall now protect my son the Marquis and your other brothers, and afford them the assistance which as a woman you are able to provide.'

Bernart of Brabant was standing there, and Buov of Commercey, and Gibert, too, these three, and the fourth was Bertram. The Queen took all of them with her and together they fell on their knees before the King.

She addressed him, saying: 'I have urgent need to beg for aid so effective that it will achieve high renown for the princes and the Empire itself, and ask that for the sake of your honour you should grant your support to the Marquis and turn Terramer out of his camp at Orange, for he is bringing disgrace upon you and upon the Empire.'

'Madam,' the King responded, 'you are behaving foolishly, if you would ask for aid for him who has dishonoured me by his treatment of you. If he had behaved with more restraint, then I should have served him if it had been in my power. He is your brother and my vassal, but what good did that do you? He has diminished my honour, and that is all there is to say. That is the way it is then. Now get up,' he said. 'I shall take advice regarding your request.'

The woman rose to her feet, lamenting bitterly. That was her way of trying to gain help for her brother, and as a result many noble Saracens later died at Alischanz. This was what the Queen said: 'Whatever princely relatives I may have here, be they count or baron, I shall disregard their wealth. Indeed, if a mere page had been born of my race he would not fail to benefit from that kinship. Whoever will help me bear this sorrow should not hesitate to lament his poverty to me and I shall so set him up with possessions that he will not need to turn away for lack of them. Let this also be made known to those who are not our kinsmen, to knights and foot-soldiers, to turkopels and to anyone who may be fit for combat.'

You ask if this message flew a great distance? It summoned a vast mass of support which later greatly benefited sweet Giburc.

Now it was Bernart of Brabant who spoke. 'If I ever had a hand which could render aid, whether by giving materially or in battle, I have it still, and now it is needed. I shall use that hand in the service of my brother, of that man who has come to me in desolation. I have suffered loss along with him.'

Then his brother Bertram spoke as well: 'Joy is a stranger to me and sorrow a familiar acquaintance. Alas, what has become of my high spirits? I have a sturdy body and bold princes, and under my command are knights for whom praise be to God's power, but all of that can still not prevent me from bearing in my heart an anguish which will continue to oppress me until my brother brings me to the place where I can wreak vengeance for Mile, my sister's son, and for the radiant Vivianz. Alas,' he continued, 'Alischanz, alas that you should ever have become so wide and so smooth and that, upon you, my joy should ever have surrendered its right to exist!' His eyes were opened up, and each tear was pushed out by the next one. You could hear the tears dropping on his clothing.

Now it was his brother Gibert's turn to speak: 'If I am worthy of the office of the shield and the spear, then, brother, I am here to fight for you. And if I have served any man so loyal that I can remind him now that I was once a source of comfort to him, you'll get to know about this, by my life. I too shall give as though my hands were the hands of a prince.'

Buov of Commercey spoke next: 'Now for the first time I find myself bereft of joy and this state will last for ever. What comfort should I look for? Joy and comfort have perished as far as I am concerned. Tibalt has brought upon me infirmity of spirit and ensured that my suffering shall remain, and that my future years shall be full of sighs. All this must turn my hair grey. Let anyone who knows judge whether Christian lands have ever shed so many heroes in battle and so increased their sorrow. If I go on lamenting like this, my brother will think I am a coward, whereas in fact he can be sure of my aid, even though sorrow may have weighed me down and still does weigh me down. I shall lead many noble strangers to Orange for him and wield our swords in such a way that Giburc shall hear them resound. I undertake to bring to him there one thousand armoured chargers which can be seen in my battalion, and on their backs men who will deal blows and thrusts on my behalf, or employ whatever form of combat the heathen may desire, whether he be carrying a bow or a sword.'

Then Heimrich addressed the King: 'My lord, go on with these celebrations now. Do not abandon them on account of our grief. It may be that God will grant us recompense. Bid the princes be seated and have them served with due respect. Noble princes of high status are gathered here from many lands. Even if joy is fleeing from us, or has already fled, from myself and my family, anyone who treats his guests aright will not make them pay for that, for they have rarely enjoyed anything so much as this.'

The King spoke to his officials: 'We shall not fall into complete despair on account of the distress of our hostess and of the others who are making their lament here: I propose to hold my feast. See to it that you accord my noble vassals their rightful places and take care that you seat them and all the nobility as befits my honour; this you shall work out for yourselves. There is not much left of the day.'

They set to at once and skilfully carried marvellous dishes to all four sides of the great hall and served them with courtesy and generosity.

The Queen went up to her brother and he took her hand in his. He was still wearing his armour. She led the grief-stricken man back into her chamber, where she bade him sit down with her in front of the King's bed. The Queen gave orders that the young ladies and the squires should remove his coat of mail and his other armour. Costly garments of fine silk were ready for him.

The charming Alize spoke to her mother and said: 'Ask them to bring the clothing which was prepared for my father himself especially for today, at his own command, and bid my uncle put that on.'

Courteously the Margrave replied: 'I intend to do without fine clothing and comfort as long as sorrow continues to thrust its thorn into my heart. I have been cut off by swords from joy and high spirits. My lady, kindly spare me from good clothes as long as I am in such misery on account of what I have lost and in my desire for Giburc.'

'I should never recover from the humiliation if you were to walk naked by my side. Brother, can you not understand how your peers would view that? It would be a long time before they decided to praise me for it.'

She asked the Marquis to put on the silk from Adramahut, even though his skin was unwashed. Then his beauty was very different from hers, for the Margrave desired that his beard, his skin and his hair should all retain the colour of his armour: Alize was quite unlike him to look at.

He escorted the Queen out of the chamber, with her daughter walking on ahead. I have not been told more precisely how the princes were seated during the meal, but the King placed his wife on one side of him, together with the lovely Alize, and then he did not neglect to see to it that his father-in-law and his wife Irmschart were seated on his other side. It was she who bade her son come to her, his beard stained by the rust from his armour, but he responded by saying: 'Tibalt has deprived me of my comrades, therefore give me my host, the merchant, as my companion at table.' This was the experience of a lifetime for Wimar, for he was sitting at the Emperor's table and eating with the highest princes in the land and with the Roman King himself.

The Margrave gave his host two hundred marks by way of reward and this did not trouble Irmschart much. For taking him in the night before Wimar received a double gain, both money and honour. The Margrave desired no food other than black bread dipped in the water which he was drinking. There was a constant stream there, trickling forth from a jug full of water. Many people observed this but they did not know why he was enduring such discomfort as far as his food and drink were concerned. Giburc had received assurance about this when she had accompanied him to the gate before he had mounted his horse. Although his brother-in-law Fabors had marshalled the besieging forces at Orange and although they had many thousands surrounding every gate, Willehalm slipped through against their wishes when he left Giburc. Her love counselled and commanded him to keep his oath to her intact and without fail. This was why he preferred to decline whatever was brought before him, or might have been brought before him, in the way of domestic meat or game, and likewise of spiced claret, mead, grape wine and mulberry wine. None of this led him to forget his oath. If anyone made as if to kiss him, he thought of the peril in which his kiss had remained behind in Orange and of how he had been driven away from it. He had sustained many other losses too, and so his breast had sunk a hand's breadth on the side where his heart was, and his joy was drowned in sorrow.

He thought to himself: 'Now the King has eaten his fill. Now he will certainly grant us what the Queen has asked him for today. I shall request his help and his support. "A drunken head will often do what a sober man lacked courage to." If he once promises me aid, the princes would think him insane if he were to break his promise and would ask why he was turning against me.'

Then he spoke out loud and said: 'My lord, ruler of princes, my affairs are in your hands. You yourself have been attacked, so it is only right that I should ask you to defend the Empire of the Crown of Rome, for the sake of which I have spent my joy. The kinsmen of your children are lost. I am beleaguered on all sides. Such towns and lands as I ever had are now in the hands of Terramer. My fish in the River Larkant are dead. All my meadows and my cultivated fields have been trampled and destroyed. Whatever advantage I once derived from the march which I hold in fief from the Empire is now in ruins. My walls have been destroyed; the fires are still smouldering; my whole march is ablaze. If ever Noah suffered great trouble in his Ark, Giburc must be suffering just as much now from the flood of heathen knights. Terramer is inflicting violence upon me. To begin with, I engaged in pitched battle with him, until that disastrous point when I found myself surrounded. Believe me, Baligan never led a larger army across the sea against your father. Force of a different kind is needed here, but I have made it clear to them that chivalry would still be practised, if only your power were backed by my desire. Now defend me: I am still capable of fighting. Take your courage in both hands, as other kings have always done.'

'I wish to take counsel in the matter,' replied Louis.

'Take counsel?' retorted the Margrave. 'If you do not do it quickly, then you are no son of Charles.'

Thereupon he leapt across the table, yelling: 'I shall not thank you much for that. You must advance against the enemy; you dare not fail to do this. Who would want to be your vassal in that case? You can have my march and my other fiefs back.'

Bernart of Brabant and the canny Gibert and his other noble brothers jumped forward and put a stop to this. The King had been sitting there patiently, but now the shrewd, well-bred man spoke to the Marquis: 'If you were prepared to honour the Empire,' he said, 'you could willingly receive my aid. If you disdain it, I shall direct my support elsewhere, but then the army which you lead against the heathens will be all the smaller. However, if I have to serve you with my forces against my will, I must be out of my mind.'

The Queen joined in and expressed herself much better than she had that morning, when the Margrave had seized her hair, and she had only just managed to escape his fury. This had now been appeased, and she spoke in a sisterly fashion: 'Ah! Roman King, my lord, what use is the radiant beauty of your daughter and her sweet and lovely mouth? She will never be accorded honour as she would be if her relatives who always fought for her renown were still alive. Their righteous deeds, their noble courage, were much more use to us than all your possessions. We two are slain along with them. Now help lament our deaths: then you will not be cutting off your help from the two of us but will be treating us with loyalty. And have sorrow of your own now for those who have bravely defended your Empire. Even supposing that they were all Jews who died in the course of defending your land on account of my sorrowing brother, you should still grieve for them out of loyalty if you have any loyalty in you. The Roman Emperor Charles never in one day lost so many heroes who were acknowledged princes.'

'Madam, I could easily be urged to mourn unceasingly for those kinsmen of yours who have died in the defence of my land, and to wreak vengeance for them accordingly if it were in my power to arrange it. But you have heard for yourself how things are. I hardly escaped in one piece, while you yourself were seized by the hair in my presence by one who called me the ruler of princes. I think you heard it plainly enough. I suffered such indignity from him. If ever a prince was my vassal, such a man has Willehalm insulted, but first and foremost he has insulted the Crown. How am I supposed to reward that? If I ignore it, then I shall be called a coward for the rest of my days, but if I must recognize that he did it intentionally this suits neither of us. If I withhold help from him it will do neither of us much good, for then I shall be fleeing before I catch sight of the enemy. Let each man, in his loyalty to me, say what he would do if he were in my position and what advice I should accept now. We must weigh things up very carefully, if he wants to preserve my good name.'

The tables were all removed and then everyone, rich men, poor men, the old and the young, pressed forward, wanting to find out why the Margrave had leapt across the table in such a bold fashion. Several of them intended to see to it that his hand was never again engaged in tussling at so high a level.

Heimrich and his retinue were standing courteously before the son of Charles. They were trying to prompt him to offer his assistance. The name of Charles was often mentioned, and it was said that the King should show that he had inherited his courage and not violate that virtue which was his by birth, that he should think of the law of the Empire which instructed him to protect the Empire and never cease from striving for its honour.

'If you now intend to permit Terramer to lay waste your land,' they said, 'then Christendom will be brought to shame and dishonour brought upon baptism. Anyone who urges you to do anything other than defend yourself and your Empire is guilty of disloyalty. If anyone knows any better, let him speak up.'

The King replied to his father-in-law: 'I shall help you for the sake of my own reputation, regardless of how your son the Marquis has erred against me and has pushed propriety close to impropriety. I shall go myself, or send such an army to your aid that his defence will be the stronger.'

'My lord, and my most noble son, you should do it in order to bring honour upon your child and also for the sake of my daughter, your wife, and to avenge the death of Vivianz,' said Lady Irmschart. 'Now, along with your princes, arrange your campaign in such a way that sweet Giburc may rejoice at it, she who is waiting for your help, for Terramer and Tibalt who have slain the greater part of my descendants are treating her with little affection. They have robbed you of many friends who brought honour upon your court whenever they came to you.'

'Madam, my second mother, I know of none who are so noble or so virtuous,' replied the King. 'Never have I seen the like of them, nor heard of men whom one might acclaim with such high praise above all others. Their soaring praise must still be sung ever anew until the Day of Judgement. I loved him truly as my own child. I summon to me all those who for my sake are intent upon revenge for the death of Vivianz. Whatever each of them may desire, I shall bestow on him, in terms of gifts, fiefs, property. I propose to demonstrate to the heroes here present that this hand is the hand of the Empire. The coward shall permit me to reward noble men. I have such vast territories that every prince may receive his share if my hand bestows favour on him.'

Some of them took his payment; some of them were in any case so devoted to him that they swore to go with him, and all the princes who had come there for the festivities set off together. Moreover, the anger of the King towards the Margrave was put aside. He who had been born of Charles now behaved in the manner of Charles, and that was Giburc's gain.

Turkopels and foot-soldiers – 'sarjants' as they are called – throughout the whole of France, knights in the retinues of all the princes and those of Heimrich and his sons, both young and old, who had not committed themselves to giving support, were warned that they would be deprived of all their rights if they did not vigorously defend that baptism which was enduring ignominy at the hand of the heathens. This pronouncement was made immediately before the princes of the realm and was approved by the noblest men. (I am not concerned with the basest men, or with whether there was a coward present; I am telling you about the end of this assembly.) The imperial command and the pronouncement made it known that they could bundle up their belongings without ado. At that time the finest knights in the whole of France were there and they all had their armour, too, or, if not, then it was sent for straight away. The roadways were overrun with knights and their messengers, all wanting to bring new tidings to the gods of Terramer and, moved by the Margrave's lament, to help Giburc to take heart.

The King proposed to view his men at Laon, on the tenth day, on the plain at the foot of the mountain, and to thank them, the powerful and the humble alike, no matter how they had come there. So now they took their leave of one another, and the festivities broke up. The King gave orders that the pledges should be redeemed, and this was done on all sides. If anyone desired his reward, this was at once seen to. Countless retainers rode away in order to return again. Knights and sarjants came, some one day and some the next. Whoever was seen arriving here or there, whether he came from east or west, found rich land and all its comforts.

The King remained in Laon until the ten days were up. Heimrich had ridden away while the Margrave had stayed with his lady, the Queen, who frequently gave instructions that his wounds should be examined carefully, those wounds which had been bound by Giburc. Thus he was healed of his wounds and made happy by the King's support of him.

One evening, the King, with the Queen and his daughter, was sitting at the windows in the great hall. He could not have witnessed better entertainment at any time, and Willehalm, who was sitting there with Alize, had to admit that. There was more and more activity between the great hall and the linden tree, where they could see noble young boys jousting with spear-shafts against shields, here in pairs, there four of them together, here charging at full tilt, there fighting with clubs. Knights were competing with each other at leaping. Whoever hurled the javelin furthest there was acclaimed: many participated in that contest, while others ran the barriers.[25] A man who was wanting to cross the courtyard could easily be impeded by obstacles of many kinds.

There was a lot of shouting from the servants who were holding the ponies. Many tambours were being beaten there. In this din a stray peasant might very easily have been turned into a ball and tossed back and forth in the mêlée. ·

It was then that the Margrave noticed a page coming along, carrying a tub full of water; he was greeted with scorn. If I can describe it like this and have no one take it amiss, he had in his one body the strength of six men. He was employed in the imperial kitchen to carry on his own all the water which the cooks needed for their preparations. It would have taken three mules, with all their strength, to stagger along with what he was carrying in his hands like a little pillow. His mean clothing and his hair bore all the signs of the kitchen. People did not treat him in a manner befitting his stature or his lineage, but it has been discovered somewhere that if a piece of gold fell in a puddle it never became stained with rust and that if someone were to examine it closely it would reveal here and there features by which one might recognize its great value. If someone throws the red hyacinth stone into black soot and it is later cleaned up again, it will once more show its reddish glow.

Thus did Rennewart, stained as he was from the kitchen, hide his fine attributes in these distressing circumstances. But remember how the eagle puts his young to the test: as soon as they have emerged from their shells he perches in the nest and picks out the best one; then he takes it gently in his claws and holds it up towards the sun; if it is overcome by cowardice and does not look straight into the sun he lets it fall from the nest. Thus he proceeds with all the others, even if there are a thousand of them, and the one which looks with both its eyes directly into the heat and radiance of the sun, that one will he in truth claim as his child.

Rennewart, that powerful man, had indeed been reared in the eagle's nest and had not been dropped from it but had flown down and was now perched on a withered branch. Those birds who should have benefited from his companionship were deprived of it: consequently they, too, were unhappy. (I would draw you more comparisons with the lad who was carrying the tub if it were not that you disdain him.)

Now a group of knights came charging up to him without stopping and his water-vessel was capsized. He endured this like a coy young girl and did not complain either.

'Such things have to go on in jousting practice,' he thought to himself, and filled it up again. Yet still he was not rid of their taunts. He was lunged at from all sides, by knights on horseback and some on foot, and attacked in such a way that once more his heavy barrel full of water was emptied. At this he lost some of his gentleness, and that strong boy who was by no means a weakling caught hold of a page and with one swing of the arm he hurled him against a stone pillar, so that the page burst open from the blow like an over-ripe fruit. Where previously a great crowd had been surrounding him they now all fled and left him quite alone.

The Margrave spoke to the King and asked: 'Did you see, my lord, what happened in the courtyard to that sarjant, the one in the kitchen clothing?'

The King replied: 'I saw it. It has never happened before that he behaved badly. He has lived at my court since he was a child and has always been well-behaved. He has never committed such an outrage. I know for a fact that he is of noble birth, but I've never found the knack, simple or complicated, by raising or demeaning him, to persuade him to accept baptism. I have treated him harshly but, God knows, if he would agree to become a Christian, I should not be slow to regret any trouble which befell him. Merchants brought him across the sea after buying him in Persia. No one saw a face or a body more handsome. The woman who brought him into the world would be honoured if only he did not reject baptism.'

Willehalm approached the King and asked him for the boy, requesting that he should let him have him as a gift. 'My lord,' he said, 'what if I were to guide him better, if I can?'

But the King refused his request. Then Alize went on entreating him for so long and so earnestly that the Emperor granted him what he wanted concerning the lad. Willehalm sent for Rennewart, who was as yet without a beard. When he came into the great hall he behaved in a very courtly fashion, yet he was ashamed and distressed on account of his poor clothing which would have been demeaning even for a serving-boy.

When the Margrave had been languishing in prison in Arabi, he had learnt to speak the languages Kaldeis and Koati, whereas the boy had not wanted to abandon his native tongue, even though he knew a lot of French. When the Margrave saw him enter he greeted him *en français*, having first obtained permission from the Princess, but Rennewart acted as if he were deaf and did not understand, whereas in fact he knew very well what anyone was saying, whoever it might be. No reply issued from his noble lips. Then the Margrave spoke to him in Kaldeis and in the heathen tongue: 'I understand both languages,' replied the boy, and Willehalm was glad about this and said: 'My dear fellow, I believe you are a Saracen. Now tell me all about your family and how you got here.'

He asked him this and that, and Rennewart replied: 'I come from Mecka, where the sanctity of Mahmete causes his body to hover in the air without support. He will compensate me in full for what I have lost here, if he is truly divine. Yet I have so often made my lamentation to him that I have despaired of his ever helping me, and now I have turned to Christ, to whom you are also subject (I assume that you *are* baptized). Since I was sold into this land, I have endured disgraceful misery. Even the King struggled with me and had me instructed in order that I should be converted. But baptism just does not suit my nature, and so night and day I have lived as if I had never had a powerful man for a father. Sometimes I do things which make me faint with embarrassment, for I am living the life of a pig. If ever a noble love takes me into her arms she may disdain me for this, for I am not accustomed to honour, even though I have yearned for it so.'

It pleased the Margrave well that the undaunted young lad could so courteously strive after acclaim amidst such shameful circumstances. He said to him: 'Put aside your sense of shame. The King has given you to me. I shall gladly give you whatever you desire, if you will serve me in return.'

The Saracen boy bowed to him and said: 'If I am to be under your command you will be able to maintain your renown through me. Sire, if you are the Marquis who has lost that magnificent army in battle against those who came across the sea, then I have been given over to you to help you in the nick of time. I shall avenge those men if I live to do so. I pledge myself to follow your advice, and you can correct me whenever I do something wrong, for youth often has little sense. See to it that I have what's necessary.'

Then did the son of Heimrich speak: 'Whatever you desire, whatever you may wish, it will never be too much for me to give it to you, if I have it.'

'You will certainly have the money for what I'm going to ask you for now, even if your march is burnt.'

No one understood what either of them was saying; it was incomprehensible to all the people present, even though they could hear their voices. The young boy who was radiant beneath the dirt and whose skin was like a dewy rose, if it could only emerge from underneath the grime, spoke and said: 'My lord, what shall I do now? Whatever you command me to do I shall do as well as I am able. I never had a master who was dearer to me, so may your favour be my reward.'

Lady Irmschart had a Jew dispatched from Narbonne to prepare the Margrave's men for the campaign. Whoever was prompted by Willehalm's distress to want to join up with him was given rich compensation by the Jew, who gave each one whatever he desired. The Margrave sent Rennewart there, too, and bade the Jew see to it that he gave to the young sarjant clothing, armour and a horse, until Rennewart himself told him that he had all he needed.

Rennewart came up and demanded just one club which he was proposing to carry into battle against the enemy. It was, he said, to be firmly bound with strong strips of steel. He asked also for a coat made of camel-hair, while his shapely legs were to be well clad in sturdy shoes and stockings of fine wool. Then he went to where tailors were sewing broad garments of white linen. For the honour of the Margrave the Jew paid for all of this for Rennewart and also offered him a horse, armour and a sturdy lance. He held back nothing, nor did he conceal the fact that he would give him exactly what he asked for, as he did other soldiers. But the boy replied: 'I mean to go into battle on foot. Let my lord give the old horses and the armour to those who want them. You shall give me a club, square-edged and made of beech-wood, so heavy that if six men try to carry it they will complain about its weight and that if seven wanted to hide it from me they would still not be able to steal it away because of its great weight. The smith is to bind it with strong bands, but it is to be smooth and bare where my hands go.'

Thus, by the hand of the Jew, Rennewart and many others were made ready for the campaign. The Margrave assigned leaders to bands of knights here and foot-soldiers there. After ten days the assembly commenced. Pitched on the plain, where the mountain rose up, you could see in splendid array lean-tos and huts, shelters of leather and pavilions. Moreover, Heimrich's son saw that many broad and lofty tents were set up against the arrival of the princes who were coming there in response to the imperial command. Giburc would have given praise to God if she had seen or even heard of this mighty gathering of knights.

The King rode down with his falcons, and everywhere on the vast plain he greeted the princes, each individually. These were anxious to hear about the Margrave's kinsmen and were full of pity for them and marvelled that he had ventured into battle with such a tiny army and had not waited in his own march for the forces of the Roman King, when powerful Terramer had been discovered crossing over in so many warships.

When the Margrave greeted them, each man showed his sense of propriety by lamenting from the depths of his heart the misery about which he had told them. The noble men declared that they would gladly take revenge for all this, both for his sake and for the sake of the Empire, and that it was only reasonable for them to do so.

The King's crier passed the word to all the battalions that next morning they should take the road towards Orleans. When the King had ridden a fair distance with his falcons, there was not much more delay. High on a mountain as Laon is, before the sun had disappeared from it he had ridden back up in daylight.

Now the Margrave found his sturdy young page lamenting: his hair and his clothing had been singed in the kitchen, but he had not been slow to avenge that same trick with another. He smashed holes in the cauldrons with his club: no pot was so solid that it did not get broken. The master of the kitchen barely escaped with his life. The young man was really angry! The Margrave calmed him down as one friend often does another, saying to him: 'I'll give you some new clothes. Your hair was too long anyway. We'll comb it out and cut it round so that it is level with your ears. Now behave in a proper way and don't make such a fuss. Tomorrow morning, at the crack of dawn, when the banners are raised, beneath which my men must make their way down in front of the town, have your host wake you up and set off your journey.' Young Rennewart promised to do this.

The King remained at Laon that night. He had resolved to ride to Orleans where, from all sides, the army would be coming together for a final assembly, the young and the old alike, who had given him their oath that they would march to aid the faith and baptism. The Queen had established a special contingent, paid for from her own funds, and had been so lavish in her provision that noble men were glad to take their share. She was ready next morning with many young ladies-in-waiting. They were wanting to see at Orleans how the King would stay behind, and how he would urge the army forward and who its commander would be.

Now the night was drawing to a close and one could see the grey light of day. On all sides, then, from the field and through the gates – I mean in all directions, wherever a road led towards Orleans – one could see marching all day long. The Queen made her way there, with her daughter who was so radiantly beautiful that I cannot compare with her the heathland in all the many different colours which it was wont to display, and still is.

Each one received the noble greeting of the Margrave, this one on horseback, that one on foot. He could be seen reined in by the side of the road on his horse Volatin, watching to see if all his men had come out of Laon. But they had made up their minds to move and there was no dallying on their part. Only his friend Rennewart came hastening up such a long way behind that many had been riding on very far ahead of him. He had overslept and was sincerely glad to see that even so the Margrave was waiting there in front of him on his horse and greeting him with the question: 'Where is your club?'

Rennewart replied: 'My lord, I have left it behind. It is helpful of you to remind me of my club. Sire, it will be no disgrace for you to wait here for me. If I bring my club along with me it will be of help to you whenever you are involved in fighting.'

Willehalm answered the young man like this: 'I'll wait for you, if you come quickly. If you have heard of anyone behind you who is heading towards me, tell him where to find me. Hurry up and bring back with you knights and soldiers of any description, and don't forget your club.'

'Now don't let time hang heavy for you,' said bold Rennewart. Without the permission of the cooks he had spent that night, despite his grimy skin, lying on a chopping bench, and they had taken his club away from him. Now he lamented his loss. He did not leave many doors standing but kicked them down with his feet. The chef lay dead, and such of the other cooks as had remained behind also found themselves in trouble. Rennewart did not behave like this for long before he found his club and this he tossed from hand to hand like a slender rod.

Now the Marquis had been waiting for his companion where Rennewart had left him and would have imagined that this wooden branch would be too heavy to be thrown about like this, and unwieldy for a mere human being. But that was how the sturdy soldier came along, and a wild animal pursued by hounds could not have leapt along any faster. There was no further delay now: Rennewart, who was in a hurry, too, ran on ahead while Willehalm rode behind.

The army had set up camp on the site of a monastery, and the King himself had come there too. This monastery had been burnt down when the Margrave had departed from it, leaving his shield behind. The income of the monastery had been a thousand marks: that was the value yielded by the property. However, if it is not too much for you to believe, that one shield which was lost in the fire had cost more than the monastery and its tenant lands put together.

The Margrave rode there too, and he took in the immense loss which he and the monastery had both sustained. Meanwhile, the abbot had informed the King and Queen of the lavish beauty of the bejewelled shield and of how no gems were set in it save the most valuable ones. When the King saw the Margrave sitting in front of him – and there were countless other knights present too – he said to him: 'It seems to me that you are too old to follow a mere whim and go into a deadly combat all decked out like that.'

The Margrave replied quite properly: 'Whatever decoration I may have I won with my own hand in victory over the King of Persia. In exchange for his life he offered me thirty elephants, laden with gold from Kaukasas, but my intention was quite different. I wanted his death much more, for that morning I had again and again kissed Vivianz, dead as he was. Whatever Arofel offered me, it was no use to him, and I beheaded the noble King. As a result Love has taken his costly shield from me, but it was too heavy for me anyway. Only the illustrious man whom I slew beneath it was fit to carry it. God knows that all his thoughts were set on the reward of Love. He spared no expense and his heart did not keep him from sacrificing himself and his possessions: he spared neither of these in his pursuit of renown, that man without blemish. Whatever Terramer may do to me now, I have struck him such a blow to the heart through the death of the noble King that he will know what grief is. My hand has slain that man who wore the crown in Samargone in Persia, in the presence of the noble princes, Terramer's cherished brother, who was favoured by the ladies. For this reason I have lost the favour of Love. If I were to desire Love, I should nevertheless have to do without it because of Love's anger towards me, for I took the life of Arofel whom noble women will bewail for ever.

'I did more, too, to advance Terramer towards grief of heart. My joust slew sweet Tesereiz. How can I make recompense for that towards the ladies who, if they can judge aright, have lost still more in him? The property of Love was laid waste: its income was consumed by his death. Tesereiz, that famous man, was so directed by his heart that if ever service were performed out of love people would have to acclaim him and declare that he practised such service and did so with good will. Tesereiz always achieved renown over and above his comrades. Moreover, he led a vast army from five kingdoms. I can compare with him no one who wears a crown and strove harder for the reward of ladies than the Arabois whose name was Tesereiz. This mighty Seziljois was born in Palerne and his lofty nobility made me reluctant to slay him. Alas, that I did not ride away from him when this man with the magnificent trappings attacked me repeatedly! Yet still I did not joust with him until he uttered the name of Arabel. He challenged me in the name of Love and this assured his death.

'*Le roi* Talimon of Boctan was even more beautifully adorned on account of the reward of ladies than was Tesereiz, but before him Poufameiz, King of Ingulie, and Turpiun, the mighty King of Falturmie, fought with me, those three. I inflicted similar suffering upon all of them: Schoiuse cut the life out of all these three. Arfiklant fought with me too and his brother Turkant as well – their land was Turkanie – and the crown of neither could prevent his being rewarded in the same way as Vivianz, whom I had seen lying dead. I later took revenge for him on Arofel.

'I will say without boasting that my hand slew more heathens, if I can judge properly, than I have individual hairs in my beard and on my head. Even though they held the field they sustained losses, and if I was defeated, this was not without suffering on their part. They will bear the marks of it for a long time to come. I call upon the dead to be my witnesses, and my stepson Ehmereiz knows the truth well enough, I am quite sure. I found out precisely who they were, each and every one of them, as they came charging towards me, from the many and varied sounds, their battle-cries, and this was because I could understand the heathen tongue. I slew all the beautifully clothed knights on whom the individual bands depended for leadership, until I found myself with no support at all. Then I preferred to flee rather than to die, but I fled fighting still in such a way that the Roman Empire is honoured by it and Terramer of Muntespir can look on the biers for many amazurs and eskelirs who were matched against me in battle.

'Now, my lord, you have behaved towards me in such a way that your men, whether rich or poor, shall take me as their example, those who are encamped upon this field and those at home as well. My lord, if I were your own child you could not feel my suffering more acutely. In helping me you will be helping yourself.

'I have told you the whole truth of how I gained this helmet decoration, and the shield and the fur cloak. He whose surcoat still gleams with such costly radiance, that same man once owned Volatin, too!'

Many of those who were sitting and standing there realized that he had suffered greatly, and this was why they did not take exception to his account, for at no point had they ever detected a lie on his lips.

The King was pleased at the revenge which had been taken and the Queen spoke too, and said: 'Brother, I shall always see to it that you profit from the fact that many women in heathendom must shed tears as I do on account of the death of handsome Vivianz, and that your brave vengeance has been meted out also on men of high birth, so that Tibalt has seen you defending the honour of Rome and you have paid back Terramer in such full measure for his crossing of the sea.'

The princes and the other vassals of the King made their way to their quarters. They had remained there at the Court to while away the evening. Some of them had come there to see the ladies while others had come to hear the news. (You ask who they all were? If I have forgotten to tell you, ask those who were sitting around there!)

Next morning, just at daybreak, a great racket could be heard from carts and carriages. The army began to stir itself and to break camp. The strangers, the first to move out and the last, rode with one accord on all the roads towards Orleans. Many banners of costly design came from all sides, as if it were snowing knights upon the King and the Marquis. Some were coming for the sake of their renown; some because they had previously given their oaths in order that they should not be deprived of their rights.

This time the Margrave was able to ride through Orleans without paying a toll, for no one detained him for it now. They had been too quick to do so the first time, but he gained for them the favour of the King and recognition of the fact that one fault balanced out the other: the death of the official on the one hand, and on the other the harm which he himself had suffered at their hands through no fault of his own. He had inflicted harm on them when he left there, and evidently at their expense, in the clash and in the joust which cast Arnalt to the ground, though later they recognized one another soon enough.

Le roi Louis was also the Roman Protector and for that reason, when he came to Orleans, there was no delay and many men accepted his pay which was readily given by him. He addressed them all, saying: 'If I live, I shall compensate you for this hardship.' He spoke then to the noble men and in particular to the princes: 'Be among the boldest, so that you can urge your men to courage. All that I have today I shall share with you. I shall gladly demonstrate to you that I depend upon your loyalty and in return assure you of my aid. Let none of you take it amiss or interpret it as cowardice if I remain here. In my one body lies but one man's strength, but in this way you can more easily be rescued. If you get into trouble you will have more reason to hope. If you are not able to fight a pitched battle, then there are many strongholds in the march. Perform your chivalry outside the gates. You know well enough that my best forces lie behind me, in the German lands: I can soon release you from captivity. I am commending my honour and my beloved army and defence of his own person, too, to the courage of that man, in helping whom I have suffered great losses through my wife's kinsmen, whom I shall always sorely miss.

'Brother-in-law, come closer to me. I have known for a long time that you are a good commander. I here invest you with my command and my power. Ask all those who are not formally committed to aiding the Empire in this campaign, whether they be of high or lowly birth, my whole retinue, not to contravene my command. Vassals and freemen, marshals and all officials, I today commend to all of you in place of me the Margrave who, in his time of need, has asked for my support.'

Then the Queen spoke, too, 'If God grants me the good sense, then if anyone supports my brother now I shall help him by averting whatever misery may befall him, as my heart counsels me to do.'

That which had been sworn at Laon was not forgotten here in Orleans. The princes in particular did not take it amiss but said that they were happier to be subject to one of their own status than to any official of the King. One marshal was to supply the food; those who wished to take a drink were to go to the Cup-Bearer; the Steward was to preside over the kettles at the appropriate time. 'The Chamberlain shall pay off the debts of those who are in financial straits,' it was announced. 'We shall gladly obey the command of the Margrave and pay heed to him and treat the heathens with little affection.'

The King himself presented the imperial colours to the Margrave and bade him remind them of the cry of 'Monjoie!' 'This,' he said, 'brought many victories in battle to my father Charles. Men both high and low, whether you are fighting in hill or valley, be mindful of the sound of this cry.'

Heimrich and his sons were not present at this assembly, and no one needed to seek them there. Each of them was making his way by a separate route towards Orange, so fast that the fish in the fords lay dead.

The princes and the King's vassals took their leave to depart on the campaign. Now young Rennewart came along, and his inborn sense of propriety urged him to take leave of the King right there and elsewhere of the Queen. The young Princess was sitting on her own beneath a tree on a grassy spot. He made his way towards her to take his leave and stand before her for a while. (If my source had not told me I should be completely at a loss to say how Alize received him.) She lamented the many difficulties which he had endured in France and then she went on to beg him to forgive her father's guilt, no matter how much the King had lost in renown through his treatment of him. 'You shall take my kiss away with you. May your nobility protect you and bring you to where no sorrow will oppress you.' The maiden stood up: the kiss was given. Rennewart bowed to her and said: 'May the highest God protect your noble kindness.' He bowed to the other ladies too and did not neglect to take his leave of them.

The army had selected Willehalm, the high-born prince, as its commander, but even so many of his peers were travelling with many large armies of their own. They had to make great haste in field and forest alike, for this was demanded of them by their leader, who was troubled by great anxiety for his Queen Giburc. He feared that Tibalt might take her love by force.

There was an anxious moment when the Margrave and his men came so close to the Saracens that he saw something with his own eyes that made his heart predict a loss greater than any which he had sustained before, even taking into account such terrors as he had experienced when he parted from Vivianz, and whatever the fifteen brave kings had done to him that morning when his manly courage had urged him on and he had defeated them with his own hand, and no matter what Tenebruns and the Persan had done to him, and Tesereiz, the Seeker after Love, and many other attacking groups, when he had acquitted himself boldly. Now his joy had to concede defeat indeed to sorrow and despair: a fire at night was what was causing him his fears.

BOOK V

Now our tale is approaching joy and lamentation, the day of assistance and the time of Willehalm's arrival, when a happy end was put to the anxious waiting through which Giburc has had to live, she who often bore arms herself. How often did her father say that he intended to force her into submission!

She said: 'I have accepted baptism for the sake of Him who created all living things, water and fire, as well as air and earth. He Himself summoned me into existence and everything that lives and breathes. Shall I renounce Christ and the Margrave for the sake of Mahmete and lose the benefits of my baptism and of the many acts of noble aspiration which the Margrave has expressed so often in the past with heroic deeds under shield and with spear and wearing a helmet, deeds which he still is eager to perform in service for my love? I was a queen, no matter how poor in property I may be now. In Arabie and Arabi I walked crowned in the presence of princes, before one prince embraced me. It is for his sake that I have determined to observe poverty and for the sake of Him who is the Highest. Where would Tervigant have found the skill that only Altissimus practised first? I have had myself baptized for the sake of Him who prescribed the course of *polus antarcticus* and the other stars, who set the firmament in motion and ordered the seven planets to compete against the swiftness of the heavens. His scales cannot deceive, those that weigh all creation so evenly that it can be called eternally constant and ever permanent. Are your gods like Him who restrains the air and orders all things so wisely, who gave the liquid spring to the well and three properties to the sun, heat and light and also motion, thus bringing light to us and taking it away? I am prepared to suffer whatever happens to me for the sake of that God who has power over all, for He can recompense me fully for it and refresh the poverty of the body with the richness of the soul. You are wasting much effort, you, father and my other kinsmen, risking life and honour to help Tibalt, who has no just claims to lay on me. Why are you taking revenge on your own child? I think you are acting foolishly.'

'Alas, unhappy man that I am,' said the mighty Terramer, 'that I ever had such a child, who can despair so totally of her own salvation and deliberately renounce the gods! Oh, sweet Arabel, don't behave like this! Whatever has happened or will yet happen to you because of me, is my very own misery. Indeed, I would lay down my life for you. May Mahmete deign to recognize that I did not want to take up arms against you at Tibalt's request, until the Baruc and his priests entreated me by our religion to do so. They told me to kill you as penance for my sins. Yet I never did betray my loyalty to that extent. I always thought of you as my child. If I find you in a state of blessedness, then honour your family and give the gods their due!'

'Alas, my great and noble father, that you persist in your folly of wanting to separate me from Him who gave the woman Eve her sense of shame to cover her breast for the first time, in which a lust had grown which led her into trouble, into the company of the devil, who is always threatening us with evil! You have been around enough years to know what the prophets tell about Adam's fall. This is what Sibyl and Plato[26] tell us of the great sin: Eve was guilty all by herself, and because of her Adam's offspring were destined for hell, except Elijah and Enoch.[27] All the others had to suffer torment. No one could escape from that. Who was it who released them from it and gained the victory by breaking open the gates and ending Adam's suffering? That was the Holy Trinity, which is one and yet three, identical with one another and equally splendid. And see, He will not die again for the sins of man nor woman. Seek His favour now!'

Then Terramer of Tenabri replied: 'But surely the three could have saved the one from death. He claimed to have been born of the house of Israel and of a virgin. If I have lost you for the sake of a man who was hanged by his own people and treated so disgracefully, then I have little confidence that our father Adam was freed from the bonds of hell by human hands. Hell is bitter and hot, and I know there is much torture there, for I have heard that from the gods. No mouth can ever adequately describe how wretched it is there. If Jesus of Nazareth has really broken open the gates of hell, why am I still being punished by your disbelief? Return to our faith, my dear daughter!'

'I can tell, father, that you are in great distress. While Jesus, the man, was struggling with death on the Cross, His life was blossoming forth from His divine strength. Father dear, pay heed to what I am saying: while human life was dying, the Godhead was achieving life for humanity. Even if your gods were greater, I should still want to remain in the command of him who always recognized an obligation to noble women especially and was therefore often seen in their service, wearing a shield and performing such feats, in which for the sake of honour the body is not spared and is preserved from dishonour by fame. Tibalt himself told me that the Margrave had wasted many a forest of spears with his jousting. And, indeed, he sought my love when King Sinagun, Halzebier's nephew, captured him in an attack, during which he had performed such deeds that his fame was acclaimed by both sides and for all time. His great nobility was rumoured far and wide among all the Saracens. I was Queen there at the time and enjoyed great wealth. I rewarded him for all his troubles by freeing him from the fetters and other irons that bound him hand and foot and by going with him to Christian lands. I served him and the Hand of the Almighty. I want very much to preserve my Christian baptism.

'To Tibalt I leave Todjerne, where you crowned me Queen. At that time, father, you still preserved your loyalty when you yourself gave me that land as a dowry. If you are going to side with Tibalt, then you will have to be angry with me. He is selling out your honour for his inherited territorial rights. He lays claim indeed to Sibilje, saying that Marsilje, his uncle, whom Roland slew, left him that.[28] Here on this side of the sea, there is much land that he claims as his inheritance. He says that he should inherit Arles and half of Provence, since your uncle, Baligan, was slain by Charles. If you are going to let your loyalty to your own offspring die for the sake of such lies, then, alas, of what value is your former courtesy? You will forfeit all your hopes for salvation by your behaviour towards me. Go ahead and give Todjerne, my property by right, to Tibalt and Ehmereiz, and let me live in poverty.'

This conversation took place during a lull in the fighting. King Tibalt repeatedly threatened Arabel with hanging, but Ehmereiz upbraided him for that. Terramer behaved like this towards his dear daughter: beseeching her one day and threatening her the next. But by no means could he induce her to cease defending Orange and herself and her depleted band of people there until the return of him who had left her to seek help from the Roman protector. She had held out with difficulty until the heathen army had grown tired of it. The stench of corpses and likewise of many carcasses was very strong there. Now Orange, the fortress, had also received many scars from stones thrown by catapults and from the trebuchets.[29] They weren't playing games! It was a matter of life and death on both sides. Terramer's experienced military advisers recommended a temporary withdrawal, since the whole land was devastated and there was not a single hand capable of fighting, save in the one city. The entire army asked him to head for the harbour, saying that as soon as they had fetched supplies from the ships and enjoyed the fresh air they would encamp before Orange again, if he asked them to, and they would do it with one accord. Terramer of Tenabri granted their request but said that he wanted an assault to take place first, as soon as night fell.

That evening, as soon as the stars could be seen, great peril arose for Giburc. All kinds of fighting men, those with slings and the advance troops, foot-soldiers and archers threatening the city, and the entire chivalry, raised an assault by night with combined forces. As a result, Glorjet, the splendid palace in Orange, was endangered. None of the Christians in the outer city, neither man nor woman, survived the fire. Giburc asked her small army to hold the core of Orange. Then all the heathens, young and old alike, turned away towards Alischanz, where Mile and Vivianz lay dead.

Now it was that the Margrave in his army perceived the heart-rending danger, since the sky and the sea were both fiery red. The many who did not know looked carefully and tried to figure out where, precisely, in the land the huge fire might be and whether that was where the Saracens were encamped. Then the Margrave told them without beating about the bush: 'Now my affairs have come to such a pass that I cannot do with any cowards. I must have heroes to pursue renown. Now, you Frenchmen, show your bravery. O father and brothers mine, alas that you are not here with me and that I shall have to attempt this battle today without you! If He who was crucified for our sakes and in death gained eternal life will have regard for my manly courage, I shall follow Giburc, wherever she is. She wanted to hold Orange until my return, and now she has been taken away. Perhaps I am still not too late for her. Let me remind you princes gathered here of how the Roman King sent you here to defend Roman honour. Don't delay any longer. Arm yourselves and your horses. Help me save fair Giburc, my wife. I will ride on ahead of you to the enemy and scout out what they are up to. The best thing we can do is to form our forces into squads, you here and those there. We shall hit them with an assault from all sides. They have indeed learned the painful lesson that we know how to fight better. So what, if their forces *are* greater? We shall have Fortune on our side.'

Immediately Volatin was brought up to him. He started out, with him his friend Rennewart and whoever was in his camp.

Meanwhile the sun rose. Then many trumpets were sounded and countless drums rolled. The noble Frenchmen wanted to gain fame at the expense of the heathens. Here on the mountains, there in the valleys, one could see the troops emerging, with their banners making it look as if all the bushes were made of silk. In addition, their helmets shone unobscured. Many large separate squads trekked along after them. The princes individually encouraged their men to bravery. Those who were recognized as good, mounted and on foot, raced on in advance of the others.

At the head of all of them the Margrave sped on until he approached the fire that had troubled his heart. His sighs of anguish could have gained his sanctity for him, for he would have died of suffering that morning, save for his manly nature. He perceived through the smoke that his palace was still standing. It was the jewel of Orange and all the march. Rennewart, the strong lad, had followed him there on foot. No other man from all his army stuck so close to him. Terramer of Tenabri and Fabors of Mecka had left the camp there, and all the kings and eskelirs had headed for the harbour with the Lord of Muntespir. Then those looking down from the palace through the smoke could see that the Margrave's army had come. The heathens were off towards the sea.

When she was told about it, the undaunted Giburc thought that they were intending to return and inflict further suffering on her. Once again she had to don her armour. The Queen acted like a man, not at all like a woman. He who had no intention of harming her – I mean the Margrave – came riding on Volatin, and his companion Rennewart came with him on foot. He had to go through a lot of smoke where the houses had been set alight. Rennewart saw the many siege-towers and catapults. He would have liked to chase after the heathens with his huge club.

Now Lady Giburc stood with upraised sword ready to defend herself, as if she were looking for combat, and with her stood Stephen, her chaplain, and her maidens attired in armour. The people inside the fortress rushed all together to the battlements. The Margrave saw that there were still people alive in there. He pushed towards the gate. There he greeted the fit and the wounded in a pleasant, friendly manner. But that still did not dispel their fears. They were ready to risk their lives again in battle even against the man who had gained the city without using force.[30] That very man was standing there before them. All those who were still alive in there, however, would have been just as happy if he had stopped somewhere else.

He called up to the battlements: 'Is the Queen still alive?', and he asked how things were there. They had no idea that the lord of the land was speaking to them.

Then Queen Giburc caught sight of his surcoat and Volatin, and she called down to him in heathen tongue: 'Sir, who are you, that you dare to stop so close to my palace and do so giving no assurance that you come in peace? You are too bold and can find a fight here as a result. I'll come closer to you and make myself so clearly visible that you will know it!'[31]

'Oh, where is fair Giburc? Is she still all right?'

From the sound of his voice they knew that their proper lord had come. His arrival relieved them of much of the fear that they had had before. Now Giburc was so overcome with joy that she fell in a faint in front of everyone, for plenty of bold help had arrived for her from France, the best knights to be found in the land of true chivalry.

Giburc was still lying in a faint, and the Margrave surely thought it was taking them a long time to open the gate. It was fastened so securely with locks that if someone inside should be tempted by an enemy to reconsider his loyalty for the sake of a bribe, it would not do him a bit of good. To guard against precisely such a danger, Giburc herself kept the keys to the fortress. They were fashioned so very cleverly. (Nowadays hardly anyone knows how to make such keys.) In a short while she regained her senses and hastened to the gate where she had heard the voice of her beloved friend, Willehalm. He was let in joyfully.

She did not have quite the fair appearance that she had when he had left her, as her sweet lips had counselled him to do, which now were kissed again and again. Alas, that he had such a rough beard to offer to her! Yet she herself was dirty from her armour. Neither the maiden Karpite fighting before Laurent, nor Kamille of Volcan was armed so well.[32] But Giburc had not fought on horseback. This tale attributes other brave deeds to her, saying that she shot the crossbow, hurled huge stones, and that her defence was marked by clever tactics. She propped up her dead soldiers on the battlements dressed in their armour and manipulated them so skilfully that it inspired fear in the enemy outside, who were erecting siege equipment against her. Such efforts had made her thoroughly dirty.

Then she looked at Rennewart. When he tossed his huge, strong, long club from one hand to the other so often, she asked: 'Who is this sarjant? Shouldn't we be afraid of him? He looks so wild.'

The Margrave replied: 'The Roman King gave me this lad and great assistance as well. Many noblemen of my rank are hastening here to us with such a desire to help that if the enemy is still waiting here, the French will fight so fiercely that the angels in the nine choirs[33] will be able to hear it and my kinsmen will be avenged. Even if mountain and valley were full of heathens, they would still have to fight.'

He clasped the Queen tightly to his breast and lamented her hardship. He addressed the others who were still alive with Giburc in the fortress, saying that they would always participate with him in whatever he might possess, be they woman or man, young ladies or other maidens. 'If anyone in the future,' he continued, 'laments the hardship that you have endured on my account and encountered while serving me, he may lay claim to my goods and my very life. You have saved this lady for me and preserved Orange, this fortress. If I can rule this march again, I shall reward you as long as I live with fiefs and with gifts.'

Giburc, the ever-faithful woman, was standing there, with her maidens, still prepared to fight, and Willehalm could not fail to see the armour that they were wearing. Some had a soft pad where the tie of the loin belt ends. (If someone gave me such a thing, I'd rather have it than a falcon!)

Now they had stood about long enough. The Queen did not fail to lead the lord of the land away to a chamber, nor to order his horse Volatin to be cared for. Rennewart stayed with the horse, and no one wanted to move him away from it until he had put it in a comfortable stall. He found an emblem from Samargone burned into the horse's shoulder as a brand. Arofel's shield was marked with a similar sign. It would have been too much for the lad, if he had realized how the horse had been obtained.

Meanwhile the Queen removed her armour, but the Margrave still wanted to remain in his. She said: 'Your coming has driven my father towards the harbour. You should take off your armour, and don't delay in telling your kinsmen and all those who have come to help you that the heathens have left here for a while and have gone, I don't know how many miles, away. My servant found out about their departure and followed them as far as Pitit Punt. He says that they were hastening away. Their coming and going have cost me dearly. May God compensate me for the loss! And He is doing so already, since your loyalty and your bravery are so evident in the fact that you have rescued me here. Now see to it that you don't neglect to dispatch a look-out. My father knows many tricks. Beware, lest his troops lie in ambush to destroy your army.'

The Margrave replied: 'Can you get a messenger for me? He shall tell the French not to lament too much because the heathens have ridden away. He shall ask the leaders especially, all of them, wherever they may be, to set up their camp in a meadow, and tell them that I shall soon come there myself.'

Soon a messenger was on his way there, and a look-out went to follow the enemy. The two sped to their tasks. Then the Marquis removed his armour and saw how the French were galloping up with many separate squads of men to gain renown, although it was still very early. These noble men wondered where the enemy had got to, but soon they heard from the messenger who had been sent out that they would find no combat there.

The French set up their camp for the night. The princes individually adorned their circles of tents as is only fitting, yet not one of them was able to equal the expanse of the heathen encampments. The field had previously been covered with many costly satins draped over the tent poles of the heathens. Now those from France were encamped there elegantly too. Their tents were indeed cut from expensive materials.

The Margrave said to the Queen: 'Madam, we would gain increased willingness from the people, if we could entertain them here in my palace and thus compensate them for their labours. Formerly I was well equipped to do so, but now servants and supplies have been burned so that there is little of either to be found here.'

'We have enough,' the Queen replied. 'I am glad that you mentioned it. We have such quantities of food and drink that all my father's knights, if we did not want to stop them, could not consume it in weeks.' She assigned to the task those who could cope with it.

The Margrave and his lady reclined in the window recesses, wishing to watch for friends. You could tell by looking at them that they had seen plenty of enemies in their time. The lively Frenchmen threw up new shelters with the siege timbers of the heathens. Yet still those fearless knights had not arrived who shared the sorrow of the Margrave so fully that they participated equally with him in the devastating events that had occurred at Alischanz. Then Queen Giburc saw many huge clouds of dust caused by the wind's stirring up dirt and leaves where many mounted units spurred their horses to get there quickly.

'Alas,' she cried, 'what are we to do now? Look, my lord, Tibalt is coming. They are riding over the field and through the brush with equal ease.'

Willehalm replied: 'They have a right to do that, for they think that we are fighting the enemy here. That's Buov of Commercey riding here from his land. God can indeed protect us from them, for Buov himself and all his men are also in mourning for my kinsmen.'

The French did as they always do. Some had ridden out for pleasure to enjoy themselves with their falcons. Elsewhere many young lads were quick to leave the bulk of the army to form combat groups. Now scouts had reached Buov and found that these were friends there. The enemy was elsewhere. Those arriving pitched camp with the ones who had come earlier. Giburc was happy about that.

It was not long, however, before she saw swords and shields flashing repeatedly through the huge clouds of dust and asked: 'Who are those people coming over there? You heard what I said earlier today. You should listen to my advice about tricks by the enemy. Indeed, Akerin, the King of Marroch, and other units of my father's army are daring enough to move among their enemies. Take steps accordingly.'

Then the Margrave replied: 'That is my brother, bold Bernart of Brabant, arriving. His son, Berhtram, was often with me and was carrying my banner when Vivianz was killed. Bernart and all those coming with him are here to avenge his son.'

These too encamped alongside the others who had arrived earlier. (Setting up camp is called *loger* in French. I've learned that much of the language. A rude peasant from the Champagne could speak much better French than I, the way I speak it. Now look how I am treating those to whom I should be telling this tale in translation! They would be better off if I used German, but sometimes my German is so involved that a man can easily become quite perplexed, if I do not explain it to him quickly. Then we are both wasting our time!)

Willehalm's army was growing. Mighty Heimrich, the old Lord of Narbonne, had brought many troops armed for battle there. He always arranged things so that everyone shared what he had. And he did not come alone this time either. The bushes were trampled down when he revealed in what a warlike manner he came riding, with his troops in massed formation. He wanted to find out for himself whether any of his children were in some kind of trouble. Then he got the news that the Saracens had ceased attacking Orange and had gone on their way.

Giburc saw her father-in-law approaching and asked Willehalm: 'Have you observed who those men are who are coming now?'

He replied: 'That is my father, and his men are all brave and bold as he himself always urged them to be.'

Heimrich's marshal came riding up, leading his lords to the divisions that had arrived previously, and the newly arrived men joined the others in camp.

Willehalm's brother Bertram came then in a manner befitting a prince, and another brother, Gibert, came too. They rode at the head of many worthy knights, their men coming on a separate route. At the same time via a third route came Arnalt of Gironde. They had arranged their routes in such a way that no one of them could be completely out of contact with the other and not be able to come to his help. None of the knights had demeaned himself by riding from his home and separate land to help his brother. Their loyalty demanded that of them.

Giburc observed all of them, the three separate armies arriving almost simultaneously. The Margrave named all of them very gallantly so that she could identify the leader of each army. That made her very happy.

The fire had made all of them – the father, his sons, each army – stay awake and endure a night march, ready to fight, if the Margrave had needed them. Their manly courage urged them to do this, and they were so bold that each one had hastened straightway towards the fire. Because they were wanting to put their manly courage to the test, each of them feared that the other would come to the aid of this one or that with his swift charge before he could, when the heathen attack with its fire was causing Giburc distress. That was why each one rode an armoured horse and was armed to the teeth himself. They sped on vying with one another. Each one came with such force that if a massed fight had arisen there in rough country or in ditches, he could have fought all the heathen chivalry in close quarters. But the heathens had found the wide open spaces on Alischanz where they were awaiting the time for Vivianz' revenge.

The Christians had set up a mighty camp on a meadow beyond the siege positions which the heathens had occupied. Those positions were completely unsuitable. What with all the smoke and stench a hound without a nose could have found the spoor there, so broad were the tracks Terramer had left. Now a group of men who had never left the path of valour could be seen coming with pierced and battered shields. The leader who had brought them was born of true manly courage. He too had journeyed the night through and pursued the heathens, fighting with them so fiercely that many of them lay dead at his feet, and he too had his trouble getting away from them. But they had had to pay their possessions to him in tribute. He had seized many of their pack animals, horses and other things there. Le roi Schilbert of Tandarnas had come as a favour to the young Schetis.[34] They had both been in the pay of the Venetians, these two who had endured so much in the war against the Patriarch of Aquileia, who did not dodge the fight, but on the contrary, gave the Venetians more than they asked for and limited their sway on land and sea with troops and ships, so that the Venetians had to defend St Mark with mercenaries and pay large sums of money for all this trouble. From there this young man had travelled here in his desire for noble renown.

Thus he had heard of the heathens' crossing and the fact that Terramer was leading the noblest and the best from there to Kaukasas. He had come to fight against Terramer and win fame. His name was Heimrich, the Schetis. His bravery could make you feel sorry for the fact that he was called 'the Poor'. That cast doubt upon his nobility too. He did not even have land enough to pitch a tent on, and he had no other income than what he earned courageously in battle with his enemies. His right hand grew around the shaft of his lance. He had great strength in jousting. No painter now alive has ever seen with his eye or painted with brush and hand such a figure as he cut when carrying his shield.

Thus the noble youth came riding to his father's camp with battered armour. But he and Schilbert had seized rich booty from the heathens, and the Christians liked them for that. Old Heimrich was delighted that le pauvre Schetis, whose young years had already accounted for so much fame with knightly deeds, had come in such a truly manly fashion. Tears of joy ran from Heimrich's eyes on to his cheeks. The Schetis was received with joy by his father and his brothers.

Up in the window the Queen asked: 'Whose large troop of men is that? Their shield straps are showing, uncovered by the boards. They have been engaged in fighting somewhere.'

'I don't recognize them,' Willehalm replied. 'I can't make out anything on them that they could be identified by. All their pennants, shields and garments are tattered, battered and torn. They have been in a fight. I have one other brother with the Venetians. If he has heard of my trouble, then it is he who has come with manly courage.'

The Schetis' men unloaded their baggage. Their courage had acquired the goods in the face of superior strength. They shared everything equally, as did the king who was there at the Schetis' request and who was called 'of Tandarnas'. The Schetis wanted people to show Schilbert respect. He asked for nothing more. It made him happy whenever anyone did. Both of the young knights had received Gahmuret's inheritance,[35] that is to say their fathers had given them nothing more than shield and spear, and their ambitions were set on chivalry. They had armour and nothing else. Their tents were scarcer than hen's teeth.

The Queen was reclining in the window, enjoying the companionship of the Margrave, who pressed her to his breast repeatedly in close embrace. She had had to do without that for a long while and had yearned greatly for it. (I would have become faint-hearted, if I had spied a woman standing there so boldly. I have trouble enough when approaching an unarmed woman to retire with honour!) Giburc was still dirty from her armour, but in his love he didn't notice it at all.

It was announced to the princes and to other nobles of theirs that they should dine in the city.

The Margrave stepped away from the windows and said to the Queen: 'It is time for me to bring my father here to you, if he will agree to come. I will invite the other princes too, for you should receive them graciously. Now see to it that soft pillows are quickly laid out all about in the great hall with rugs in front of them, and on the pillows quilted coverlets made of brilliant silks which people can see are expensive, if anyone chances to notice them.'

He rode down to his father and joyfully welcomed his brother, the

Schetis, who supported himself only with what his spear and shield could earn. I'll tell you what his best business was: he busied himself rightly with weapons! *He* didn't lose any sheep that a wolf had killed or that had run away. Wherever a city or castle burned, *he* didn't lose a wisp of straw. Hailstorms did no damage to *his* crops and *his* foliage. Possessions were burdensome to *his* limbs.

The Margrave asked his father to dine with him in the city together with his two guests, so that they might see the Queen inside in the great hall. The King of Tandarnas, whom the Schetis, Willehalm's brother, had brought, thought that was a splendid idea. Willehalm received him with the utmost respect, as if all lands served him. Wherever he found people in distress he greeted them and welcomed them so warmly that they were happy to see him. The Margrave found Heimrich and all his sons sitting right there in front of him under a canopy. He welcomed them and promptly invited them to come and see the Queen, saying that their arrival had made her extremely happy. They did not in the least mind seeing her, as courtesy required. Then he rode to the other princes whom the Roman King had sent. He told each one separately that he was invited to join him in his palace Glorjet. He told them that part of it was still undamaged by the fire, although his land had all been laid waste. They should enjoy with him what was left, and he would gladly offer it to them.

The noblemen of the army were asked to ride on ahead into the city. The princes each rode with three others. Their company was no larger, for all the high-ranked men they had brought. The counts reacted in like manner, and the barons like the counts. Each one thought it quite enough, if one companion rode with him. They told the other knights to be at ease on the field. That was done in accordance with good breeding. The French are not greedy, but they are eager to gain fame in fighting. If the Margrave had taken back his invitation, they would have been so polite as to have done without his food. They thought that so much had been lost that they would find little there anyway, and it would be a sin against the emaciated people of the city to accept their food. Therefore each nobleman left his army with not too large an escort.

Now Giburc could lay aside her surcoat in honour, and she and her

ladies could wash the armour rust from their skin. She said: 'The wheel
of Fortune is round. I was beset by sorrows for a long time. Now I am
partly relieved of them. I urge all of you, my ladies, to put on your
best clothes. You should deck yourselves out, do your face and hair so
that you look lovely, so that a knight seeking love and offering
service in return for love will not quickly have too much and that
parting from you will be painful. Do that first of all, and put on your
best courtly manners, as if you had not suffered from the enemy.
Don't be too talkative, if they ask you about our troubles. Just say:
"If you can bring yourselves to do so, don't pay any attention to our
tale of woe. We have outgrown our lament. The consolation of your
arrival has freed us from the oppression of our enemies. If you will
grant us your help, then we can indeed forget our sadness." Act like
good hostesses. There was never a prince so mighty that he would
not listen to a maiden's word. Sit here or there, but if a knight
mingles with you, behave towards him in such a way that he will
recognize your pure virtue. A lover always finds courage when near
his beloved. Your womanly tenderness will bestow high spirits on
the man. I want to make myself pretty too. If my hair was all tangled
and my skin marked by chain-mail, that shall cause me no more
trouble. I shall wash off this rust that I picked up from my armour.'

This was soon accomplished, and the ladies and the palace were
delightful to behold. One had to say that all the women were in fine
array. All round about in the great hall there were many carpets, and
on them the cushions with their coverlets. Now it was time for the
prince to ride in. The others had all waited for Heimrich and his
companions, and now he came riding in at the head of his men. All
those came dressed in fine clothing who had in mind to see the
Queen. And they found her in her sweet beauty, standing there
resplendently before them. Both the gown and the cloak that she
wore were of silk from Alamansura, so skilfully worked and costly
that no more expensive effort could have been put into embroidering
it, if Sekundille had given it to Feirefiz. The cloak hung open with
laces untied. She was beautifully formed and proportioned. I don't
think anyone without God's artistry could have designed her better.
She won the favour of the hearts of all those who turned their eyes
towards her. They declared that her belt was extremely expensive,

adorned with jewels, so that it flattered both her hips and her sides. Now and then she opened her cloak a little, and if any eye peeked in under there, it had a view of Paradise itself.

Now her father-in-law, that grey-haired man, came up and dismounted in front of the palace. With him came the King of Tandarnas and his own youngest son, Heimrich the Schetis. Both were deserving of the reward that Love sometimes offers for service. Heimrich of Narbonne rewarded the young King for having come by telling him to precede him. Now they saw Giburc standing at the window by the wall. Heimrich led King Schilbert by the hand up to the noble Queen and asked her to kiss him, as indeed she did.

Then she greeted her father-in-law and would have kissed him, but the courtly gentleman said: 'My lady, we should not do that yet, neither I, nor any of my sons, until the princes who are less familiar to you than I and my children have received your kiss of greeting. We should not be improperly hasty but, however you wish to honour us, we shall serve you accordingly. We have received much more honour through you. We shall always speak of your loyalty, for we have found you today to be so fearless that neither Olivier nor Roland was found to be more courageous. You are courageous and have the manners of a proper lady, too.'

Having said that, he began to summon the princes and named them, all of them, by both name and land. He led each one by the hand up to his noble daughter. He could not have conducted the reception with greater propriety. The princes and all the nobles could well be satisfied with that. Now the ranks of the ladies were interspersed with knights. And of course the Queen did not forget to receive Heimrich and his sons.

When that was done, her father-in-law sat down next to her. Thereupon new grief arose, which caused their eyes to well over. The face of that sweet, lovely creature was wet with tears. Heimrich's white beard was sprinkled with tears too, as he said: 'Your faithfulness and your womanliness, Madam, have taught us that our heartache will be turned to joy. You could have disgraced us, if you had not remained steadfast towards us. We would have been forced from our position of high honour, and if you had not stood by my son, this land would have been lost and Orange, the fortress, as well, that best of all towns, which has endured much punishment through assaults. But your loyalty directed you, and still does, to do that which demonstrates your renown. My son, the Marquis, and his kinsmen everywhere can say what a friend should expect from friends. You have made ample compensation for the deaths of our kinsmen. If we did not now gladly wish to serve for your favour, it would be an unforgivable sin on our part in the sight of God. We shall remain for ever faithfully at your service, if we have any sense at all. If my son ever brought spear to bear on an enemy for the sake of your love, you in your loyalty were mindful of that when Terramer marched in force against Orange for Tibalt's sake and the flood-tide of his army swirled around you, for, virtuous as you are, you did not fail to accord Love its privilege in such a way that brave men shall always think of your reward and not waver in their service, if they seek the love of noble women. My lady, grant me one request: for the sake of my service and the other princes who are here, please stop your weeping and moderate your heartfelt grief.'

The Queen's hand was lying in his, and she acceded to his request with difficulty, as her weeping and sobbing became mixed with words. She spoke to her dear father, telling him of such sorrow as was known to her personally and of her immense suffering, which was both so long and so broad that all heathendom felt its effects, and all Christian lands participated in it. She said: 'I came too soon into the mind of Him who brought me into this world from the void. I am the scourge of the creatures of Him who creates and maintains Christian and heathen alike. I was a loss for both of them. Suffering arose through me for them and for us. Thus I have paid a price for your son, my lord, and for his nobility in that your relatives and mine have sacrificed their noble lives on both sides. High-born prince, of pure nobility, how was I to have silenced my sorrow when I saw him whose brave fruit had sprung up towards joy with such manly bearing? I lament the fair youth Vivianz, who must always be the first to receive my sigh-filled greeting instead of my laughter. What has bitter death done to that handsome, sweet, pure young lad! Every other man's countenance was like a fog when his radiance came into view. He won fame before all others by himself, for his splendour was a second daylight. Where his body lay dead on Alischanz, young little suns could have arisen from his dazzling brilliance. But now I will let no new day dawn without lamenting noble Mile and the others whom we have lost. I was born to be the target for suffering.

'Now, my lord, since joy has fled from my heart, I hope that you with your sense of propriety will not hold it against me. Allow me to benefit from the fact that you are like a tree trunk in your manly loyalty. Listen to how many kinsmen Death has snatched from me on Alischanz. It is only proper that I mourn them, although they were not baptized. My relationship to them makes them a loss for me. My father told his men to ride away. Then under this window, where he stood in tears and where sorrow wrenched joy away from him, he told me how many noble relatives we had lost, whom Love, even more than his own request, had prompted to come here. He began to recount the deaths of the nobles, beginning with le roi Tesereiz of Latriset and telling me whoever else met his end on Alischanz at the hand of the Christians, who also paid with their lives while fighting there. These are the kinsmen of mine whom Death claimed: le roi Pinel of Ahsim and dear King Tenabruns, who came from Liwes Nugruns; both Arofel of Persia and Faussabre of Alamansura, my uncle and my cousin; King Turpiun, whose land was called Falturmie and King Galafre, who wore the crown of Kanach and whose death was a real loss to Love; and King Noupatris – if a branch of Love ever bloomed in human form, then it was he in his splendour. Love had sent him here from Oraste Gentesin. He was found dead in his fine trappings. The death of le roi Talimon of Boctan will cause mourning to resound in heathen lands. The death of these two, le roi Arfiklant of Turkanie and le roi Libilun of Rankulat, will checkmate joy in both their lands. Now believe me when I say this: twenty-three kings were lost there and countless numbers of those who as eskelirs were considered as powerful as princes. So many of them died there that no one could say precisely how many. They cannot even estimate how many emerals and arnazurs sudden Death carried away from them. I have named only my kinsmen, who lived until their end with their noble honour unsullied and who always strove for renown.

'It was naive of my father to ride out in force with his army against his own child, but however many of our relatives died because of me, he would gladly have lost all of them, if I had been willing to renounce Christianity and worship his gods.

'Then my son, Ehmereiz, offered to compensate this land for damages, saying that wherever it had suffered loss as much as one byzant worth, he would weigh out hard cash, according to Charles's weights. Vineyards, trees, sown fields, all the meadows and the heath, both horses and cattle, all the farms to the last straw, the birds, the game and fish, all that, he would have paid for ten times over, if I had wanted to renounce my faith in God. Steadfast Matribleiz, the King of Skandinavia, who everyone knows is to be trusted and who both here and elsewhere has preserved his loyalty, was to protect the assessors, ensure safe conduct for them and pay out the money in cash.

'Then I said: "Son, what are you thinking of? Some other kind of speech would be more fitting. Do you want to put me up for sale and thereby demean yourself when I am paid for just like a cow? You are my son of lofty lineage, but what you propose will damage your reputation. If you are as wise and manly as the Margrave ever was and if someone would give you all the mountain Kaukasas – that would be a rich reward, for it is all solid red gold – you would not want to accept it for a woman who was just as beautiful as I still am today. Your offer is ill-made. I have committed myself to the Margrave, and no one can offer such wealth as to separate me from him."

'This displeased them all. For my apostasy they offered more ransom, loyal and noble men. My nephew, King Halzebier, offered to free from chains eight princes captured under his banner and to send them to France in exchange for me. For him, my return could serve as recompense for loss and heartfelt pain. Twenty thousand of the men from his realm lay dead there. Falfunde must mourn for ever its eskelirs whom Death could not pass over. I asked who those Christians might be who had survived and was told their names and the damage for which this land must pay. He who created weeping and laughter can see to it that they are freed. Let me tell you their names. They are Gaudiers and Gaudin, Huwes and Kibelin, Berhtram and Gerart, Hunas of Saintes and Witschart. Death did not deter them.

'All those who came to help the Margrave from your family died except those eight. Rich and poor knights died as well. Graciously accept the fact, my lord, that that causes me great anguish. Those were my best friends, who died there in battle. Their cemetery is a broad field, consecrated and hallowed by angels. It happened this way: the blessed bones and bodies of the Christians were discovered entombed in many beautiful sarcophagi never fashioned by human hand.'[36]

No one sitting there was so callous that his heart was not moved to the point that tears welled from his eyes. There was not a person there who did not lament what the Queen had just said. Nevertheless, they took great joy in her assurance that the Count Palatine and his seven relatives still lived. Then the table-cloths were brought in.

The Margrave himself heard for the first time that the Count Palatine Berhtram and seven others were still alive. He said: 'God has the power to bestow joy and sorrow on whomever He will. He may well have happiness in mind for me after all the sorrow, if His grace is directed toward me.'

Heimrich and all his sons thanked the Queen for having rejected her father's advice and for not having accepted the separate offers of her kinsmen or her son. They said that she had done honour to God Almighty and to the Margrave in her noble love as a proper woman should and had increased her claims to salvation.

Then Bernart of Brabant spoke, saying: 'My son, the bold Count Palatine, was always seen in the midst of the enemy. The other seven, each one of them, are blood relatives of mine. The eighth is indeed my own child. No one of them is so dear to me that I would not let his skin be cut into bowstrings before I would see Tibalt take Giburc from us by force or bargain her away from us and rob us of our honour.'

'From what you say, Madam,' said the Margrave, 'the heathens have not forgotten you and still have their eye on you. But they must admit that however many relatives of mine they have, I have in you a security for them indeed. They will have to take some other hostage, if they are still fit to fight.'

The Margrave was very sorry that no more knights from the army had come into the great hall. He said: 'In other times you have seen more of them here. You can blame my father-in-law for the deaths of my kinsmen and the devastation of the land. Such is the dowry he gives to me. Many men, more powerful than I, have attacked me. This would have been avoided, if Tibalt had been acting on his own. Such an expedition would have failed, for without Terramer's levies not one of his gods would have helped. Father, please take charge of the seating of all the princes,' he continued. 'Give the orders here as in Narbonne, and do it for God's reward. Tell your household officials to serve us up here today. Whatever stewards, cup-bearers, marshals and chamberlains I had were killed when they "served" the heathens and did not budge from the flag until they poured out their own pure blood. My loss of so many devoted hearts is immeasurably great, and I mourn them all, as indeed I should, for now I am in need of them. Ask your people to lend a hand.'

'I have already thought of that,' said Heimrich. 'You men of mine, do as he asks. You know the straits the Margrave is in. Serve us his bread courteously, just as if his men were still alive, who often served it to us with such finesse and presented it to us in such great abundance. I need say no more to you about it: act as if we were at home. What my son has, is mine as well. I think my lady, in whom I have never doubted, will grant me that too.'

'Indeed, Sir,' she said, 'most gladly. And if all of Todjerne, Arabie and Arabi were free of heathen rule and were at my service, I would put them all at your disposal. I gave all that up for this poverty. Our possessions, your son's supplies that we have so narrowly defended, we should not like to consume without you and those to whom you will distribute it. My heart awaits your command and that of my brothers, your children. I shall gladly be a household servant to all of you after our losses. Steadfast help is now at hand for which I often looked to you when the heathen storm beat against Orange.'

'My lady,' said the grey-haired man, 'in whatever way I may or know how to, I shall be happy to serve you, and if anyone needs my help, all my relatives and my sons stand faithfully at your service.'

Then he asked the Queen to remain seated and told her that she and the other ladies should stay right there. 'Let me be the host today. I shall return to you presently,' he said.

With her leave he went away, holding a staff in his hand. Graciously he showed the young King of Tandarnas where to sit, on the one side of the great hall which was opposite the Queen. He told the Schetis to sit next to the King and Buov of Commercey and Bernart of Brabant. Those four had one wall. The princes from France whom the Roman King had sent there, he seated in a manner befitting their knightly status and gave orders that they be attended to nicely. Noble knights were assigned to wait on them.

He asked for God's blessing for the food they were about to eat and told them to partake freely of it, saying that whatever they were eating there had been preserved by ladies' hands from the overwhelming pressure of strong enemies: 'Many unbaptized strangers did not hold back their rage here, but Orange was defended by ladies who have earned renown here. They proved resolute in their defence. Since they have preserved it for us, you shall all enjoy it, each one of you as he wishes, princes, counts, this one and that, barons and all the other knights. Don't think of any lack of food. Orange is well supplied, thanks to those who saw to it before we arrived but are now dead on the field of Alischanz. Their deaths have brought us here. Let us eat what they left for us. We should rejoice in their departure, for where they are now, their wealth is increased.'

The old count left the princes and went on busily. He began to seat the other princes, his sons, who had not yet been seated, on another side of the great hall: Arnalt of Gironde, Bertram and Gibert and Willehalm, the host himself, for he knew all four were noble.

You ask who was sitting with the Queen at that time and who ate with her? That was old Heimrich. Those who carried the food in and served it, did so with excellent manners. They let it be known that there could be no lack of anything. They had mulberry wine, claret and grape wine and fine food as well, yet their eagerness to serve was even better than all the food. Brilliantly dressed ladies sat there, lovely to behold, but old Heimrich was not interested in such a feast. Not one of them was so beautiful as to succeed in capturing his heart and mind, except for his son's wife alone. Those two ate very little because of the many questions which he asked about the troubles the Queen had had, and he lamented heartily when she described them to him. She derived her nourishment more from joy than from the food, although the sensible old man chided her for that.

While much was being served and enough had already been served in the great hall, Heimrich, grey in years but not weak in spirit, ate less than any other man. When he asked the Queen while they were eating which heathen besides Tibalt bore the greatest enmity towards her, she replied: 'All the noblemen were hostile to me, as far as I know, except my son Ehmereiz. He had many knights here, but no one from his camp raised bow, shield or sword against me. He didn't want to stoop so low as to cause me fear from the people who were under his command. Two kings who had been sent by women lost their lives on Alischanz and their mourning armies came here to Orange, but my gates, towers and walls suffered no damage from them. Noupatris brought some of them from Oraste Gentesin. Tesereiz' army declared that for the sake of his reputation their suffering should not be avenged on me and all other women, since it was after all in the service of women that Tesereiz had met his death. However, when the Margrave met them in battle, that would be the time for their revenge. Noupatris' knights were here with the strength of a great army. Those whom that Seeker after Love had brought disdained whoever showed himself in an attack on a poor woman like me. Since the lord of this land had been defeated and had ridden off for help, they maintained that noble men should act towards women in such a way as to be ever at their service and to seek reward in return. Many an army was here without its leader, and from them I suffered severely. Only Noupatris' people and Tesereiz' army kept apart from the others, as I explained. But I am sure they were not lacking in courage.

'Ten brothers of mine showed their hostility towards me here. Many a strange knight from Griffane and Vriende was here for the sake of my sister's son. Poidjus and my other relatives were not reluctant to do whatever they could in their hatred towards me. Tibalt's whole family was here with a mighty force. I should have liked to have more friends among them, but now they are intent on inflicting anguish on me.'

Thus the sorrowful woman sat with the dew from her heart flowing from her breast through her eyes and running down her beautiful face. Then her estimable father spoke to her, asking her courteously to conceal her weeping, for the Margrave and his guests should be entertained, unburdened with mourning.

She said: 'If you say so, my mouth will try to laugh, but even if I jest now, my heart must still be sorrow-filled.'

'Now control your grief,' he replied, 'so that your behaviour will be proper and no one will become alarmed at it. The coward and the bold man are sometimes one and the same person. I am confident indeed that my sons will not lose their courage, but I cannot always say the same for those who are considered my equals. Some princes are just not made for fierce knightly combat. We should show the people high spirits and encourage them. "Good encouragement has made many a coward bold."'

BOOK VI

Is that oath now no longer binding, which was sworn that evening when the Margrave left Orange? He had been urged to do so by Giburc, who herself asked him to ride away for help, out of the city and into the land of the French, to see if the authority of the Empire, his father, his brothers and his other kinsmen would size him up in such a way that he would gain their support. He secured their aid and now they are here.

You have certainly heard both about his departure and their arrival. From now on he can eat more than bread: Giburc has been released from the clutches of her foes, even though she is still weighed down with misery. The Margrave was very glad to eat and drink whatever was set before him. His friend Rennewart, that sturdy youth, made his way in front of the visitors, intent on gaining renown for himself. In his hand he was carrying his huge club as though it were a piece from a shattered lance. All of them wondered what he had in mind, the Burgundians, the Bretons, the Flemings and the Englishmen, as well as the Frenchmen and the men from Brabant. It was the son of the most powerful ruler of the time who had come in and there was no disputing this.

Down the middle of the great hall were many marble pillars supporting lofty vaulting and Rennewart leant his heavy club against an archway. They wondered what he was up to, when he looked around him so wildly, and some of them were afraid that through no fault of their own they were going to have trouble with him, though as a matter of fact he knew how to avoid that, provided that he was not provoked.

Since his skin was sweaty and dust had settled on it when he came on ahead of all the others as his manly courage prompted him to do, here and there a bead of perspiration had removed the grime from the shining skin of Rennewart, the bold young squire. He looked like a dewy rose when its rough outer skin splits and reveals in part the petals underneath. If he ever gets rid of all the grime he will shine like the flowering meadow.[37]

The powerful man – no weakling, this – had eyes in his head like a dragon, huge, clear and shining. Although his beard was only just beginning to grow – he was not yet old enough to have a proper one – he had been obsessed with thoughts of fame since he had set off from Laon on this march. Alize's kiss had caused his beard to sprout. You could have counted the hairs on his chin which did not get in the way of his mouth very much.

You could detect in him the nobility of the mother who had borne such a child. His whole face and all his limbs were perfection itself, and his handsome appearance earned him the approval of women, so that not one of them was ill-disposed to him. I shall have plenty to say to you in praise of him if he gets closer to renown, and if I am still clever enough for that. One thing you can believe, for no one could take this away from him: through the grime he shone forth like the young Parzival when Count Karnahkarnanz came upon him on his knees in the forest, so radiant in his beauty.[38] Right now you are to attribute a similar beauty and a similar strength to Rennewart, as well as the same inexperience. Neither of them had been brought up in accordance with his lineage and so they were robbed of their nobility.

Heimrich addressed a question to the Queen: 'Who is this coming in before us, looking so strong and so vigorous and with such a huge club?'

Giburc, who was always so kind, replied: 'My lord, it is a sarjant who, in the course of his short life, has not, I think, received his due. I believe that he should be treated better. He is brave and far from sluggish. He came on foot ahead of the men on horseback and would have liked to go straight into battle, if he had encountered some of the enemy. Sir, the Marquis told me that King Louis gave the lad to him. He is certainly not hideous to look at. Since the death of Charles l'Empereur and the mighty Baligan, no mother in the kingdom of either of them has given birth to such a lovely child. Moreover, he is modest and well-behaved, and as easy to train as a young girl, for he is glad to do anything one asks of him. Since I saw him this morning for the first time my heart has been telling me something about him which often causes me to sigh. Before long something, whether joy or sorrow, is going to happen to me because he has come here. I must say that he is like some members of my family to look at. My heart gives me no option but to love him, I know not why. It may be that he hates me.'

Rennewart, the young sarjant, went up to his master, the Margrave, who soon became aware that his friend was standing there in front of him. He greeted him kindly: 'I must ask you to do something for me,' he said. 'Go before my lady and that gentleman with the snow-white hair: they are both worthy of your service. Look at his lively manner. I am always pleased to see him. If I tossed that old falcon in the air he would surely catch the crane.[39] There is not a timid bone in his body.'

'My lord,' replied Rennewart. 'My service will not fail him, nor anyone who wishes to have it and asks for it nicely.' With that the brave lad stepped courteously before the lady of the land.

Heimrich called across to Willehalm: 'What if your visitor goes ahead and vents his anger on us? We have done nothing to deserve it.'

'I shall take the responsibility for anything he may do to you in his inexperience,' replied the lord of the land. 'He was the first to arrive with me this morning. He knows how to be a good friend and a foe to be reckoned with as well.'

The table was short and wide. Heimrich invited Rennewart to join them, to sit on the carpet at one edge of the table near to the Queen who did not, of course, object to that. Rennewart sat down with due courtesy, and Heimrich looked him up and down. The boy blushed with embarrassment at being so well treated there. The Queen made no ado but graciously placed a piece of the table-cloth across his lap, and, even though he did not speak, he bowed his thanks to her politely.

Although the Queen was sitting higher up than he was, his head was much higher still, and this, of course, was because he was so tall. Thus the two of them were able to demonstrate that they were very much alike, as if they had both been pressed out just a bit too hastily from the same seal, so that the only difference was his tender beard, and I should have been glad if that had not been there, for then one could easily have mistaken the man for the woman, so similar were they to look at.

Right away then, at the request of old Heimrich, Rennewart was provided better than he had ever been before, with mulberry wine, grape wine and claret. He stuffed his cheeks so full of the food which he found in front of him that there would not have been room for a snowflake in there, and ten bees would not have been able to suck so much from the bowls, unless my tale deceives me. Yet the two people who had had it put on the table for him did not eat much, for they were ensnared in the bonds of sorrow. Even so – take note of this – they acted as though they were happy.

Many pages came along, wanting to seize his club or carry it away, but a rude farm-waggon would have creaked and groaned under its weight. Rennewart laughed and said to them: 'You are making fun of me. Stop playing about like that with my club or I'll make someone angry. You want to carry it in your arms like a child to be baptized. I swear by the twelfth apostle who lives in Spain – they call him Santiago there[40] – that if you do not stop this nonsense someone will live to regret it. I should be able to eat more of this food than a tiny sparrow if it were not for you and your games. Now just watch your manners.'

Rennewart was eager to get at the food, and no one needed to offer thanks for what *he* sent forth from *his* table.[41] Spiced red wine, claret and mulberry wine too, these strong wines pleased him better than the water in the kitchen. He ate all of the food, disdaining none, but, unfamiliar as he was with wine, the excessive drinking got the better of his courtesy and restraint and excited him to wrath, that noble lad of high birth.

Many young pages were pressing against the club until they finally knocked it down and caused a terrific din to resound throughout the great hall. Rennewart jumped up from the table and headed towards them but all the pages had scattered so completely that he could get at none of them. He seized the club in one hand. One page had run away and swiftly slipped behind a pillar made of blue marble, but Rennewart caught sight of him there and thrust out at him with such force that sparks flew out of the pillar and shot up towards the ceiling. The page scampered from the room, so now there were no pages left in the great hall. They were crowding out of the door, each one trying to get ahead of the others. The table-cloths were folded up but not carried away, for those who looked after such matters had fled and did not dare to venture up to Rennewart and encounter his bitter brand of tenderness.

Those who had been eating there rose to their feet. The Queen did not remain seated either but asked the princes to go and rest, saying to all of them: 'Have your retinues take with them whatever they please in the way of food and drink.' And Heimrich, the shrewd old man, added: 'Those whose supply-train has not yet come need not be ashamed to accept this offer: you will be given whatever you wish in plenty. That is my advice to you all.'

The princes went to their camp-sites and the Margrave had a horse brought for him and rode down with them. Thus he rode this way and that, here over meadows and there across fields, and if any camp was without provisions, he ordered supplies to be brought down to the people there, so that they had no reason to complain of any shortage. When he had ridden down, the Margrave requested all the noblemen in the army to eat and drink well, and to rest for the whole of the day, adding: 'As soon as day breaks, you are to hear Mass sung in my chapel, and I shall take counsel with you there.' They gave him their promise and did as he commanded. All the princes, counts and those who bore the title of baron, every one of them, and all who were put in charge of a detachment, had ridden into the field.

Inside the town, Giburc was attending to the needs of her beloved father-in-law, Heimrich. Many lovely maidens, who were well versed in courtly service and were glad to be there now, were standing by his bedside in a chamber. Heimrich lay down and Giburc seated herself on the carpet before the old man. Young girls removed his boots in order that Giburc might massage his legs before she left him. Weariness and sorrow caused him to fall asleep straight away, even before they had gone out of the room, for he had been riding all night long in full armour.

And now the lord of the land – I mean the host there, Willehalm himself – came up again and did not fail to take advantage of that companionship from which previously he had often derived both joy and pain. He and the Queen went to a bed and made love so tenderly that for both of them there was recompense for what the battle had inflicted on them at Alischanz through the loss of their kinsmen, so mutual was their compensation as they lay there.

When the generous Anfortas was in the service of Orgeluse before he parted company with joy and the Grail provided for his people, and Queen Sekundille ventured to offer him love and sent Cundrie to him with such precious wares, which he accepted from her out of love and out of love passed to another, the acquisition of all the crowns and all the lands of Sekundille, with the bequest of the Grail itself, could surely not have compensated for the enormous losses sustained by Willehalm at Alischanz.[42]

In his arms now a slender shoot was blossoming forth from sweet love. In her pure tenderness Giburc snuggled so close against his chest that he was recompensed: he claimed her as his compensation for everything that he had ever lost. Her love afforded him such aid that the Margrave's sadness was streaked with joy. Sorrow had ridden away from him so far that no spear could have reached it. Giburc was the guarantor of his joy.

Sometimes joy does follow on from sadness, and joy has assumed a familiar custom which applies to men and women alike, for sorrow is our beginning, and with sorrow we come into the grave. I do not know how it is in the life beyond, but that is how things are here. There is not much joy in this tale. I should need to be very clever to discover any joy in it, although I don't begrudge good to those who have not done me any harm and do not harm me now: such people will not suffer at *my* hand. A wise man once advised me to perform good deeds, whenever I was able, which would be more to my credit than following the example of the false: that way I might gain renown.

Yet no one should despair if he has to endure suffering as well as joy, for a man who has joy as his constant companion has never really experienced ease. Indeed, a man's efforts should be directed towards joy *and* sorrow, and true womanliness also knows this dual companionship, since sorrow has always been associated with joy, as its floor and its roof, and its walls, on the sides, at the back and in front. No one should rail against great sadness, for even if so far he has avoided it, it nevertheless is right there, at the heels of his joy.

The Margrave took his ease, and his whole army, too, was well encamped, and his men very comfortable. Only Rennewart could still be seen coping with trouble. A great many pages would not desist from constantly running about and leaping around and did not tire, some of them, of hurling things at him. Many of them he had been chasing away all day long, and so he had been playing at fighting until after the time for vespers. Yet, even so, he injured none of them as he had done before at Laon when the jesting had got out of hand. There were plenty here who were taunting him, not having encountered his fury, but he did not give vent to that at all.

Now night was drawing nigh, and the noble, high-born youth sped away from them. The young man was carrying his club, for he was anxious to hide it from them. They plagued him from behind but after a while they grew tired of this and he too was overcome with weariness and, for all his nobility, he deigned to seek out the kitchen where he lay down to sleep. His soft little pillow was his hard club, and he did not rest there for long.

Poidjus, his sister's son, had rarely lain like this, the King of Vriende who had in addition under his control the lands of Griffane, Triant and Kaukasas. I think *he* had a better bed when he lay down to sleep. This uncle of his was enduring hardship which he would have been spared altogether if only someone had known the true story, of how this high-born child had been stolen from the breast of his wet-nurse and plunged from wealth into a state of poverty. Such is the intricacy of fate. The child was brought up by merchants who kept him until he reached the age of understanding. Their sole concern was money and they believed that his noble lineage would be a great asset to them. They mentioned to him quite correctly the names of nine kingdoms where his father was the ruler and regaled him with tales of how the most powerful Saracens had to obey his command, in the north, south, east and west, and of how two of his sisters were queens and were so lovely that they were renowned above all others for their beauty. They spoke to him in particular, too, of truly marvellous wealth, of the lands of his ten brothers and the names of those brothers as well.

The merchants were cultivated men and they taught the child French, for they had in mind to bring him as a gift to the Roman Emperor. The child was so good-looking that it could truthfully be said of him that no lovelier face had been seen since the day when Anfortas was cured by Parzival's question.[43] The merchants warned the child that, if he wished to stay alive, he should keep silent and tell no one at all, neither man nor woman, from which land he had been abducted. Otherwise the men from Samargone would have come back for their wares.

Louis King of Rome gave instructions that he was to be well looked after. The child was renowned for his beauty and the maiden Alize, too, was beautiful, as I have told you. When they gave him to her as a playmate, the seed of their love grew to maturity, and they sustained it to the end of their lives, each enduring grief on account of the other. The King wished to have him baptized – he had been sold in Tenabri, you see – but he resisted this doggedly, and so he was denied the honour of the company of Alize, which caused them both distress. Alize was the epitome of loyalty and for this reason, when the two of them were together, the boy confided to her all about his family. Then he had to leave his lofty status for a lowly way of life and cope with humble tasks – and all in order to force him to be baptized.

The boy bore a grudge against his father and his other relatives because they had not secured his release. He thought that they were violating their own loyalty, yet his anger was not justified, for they did not know anything about him. If a messenger of his had come to them, or if anyone had demanded ransom money, such sums would have been offered for him that the French would be weighing the gold to this day. Many of his high-born kinsmen died because of the indignities he had suffered. He fought for Christendom and gained the victory and that was how he avenged the ignominy and the suffering which he had endured in the presence of Alize. It was her love which urged him on to fame, and matters will not always stand like this for him: the love of Alize will protect him. Whatever degradation he may have suffered, Alize's love wrenched this from him shortly afterwards in the course of deadly combat.

The cooks had been told that, at daybreak, a great deal of food was to be prepared, if anyone wanted it, and that all the princes were to eat in the great hall. Because of this many kettles had been hung up over blazing fires. Then something happened which proved to be the end of the chef, who behaved as I shall now relate to you. He took a glowing brand and went right up to the wall where he could see Rennewart asleep. There was no need for anyone to deprive him of such miserable repose. The cook singed his young beard and burnt his mouth a little too, but his flippant behaviour was his downfall, when the boy whose sleep he had disturbed like this tied him up as though he were a sheep, trussed his arms and his legs together and hurled him without further ado under one of the cauldrons, into the huge blaze. This was how he came to lose his life. Rennewart did not have salt fetched to sprinkle over him but piled on him brands and pieces of coal. My lord of Vogelweide used to sing of roast meat: *this* roast was long and thick and would have been ample for his lady, for whom he always had such an adoring heart.[44]

Only Rennewart remained behind, for sheer terror had driven the others away from him. They were afraid that they would be landed with the bill. One cook fled this way, the other that, and then they peeped in through the wall and heard how young Rennewart was mourning for his beard and what else he was bewailing.

'Wretched man,' he said, 'I thought that I had been freed from bondage when the Roman King gave me to him who is acknowledged before all others as the highest eskelir and who in truth is incapable of any false deed. If only they had allowed me to benefit from the enormous loyalty which I have pledged to him! If he knew me for what I am, he would be sorry about this. This beard of mine which has been burnt was sown upon my mouth by the love of her who gave me her kiss to guide me on this journey. Her love has done more to pull these hairs out of my chin than the few years I have lived, or that shameful treatment to which her father subjected me. I know for sure that she grieved on my behalf whenever she saw how the King was acting against his natural courtesy in his behaviour towards me and when I myself investigated the whys and wherefores of chivalry in tournaments and battles which I would often run to in order to observe the art of horse-riding, or how one should behave towards ladies. Whenever I was in refined company they chased me away with their staffs. The lord of this land has been disgraced because his cook has burnt me like this. Moreover, the children of the mighty Terramer are mocked through me, ten of whom are powerful kings in vast realms and themselves have great kings as their vassals. Those whom I know to be my brothers must share in my ignominy, Fabors and Utreiz, Malarz and Malatras; if our origin, born as we all were of one mother, was in loyalty, then Glorjax and Passigweiz, Karjax and Matreiz, Merabjax and Morgowanz will have plenty of grief on my account. If we are born of perfect loyalty my wretched life in exile represents disgrace for those ten too. The King of Kordes should allow me to benefit from his great wealth. Happe and Suntin, Gorgozane and Lumpin, Poye and Tenabri, Sembli and Muntespir are all under his command, yet I am receiving no support from him. If only his noble eskelirs would tell him about his ill-treatment of me! After all, I *am* the child of Terramer.'

Through the wall they could hear him lamenting like this.

By now day had come and the sun was breaking through the clouds. Princes came riding up, and when they had all assembled, a Mass was sung, in honour of God and for their own sakes too. The Margrave sent someone to find out if the food was ready yet, but those who were employed as cooks had fled the deadly toil, and no one had made up the fires. The Margrave was told that Rennewart was bitterly lamenting his singed whiskers. Some of them had heard him saying something about his noble birth, but not all about it. Willehalm sent the Queen to him, asking her to calm his rage.

'The chef is dead,' he told her. 'Use your diplomacy to get my friend away from there.'

And so, in order to find the young man, she went to where she never again set foot. Very courteously she begged him for her sake to cease complaining of his loss, to calm down and put aside his bad temper.

He replied: 'My lady, you are so kind. Whatever you tell me to do I shall do, but look how I have been brought up. Many people are being deceived about me.'

The Queen led the boy away and offered him better clothing, in a room where tailors were sewing many different kinds of surcoats.

He, however, said to her: 'Madam, I am sorry that you had to walk so far to fetch me. As far as I am concerned, you can give your clothes to those who are your subjects. Poor I may be, but lots of men in this army need them more than I do. Just leave me my club as my defence.' (He had brought the club along with him.)

Giburc began to lament his singed whiskers and all the time she did not take her eyes off him, for she discerned something in him which startled her deep in her heart.

'My dear friend,' she said, 'if you permit me I should like to ask you where you come from, if you will allow this and not get angry.'

He replied: 'Madam, believe me: I am a poor page, and yet the child of very noble people. This I must admit if I know how to behave properly, but, my lady, for the sake of your own honour, do not ask me any more questions, for this will be the best thing for both of us: just leave me in my wretched misery.'

The boy was still standing in front of her and the lady's heart was telling her something which she did not find out until a long time later. She asked him to sit down next to her and tucked part of her cloak around him.[45]

He said to her: 'Madam, the finest knight who ever fastened his helmet with his own hand would be glad about this, but if anyone sees me sitting like this he will accuse me of behaving in a most unseemly fashion and mock at me because of it. My lady, spare me this for the sake of your god.'

Giburc said to the young man: 'What other God should I have but the One whom the Virgin bore, if you know anything of His power?'

(The Queen wished by this means to discover whether he was a Saracen, for she did not know what his religion was.)

He told her: 'Three gods are known to me: the holy Tervigant, Mahmete, and Apolle. I am happy to follow their commandments.'

The Queen sighed before she spoke and all the time she gazed at him, for her heart could see that he was certainly born of her race, however he might have been lost. She acted entirely in accordance with her good breeding, taking his hand into her hands and saying: 'My dear, good friend. Have you a father or a mother, brother or sister? Do not be afraid to speak out and tell me without embarrassment just one thing: the name of your family.'

Rennewart replied like this: 'I had a sister at one time who surpassed all others in beauty, a maiden who took away the radiance of the sun when people saw them both together in the morning, when the sun was breaking through the clouds. She was given in marriage to a man who has achieved much fame though he behaved badly towards me too, when my brothers let me down as they did, for he has left me in a state of distress for so long and has not been prompted by true magnanimity. I am justified in hating him and my whole family. They have cut me off from their gods and have still not sent a messenger to me in my trouble but have brought shame upon their famous name through their treatment of me.'

Then he added: 'My lady Margravine, if you do not mind my saying so, you must have looked like one of my sisters when you were young, and, if you were powerful as they are, you could easily be the child of the man who has brought dishonour on himself by his ill-treatment of me and against whom I shall always struggle for revenge because of my misery. My father and my other relatives are too grand for me. I tell you this because I recognize your true courtesy, but you must not treat me any better on this account. Keep quiet about what I have told you. They want me to live in this lowly station. If I was born of noble people, they have sacrificed their good fortune by their treatment of me.'

Giburc asked him on his honour if the Marquis of Provence would really have his support and he replied: 'My lady, I shall uphold his honour absolutely. In doing so I shall have my revenge for the shameful suffering from which the heathens should have released me a long time ago.'

Giburc said to him: 'Then I wish to give you a suit of armour in which you can protect your young life whenever you become involved in battle. It is quite big enough for you and made with skill and artistry. Thus nothing that they may do to you in battle can defeat you. King Sinagun was wearing it in the battle during which he took the Marquis prisoner, when the great defeat was sustained and King Tibalt was put to rout. The undaunted Willehalm pursued them until all of them, bold and timid, high and low, began to regroup in strength. The heathens, one and all, acquitted themselves with the utmost valour. Sinagun, who always strove for renown, forced the Marquis to surrender, for he had ridden too far away from the Christians. Thus Willehalm himself was conquered without a victory for the heathens, and led away into the land of Tibalt. I was unhappy when I saw him in chains and other irons. I had inherited the crown of Todjerne, and the generous King Tibalt of Kler held sway in many lands at that time – even today he is the leader of a vast army – and he had given me the crown of Arabi. I do not know who is now the Queen there. My nephew, King Sinagun, the son of Halzebier's sister, left me his own armour and his captive who had performed so many illustrious deeds. The armour and the Margrave both escaped with me, and that is how I came to have this armour.'

She gave orders that the armour be brought before him. Schoiuse had often struck out at it but it was so excellent that it had withstood the blades of Schoiuse and all other swords as well. The helmet was thick and hard, coming down far to the shoulders, decorated with jewels all round the edges and fitted with precious straps. The chain-mail leg-coverings and the hauberk gleamed; the sword was long and shining and quite perfect on both its cutting edges. Both the blade and the groove between the edges were smooth, the hilt sturdy and broad. No one in Nördlingen has a wider swingle.[46] With this sword the valiant Sinagun had fought and won fame, but it did not please Rennewart, who considered it too slight for his enormous strength. He pulled it out and tossed it aside, saying: 'My lady Margravine, just let me carry my club, but I won't refuse the armour, although I can't do much dressed up in it. Nevertheless, have it put on me.'

Young girls, as well as the beautiful lady herself, helped Rennewart into his armour, and, when he had it all on, the young man fastened hefty shoes over his leg-coverings of chain-mail. His spirits began to soar with pride, constant as he was in his pursuit of fame. His coat was rather the worse for wear, nevertheless he wore it as a surcoat. Every lock on his head was covered by the sturdy, precious helmet.

'Now may this sword be my comrade,' he said. 'Let me put it on. The Margrave can absolutely depend on me to serve him as well as I am able, if only he will give me the chance to fight.'

Giburc the Queen asked all the maidens to keep him company and to comfort him in all his trouble. 'I shall soon come back to you,' she said, 'but you must allow me to go to church and not raise any objections.'

Duly armed for combat, Rennewart sat down among the young ladies, who helped him while away the time.

The Mass was sung, and afterwards all of them, old and young, princes and counts, whatever their names were, and those who were appointed to command a detachment, were summoned to a council, just as to this very day people are glad to call together men of high rank. Giburc was granted leave to attend, together with many noble men. Now hear what they did: the Queen sat down and so did they. Only the Margrave remained standing, and he spoke as follows:

'I am addressing all of you who are my companions here, my father and my brothers and those other relatives of mine, and those whom the Lord of the Empire has sent here to protect baptism and our Christian faith. Listen, all of you, to how things stand with me. My father-in-law has attacked me. The breasts of Christian women have been cut off, their children martyred.[47] Their menfolk have all been slain and set up as so many targets. Whoever shoots at them gains in respect among the heathens. This is how Tibalt and the mighty Terramer have vented their hatred in my march. Eight of my kinsmen who responded to the dictates of loyalty and hazarded their lives by riding with me have been taken captive; seven of my princes, too, have been slain, the noblest in the kingdom. I beg you, one and all, take pity on me, bereft of joy as I am.

'I must remind the Frenchmen that, when I accepted from the Empire in fief that land to which Tibalt now lays claim, I was granted the following pledge: The Hand of the Empire swore to me – and twelve men who were acknowledged as the most powerful in France gave their oaths too – that if ever the fighting threatened to overwhelm me they would come to my aid with an army of excellent knights within a year. I have been waiting seven years for that. Now Tibalt has defeated me, though I have inflicted substantial damage on him. I played the part of a merchant until I had conquered that fine city of Nîmes with my waggon.[48] After that, while I was in prison, I sought the love of Tibalt's wife, the Queen. Kind as she is, she granted me all that I desired of her but she did this – and then when she crossed the sea with me – more on account of baptism than through any worth of mine. Since then King Tibalt has very often inflicted great anguish upon me. Those who have treated Almighty God with contempt are still with us in this country. Now – if I may put it like this – honour the Virgin's Son through me. Help me avenge my kinsmen so that we may gain such ransom from the heathens as may open up the fetters of Berhtram in prison. If now I may benefit from my kinship and from the oaths which have been sworn to me, then joy will still be mine indeed.

'Let my father and my brothers speak first and after that let my kinsmen and the chief among my vassals speak as their courage urges them to do and so demonstrate their loyalty by their behaviour towards me. If you command me to keep quiet about it, then it will be my duty never again to complain. Let each one be mindful of his honour as a knight in accordance with that benediction spoken when he received his sword: anyone who wishes to practise chivalry aright must protect widows and orphans from danger, and this will bring him lasting gain. He can, moreover, direct his heart towards service in pursuit of the reward of ladies, when one learns to recognize the sound which comes from spears cracking through shields, and to know how women rejoice at this and how a beloved woman soothes the anguish of her lover. Two rewards are waiting for us: heaven and the approval of noble ladies. If I am brave enough I must now seek to gain these things on the field of Alischanz, or die in the attempt.'

Up stood old Heimrich and spoke to his son in a fatherly fashion, saying: 'You may now be seated. It is my privilege to reply first, for I am the oldest man present. My peers, princes, all of you, do not take it as an insult if I speak before you do. My son shall not bear his grief alone: I share it with him. I do not deny that my heart declares him to be my son because he is in trouble, but even if he were my vassal – which God has not deigned to grant to me – I should certainly still wish to help him since he has gained too much renown for the Empire and continues to bring honour upon it with his acts of courage. Whosoever is not deserted by good fortune will preserve the nobility of the Roman Empire by his valiant efforts. Since Terramer of Tenabri has led all the men who live as far as Vriende, into battle against us, all the noble people from Marsilje to Kaukasas, we shall find all the more hostages to take. He has brought with him across the sea no king so powerful that he could not easily lose his army.'

Bernart *le fleuri* stood up and said: 'Brother, Margrave, my son Berhtram carried your banner and dared indeed to spur his men on. I believe that he too was valiant. Now they have more than enough trouble, those princes who are in captivity with my son. Those of you who have entered our service and have accepted imperial payment, or who are here in any case in all your princely power with a vast company, both for the sake of the Empire and for our own sake, now, all of you, you heroes, help to break open the bonds of my son Berhtram and to avenge the death of Vivianz. I am speaking on behalf of all my brothers. I am so confident of their loyalty that our hearts are as one, and this is why none of them has spoken yet. Now our visitors are to speak, those who have come riding here in such force from France. Come on now, take your turn bravely! I am not referring to our relatives as "visitors": that would be to violate kinship, and my father and we ourselves are relying on our kinsmen. You, Frenchmen, speak up now and tell us what we can expect from you, and let us have a look at your courage.'

He who is telling this tale will now explain to you why the princes whom the Roman King had sent there are not mentioned by name. This is because some of them turned back and brought shame upon their princely rank, whether they had received this through the sceptre or the flag.[49] If anyone wants to remind them even now of their ignominy, let it be said that, after all, they did return. Young Rennewart turned them back at the narrow pass at Pitit Punt, fifteen thousand of them in one go, between Orange and Alischanz. You think that he who was bearing the enormous club was dumber than an ox, and yet he was the son of the most powerful man reigning at that time. But enough of that! There were many princes sitting there who declared that anyone who was not satisfied that Orange had been freed from the heathen should try to find better aid and that, for their part, they did not wish to go any further with their travel-weary armies. It would be no shame, they said, if they did not fight, since the heathens had ridden out of the country and away to their ships. 'If anyone will deal with us,' they added, 'we shall ransom the prisoners in exchange for goods.'

Bertram of Berbester said: 'It was never right for a noble man to retreat from fame, and if anyone urged him to do so he should never again treat that man with favour. Now, heroes, remember that you have endured suffering to gain much fame in France. If you forsake the Marquis now, when he is in such dire straits, this will not match the intention of the lady of any one of you. I know, too, that He will hate you for this who on the Day of Judgement will come forward bearing in His mouth the sword which will lay low the bold man and the coward alike. Lucky for those whom He claims as His children! If only we may behold the five wounds which are still open! He shed His blood for us. Whoever now would turn from God would come to a terrible end and such a man's soul would go to hell. His flesh and blood gained blessing for us, He who came riding with no thought of flight. He was seen approaching on an ass to the place where later a blind man pierced Him with a spear, though He could easily have escaped even those who could see.[50] Anyone who wishes to preserve the blessing of the Cross for himself should grieve for how He hung upon the Cross, Jesus, when He accepted death for our sake.'

Then Buov of Commercey said: 'Frenchmen: you have always acted with courage, and yet you have really been too quick to abandon it. Let every bold knight behave as his finest nobility prompts him to.'

The Frenchmen were ready to have second thoughts and to avenge Vivianz on the hostile mass. Each Christian was matched in battle by fifteen others who had been brought from distant lands. This is how the Frenchmen behaved: that which they had sworn at Laon and at Orleans before the Roman Protector was no longer withheld. Declaring that all the Saracens must be their foes they took up the Cross with one accord. The noise resounded and reached the army outside, and many a knight rejoiced at this. The noble men all desired to take the Cross, and this the many priests arranged for them, for knights and sarjants alike. Stalwart turkopels everywhere took up the Cross without exception, too. They cleansed their hearts and thought only of Almighty God.

In the individual armies of the seven brothers some men were preparing for battle, while some were still asleep; others were checking their weapons, their shields and their banners. There again, some were polishing their armour until it gleamed, while others were directing all their efforts towards decorating their helmets. None of the appropriate straps and ties was forgotten. Many brightly shining objects could be seen, armour and trappings, which later were to become murky with blood. Some were exercising their steeds, while others were riding around for pleasure on their lovely saddle-horses. At the same time, many undaunted men were enduring pangs of fear, as they came to realize quite correctly that the battle would cost no less than lives on both sides, willingly offered up to Death. The first battle at Alischanz had brought death to Pinel and because of this his kinsmen later caused suffering to Christian men at Alischanz. The death of Vivianz, too, later cost many noble heathens their lives. Thus revenge matched revenge.

Giburc was the cause of all this misery. She stood up now and spoke courteously before the assembly of princes dispersed. 'If any man present is loyal and chivalrous,' she said, 'then let it please him to listen to what I say. God knows that I have laid up in my heart such a store of grief that my body is hardly able to bear it.'

She asked those who had risen to their feet with her to be seated and not leave. When they had all sat down she said: 'If I am responsible for the many deaths which have occurred on both sides and because of which I must endure the hatred of Christians and heathens alike, may God grant recompense to them through me. I hereby remind you princes of the Roman Empire that you will be increasing the honour of Christendom if God so honours you as to allow you to avenge the death of Vivianz in battle against my kinsmen and their army on the field of Alischanz: you will find them formidable fighters. And if you defeat the heathens you should act so that your salvation will be assured. Pay heed to the advice of a foolish woman: spare the creatures of God's Hand!

'The first man whom God created was a heathen and you should know for a fact that Elijah and Enoch, heathens though they were, are saved from eternal damnation.[51] Noah, too, who was saved in the Ark, was a heathen, and Job was certainly also one, but God did not cast him down on that account. Think also of the three kings, whose names were Kaspar, Melchior and Balthasar, and whom we must consider as heathens who are not destined for damnation. God

Himself, at His mother's breast, received His first gifts from them. Heathens are not all condemned to perdition. We know it to be a fact that every mother who has borne a child since the time of Eve gave birth to one who was indisputably a heathen, although each child was encircled in the womb by baptism. Baptized women give birth to heathen children, even though baptism may have surrounded the child as it lay there.[52] The Jews have a different custom with regard to baptism, for they perform it through circumcision.

'After all, we were all of us heathens once. It pains the person in a state of Grace if the Father has condemned His children to perdition. However, He who has always been compassionate will show pity for them. Now believe me when I say that mankind wrested that place in heaven in the Tenth Choir from those angels who are now so hostile towards our race.[53] They behaved so defiantly towards God that they betrayed His noble and steadfast power. Those very comrades in arms had to fall because of their thoughts, for God, who knows thoughts undisclosed, did not allow them to express those thoughts in deeds. This was why man was conceived. Both men and angels had incurred the wrath of God. How is it that man now has more hope than the angels? I shall explain this to you: man was ruined by bad advice, while the angel, by his wicked cunning, selected eternal damnation for himself, and all who joined up with him encountered the same grievous end. To this very day, these wicked angels pursue mankind, as though the Choir were their inheritance, whereas it is in fact bequeathed to those who know how to avoid incurring the anger of God who grants eternal bliss.

'Whatever the heathens may have done to you, you should allow them to profit from the fact that God Himself forgave those who took His life. Have pity in the battle, if God grants you the victory. Our Father Tetragrammaton[54] offered up His virtuous life for the guilty ones and so rewarded His children for their forgetfulness. His love which is so full of mercy embraces all miracles and in His loving loyalty He will not cease to hold out the helping Hand which first brought into being both land and water: all creatures contained beneath the heavens have need of this. That same Hand allows the planets to run their full courses both near and far. Never ceasing in their activity, they bestow warmth and cold alike, sometimes creating ice, then bringing sap to the trees so that the earth may seem to be shedding its plumage and the month of May instructs the earth to accomplish its moulting process and to bring forth flowers in succession to the frost.

'I serve the Hand of God the Artist in place of the heathen god Tervigant. Its power has led me away from Mahmete and towards baptism. Because of that I am enduring the hatred of my kinsmen, and of the Christians, too, for this reason: they believe I brought about this conflict out of desire for human love. It is true that I left love behind me there too and great stores of wealth, and lovely children, with a man of whom I cannot discover that he ever committed any wrongful act since I received a crown from him. Tibalt of Arabi is innocent of any misdeed. I alone bear the guilt, for the sake of the grace of Almighty God, and also to some extent on account of the Marquis who has gained such high renown.

'Alas, Willehalm, true fighter, that my love should ever have become so bitter for you! How many supreme men have lost their lives gallantly in your service! Rich and poor alike, all of you must believe that the loss of your kinsmen sears my breast. Indeed, my joy lies slain with them.' She wept copiously, convulsed with misery.

Gibert, the brother of their host, leapt up and pressed the noble Queen to his breast. Her heart shed many tears out of her eyes and down her cheeks. The council dispersed. The princes went into the great hall, where many tables were splendidly bedecked. The courteous Heimrich spoke to all the princes individually and told them that they were all to sit against the same wall where they had been seated on the previous day.

The maidens were summoned and they came, and with them Rennewart. His incipient beard had been singed, but his armour was expensive and brightly shining; he himself was handsome and strong. He laid his club down and many knights went up to it. However, none of them had sufficient strength – they all lacked the power to lift it from the ground, except for the noble Willehalm, who jerked it up above his knees, something the others could not do, not one of them. Rennewart took hold of one end and that young sarjant swung the club above his head like a sapling. His strength stood the Christians in good stead.

When there had been enough playing about, water was brought to the princes and to many lovely ladies, as well as to all the noble knights. Each one was sitting in his place, and Heimrich asked Rennewart to be seated beside the Queen, on the rug, at the head of the table. When he had sat down he had to eat, just as he was, in armour. It must be said of his sword that if Neidhart had seen it being carried over his local hill he would have complained about this to his friends.[55] The Margrave did not object, even though Rennewart was sitting very close to the Queen.

Never had better food been seen and so willingly served in such a devastated land. If anyone knew how to live on goodwill alone, he received this from his host and hostess, and neither of them made the mistake of carrying away what anyone who was proposing to fight the enemy could eat right there. By the time they had eaten, it was far on into the morning. The princes took their leave, wanting to press on and eager for battle. Giburc was weeping as she kissed them.

Before they had reached their encampments, the tents had all been dismantled and the army drawn up in groups, and the field adorned with many banners. Giburc came quickly to the windows with her many maidens, to watch how the plain was being covered with many companies of knights and all their princely forces. From all sides there came marching along the roads towards the sea such a powerful army that the angels could have seen it if they had known anything about helmet decorations. On their helmets those men there had fixed many costly and beautiful ornaments. Moreover, the whole field could be seen glistening with the finest silks worn by these noble and high-spirited men. Never in the whole of Christendom had there been seen such an assembly of the friends of the lord of the land.

So they are about to depart: they are all set to ride against the heathens. May God, who takes care of everything, direct all this. He knows well enough who will be victorious there.

BOOK VII

Rennewart was able to see how one knight positioned his shield at his neck, how the other tied his helmet on his head and how look-outs were sent out in the direction of the enemy to protect the army. Special detachments were positioned both on the fields and on the road to offer resistance to the enemy forces, if they should return. Terramer's tracks were broad indeed and nowhere narrow either on the hills or in the dales.

Rennewart ran around amongst all the men, wanting to find out all the different techniques they had. When he found his master they had already travelled a good distance. Terramer's son came running, not walking, up to the Marquis and Willehalm asked him about his club, saying 'How are you going to help me?'

'You've got to count me as the worst among all these troops, if you are looking for a bad apple!'

Rennewart was much ashamed. He considered it a great disgrace to have forgotten his club. You see, he had run immediately from the table when he heard the trumpets sound, and when he saw so many intricate decorations on all the helmets – there is no woman so old that she would not feel rejuvenated and turn her attention eagerly, if someone paraded those knights in front of her – the many splendid units caused Rennewart to forget completely that he had ever owned a club, so eager was he to get under way. Yet all the time he was wearing his sword.

The noble page said to the Marquis: 'My lord, I shall go and fetch my club. Let me endure this humiliating task, for if I were really a man, the club would be with me now. I shall quickly catch up with you. And even if night should draw nigh, I shall still find your tracks and those of the heathens who rode here before.'

The Marquis said to Rennewart: 'You can save yourself the return journey this time. I'll provide you with another messenger who will go and fetch the club for us.'

A squire on a good horse was sent for the club. He rode all the way back to Orange, where the club had been laid down. Either a cart or a waggon was needed to carry it back to the army.

Heimrich and his sons and also the other princes arrived at a pleasant spot, where the army was ordered to camp. The field was splendidly decorated: pavilions and many tents, shelters of leather, lean-tos and huts were set up there. Before the army had settled down completely, Rennewart's club arrived with the rearguard. He was happy about that. They camped there overnight.

In the morning the army began to move towards the heathen forces. You could hear a cacophony of trumpets and other noise there. Now Rennewart wanted to run around and see everything again, those far ahead and those near, here one detachment, the other there; he wanted to inspect all of them more closely, their shields and their banners too, until he had forgotten his club once more.

After the army had moved some distance away, the camp-sites were burned. Now the young sarjant noted to his chagrin that the club had not come along with him in his hand. Anger rose in his heart, for if he had suffered great embarrassment yesterday, it was twice as bad today. He said: 'Now my stupidity has really struck again! It never seems to leave me alone. If one keeps frustrating the desire of a wild falcon – and I've seen that myself – he later becomes shy and timid. I alone have frustrated my own desires.'

Back along the road he trotted, his legs showing their speed. He went all by himself. A horse would have to break out in a sweat to follow him at that pace, so swiftly did he hasten back. And yet he was wearing full armour! His good breeding could not keep him, brave man that he was, from choosing great rage as a companion instead of high spirits. 'What kind of miracle can this be, that I have forgotten my club now for the third time?' he said. 'The fact that nobility keeps eluding me in this way, will, I think, help those heading for death to reach their destination. Do you suppose He who can perform all miracles is testing me to see if my bravery is ready? Out of propriety and out of shame I neglected to tell anyone that I had turned back. That will only increase my disgrace, for they will think that I have fled. One thing I have decided: that if my master is attacked there my kinsmen will share in my great disgrace. Many noble men who are my kinsmen will be brought to shame for this, for people will think that my turning back came about through cowardice, and that would disgrace the kiss that was given to me by the niece of him at whose side in battle both my heart and its desire will be. Even if I say nothing about this it will still be talked about without me.'

Now the bold young lad arrived at the place where the huts of branches, reeds and straw had burned or were still burning. He could not remember where his sturdy club was lying, and he searched high and low for it.

The club had been charred, and it took him a long time to find it. The fire was extinguished, but the club was black like the other coals. (Now, don't worry: if it was better looking before, it is now tempered better and tougher.) He snatched it from the fire and ran towards knightly enterprise.

The Margrave had come so close to the enemy that he had taken many of his supporters up on to a mountain to have a look. He had ordered the army to halt on the slopes and on the meadows. Terramer, mighty by virtue of his lineage and his immense wealth, lay encamped by the River Larkant between the mountains and the sea. His forces could be seen spread over the broad field of Alischanz. If I were to name for you all those who were camped there with large forces in their own individual camps and if I included names *and* countries, I would have my work cut out for me. The field was so densely covered with camps that those who were watching could see nothing but tents and the sea. At that sight many who previously had often fought bravely and gained renown in France seemed to have second thoughts.

The Margrave spoke to them all, saying: 'Now let each one with his companions weigh the hearts of his friends against the strength of the enemy. Let each man who is here for God's sake or mine consider what he wants to do in battle. There lies the son of Kanabeus, mighty Terramer, with such forces that we shall indeed find opposition.

'Now I must ask you – the time has come for this – who wishes to venture into battle. God shall send such courage into all your hearts that you will do justice to yourselves. I have full confidence in all of you, yet this army of God would be destroyed if one of us should start to flee. Let every man in his courtesy speak as his heart prompts him to. Since many a charge will now require us to counter-attack, if anyone does not have it in his heart to push ahead but wants to turn back, let him rather choose here to turn back now than increase the chances of flight in battle. Let each prince talk to his men. If God gives someone the good fortune of achieving eternal salvation this very day in the decision of the battle, his participation in this campaign was indeed blessed.'

Louis, who wore the crown of Rome, had sent many princes there with a vast company of knights, but almost all were disgraced there. Many took it into their heads to want to return hastily to France when they saw such a flood of heathens encamped before their eyes. Some got ready and took leave to travel back. They regretted that later with shame. Whatever entreaties had been made of them at Orange in the great hall were made much more strongly here. They took leave immediately, saying that they could maintain their renown within their lifetime at home in tournaments and matches. They didn't want to serve as anyone's quiver for a single moment, waiting for him to stick his arrows in them. And so they began to retreat. Their disgraceful about-face was a dishonour to the crosses that had been affixed to their clothing. I hope you will not laugh when you now find out what happens to them when they come face to face with Rennewart.

The manly undaunted hero who had earned much renown (but now it is the Marquis I am talking about again) spoke, saying: 'Those who have now stayed here will earn eternal fame. They will never be rejected by the pierced right Hand, which spilt its blood for us on the Cross as a ransom to hell. That same Hand has never yet ceased to give eternal reward to whoever has earned it with simple devotion. Those of you who have remained here are destined for salvation. Only when someone removes the husks, does he see the true kernel. We shall find out yet today how God's right Hand will reward us. No star is so purely brilliant that it does not become dull from time to time. Never mind! Let them go! What difference does it make that those dandies have left us? If the women at home know what is proper, they will show them such disfavour for that, that they would be better off if they had stayed here. We here can do penance for our sins and keep the favour of noble women too.

'Now, father and brothers,' he said, 'see how many units we want to form with the number of men we have. That is for experienced men to decide.'

The pay promised by the Roman Queen was earned there now with glorious deeds, and none of those whom Irmschart of Pavia had recruited for the campaign wanted to flee from the heathens. The troops of his sister and his mother stood by the Marquis ready to fight. Those who had often summoned up courage before and had experienced many an onslaught formed up in five battalions.

Meanwhile the fleeing troops had come to the narrows at Pitit Punt. There they encountered opposition. All the while they were retreating they had desires of many a kind: one wanted to see the ladies, the other wanted to pamper his body with many nice things after the great discomfort of hard camp life. On the other hand, a third wanted to be leeched and make himself forget all the trouble. He said that no matter how good a tent might be on meadow or on field, he would prefer a chamber well equipped with soft cushions. 'Let the fools fight with so many Saracens,' they were thinking and added: 'Let us leave these toils for a place where we shall find plenty of comfort. Why the arrows of the Saracens are poisoned like the bite of a snake!' (They didn't want any goblin shooting *them* through the knees.)

When Rennewart saw them fleeing he sped towards them in anger. Before he said a word to any one of them a good forty-five lay dead at his feet. They could not escape from the great danger of the narrow pass. It seemed a long time to them before they found out why he was treating them so sinfully through no fault of their own.

The rich nobles asked why he was carrying on that way. He let the fury of his first attack just get closer to them and gave them more than they bargained for. They were unprotected, without armour. Some did not defend themselves at all, but others did. Yet neither course of action could save them. Precious few of those whom he could reach with his huge club were spared by him. They rued the fact that they had turned back.

Many among them maintained that they were getting their just deserts. It was the Hand of God, from which they had fled, that was punishing them. 'We haven't enough space to be able to put up a defence against this attack. If Rennewart would lead us back under his command, he could gain in us a force to oppose the heathen army. Here, unarmed as we are, we can't even defend ourselves.'

By now Rennewart had felled countless soldiers on both sides of the road, and he began to take pity on all of them. When he had finished swinging his club he let them appeal for a truce until he could hear how their turning back had come about.

Then from their midst a clever man spoke, saying: 'You have inflicted this tremendous and terrible damage upon us for no reason at all. Many a man lies slain here before you who never had any part in the insults that the Roman King Louis offered you in such plenty, thereby damaging his reputation. Now follow our advice. Turn back with us. We shall raise your nobility so that your disgraceful suffering will have an end as you wish it to. If you are ready and willing to serve women for their love, then what you gain in joy will vanquish great sadness. But if you wish to hang out in taverns you will be so pampered that whatever delights women can provide would be as nothing by comparison, as I shall describe to you now.

'We shall drink to lots of love-making and hang our glass bottles to cool in sparkling springs where green clover and other grass may grow under the shade of a tree. We shall spice our wine with good sage. Thus we shall enjoy life to the full. We shall also hear the wine run from the spigot like a deer leaping from the chase. We are all too wretched in the heat on this moor. There we shall have many delicacies to treat ourselves to.

'You should decide to turn back. All who are here will advise that. The Margrave would fight for nothing. Yet all wise men know that "a strong boar sometimes flees from a cowardly dog". Wherever the Margrave can find a fight that is a pastime for him like a child playing the game of rings, but he will just lose another army!'

'Can't I find any courage in you at all?' said Rennewart and launched at them again. The undaunted young man cancelled the truce and now their second punishment began.

Towards the bridge was a gorge with high cliffs on each side. No one could avoid the fight nor could anyone escape, for on either side of the bridge lay a swamp, and no one could pass through it. Rennewart ploughed a deadly furrow with his huge club, yelling at them: 'If you will pledge your help to me against the heathens, I'll spare your lives.'

To escape his club they swore their oaths swiftly, turned around and started back, all of them, rich and poor alike. When they had all come out on to the plain before the gorge, Rennewart moved in front of them. They all followed after him, while he set out on foot ahead of them.

The imperial banner had been taken down because the imperial troops had deserted Willehalm and his men. A fine gold star on a bright blue silk background was floating above the heads of the Marquis' men, as he himself had ordered it. Beneath it Arnalt of Gironde was riding next to the Marquis.

Now old Heimrich was leading the second strong battalion. And who was the leader of the third? Mighty Buov of Commercey and bold Bernart of Brabant, both known for their courage. The fourth battalion had appointed Gibert and Bertram as leaders. And who was the leader of the fifth? The Schetis and the King of Tandarnas. Those two had decided that they wanted to lead the attack. I shall not say how many thousand men each battalion had. What could such a handful do anyway against the army from all the heathen lands?

The Margrave assigned a special battle-cry to each battalion. All his men were to cry 'Monjoie!' while fighting against the superior forces of the strong enemy. The troops of old Heimrich had 'Narbonne!' as their battle-cry, a fearful sound for the enemy. The third battalion cried 'Brabant!' Bernart's banner was carried in the hand of the mighty Count Landris, who had earned much renown in fighting. And what did the fourth battalion cry in fighting against the superior forces? Their cry was 'Berbester!' Some of them were performing knightly deeds for the sisters of the others, for noble Love inspires courage. The fifth battalion cried 'Tandarnas!', for the Schetis was still without a land of his own.

Now Rennewart came running up before they had started to ride in their formations towards Alischanz. He was carrying his club, which was all bloody. He asked right away where the Margrave was. The latter came riding on Volatin and stopped before him. Then

Rennewart said: 'My lord, let those whom people here consider cowards because they fled be my men. They want to fight bravely for me now. They have seen the error of their ways, and their great nobility has inspired them with such desire that they want to help me fight against King Tibalt of Kler. None of his weapons can help him now, neither sword nor bow. I was their sergeant-major long enough with this stick to get them to turn around and seek fame.'

The Margrave saw that what he said was true, for Rennewart's men were raising many clouds of dust on the broad field with their large units. He saw many naked swords shining and many decorated helmets gleaming through the dust. Many banners and beautifully painted spears did he see coming towards him, and with them many sharp lances. St Denis *de France* was not prepared to let his land be disgraced, and even today, wherever it is told, noble Frenchmen are loath to hear about the desertion. They prefer to hear about the return. (I did not like to hear about their flight either.)

The Margrave spoke to Rennewart, saying: 'If you are responsible for this return, then I am lucky to have you! If you are of such lineage that my hand can enhance your station (I mean, if you stand below me, not above), then, if Almighty God grants me life enough, I shall bring you to such renown that no prince's soldier was ever honoured more than you. Your nobility will be raised. But if you are of higher status than I, then I shall serve you, as will all my family. I have the right to make such a pronouncement to them.'

'My lord,' Rennewart said to the Marquis, 'if with my own hand I can gain renown in fighting with the Saracens, I shall gladly accept your reward. And one special reward that I shall not mention: the very thought of it is too much for me.[56] If you free me from my heartfelt pain that will redound to your honour.'

The French came riding up to him then with many detachments of men. The Margrave took the leaders aside and said: 'Since courage has now admonished you to recognize yourselves, your eternal salvation has sent you back here to the Almighty Hand that smashed the gates of hell and declared redemption for Adam and many of his children. Through that very Hand a huge rough nail was driven, but that wiped out the gains of hell. You were seen in a state of doubt before, but now one must rightfully ascribe courage and salvation to every Frenchman. Peter, the Gatekeeper of Heaven, who knew God's secret[57] and kept silent about it for many years and then later saw it revealed openly was struck by doubt three times so that he denied God.[58] Yet later he gained high renown. His courage was so great that he alone drew his sword to defend Jesus against the Jews.[59] Just so will the French soldiers return to help God and so increase their chances of salvation.

'Now fix your cross insignias on again. It is only right that the imperial banner should carry the sign of the Cross, copied from the Cross on which our salvation was won. When the imperial troops left us we treated their banner with disdain, stuffing it into a sack, but your return has blessed this day for us, for it restores the honour of the Cross.'

He returned the broad banner to them and continued: 'Since you have decided to fight, group all your forces into one battalion. That will be a powerful one. I am confident of your support. Rennewart shall fight under your banner. Encourage one another to boldness. Let your battle-cry be Rennewart's name.'

Then the pages did not hold back but cried aloud: 'Rennewart! You shall keep the deserters for your own!'

Prompted by a desire for fame, one of the knights in the Queen's pay had stolen away from the army of the Marquis. For that he was later said to be courageous. He spied a look-out waiting, who had ridden out from the heathen army. There was no avoiding a joust. No one else had seen him waiting there. But now such a joust took place that you had to give credit to both the Frenchman and the Saracen. The heathen made his charge so strongly at a gallop that it resounded with a great crash. The Frenchman was riding a very fast horse, and he spurred it on so hard that his spear passed first through the Saracen's shield, then through his arm, aimed with its thrust right up to his breast.

The Frenchman returned with the heathen's spear impaled on his shield, while the Saracen returned to Terramer. They found a spear through his shield at the point where the four nails are located. (This is the way look-outs *should* come back!) Quickly the news was spread through Terramer's camp that the Carolingians had come to Alischanz in full force. Tesereiz and Vivianz were to be avenged on either side, and now the time of decision is approaching when swords will decide who will carry off the victory.

The look-out spoke angrily when he saw Terramer sitting there: 'It looks as though you are ignoring the trouble which may befall your army. You are encamped here unprepared to fight and will have to pay for that this very day. What will your army do about the fact that the French are approaching? You could have thought of that before! Three nights ago the harassing by the French was able to hurt us wherever the quarters were cramped. Their battle-cry was "Tandarnas!" You lost men and material there. I was unhorsed in that very spot by the light of the moon, but in turn my joust hurt the knight who felled me from my horse, and I did the same to him in return. Whatever anyone suffers for your sake is of no more importance to you than a little gadfly attacking an aurochs. Willehalm, the bold fighter, is leading many renowned jousters from France. I am the Castellan of Kler. I have fought against the French army eleven times, and I'll do it again today. Tibalt is my lord, and he will be the first to ride against the knights this very day if you will allow him to. Now I beg leave to depart.'

Terramer spoke to the look-out, saying: 'I am sorry about your discomfort, brave man. Your fur cloak is soaked with blood, I see. You should justifiably be treated better than someone who missed the joust that you in your courage entered into. You have brought back the markings of a look-out. Now tell me, sir, without delay, how the French are situated. I would be sorry if they escaped us.'

'Now believe me,' said the Castellan, 'before the day is out Willehalm's army will risk many lives in knightly combat. It can well cost us a lot that Arabel, my lord's wife, was ever weaned from mother's breast. You will see them coming towards you soon with six splendidly decorated battalions, in which those who are eager for glory are riding. That will cause many a knight's lady to weep. I heard the battle-cry of each individual battalion. Where the imperial standard flies they are all crying "Rennewart!" I've never heard that before in their campaigns. The French intend to risk it. That star in the Margrave's banner shall shine to the detriment of your vassals and kinsmen and the foreigners from Vriende. Now you should alert Ehmereiz. He brought fourteen kings with their separate armies across the sea with him and lost seven of the kings here. If the men of the dead kings will now show their lament for their dead lords in bravery, the French will have a hard time of it. We have even more forces with the same anguish.'

Powerful Terramer spoke as was his right, saying: 'If you are that Castellan of Kler who has tempted fate so many times in combat with spear, whatever you wish of me in fiefs or gifts, depend on me for that as long as I live. In addition you will have the reward of ladies and loud acclaim in many lands where they will speak of your nobility, which is enormous. But tell me,' continued the King of Tenabri, 'if you were so close to the French that you could hear their individual battle-cries, whether Louis is amongst them, whose head wears the Roman crown. If so, then *all* my forces will be mobilized. You say that the imperial banner is approaching. Then it is only fitting that I mobilize everyone, whomever I can, against that threat. The day of retribution has dawned on which we shall lament Pinel's death with the suffering of the Christians. The two kings, Tesereiz and Noupatris, had great renown, as did my brother Arofel. If I do not avenge them, I shall ever be bereft of joy. I ask all of you, each and every one, soldiers of the princes and kings who lost their lives here defending our gods and fighting for their ladies and who met death on Alischanz, let each one of you be unceasing in avenging your lords and kinsmen. You have all heard of the approach of those guilty of their deaths.

'In my youth I used to get all decked out for the ladies. I leave that to you young men now. When my first whiskers appeared Love held me enthralled even more than any of my gods. For the sake of the gods and Love we shall strive for the reward of fame this very day so that Louis' Romans will die before we do. By rights I should be lord in Rome. You have heard me complain for a long time that my head should wear the Roman crown, for which my uncle Baligan lost many noble men. My claim to the Roman crown is this: noble Pompeius, from whose family I am descended – and I've never given up my claim – was driven from the Roman throne. Since that time many a king has remained illegally in possession of my inheritance. I believe many will yet die for it.'

Many powerful lords, kings from many lands, were summoned

before Terramer in the name of all the heathen gods and of Terramer himself. They spoke of the disgrace that holy Tervigant and Mahmete had suffered and their noble god Apolle as well. They spoke too of the toll that they would have to pay to Death. They said that their lives would be worthless if they did not take more adequate revenge for the loss. Many sat at this council of war, eskelirs and emerals, amazurs all together, and the highest kings in the whole army. Some had come across five seas with many detachments. (I should not be surprised if the seamen had charged them for it!) There, too, sitting apart from the others, were many princes who had lost their lords. This was why they had vowed to campaign against the Christians. They had wanted revenge for their own heartfelt pain and to bring honour to all their gods. They wanted to destroy Orange and Paris. After that they wanted to push further against the Christians for revenge. Terramer wanted to take possession of the imperial throne in Aachen and then move on Rome to preserve the honour of his gods, so that those who wanted to live with Jesus' help would be killed. He wanted to wear the Roman crown in splendour before his gods and before all heathendom.

When the look-out had thus had his say, the army was turned around. Terramer was courageous indeed. He said: 'I ask for all your help. Charles' son is riding here against me. Since the Christians have hoisted the imperial banner, they must be bringing their true leader, whose father did much harm to me. Listen all of you to my command. I want to have ten battalions, each of which will be better manned than three of the largest battalions that my uncle Baligan led into battle against Charles. No matter how many men I have lost, I still have so many soldiers that no one can count them. Whoever lost his lord or kinsmen or other close companion here, let him wreak vengeance, if he will, as his courage prompts him.

'Nephew Halzebier, your banner shall be the first one today to advance against the enemy's knights. I can trust you in your bravery. Take under your command the princes of Pinel of Ahsim, whom Kator had sent to me splendidly equipped from his land. He had no other child. I shall always mourn Pinel. The father is slain along with the son, so terribly will he lament, I mean. I assign also to your banner the men from Oraste Gentesin whom dear Noupatris led. They earned much renown with their lances of bamboo. They will be eager to joust today too. A woman held the heart of their lord, and for her sake he lost his life here. The same thing happened to the princes from the land of Kanach with Galafre. I shall put under your command all five armies of those love-seeking kings, Eskelabon from Seres and *le roi* Talimon from Boctan. Their lords always fought for Love until Death rode them down.'

Halzebier was very happy. He considered it a great honour that he should rush out and be the first to engage the enemy. Apart from his own army he had the armies of five lands to help him.

Terramer spoke to Tibalt, saying: 'Remember, Sir, that you were always reckoned among those of unflagging courage. May you feel today the pain of my daughter's having deserted you, prompted by her evil star. A fortunate woman who had a proper woman's attitude would always want to love your generosity and goodness, your knightly attitude of mind and your handsome physique, and your wealth and your lofty lineage as well. True love should have remained with you. Now you shall act boldly, you and Ehmereiz, your son. You have a huge flood of soldiers here. And Ehmereiz, your high courage, whether you get it from your father or from me, will gain renown for you. Be brave like your father. Then you will be preserved from disgrace in all lands.'

The brave and courteous Arabois, Tibalt, said: 'My lord, you are speaking as befits your breeding. But worthiness has shown its heels to me long ago. If I had renown, it was lost. You gave me what I asked of you, but she checkmated all my joy and vanquished all the high renown in which I had previously been viewed. My shame has been known far and wide for a long time. Since then I have been able to send some anguish to your daughter, who has shamed me so. I know my son Ehmereiz leads such an immense army that if we ride together and join our forces, we shall give battle to all the Christians who come for either cause, for the Empire or for the Marquis.'

The lord of Todjerne was elaborately decorated. They both liked to fight, Tibalt and Ehmereiz, and their charge was powerful.

The heathen battalions are now two. The French came riding up at an easy pace, and Halzebier moved to oppose them, ready for the fray. Then sorrow was heaped upon sorrow.

The leader of the third battalion was Sinagun, the King of Bailie, who was always free of duplicity. Let me tell you, if I can, whom Terramer assigned to him and what their separate battle-cries were. The soldiers of King Tampaste and those whom King Faussabre had brought from Alamansura were there too, beautifully decorated and skilled in the practice of chivalry. And those whom King Turpiun had brought from Falturmie hurt the Christians with their fighting. Those whom King Arfiklant and his brother Turkant had brought also rode with Sinagun, and they fought well there. The army of King Poufameiz of Ingulie, that splendid knight, also rode in Sinagun's attacking force. No ears had ever heard of a disloyal act on his part. He had the favour of women until his death in knightly combat, for he had offered himself in service to Love. All these armies had been deprived of their lords. Because of them the Christians had already lost many knights, and God had received their souls into heaven before the new attack began.

Terramer of Suntin spoke, saying: 'You ten sons of mine shall command the fourth battalion. Think of the unshaken courage that I had at your age when I was accorded great renown. You are the kings of ten rich and powerful lands. Each one of you has as vassals many kings who do not disdain to receive their crowns from your hands. Fight against the noble Christians and extend the territory of our gods with victory. You shall also have in your command the splendid army of your uncle, those from Samargone and the princes all the way from Persia. Arofel had often instructed them closely there in matters of chivalry so that their renown increased. Just remember today that he in whose camp you were staying always treated each of you as his own son until he lost his life for your sake. Alas, who shall now cherish courtly love since such high renown lies slain? What amazing feats did the Persan perform! If women have a sense of loyalty at all, they will be heard mourning for him: we are, after all, all born of women.

'Fill your young years with high spirits. You have noble lineage and such wealth as easily to be masters of an entire race of people. The sweetness and lovely appearance of women shall show you the way today to increase your fame against the enemy, those who themselves come with renown against you. Why was the Marquis called "Willehalm the Fighter"? Again and again your sister's love has turned sour for him in the pursuit of glory against men of inborn courage. All ten of you shall this very day venture into the ford of battle ahead of me. If women will deign to do so, some of them will give you their reward for it. Old Heimrich of Narbonne is setting his sons against me. I have ten sons whom I shall send to receive him.

'Now Poidjus, mighty King of Vriende and Griffane, act valorously today. The fifth battalion shall be yours. The army of Tesereiz, my nephew, the bold Seziljoises, shall harass the French today under your banner, whereby swords will resound against helmets. Take Tesereiz' princes under your command. Believe me and all of them too, the Grikuloises and the Latresetans, when they say that their lord's heart was weeded over so well that no duplicity was ever found in it. He ruled as king over five lands. Because you were a stranger coming to us from Vriende and on account of kinship and his loyalty, not because of your power and wealth, he was subordinate to you, serving you just as if he were your vassal. Him you shall avenge today. Good women will always express their lament at his death. From the first day until Judgement Day dawns, Tesereiz must be honoured before all the race of Adam if anyone chooses to judge honour properly.

'Now Poidjus and Ehmereiz, sons of my children, you who are here with many troops: wherever you two are engaged in battle and also my ten sons, my heart will suffer the self-same anguish, the blows will be landing on my own body. This is the straight truth and not slanted: Halzebier and Sinagun, each one is as dear as a son to me.

'But even more of my kinsmen are here. Aropatin of Ganfassache, your realm is a vast one. You shall lead the sixth battalion into battle today. You will want to have with you the kings and princes, your vassals, who pledged support for your campaign. It will benefit your crown if you suffer anguish in battle yet today, fighting for the reward of the gods and for your own renown if Love will guide you and if you earn the reward of women justly where blows are received and given. If your heart is set on battle you have so many good knights who will inflict damage on the French. The clash of your rushing onslaught shall press them hard indeed. I know that King

Matribleiz is in your camp with powerful forces. He has many men there brought from Skandinavia. He didn't leave a single knight behind in Gruonlant and in Gaheviez. Proud Glorion, King of Ascalon, is here on your account. "Mix manly courage with your youth; old age has virtue then in truth!"'

Then Terramer said: 'Brave Josweiz, just think now, if you ever at any time received a sweet promise from the lips of a good lady for having performed knightly deeds: let Love give you advice. You shall preserve the honour of the gods today, O son of brave Matusales! Matusales sent you to me. My kinsmen and I are relying on you, for you are the son of my children's uncle. All those who live from Hippipotiticun to Agremuntin are vassals to your crown. You shall fight today for the reward of the gods and lead the seventh battalion. Korsant of Janfuse received his crown from your hand as did Rubual of Nouriente. That King has all the characteristics that I know are found in a noble heart. Pohereiz, King of Etnise, always eager for glory, has also come here on your account as has the King of Valpinose, steadfast Talimon, for wherever he opposed enemies he still had a noble disposition. These four kings are here because of you. Now your revenge must fall upon the daughter of your aunt. She was my daughter once before she succumbed to Jesus. That was the root of her misfortune. For her sake Frenchmen and Germans are attacking me here on this plain with their knights so that I cannot profit from my immense power and the gods.

'Poidwiz of Rabes, you shall have command of the eighth battalion. I shall assign to your banner the men of Tenabruns, the noble King of Liwes Nugruns. Their lord has never left the path of honour. The army of Libilun of Rankulat shall also follow your flag, and they shall hack notches in many a hard helmet before the day is out so that the sand will be covered with blood. The army of King Rubiun shall also fight under your command. The blacks from Azagouc are a stone wall against attacks. You also have many turkopels and are very powerful. Except for me, no king has an army here that has so many kinds of arms.

'My daughter Arabel is causing me heartfelt pain,' said Terramer then. 'I must lament that to my good friends. You, King Marlanz of Jerikop, shall lead my ninth battalion. You have never brought a shield or spear back from battle in one piece wherever you opposed enemies. Now for the sake of your nobility help me avenge my suffering today. I shall put under your banner the son of King Anki, and King Margot of Pozzidant shall also be under your flag, as shall King Gorhant of Ganjas. His skin is horny all over and pure green like grass. His men are bold and swift. You should not spare the enemy at all. May the gods protect you.'

Now the Christians had arrived, and many a loud clash of spears was heard on Alischanz as a result. Pieces of broken lances covered the field. The jousters on both sides began to fight in a massed attack, the French and the Saracens. May Jesus protect His own! Tervigant will have to take care of the others from all the heathen lands. Terramer had that very god and his other illustrious gods as well put up on many high masts. However, that was such a heavy burden that carts wheeled them along, and armoured water buffaloes pulled each one separately. Strong men (they weren't boys!) drove the buffaloes with goads. Terramer observed how his gods were decorated with gold and jewels clear and pure. (He himself was completely duped to believe in them and to rob his old age of wisdom just as if he were still a foolish youth.)

But now finally his tenth battalion was arrayed for battle. He spoke, saying: 'I have nine kingdoms under my sway, not counting those of my sons. All the princes who have come from those kingdoms shall be under my banner and the men of all the dead kings as well whose lords have lost their lives here, except those whom I have previously ordered to battalions and sent ahead. The others shall await my orders,' said Terramer of Suntin.

'Ektor of Salenie: no lady friend, I think, sent you here,' said Terramer, 'yet I believe no one shall see you turn while you are still alive. One must acknowledge your manly courage. My father, Kanabeus, who raised you, never fled. You are wearing your crown as standard-bearer in fief from me. Let me remind you of that now. Take my standard into your hand. May the gods protect those who ride with you under it and fight for me today. Whichever kings hold fiefs for taking care of my armour, let them bring it all ready to me now. I want to fight!'

Then Terramer sat down before his tent on the plain on a couch covered with a costly gold cloth embroidered with silken thread just as he had desired it. Putegan of Ormalereiz of noble family came up. He wore his crown in fief for sounding his horn whenever the father of sweet Giburc wished to ride armed into battle. He ordered his horse, Brahane, to be saddled.

Terramer, the shrewd man, said: 'Charles' son Louis thinks he has sneaked up on me, as his marquis did when he came riding out on to Alischanz. He didn't wait long enough for me to see to arranging my army for battle. As a result I suffered heartfelt losses. My gods in all their sanctity and good women too should take pity on me because I lost so many worthy men from my family upon this very field. My own brother met his death in combat here, I am told, at the hand of him whom my daughter loves, who has not stopped to think what she has lost for his sake, having renounced our gods and given up her extensive lands, her rich and powerful life in exchange for poverty here.

'She deserted Tibalt, too, that dear, upright, generous and rich, handsome, brave man who never allowed even a bit of disloyalty to enter his heart. How does sunlight pass through a gem without making a slit? Just as little did anything that could be called an ignoble thought lead Tibalt, that courageous man, astray. His heart was ever blind to falsity. That is why I chose him as a son. I gave that man whose courage was so firm the reflection of the sun, Arabel, the very beautiful, when they were both young. I shall destroy her now, and yet her loveliness blossomed forth from my heart's blood. It grieves me most sorely, but I have read about David's having to fight against his child. David gained an ignominious victory when Absalom lost his life: he would gladly have died in his place.[60] Now that same suffering is imminent for me. If Louis is defeated yet today I fear the revenge he might take, and I always have feared that sweet Arabel might squirm beneath his sword. Indeed, they cannot bring about my death any sooner anywhere. If the Christians hate me, then it is better for those worthy men to preserve their renown and to turn their hatred towards me as much as they can and not to stop doing it.'

Thus the loyal heathen sat there on his couch lamenting bitterly. King Grohier of Nomadjentesin brought him his mail leg-coverings and his protective pad. The leg-coverings of chain-mail gleamed brightly. A sturdy under-jacket and a sleeveless coat of mail – King Arthur at Plimizoel[61] found nothing better among his knights – were brought to him by King Oukidant, who was from Imanzie. The King of Barberie brought him a hauberk. It had been made in Jazeranz by a master craftsman. A costly helmet made in Assigarzjunde was brought by a doughty king, Samirant of Boitendroit. It had been made by Schoit, the son of skilful Trebuchet.[62] The King of Hippipotiticun brought him a shield. Such servants would have been too much for a poor man. A lance, sharp but not heavy, made in Siglimessa (its blade was a griffon's claw), was brought by King Bohedan of Schipelpunte, a noble man. Akerin, the King of Marroch, brought him a quiver made out of a ruby, and a sturdy bow. Terramer did not put aside what each one brought, he put it all on and armed himself. Ladies had sent him few gifts. He did not wear a helmet decoration, he left that to the young knights. Then Klabur, a high-born king from Tibalt's family, fastened on the spurs.

When Terramer was fully armed he stood up in all his noble power and wealth. Then the brave son of bold Kanabeus spoke, saying: 'How are we to do knightly combat with all those Christian sarcophagi in the way? My powerful mounted charges cannot press forward effectively against Louis, the Roman King, nor can they drive him back. The Christians think it is to their credit that Jesus, the sorcerer, has strewn their battlefield with many sarcophagi. Their flesh and bones lie in there still undecayed. He who wore the thorny wreath, that savage hat, on the Cross has worked such wonders for them.'

'All of you who have brought my armour,' said Terramer, 'you here and there, to whom I have given immense lands as fiefs for your services and crowned your heads, shall serve for your fiefs today by fighting against the Christians. You eight lead large armies here, and your men are well armed with swords, bows, lances, battle-axes. Ride at my right hand along with the carriages of the gods. There you will find Apolle and Tervigant, Mahmete and Kahun. Kanliun, the King of Lanzesardin, shall protect them with you. That is my oldest son, by my first wife. I have chosen him to protect the gods because of his bravery and have included him in my own battalion. He will watch out for them and me.

'You nine kings shall ride at my right hand. In the same fashion at my left hand in the battalion shall ride the King of Nubiant with his fourteen sons. Purrel will display his manly courage today, as will the proud men of Kordes and the fighters of Poitwin and strong Kliboris, the King of Tananarke. *Le roi* Samirant of Beaterre and *le roi* Oukidant of Norun shall form up to the left of me, as shall King Krohier of Oupatrie: you shall hear many kinds of battle-cries in his army. King Samuel shall fight at my left hand and King Morende, too. He has come to me from afar, from beyond Katus Erkules, believe me. It has been over six years since I issued the call for a gathering. If anyone were willing to follow my call at that time he could surely have heard it. King Fabur shall fight alongside Morende. He has brought many an amazur across the river Fison.[63] I have also thought that Haropin, the old knight from Tananarke, should fight at the side of his son, courtly Kliboris, whom I raised. Neither one of them ever fled. Wherever one heard savage onslaughts they seemed so tame to them that they stood firm against them in all the din. All these noble kings shall form up on my shield side and protect me and their reputation.'

Mighty Terramer spoke to one king, saying to him that he wore his crown to have a thousand clashing tambours sounded and tossed. Zernubile of Amirafel ordered his men to do that. He ordered eight hundred trumpets to sound the signal to gallop. People are still aware that trumpets were invented in his land. They had been brought from Tusi.

Then Brahane was brought up to Terramer. The horse was completely covered to its hooves with a caparison: a silk covering gleaming like fire and worked expensively in Suntin lay on the armour. The King of Tenabri mounted. On either side of him rode many good, brave knights. Women caused each one to yearn for them. The water buffaloes that pulled the carts with the gods were started. (Theirs was a paltry faith, those deceived by the gods which were affixed to the carts!)[64]

Now let Terramer ride! Hear how the first knights were fighting. Terramer's help will come too soon for the Christians after all. Now hear who is doing such deeds that he will be praised for them. If my source so directs me I shall tell you the names of many who bore with them such a brave heart there that they gained renown when the reports of their deeds were brought to us in Christian lands. Ladies on both sides had sent such dauntless knights to fight there that the Christian army and the flood of the Saracens suffered great punishment, acquitting themselves in such a way when Death sowed its seed amongst them that people can still speak of their deeds with great respect. That was a day with a noble end for them. Many came out to joust in individual combat, but one saw also many knights who, after attacking a group single-handedly, wheeled and turned to await the charge that the whole group levelled at him. Many a man shattered his spear by aiming his charge so that he thrust himself into the heathen knights like a sword into its sheath.

BOOK VIII

The men on both sides were skilled in such matters. That was how the battle went. Jousters from five battalions came riding up with the Schetis, the King of Tandarnas and all those whom these two commanded, to oppose the King of Falfunde. Halzebier was grieving for the death of Pinel of Ahsim, whose brave army was riding at his side, decked out in costly splendour: they received the charge of the Christians and made them pay for it. Riding with Halzebier had come more men who were wishing to joust but who had refused to fight with Giburc at Orange. It seemed to them that they could gain honour by taking their revenge now that the Margrave was arriving.

King Noupatris of Oraste Gentesin was manfully avenged with lances made of bamboo. Even if the tips of the lances broke off, the remaining splinter still struck shield and armour, the sharpness of the bamboo piercing them both. Anyone who wished to have the advantage in such jousts certainly needed his spurs to move his charge from gallop to full career.

The army of the King of Kanach could be seen alongside Halzebier, so that their fighting caused trouble for the Christians. Noble princes – vassals of King Galafre they were – were thinking of their master, who had been slain by Vivianz in the course of combat: their revenge brought death as its reward. King Eskelabon of Seres, whom young Vivianz had also slain on the field of Alischanz, was mourned with many jousts and with swords too, so I am told. The men of Boctan were fighting well on that plain beneath the banner of Halzebier. No one needed to urge them to take revenge for their lord, King Talimon. They did not spare anyone. Thus the army of Heimrich the Schetis was soon at the receiving end of great trouble from the strangers from across the sea: many of his soldiers and the company from Tandarnas were hurled on to the grass. Halzebier himself was fighting there, and all the Christians who rode out against him received their deaths from him and for this they gained God's reward.

Now King Tibalt of Kler and his son from Todjerne came along with a magnificent army. They were heading for the place where the star was shining forth from the Margrave's banner. Ehmereiz urged all the kings and princes who were riding in the battalion to think of their reputations. They turned towards the Marquis.

The proud Frenchmen who were grouped under the imperial flag intercepted the Araboises. The strong young Rennewart could see many costly silken coverings upon the heathen chargers. Tibalt and his men, and the Saracens of Ehmereiz, were all decked out, thanks to the ladies. Compared with the cape of Ehmereiz, the radiance of the dewy heath in maytime would have paled in splendour. So brilliant was it that the flowers were put in the shade. This type of silk was called 'pofuz'.[65] An ostrich could easily have hatched out all its eggs upon it, assuming that they had been well protected in other respects.[66]

Giboez, Castellan of Kler,[67] was in charge of the banner in Tibalt's army. When he heard and saw how they were slashing there, with blows and thrusts, he was distressed that his master's battalion was not the very first to fight, for he was full of daring when it came to combat. Trohazzabe of Karkassun was bearing the banner of Ehmereiz. His heart never felt a twinge of cowardice: no one could say such a thing of him. On any day when he did not catch sight of an enemy he was restless among his friends.

When the pennants were dipped as the lances were levelled and the heroes fighting beneath them on both sides demonstrated who dared to defend his life and honour there and hazard his very being, and who was able to do this too, just hear what Rennewart did. He pitched in boldly to the attack and slew both men and horses, for he did not think out properly who it was he was supposed to be attacking. Since there were such costly silks covering the heathen steeds, he thought he ought to be fighting with the horses as much as with the people.

I'm not able to describe very well how the fighting went there, for many a charge rapidly became entangled with another. If I had ever heard that anything was whiter than snow, then I should have to compare with that everything which Tibalt was wearing, all of salamander.[68] The covering of his shield was made of salamander, and all that could be seen on top of his armour, his cloak and the caparison of his horse. His suit of armour, costly as it was, was not the gift of ladies. He had ridden out in person to joust upon the plain. The Count of Champagne, the high-spirited Champagnois, the rich and powerful prince Gandaluz, approached the generous Arabois, and I am told that such a chivalrous joust was performed by these two men that both of them deserved acclaim for it.

Meanwhile Ehmereiz was engaging in combat. Tibalt's main force had not yet arrived in its entirety, those men, amazurs and eskelirs, to whom the individual bands had been assigned. Between Wissant and Steiermark[69] there are not so many knights as Tibalt had mustered and who had ridden out just from his one camp, in the hope that Queen Giburc might be their lady still. To this end they would now seek hostages, or die by the side of their lord.

Giboez the Castellan ventured to attack with levelled lance in search of ransom. Boldly he led those who were fighting to regain Giburc so that they came at a charge. They believed that King Louis had come on behalf of the Marquis. Then the imperial troops were ridden through ceaselessly and surrounded by the Saracens, but again and again the French army regrouped and felled many heathen knights.

Duke Trohazzabe, bearing the standard of Ehmereiz, had previously attacked the Frenchmen, and the bridle of Ehmereiz had been seized and his horse led away. However, the expensive silk shimmered so brightly in the sunlight that the whole flood of Saracens could not fail to see their King's predicament and his men rescued him.

Many dauntless Christians were striving for the kind of ransom which could be exchanged for Berhtram, while Ehmereiz was fighting to gain ransom for the woman who had borne him. Then Sinagun, the attacker and the standard, arrived with his battalion. Of him no eye saw nor ear heard tell that his heart ever faltered or that he ever harboured the kind of thought which cut him off from fame. In this he remained firm. His hand, his sword and his lance had time and time again rolled three winners for him and many other honours. One winner was Generosity, the other Courage whenever he was fighting, the third was Manly Goodness. That was the nature of the man. My source tells me that his horse was called Passilivrier. It was swift and like a dragon to look at, as if its markings were all lined with sparks of fire. It leapt along unhesitatingly beneath him at the head of his battalion. If any lady had sent him there with promise of reward, her messenger was not disgraced.

King Sinagun of Bailie was daring indeed in the performance of that which is still today called fierce fighting: for this his courage was well known. He made his way towards the thick of the battle, where, along with Arnalt of Gironde, the Margrave was fighting with all his might for his honour and his life, for the love of Giburc and in order to retain possession of his land. These two men were leading one battalion.

Sinagun was struggling to reach that spot where the star was shining forth with such radiance from the banner of the Margrave. (Let none of you get the idea that it was the star which – so the story goes – guided the Three Kings. This star here was providing much jousting for the Saracens!) Sinagun, who had endured a great deal of suffering for the sake of the favour of the ladies, was the first one to engage in a joust, mounted as he was on Passilivrier. (That horse was swifter than a deer!) A count from the land of Arnalt – Gifleiz was his name – came forward to meet this joust from the King, as was quite appropriate for both of them.

When Sinagun came galloping towards the Marquis with his battalion, the leaders of both detachments performed such deeds of chivalry that God and the ladies too should give thanks for it. Many knights, high-spirited yet not without sorrow, were riding with Sinagun, and these had experienced a day of real grief when they had lost their master and their kinsmen. For this they were lamenting, too, and because of it they endured still more losses on both sides, as well as fresh heartache at the hands of those who dared inflict it.

You could hear the sound of wood from many forests cracking there. (They could have done with men who knew how to make lances, but they're better off where they are, fixing the shafts to the tips, for if they had been in the thick of the attack, there would have been fewer lances of their making!)

Many fearless knights from six kingdoms preserved their honour there. Sinagun's company was strengthened by many princes who had suffered the loss of their liege-lords and were about to die themselves.

The army from Naroklin took very fierce revenge for their lord King Tampaste, and the army from Falturmie, led there by Turpiun, fought well in Sinagun's battalion. The princes from Alamansura certainly took their revenge for Faussabre, Terramer's sister's son. Then another army dared indeed to avenge the generous Turkant and the gentle Arfiklant, who had come from Turkanie. Let me tell you the name of the sixth king whose men were also riding with Sinagun and who had fought boldly against the Christians: that was Poufameiz of Ingulie, of whom this story of mine relates that, young as he was, he always strove after high renown as long as he lived.

The Christians suffered misery and gained the twofold reward. Noble ladies bestowed reward on those who came back alive, but those who died there went into those Hands which are able to grant payment above all other payment. Those same Hands are a protection and a shield against the cunning of the Devil.

I cannot tell you properly what all the individual heathen battalions were shouting, what they were yelling as they fought, but the cry of 'Monjoie!' was not silent either. Now the ten brothers of Giburc all came riding in bold and manly fashion. High-born kings with large fiefs were riding together, along with Terramer's many sons, and eskelirs of princely status, and countless emerals.

Now the forest really thundered with the crashing of lances and spears, and then there came at a gallop many detachments of the ten young kings untouched by any cowardice: Proud Spirit rode along with them.

Bernart of Brabant, who had always been known for his courage, and Buov of Commercey were riding beneath one banner, Fabors of Mecka came forward for a joust and Glorjax, Malarz and Utreiz all came in advance of their main force. It would be impossible for anyone to describe to you in a few words the helmet decorations of the four brilliantly dressed kings, but it was plain to see that they were costly ones.

Sturdy Count Landris brandished his banner aloft in his pursuit of fame, and Duke Bernart rode at full tilt in a mighty onslaught on

Terramer's sons, for he was looking out for hostages to exchange for his son Berhtram. He jousted with Fabors and seized his bridle. The horse which Bernart led away was bearing a costly load, and it seemed to him that he had in his hands a goodly ransom for his son and his other kinsmen. What can the Saracens do now but go to the rescue of Fabors? All the decorations on his helmet and on his cape, whether he had purchased them himself or been given them by ladies, had been battered to pieces in the fray.

Charge! How many transactions did the Christians make, taking in and paying out without carts![70] The scales of some of them tipped so quickly that they were plunged into death. They suffered losses on both sides, Saracens and Christians alike. Noble Buov did not attempt to spare the tall turbans of the heathens.

The sons of Terramer were opposed by those who were out to release Kibelin, Berhtram and Gaudin and their other kinsmen who were lying in captivity. They tried desperately to do this, and you should give Terramer his due for providing his sons in advance with arms which no one could take from them with a sword. These men were also seeking revenge for the suffering which had been inflicted on them. Their kinsman Arofel the Persan had been slain at Alischanz and his men were mourning him there with the edges of their swords and with their shouts. Their cry of 'Samargone!' accompanied many an onslaught. Arofel was recalled by his men in acts of courage in that battle, he who had himself many times led them nobly to confront the enemy. Many princes from the kingdom of Arofel were there in full force, but Terramer's sons still missed Arofel himself, for he had been a second father to them. Never did the sun shine on any more faithful king, alive or dead.

Many helmets were battered to pieces by those who were fighting bravely alongside the sons of Terramer. On both sides there was seeking and finding in plenty: one group attacked with lances, another with swords. The turkopels also acted with one accord and, shooting, pulled many a smooth arrow-shaft all the way to the tip. Then the bows began to chatter like storks in a nest.

When the battle was raging furiously on the plain, Poidjus of Griffane approached with a great flood of knights. (May God protect the Christians now!) He was King of Vriende too, and Tasme, Triant and Kaukasas were all subject to him. And so the son of Terramer's daughter arrived with a powerful battalion. His standard was borne by Tedalun, the Burgrave of Tasme, who was also chief forester in charge of the forest of Lignaloe.[71] He held the 'cutting rights' in Kaukasas and the right to exact a 'tithe' in many a desolate harbour. Whatever gold was scratched up by the feet of griffons there could well make up to him for any poverty.[72]

The whole of the battlefield was splendidly illuminated by the battalion of Poidjus with its many costly silks. Neither the sun nor fire could have emitted a brighter radiance. You could tell by looking at his men that he had great wealth at his disposal at home, for expense weighed lightly with him, this Poidjus, and he himself was so richly equipped that I dare not speak of the cost. (It is enough to frighten the daylights out of a poor man like me!) If he were to deign to do so, a rich man should tell you about this and describe exactly how the covering of the armour of King Poidjus was adorned and lavishly embroidered. All other costliness was as nothing in comparison.

No one will believe me if I say how he was dressed from head to toe. If such trappings had been sent to him by a virtuous woman without his having earned this token of her love, it was a sin on his part if he did not for her sake perform such deeds as to this very day are regarded as demonstrations of high valour.

The helmet of the fearless King Poidjus was fashioned with great skill out of the precious stone 'antraxe'.[73] Enormous expense was of little account to those proud and carefree people of his. (Just think: if a duck were to drink up all the water that it could find in Lake Constance, this would do it harm. I feel the same way about the army of Poidjus, which had come there across five seas.) If they had expended all their wealth on their armour, their steeds would not have been able to carry them. I hear it said that in Vriende all the rivers which are known there and which flow from Kaukasas are lined with precious stones of many different kinds. Some of them made night into day with the radiance which they gave forth.

The King of Griffane had many sources of wealth and mountains of gold were at his disposal. If I were so inclined I could easily get hold of a head-dress of laurel leaves from the Spessart when May, according to its nature, was endowed with dew and sweet breezes.[74] Who would accuse me of boasting about *that*? It was no more for Poidjus to sport great wealth.

If the men from Vriende now waste a whole forest of lances jousting on the plain, and the men from Griffane too, this will add honour to their power and riches. A large army, free of any cowardice, that had been assigned to their battalion showed them how. It was those men who had left Giburc in peace at Orange who were now getting ready to fight, in the belief that it would be honourable to fight now that the Marquis had arrived.

This was the army of Tesereiz who had always been on guard against dishonour and whom Love had deprived of his life. To this very day good women should be glad to recall his nobility without faltering, since his heart never flinched from serving them so devotedly that his high renown equalled and far surpassed that of his comrades. During his lifetime it was said in praise of the proud Latrisetan that he would never have a peer who could come so close to him that it might in any way damage his reputation. Nor did he ever lose the favour of ladies by committing any dishonourable act.

For the sake of wealth and in pursuit of other kinds of fame as well, the mighty Poidjus had led many princes out of many vast duchies and from many marches, and their troops were very active when they entered the battle. Now Bertram and Gibert, who have not yet engaged in fighting, will pay them back for that.

Charge! What a fight they had now! How the lances did spurt into the air on both sides, whether for the sake of the reward of women or out of sheer bravado! That is what the jousters did. I want to tell you truthfully that neither in the past nor nowadays have I ever seen so many men in splendid trappings perform such a fine display of chivalry anywhere. (Why should I lack the courage to do this? If *those* men dared to fight there, then *I* can dare to tell of it!) The enormously rich Tedalun, the chief-forester of Lignaloe, was bearing the beast 'ezidemon' which Feirefiz had used as his emblem.[75] This was lavishly embroidered on the standard of Poidjus, and that standard came charging along in the hand of bold Tedalun, who was seeking ransom for Giburc, his lord's aunt.

On both sides many knights were hurled on to the grass. The

battalions were joined together in mutual hostility, and the men found whatever they were looking for, one a blow with the sword, the other a thrust of the lance. Revenge was taken by the Christians for Vivianz, who did not die in such a way that his fame died with him. Anyone who wishes to attain salvation should honour you, Vivianz: you are bright and lustrous, and in the company of God. How your death grieves me, even though I know your soul will never burn in the fires of hell. That tribulation is hardly for you, son of the sister of Bertram of Berbester and of the manly Gibert.

Many swords were sounding in their two retinues, on account of their kinship with you. If they know how to value loyalty, liege-lords and lady-loves should grant reward for such fighting as took place on both sides, or so this tale tells us. Many lances lay broken there. There, too, at that same time, the handsome, sweet Mile, whom the high and mighty Terramer had slain in joust at Alischanz, was amply avenged, to the anguish of the heathens. Mile was the son of the sister of Vivianz' mother.

They went for their opponents as if they were supposed to be chopping down tree-trunks: they would not have hacked away with greater force if they had been doing so.

It is said of the Christians that they splattered the costly, brilliant silks of the strangers from Vriende with the blades of their swords, so that the blood flowed over their radiant beauty and almost all the silks were coloured red.

Now Aropatin of Ganfassasche came with his battalion, like a hailstorm over the Christians. All who might be there, young and old alike, for the sake of God and for the reward of ladies and for the son of the lord of Narbonne – all the Margrave's troops in fact – Aropatin could easily have taken on in battle, such was the size of his force. (Now I hope he will succeed as Welf did with all his power when he marched on Tübingen: *he* withdrew without a victory.[76] That is what I wish for Aropatin, and that is how I think it will turn out, too.)

There was a chessman in his banner, the rook: this signified the broad reach of his power and the fact that people on land and water rendered substantial tribute to him. The lands between the Geon[77] and the Poinzaklins were all subject to this young King, and in

addition he ruled in Ganfassasche by right of birth over many
splendid princes: this was how he came to have many knights at his
command. How many trumpets sounded out to herald his arrival!
And how skilfully the men ahead of him rolled many drums with
bells attached! Fluters could be heard there too. The battalion of King
Aropatin was sumptuously decorated, of course, with many special
trimmings. He himself was guided by his manly heart and the
thought that he was struggling for the favour of ladies: moreover, he
behaved as was fitting to their reward. Up to now old Heimrich had
not entered into battle at all with his powerful forces, but there with
Aropatin were the King of Skandinavia and the King of Ascalon, and
now they advanced on Heimrich of Narbonne, the father of the bold
Margrave, who was urging his men into battle as he had often
spurred them on before. Thus armour was pierced by jousts from
many lances. Many shields once whole were shattered and many
helmets struck in such a way that swords resounded through them.
This was how the men from Narbonne received the young Aropatin
and the proud King Glorion and the steadfast Matribleiz with many
mighty onslaughts. The cart of Mahmete may well be too far away
from the men from Ganfassasche: let's see if that causes them any
trouble!

Then old Heimrich struck up a tune with swords for the jig which
had often swirled around him. This was the inheritance which the old
man had bequeathed to his sons. Since he had chosen as his son
someone who was not his real child his own sons received and dealt
out suffering in foreign lands. The men from Ganfassasche are
now in trouble in the face of the superior strength of Heimrich's
company.

Let's see whether mighty Aropatin can find combat there! Just he
on his own had an amazing number of units there with him, and his
buoyant heart urged him always into the thick of the fight himself.
White flowers and green grass turned red in his tracks. The armies
from Skandinavia and Ascalon fought well. The sound of many
clashes could be heard when the main attack took place.

Whoever held a shield to his neck and carried it properly as he
charged through the dust was doing justice to his knightly calling.
On the plain of Alischanz there occurred such a battle with swords

that, no matter what was ever told of Etzel or of Ermenrich, their fighting could not be compared with this. I have often heard it said of Witege that on one single day he smashed eighteen thousand helmets as if they were mushrooms.[78] If anyone were to have that many lambs tied up and brought before him and if he were to slaughter them all on one day he would have to go at it pretty fast, even if they were already shorn!

People should describe fighting properly, and then tales will be told straight, for battle and love both demand understanding. The one comprises comfort *and* suffering, the other nothing *but* discomfort. If a man strives properly for the reward of women he must from time to time endure great pain: if then the sweetness of love makes compensation for such pain, the reward of love will be received wherever this occurs.

Old Count Heimrich was so daring that he urged his young knights towards the pursuit of love. A noble man who followed his advice never lost the favour of ladies. His men performed in such a way that if an emperor had been paying mercenaries he would not have found men like these to venture into such severe peril as to suffer death for his sake. There was no thought of peace there. His men hurled themselves about in response to the many battle-cries. A tournament at Kitzingen[79] would have been of little account there, where they were having to use their bloody swords in a different fashion. There was no comradeship at all between the heroes on opposing sides.

Now the son of Matusales, Josweiz, who craved for love, came riding up and launched his powerful attack with many units. They trampled indiscriminately over heathland and sarcophagi. The mighty Matusales had sent his son out from Hippipotiticun with powerful forces. A prince was bearing his standard, upon which could be seen a swan, embroidered expensively and with great artistry. The swan was all white, with the exception of its beak and feet which were black as a raven. This was because Matusales had completely white hair and skin and because a Moorish woman from Jetakranc was the mother of his son Josweiz. The swan has two colours and so had Josweiz too. For this reason the campaign of Josweiz was conducted beneath the swan and with him came many rulers marked with this same coat of arms. Twelve princes bore shields which he had given in his generosity and because he was wealthy and noble. He came riding into battle accompanied by four other kings.

The shield, the helmet and the cloak of Josweiz of Amatiste were fashioned with artistry and great expense. My tale reports that noble love had prompted him into battle. I only wish I had the ability to do justice in my description to his handsome appearance, his youth, his magnanimity and his other fine qualities, since in truth he was of an age to be courageous. The men in his battalion were beyond control, so fiercely did they fight, but there is not one of them alive today for whom I would have to say that just as a favour.

The King of Valpinose broke away from the battalion with his men. King Korsant of Janfuse could be seen riding after him, with King Rubual of Nouriente immediately after him, and close behind him proud King Pohereiz with a powerful attacking force. The latter was from Etnise and was striving for renown there. Following them came the forces of Josweiz, all his men with their swords unsheathed. Since they had missed out on the initial jousting, none of them proposed to use his lance.[80]

Josweiz was very much annoyed that he had obeyed Terramer and that therefore six whole battalions had engaged in battle ahead of him. Angrily he rode alongside his standard: above him could be seen the precious swan gleaming white as snow. He turned towards where, at the head of Ehmereiz' battalion, Trohazzabe was having trouble. There the proud Frenchmen had been inflicting enormous damage on Tibalt the Arabois and on Ehmereiz.

Rennewart had been wielding his club to compensate himself for his frequent loss of esteem in France and had displayed very clearly his hatred for the heathens. Anyone who rode up on a horse in front of him he crushed to a pulp: thus many heathens died at his hand. He did not seek to take hostages, for Berhtram was no relation of his. Rennewart could be seen there, at the head of his troops, but the Frenchmen, too, had many terrific blows rained upon them, and they began to cry out 'Rennewart!', for they were eager to save their lives. This battle-cry had been given to them when the Marquis had formed them into one battalion and reinstated the imperial standard. The Frenchmen came to know what trouble was. If they had gone home comfortably across Pitit Punt they would not now have been so violently trampled on by so many troops.

Ehmereiz was rescued then and King Tibalt of Kler, too, by the army of proud Josweiz. It was only right that Josweiz did this, for King Ehmereiz was the son of the daughter of the sister of Josweiz' father, and the attack by his mighty kinsman came in handy there. Now thunderous charges like cloud-bursts were delivered and received.

And now came Poidwiz of Rabes, that brave and high-spirited King, who was leading many fine knights. We hear it said of his courage that he was never seen in action among his enemies without emerging victorious. He had engaged in many jousts in which he had spent his full supply of lances. I should not wish to choose *him* as a forester, because he caused the whole wood to disappear when he fought. People say of his jousting that the Black Forest and the Virgunt[81] would be laid waste by it.

(Now I suppose someone will be saying that I should stop this lying, but why does that someone not want to let someone else cut down a forest? Let him mind his own business!)

King Poidwiz of Rabes came riding into battle, but not at a trot or a canter: he came riding as a man does when the spurs cut deep wounds into the horse's flanks. He was furious with Terramer for giving him the order to engage in battle only after seven other battalions.

'Even if I had never fought before,' he said, 'I am leading so many noble men from the realms of other kings that I should by rights have led the first charge. No one need tend the wounds which I might have received in the attack, but I have come into this battle like a hailstorm upon a field of grain.'

Ahead of him there was the sound of trumpets blaring. Nothing could prevent his banner from making an attack from the right with a great retinue and immense strength on the flanks of the knights who until then had been fighting fiercely, with neither side gaining a victory. There were no boundaries round the fields, and friend and foe were pressed together in the attack conducted by Poidwiz, and many groups of knights were split apart.

The pressure from Poidwiz gave the entire army such a jerk that the Christians and the heathens merged into one mass – all of them who were known to be present, bearing arms on either side in the battle – as if they had been crushed together in a press, old and young alike, rich and poor without exception. They were cooped up in this vast expanse, locked in with swords. Many lives there bore the seal of death and many a man present could speak of the burden of battle. There were blows from swords and thrusts from spears and plunging attacks. They were able to come to grips with one another better than I can say, and I shall bear no grudge against any man who can describe it better to you. Imagine the waves of the sea billowing up and down: this was how the battle went everywhere, whether on the plain or over the hills. They endured much hardship, those men who had entered the battle with Poidwiz, those three armies which were much acclaimed. One of them had been led from Liwes Nugruns by King Tenebruns, while the army of the King of Rankulat hacked out many paths there with its swords and the knights from Azagouc, the third army, took revenge for their lord, King Rubiun.

What can the Christians do but defend themselves as long as they remain alive? God alone can help them. Poidwiz was too much for them: their forces were losing strength, not gaining it. The Christians were depleted, while the heathen army increased on the field of Alischanz. If ever an army became pregnant, one could say this of the heathen battalions. If it was not a case of one giving birth to the others, then it was a miracle where the flood which was performing much exemplary chivalry there was coming from.

The battle struck down one man's companions, this one's lord, another's kinsman. How many hosts from both sides lay slain there, struggling into death from battle! How many beautifully equipped men were strewn before the horses! They would have been spared this if they had stayed at home, for there the weary horses are delighted if someone throws down dry straw beneath them. How many horses fell there, too! Some of them were lying on top of princes, others on top of amazurs. Poidwiz had become practically a neighbour of the Christians, but his fighting could no longer bother those who had previously been fighting fiercely.

Now, for the first time, the field could be seen blossoming with noble knights, as if a mighty forest were springing up out of the earth, and in it many lovely patches sparkling with dew. Then with trappings gleaming came the company of King Marlanz of Jericop, broad and long and densely packed and with many separate bands of men. (If the Emperor Otto had ridden back so splendidly from his coronation in Rome I would agree that that would have been quite enough.)[82] Look how many skilled knights King Marlanz was bringing with him! He was not in too much of a hurry. It seemed to him a good idea to have waited until those ahead of him had fought ferociously. He was wanting to see how they had slashed their way on the battlefield. The carpenter has to wait to see how he should cut with the hatchet after having first used the axe: this was exactly what Marlanz was wanting to do, too.

Poidwiz had proceeded quite differently, for he did not know how to follow a chalk-line when chopping. Do you suppose the sarcophagi of the Christians were now being trampled over by heavy hooves? Certainly they were, and this was even before the army of King Marlanz of Jerikop brought the full force of the attack to bear. He deserved to be acclaimed for his courage there. I can hardly attribute to the sun such radiance as his men gave forth from their gleaming helmet decorations and their expensive silken garments.

The King of Orkeise did not wish to delay any longer, and he brought new movement into the campaign. This was Margot of Pozzidant, who could be seen in all his trappings and riding on a mare, which wore a covering of chain-mail. Over this was stretched a silken cloth. All this was too much for the mare. (It is not our custom here at home to dress up mares like this: we ride stallions into battle.)

Margot had brought a king there – his name was Gorhant of Ganjas – who thought it was no disgrace that all his men were without horses. They were faster just as they were, on foot. They caused many Christians to make payment with their lives in that battle. They did not need any armour other than their skin, which was of green-coloured horn, and they carried steel maces. The enormous horny contingent was moving forward with King Margot, who was himself assigned to the army of Marlanz, but his battalion did not remain intact any longer. Margot, who had travelled so far to be there, and his men attacked with such force that, even before they had completed the charge, the field was beginning to tremble with its impact.

Now the wedge is plunged in as King Marlanz of Jerikop hurled himself with tremendous force into the enemy army and caused the swords to clash. If the knights had been pressed together before, they had even closer quarters now, Christians and heathens alike.

Side by side with Margot of Pozzidant was fighting the army of King Gorhant with its steel maces. They hammered ridges and slants into the roofs of the helmets with huge strong blows. (I should not like to have carpenters like that today: I should not be able to pay their wages!) In many languages they uttered cries in differing tones.

Now Terramer can honourably forget the journey to Aachen, for most of the noble Roman princes have come to meet him at Alischanz, wanting to make it known to him that Vivianz and the noble Mile have been slain. If he was wanting to wear the crown and bind them to his service, then he must first make reparation to them for this.

Many fine bold knights were beaten with maces by the horny-skinned henchmen. (Could any hat from Beratzhausen have come crashing any harder against another?)[83] They were in great danger as a result. Now everywhere six battle-cries could be heard, shouted out by the Christians at the tops of their voices. One of their cries was 'Narbonne!', while a second shout resounding through the army as a rallying-cry was 'Brabant!' The third cry – 'Rennewart!' – was assigned to the Frenchmen who were being treated with very little tenderness there. The fourth battle-cry was 'Tandarnas!' and 'Berbester!' the fifth which greeted Marlanz. Nor did the Margrave's battalion refrain at all from shouting 'Monjoie!', crushed together as they were, as though an iron chain had been forged round them. They flogged each other with their swords.

The Christians were hardly able to slash their way through to enough space to reassemble. The beautifully equipped knights – some of them from the family of Terramer – formed a bridge for them across a bloody ford.

The Christians have finally assembled. What if they *have* suffered losses? Now they are going to inflict losses themselves. So Rennewart set to and dealt mighty blows with his club. The men who had previously been grouped separately were now fighting side by side, brought together by their battle-cries and the pressure that Poidwiz had applied. The Christians were bothered a great deal by dazzle from many directions: the heathen silks were flashing in the sun. The battle rose and fell, like a goose bobbing up and down on the waves. And so the field of Alischanz was bathed in blood. Both their liege-lords and their ladies were well served there.

The chief of all heathendom was now mounted on Brahane. The battle was stretching out towards the spring close to which Vivianz had died. The battalions assembled from many lands had now crossed the River Larkant, together with the carts with the gods. The son of bold Kanabeus had ordered that, on pain of death, they should travel with the gods, those men who had been assigned to do so, but they were fooled in this, for Mahmete and Kahun and whichever other gods were there – Apolle or Tervigant perhaps – could do little to help them.

Alas, that he is coming now, he at whose hand the Christians must endure sorrow and profound suffering! Now I am referring to Terramer, who was well able to inflict anguish on the Christians. But enough of that: before they die he will suffer damage from them too, so that his heart and his mind will be filled with misery and brought to shame as well.

I should not like to try to estimate the immense size of his tenth battalion, but if someone wanted to bottle individual drops of rain he would need to have a great many stoppers, and even so it would be a miracle. That is how I see the Lord of Suntin. On either side of him, in front of him and behind, could be found many huge detachments, who did not even speak the same language. Many men were riding there who were incapable of communicating with one another and did not know what the others were talking about, whether their intentions were good or bad.

Alas for Christian people! The caresses of virtuous women, their favour and their love, and the superior gain as well – I am referring to eternal repose – are now inflicted on you with the point of the spear and beaten on to you with many hands. Any man of loyalty must mourn for you, for it is loyalty which has sent you into this peril. Since the first time you were offered battle you have been fighting for nothing: you have been waiting until now for a proper battle.

Here comes the Lord of Tenabri with his gods close by him! As you have heard me say before, there was the rolling and the crashing of a thousand drums – tautly stretched, no slackness here – and you could hear as well the din of eight hundred trumpets blasting. The ocean could have been stirred to its very depths by the racket and the trembling.

If I want to I can describe the many costly helmet decorations which came riding there in the army of Terramer. Many kinds of creatures in different colours they had fixed upon them, not sparing the expense, symbols of birds and animals, all the wonders of the sea as well. They were bringing with them into the fray many different kinds of battle-cry. One wore a fish, another a dragon fixed upon his armour. The battalion came riding in full force on to the field of Alischanz. Those precious agate stones are *really* not so varied in appearance as the decorations which the knights wore in their pursuit of noble love, and many of *them* were slashed through by the Christians, no matter what their shapes.

Now the King of Tandarnas and *le pauvre* Schetis did not need to rush ahead in pursuit of fame. Any man who had been borne into battle by the dictates of his heart found battle there in plenty.

Ektor of Salenie raised the banner high, so that if the Christians wanted to they could still not reach it with their swords. The pole was tightly bound with metal thongs. Ektor of Salenie was a fearless king. The cry of Terramer went up – 'Kordes!'

Alas now for the murderous slaughter which occurred there on both sides, when that standard entered the fray and produced an enormous clashing of swords! There was a great crush of troops trying to get ahead in battle, even though they had heard and understood Terramer's edict that any man who broke out of the battle order would be punished with death. Then did the rule of death become familiar in that battle. On both sides they made pledges which could never be redeemed until the Day of Judgement, when all mankind will receive life restored to it.

There were many separate skirmishes. If anyone can have them fight as befits chivalry, let him take on the telling of this tale with my blessing and tell with words how, in the thick of battle or on the edges of it or anywhere courageous men were riding, they fought there for the reward of women and for their favour, and how one onslaught gave way to the next after regrouping. I'd be grateful to anyone who did not let the story of this fateful battle come to nought. [84]

BOOK IX

Alas, Giburc, saintly lady, may you in your blessedness afford me the chance to see you with my own eyes there, where my soul will find repose! Because of your sweet renown I shall continue to call upon you yourself and those who defended you and thereby saved their souls from the Devil's bonds with their courageous hands.

What did it avail Heimrich's sons that all seven of them, their father and all the Christians had rallied together? The tremendous onslaught scattered them with the sound of blaring trumpets, and there must have been a thousand tambours beaten which stirred the River Larkant and made the plain tremble as the bed Lit Marveile did when noble Gawan lay on it.[85] That is just the way Alischanz was trembling now. You could see amazing animals and birds bobbing up and down on many sturdy helmets, and trees with branches and twigs, too, all richly decorated. Seeking the reward of ladies, many Saracens came, some swiftly, some more slowly, splendidly adorned, towards the son of Heimrich of Narbonne across the River Larkant.

Charge! Charge! Charge! How they did race out of the fords, those many groups of men whose lives were to be ended before day became night! The brave, powerful forces kept coming, and then the great throng headed towards many an anvil, that is to say: Christians, protected by baptism. The attack was made at full speed, the horses spurred to their utmost, so that the carts remained alone behind, with the mighty gods mounted on them. With Terramer rode the King of Lanzesardin, and he it was who had left the gods all alone. That was noble Kanliun. The son much preferred to follow his father rather than the gods. If someone dammed up the Rhine and the Rhône for a fortnight and then suddenly removed the dam, it would not have produced as great a flood as Terramer's forces did, for he literally swamped the whole Christian army. Yet the Christians kept fighting

so valiantly that there will be enough to tell of their deeds on
Judgement Day and in all the years between, so great were the
heathen losses. But the heathen attack was made so massively by
their overwhelming strength and so swiftly on many a beautiful
charger that the six banners of the Christians were soon riding apart
from one another: some had only a small following. They were split
off from one another in groups of unequal size in the press of battle.
Thus they fought for a long time with many a Christian of necessity
under the command of a different leader from the one to whose
banner he had been assigned. Every Christian fought well, no matter
which of the six banners waved above his head, and their battle-cries
were mingling too.

I feel great pity now for Heimrich himself in that he in his old age
paid so dearly for eternal honour and that his family was baptized
there a second time, this time in blood. How do you suppose he felt
when he saw his children and his children's children and himself in
such danger, and his kinsmen and his vassals as well? His heart must
have been full of sorrow, and yet there was courage mingled with
that sorrow. No matter how many heathens they killed, these were
not enough for him and his companions who were bearing his
shields.

Old Heimrich was wearing a riding coat of samite and under that
had been put a silk lining with mail and silk quilted and sewn in layers
in between, and he was wearing gloves fashioned in the same way.
The coat also had a neck-piece that was closed together at the throat,
and the coat was slit up to his waist. The buttons on it were emeralds
and rubies, and on the front and on the back a sign of blessing – he
wanted to wear that in battle – cut from a border, a cross with three
points, made like the letter that God gave to the Israelites to write in
lamb's blood on the doorpost and over the door for their protection.[86]
Wherever that letter was found, God's revenge, which was intended
for the sinful, had to pass by. It is true, as we have heard, that the
Cross on which the Son of the Virgin hung in anguish until He in His
humanity suffered death on it for us had three points, although since
then many a cross has four. Heimrich wore one like that affixed to his
riding-coat on a brown samite background when his son's father-in-
law brought his overwhelming attack to bear against him.

You have all been screeched at by a jay in the woods: in the same way on this occasion that old Count's presence was made known there by his fighting. He and his men cleared such room with their swords that many a unit wanted to turn away from them rather than increase their losses there.

Zernubile of Amirafel came rushing up with a detachment. That very King wore his crown in a large realm for being in charge of the sounding of tambours. He came up against Heimrich and performed such excellent chivalry that he thought he had all the Christians tied up in a bag, but his way was barred by blades, and you could hear a great clash of swords there.

Then King Zernubile turned towards the man who was wearing in battle the beard white as snow, unprotected by a ventail. Below his eyes Heimrich's face was not enclosed by a visor, yet his helmet did have a nose-guard. Zernubile found many a cross affixed to the garments of those who countered his charge with their knightly deeds and split many heads so that the tongues in the mouths could no longer utter a battle-cry. Zernubile put his trust in Mahmete and turned towards the old Count, spurring his horse to the attack. Zernubile wore on his helmet and on his cape many things that a noble lady gives to her friend out of love for him. If he gained renown on that occasion, it never happened again thereafter, for Heimrich avenged his daughter's son, brilliant Vivianz, there on that splendid heathen, who was wearing so much helmet decoration. The Count of Narbonne split the King's helmet all the way to his teeth.

If I yearn now to lament his death that is only because of our very distant kinship. After all, those who endured danger on both sides and escaped with their lives, even if they never fought again with lance or sword, would all have died since then.

When King Zernubile had been felled to the clover, his death was avenged viciously, for his men hacked and pierced many Christians for whom the women at home would mourn.

Bernart of Brabant was still at his father's side. He had remained there when the great assault drove the others away from him with the clash of its charge.

Here comes Kliboris of Tananarke flying like a dragon! He had a boat on his helmet and his many other individual helmet decorations appeared to be very costly, for translucent jewels, some not small at all, hung from threads of spun gold and sparkled in the sunlight with every movement of his head, as if fiery sparks were spurting from his mouth, glowing as they flew up and down. Thus Kliboris came charging up.

Bernart of Brabant was sure that he was bringing him the day of his death. So many of the Christians lay both dead and wounded before Kliboris that if I should tell you all of them – who had been slain there, how another avenged his kinsman, how this one came riding up with a group, how that one spared neither horse nor rider, and who won great renown there in the army on all sides – if I were to describe their individual feats, then I would have to name a lot of men for you!

The King of Tananarke fought his way to Bernart of Brabant and struck him a blow which split the helmet wider than a hand's breadth that went all the way to his coif. If his hauberk had not been double, it would have been the end of him right there. Bernart raised his sword, Précieuse – its edges were both keen – which that King had carried whom the Emperor Charles had slain.[87] The sword had been taken at Roncesvalles, and from there it had been brought back home in all its splendour by the French. Later it came into the possession of Bernart, who dared to perform manly deeds. Haropin's son was slain then with a blow from this sword that went through both boat and helmet. Those who receive the reward of women should lament the loss of the splendid beauty of his helmet decoration. The strong, young, handsome stranger lay slain beneath his horse. A wave of blood poured into the boat. Any sailor who had been in there would not have managed to survive!

Poidwiz, the son of King Oukin, also gave evidence that he had often gained high renown through bravery in many a joust with lances, and right now he brought death by the sword to Kiun of Beauvais and five courtly French knights, his comrades. He slew them by felling them to the grass beneath their horses, right where young Heimrich stood. Enraged, Heimrich attacked Poidwiz. He rushed up to him and quickly turned him around, chasing him towards King Grohier, through his camp, right up to his tent. There he paid him back with death for Burgrave Kiun. It was only right for

Heimrich's son to avenge him, for he was his kinsman. And Poidwiz too lay slain, that bold jouster who had often risked his life for the sake of noble Love. His kinsmen and noble-minded ladies did indeed mourn his death at that time far and wide in many lands. *Le roi* Oukin of Rabes mourned his noble son Poidwiz, too, of whom one must tell of excellent knightly deeds. Of what use to him was the strength of the great army that his father had sent to protect him, with many separate units? He had become separated from them in the course of the fighting, so that he had ridden too far away from them. 'Whoever does without his men is bound to end up in defeat.' That the Schetis slew him by himself arose from the fact that his horse carried him through the camp of King Grohier, and there the headstall was cut off by a blow through the head-covering, so that the reins came loose. As a result, the Schetis turned Poidwiz around, so that his back was turned to him, and killed him.

Clang! O how the swords clanged! And how the sparks leapt from the helmets when the Protector of Baldac undertook battle himself! He was a daring man and knowledgeable in such matters. It was of little use for someone to oppose him. Nevertheless, at that very moment one knight under the imperial banner began to encourage the French and his friend Rennewart. He dug his spurs mercilessly into his horse's flanks, crying out to Terramer: 'Come over here, you grey old man! You've done us a lot of damage, but I'll do battle with you, if that's what you're looking for!'

Count Milon of Nevers was the name of that bold man, but the hand of mighty Terramer cut the life from his body. Rennewart was grief-stricken at this deed. He thought that the loss of his noble companion-in-arms was too great, and he promptly avenged it. He killed four noble kings, Fabur and Samirant, Samuel and Oukidant. Then, on the left of his father's battalion, he caught sight of the fifth king, whose name was Morende and whom he also slew. That was how Milon was avenged, but cries of 'Shame!' arose at Rennewart's uncourtly, crude behaviour.

Some of the men from Falfunde turned towards the sea, for they did not want to fight any longer. It is said that their lord, Halzebier, with his battalion, was the first to see the enemy that day and that he had begun the attack. Here a tired man, there a wounded one, departed towards the sea to their ships, but they were fighting as they went. Rennewart hastened after them. Men of the Marquis followed him all the way to the shore wielding their swords, although he had asked none of those who yelled 'Monjoie!' to come along.

Then the Count Palatine Berhtram heard the battle-cry in the hold of a ship where he and seven of his kinsmen were being held captive under extremely wretched conditions. They recognized the cry 'Monjoie!' Their guards were from Nubiant. The men imprisoned below decks there cried out 'Monjoie!' too.

When Rennewart, the strong lad, had come to the place where the bark from that warship put ashore and when he had stepped aboard the warship, he hurled many a man over the side. The men fled to the ends of the ship, some even into the hold, thinking to save their skins, but Rennewart broke away the planking in search of them until he got them all out. The eight captives cried 'Monjoie!' and Rennewart heard their voices clearly and that they were yelling in French. Many a bitter roll of the dice took place there for the heathens, for with his strength Rennewart threw many of them fully armed into the sea. Their resistance availed them very little. Then he forced the men from Nubiant to unlock the fetters, the manacles and the shackles. He was able to exercise sufficient restraint as not to slay any of the guards, but they were frightened enough as it was.

Then and there Kibelin, Berhtram and Gaudin, Hunas and Samson were freed. Rennewart rewarded their guards by leaving them alive. An inborn sense of chivalry made him do that since they were lying there defenceless without sword or bow. The men from Nubiant stayed there, but via the bark and on to the shore came these eight princes who increased the losses of the heathens: Berhtram and Gerart, Huwes and Witschart, Samson and Gaudin, Hunas of Saintes and Kibelin. Before they acquired new armour the lights went out for many a Saracen, broad daylight though it was, for these eight could not fight before they were given battle-dress by the one who preceded them in combat with his club. He slew many heathens there, many a man who wore armour which would be fit for an emperor to wear if he should be in battle. These eight high-born princes, noble heroes all, had their choice of chain-mail leg-coverings and spurs, hauberks, helmets and swords.

Rennewart brandished his branch: I mean he swung his club, which clanged on helmets and shields in such a way that rider *and* horse died under the blows. When so many horses were thus being lost, Berhtram called a halt, and Rennewart heard the prince's advice: 'You should knock the knights to the ground, whether they are armed or not. Spare us enough horses so that we can ride, and then we shall help you better fighting on horseback than on foot.'

'I can only agree with your advice,' said young Rennewart. Many of the Saracens felt his blows then. He thought: 'If I could get mounts for my men, they would make their swords resound.'

However many knights he felled then, he did not lose any of their good horses but led them away to these eight princes. (Landgrave Hermann of Thuringia would surely have given them horses too. He knew how to do that all his life, especially in such a great battle, whenever the request came in time.)

But enough of such talk now! Hear how that fighting was going on. Essere, the emeral, with the splendid helmet decoration, a prince of Halzebier's army, was defending himself, still undefeated, with his group of men there. Rennewart came forcing his way through to get to him. He thrust his club through Essere's body a good fathom's length, despite the armour, and that was enough. Kibelin got Essere's horse, and he killed many a Saracen while riding it. Now these eight princes of Willehalm's family are all mounted and well equipped. They were accompanied into battle by the servant of their niece Alize.[88]

Now they say that Halzebier was fighting in front of them like a wild boar, but he in his courageous strength was tired because he had been fighting all day long on horseback or on foot. Even today his reputation is rewarded with praise for that. Now Samson recognized him by his shield, which was battle-scarred. They took terrible revenge for Vivianz then with their swords and for the fact that Halzebier had delivered these eight as prisoners to Terramer. Were it not for the fact that Halzebier had initiated the heathen attack that day, these eight would have suffered more at his hand than they did.

The attack against the King of Falfunde was started, and they hurt him as he did them. (O God, that You allowed it to happen!) Hunas of Saintes lay slain by his hand. The seven who were left received intense pain from their wounds before they felled the powerful King to the grass, killing him. His noble body covered with sweat grew cold before he died, he who always strove for a renown that was too much for other kings. He set such a magnificent example with boldness and generosity that other kings, his peers, simply could not equal it. Thus that faultless man died, free of ignomy. People say that his hands were equally adroit in fighting and in giving. Courtesy with loyalty, all these noble qualities he possessed all his life until death. Many a prince from the six armies that he had led and that had been assigned to him that morning lay dead around him. Terramer would have liked to save him.

Many battle-cries were heard there, and then it turned into a *temperie*, or, as we say, a mixed battle. It was difficult to distinguish the Christians from the Saracens. Alischanz must ever be a blessed spot since it was wet with so much blood which flowed from the pure bodies of those who are now saved in God's sight. May we share in their martyrdom and holiness! Happy the man who fought there so that his soul gained the victory! It was a blessed thing for him.

Charge! How the Marquis gained renown there for both lives, the praise of this short life and for that one which stands high above us! Wherever splendidly adorned heathens charged at him, he struck down countless ones.

Rennewart later got a horse named Lignmaredi. It went running past King Oukin with an empty saddle. Oukin exhorted all his men, saying: 'Alas, where is Poidwiz, in whom lay the source of my delights? Here comes his horse, the one he was riding, that he won with his own hand at the foot of the mountain at Agremuntin. Alas,' he said, 'my son, shall I ever see you again? Your friends and your enemies must admit that your hand won many a victory. You surely inherited victory from me, for victory never escaped me, until today, if I have now lost you to the Roman King Louis. If the Christians knew your reputation they would not want to see you die, if they are taking hostages and if they knew your virtue. I have never found your equal on earth. I must be put to death myself if I do not try to find out what has happened to you.'

Thus the grief-stricken old man came riding up to the Marquis. The latter knew well how to keep him from ever lamenting for anything again! Yet Willehalm's helmet was cut through by Oukin's hand so that if you wanted to examine it you found a bloody cut there. The Marquis had to admit that a hero was opposing him there whose body had never been harmed by any weapon. All his armour had been fashioned with great skill and sturdy strength. He himself had always been seen fighting in many an attack, and his reputation was enormous. From youth to the days of his old age his hand struggled for the prize, with generosity, with manly deed, of which one has to speak with praise, for he never yielded to fear in cowardice.

Willehalm, the prince from Provence, received many bold blows from his noble hand and had to defend himself if he wanted to save his skin. He swung Schoiuse towards the place where Oukin's shield hung near the knot of the helmet ties. Both his neck-covering of quilted silk and his stout head-covering of steel were thick, but all their sturdiness was of no avail, for his head was sliced off like a slender switch. You could see his body sitting headless in his saddle, and his shield followed by his body fell to the ground into the dust under his horse. Thus the faultless knight died.

King Arestemeiz and the King of Belestigweiz and mighty King Haropin, all bold in the fray, came up with separate groups of men. If someone had time to look he could see quite a sight there. Almost all their men had been sent there splendidly decorated by their ladies. Not one group of the three kings had yet got close to the Christian knights. The Larkant had been in the way, and many a narrow ford which they had to cross. Only now were they approaching the battle.

Meanwhile even Rennewart was taking a rest. Do you suppose that his singed young beard was covered at all with sweat and that sword blows had landed on his club anywhere? Yes, indeed, you could see that the steel bands surrounding the club from the end to the handle were almost all hacked to pieces. But you could well count those who had done that among the dead! Now the battle had been forced so far away by the pressure of the three kings that the Christians had given up a lot of ground. Rennewart did not like that. He saw how the men were being replaced so that whenever tired troops left combat many others entered with fresh strength. There were so many heathens that they had never been counted. Many a charge resounded with such a din that the Christian army began to tire in the battle.

Rennewart came to their aid. He headed for where Gerart and his kinsmen were fighting boldly against strong King Haropin, the old Tananarkois. They had come upon the group of the Burgrave of Beauvais. They had previously suffered the loss of their lord, who had been slain, but they were still carrying his banner nobly. Rennewart recognized them quickly and the fact that the imperial banner had been moved away from them by the attack of the three rested groups. Iwan of Rouen in Normandy it was who carried the imperial standard. His heart and all his limbs were strong and bold. He had thrust his way that day without ceasing through many troops where sword blows rained about him. When he caught sight of Rennewart he forgot that he had suffered anything in combat that day, regardless of how things might eventually turn out.

The Christians regrouped but suffered new losses, for then the King of Nubiant came up with his fourteen sons, who were known as kings in separate lands. The Christians thought that it was snowing knights from the sky. Old King Purrel's beard was greyer than hoar-frost. Many bold knights with helmet decorations rode in troops with his sons. All the Christians there were still gambling with their lives in the battle. If there were any more elsewhere, they did not see such suffering as this story relates to us now. The company of the King of Nubiant was the last across the Larkant, but now they are storming to the front.

Purrel, the mighty King, was armed in a strangely wonderful way. His hauberk was a skin whose hair was greener than the grass that grows at the edge of a meadow. Neitune was the name of the dragon from which the skin had been removed. It was found to be as hard as a diamond and there was also a shield made of it too, firm all over, and it was the very best that came against the enemy in that company. The green of emerald and *achmardi*[89] was nothing compared to the green attributed to that shield. Muntunzel was the name of another dragon from which King Purrel's helmet had been fashioned. This is a true story, and you should take it as gospel that the hair of this dragon shone in four different colours just like the rainbow. The skin inside was the same. It was impervious to shot, blow and thrust. The

King could take comfort in the fact that he could never be wounded so long as he remained under it. The skins of this dragon were not too thick nor too heavy. Those were skilful people who made such equipment. (You can't find it in the Sand in Nuremberg!)[90]

Thus King Purrel came with the sound of many bright horns, so that the noise spread over the entire army. The Christians were, of course, displeased by so many new strong enemy companies, but their six banners all rallied to one another. Purrel's son Alexander and another of his sons, Bargis, and Purrel himself were sure that victory would be theirs. All fourteen young men rode at full speed ahead of the old man. If noble ladies rewarded those who escaped with their lives for that, then they were right to do so. Although those men were serving for love, I myself would hardly have contributed to their gaining it there. They learned soon enough how one must earn courtly love and the favour of noble ladies in battle. Purrel could see his sons being hacked to pieces there, along with many of his other men. He knew how to put up the stakes and collect them in such a game of chance, for he had grown from youth to old age with thrusts and blows. He had heard the cracking of lances many times, and his heart escorted him towards proper manly courage. Although one speaks a lot about kings, the deeds of the poor man are not mentioned. Ordinary knights were expected to fight, but a king could well wait until he had heard how the ford was secured. But Purrel, the husband of Baligan's daughter, always gained renown whenever he accepted battle with the sword and attacked.

Now he soon became well aware that one of his sons, Palprimes, was in difficulty, in the vicinity of the imperial banner. He wore such costly armour that you could see his trappings among many groups of men. Purrel's horse carried him swiftly to the aid of his son, where he slew Kiun of Munsurel and Remon, the baron from Anjou, whose renown was brilliant. Thus he protected his son. Noble Girant from Bordeaux also lay dead by his hand. Anselm of Poitou was killed there, and his father who was called Huc of Lunzel suffered the same fate. These five were slain by Purrel.

But he caused even greater losses. You could see the King of Nubiant hacking a road through the battle. So many of the Christians fell that there was a wide space around him. Rennewart leapt into the ring so that he could swing his club, and you could begin to see his traces. Then King Purrel rode a strong, bold and swift horse, armoured to the hoof, one which always obeyed his command swiftly when he gave it. Rennewart paid him even more than he owed him. His club was raised high against the shield that was greener than grass – Purrel's helmet resembled a rainbow – and then the club smote helmet and shield with such a severe blow – this was no caress! – that the club splintered completely. You ask whether the heavy fragment of the club flew up into the air at all? I'll say it did! When it came down it smashed through the helmet of a knight.

All Purrel's limbs cracked. Although Kiun of Laon, the smith, had made the club carefully, its steel bands still burst. If it had not been for the dragon armour, Purrel would have been completely smashed by the blow. His friends had good reason to praise the armour! See whether he suffered any harm beyond that: from that one blow the horse lay dead and the king unconscious. Blood streamed from his ears and nose, making the green grass all red.

Rennewart then fought with his fists against any of Purrel's men who attacked him. He continued fighting with his fists because he had forgotten the noble sword in the sheath at his side. You never saw anyone fighting more manfully with his fists than he did. Kibelin rushed to his side riding the horse that had been taken earlier in the attack on Essere, and he told him to draw the sword. Rennewart quickly granted his request. Charge! How the sword was tested! Neither armour nor man was spared by its edges. Anyone who did not run away from him had to forfeit his life. Rennewart tossed the sword about in his hand, praising its groove and its edges, saying: 'My strong club was a little too heavy, but you are light and battle-worthy all the same.'

Great losses were suffered on both sides over the head of King Purrel, for the Christians and for the heathens alike. Attacking charges were made on both sides. They hurled spears and other missiles. The flow of blood from the Christians and the noble heathen dead began to turn the field red. Purrel's men rode without lances except those who were riding well equipped in the service of Love. Some of them had stayed there to see how their ladies would reward them, but Rennewart, who was also intent on happiness in love, did not spare them. Purrel, the grey old King, was carried away by force. On foot as they were, his men proved that they were not afraid. Many wounded knights, we've been told, carried him on his shield far across the heath to the sea and on to a swift ship. They saw that he was suffering. That mighty foreigner had gained renown for his old age by his own hand. The fourteen young men, sons of the King of Nubiant, were found by their uncle, Sinagun, as they were about to flee. They were so badly wounded that if he had not come on his dragon-coloured horse with his tired men to help them, the French would have overwhelmed them.

Then mighty Terramer saw the anguish of his kinsmen and began to encourage all his men. Ektor of Salenie carried the banner of the Admirat in fine style. Poidjus had previously seen that Halzebier had been killed. He told that to Terramer, who learned of even more losses. Rennewart had slain Goliam, the King of Belestigweiz. Before that, Rennewart had withstood many a fierce attack. Giboez, the noble Burgrave of Kler, had been wounded by him, and Tibalt had turned away with all his army. Trohazzabe of Karkassun, who carried the standard of Ehmereiz, had never fled before until he saw that Duke Bernart had slain Ektor, who was ever preserved from all cowardice.

Then the defeat became immense when the banner that the Protector of Baldac had entrusted to King Ektor lay on the ground. The imperial colours flew on high, as did the banner of Brabant, which Landris held in his hand. The Provençal flag, richly adorned with its star of gold, was also flying high, and old Heimrich's banner and that of Tandarnas, under which the Schetis fought, all five survived against the many difficulties that had beset them. Many a bloody sword followed the banner of the two, Bertram and Gibert. They put to flight the battalion of Terramer's sons. Of what use was his army from many lands now? The knights had to suffer danger with him. The core of the heathen fighting strength, Poidwiz and Halzebier, lay dead, and many noble soldiers were fleeing.

Whoever bears the imperial name, the one whom the heathens call 'Admirat', is also Protector of Baldac. Terramer had both titles, for he was Protector *and* Admirat. You know what Roman rank is vested in the Roman Emperor in Rome. The Roman crown ranks high with respect so that it has nothing equal to it, so acute is the fear of the Roman crown. Whatever other crowns are made and worn on Christian heads, all their power is nothing compared to that and they have no power at all. Just so did the son of Kanabeus have sovereignty over all heathendom both by virtue of his lineage and also his power, and his inheritance from Baligan had made many kings subject to him in fealty. Yet however powerful he may be, Altissimus is still mightier. He caused the battle to go thus: whatever amazurs and eskelirs were there with the Lord of Muntespir, all his kings and emerals had to flee in defeat from the battlefield with losses all around.

The Christians increased their chances of salvation, for with their swords they turned all the heathens about. In truth it was the Hand of God that helped all the Christians most in this wherever they were fighting, that much I know. A more courageous victory was never achieved in many years. Those who had been graced with baptism acted like the noble hunting-dog who does not give up the scent and keeps following it without stopping to shake himself after having swum through water.

But still many of the Saracen knights regrouped. Fabors and Kanliun and Ehmereiz, Tibalt's son, showed that they could rally their forces even in retreat. Wherever they found their kinsmen or vassals being pressed, they helped them then in a way that did honour to their chivalry. Still the Christians kept attacking them sharply at a gallop. If they could have charged at full tilt on their wounded horses, the heathens would have left more forfeits there.

The Admirat fled on his horse Brahane: he simply had no choice. Some of his men headed for the mountains where later many of them were killed. Others headed for the sea-shore. Many a prince who normally took just a bundle of twigs with him was seen heading for a bath now in full armour. Some also fled into the swamp. Many a silken tent-rope was trodden to pieces in their wake, and horse and rider sank into the River Larkant. But many a Christian hand found plenty of courageous combat, for whenever gaps opened up through which they could break, they found slashing and thrusting under the banner of Josweiz, that high-spirited King, who had a swan depicted on his banner and on his shield. That noble, generous King had to abandon the ford, but he did so without disgrace, and he returned repeatedly, greatly increasing his renown. He protected many a Saracen who would otherwise have been lost there.

The six battle-cries that had been assigned to the Christians that morning were now forgotten here and there when the defeat, so wide, so great, had been meted out with swords. You could hear many new cries there. Each knight promptly yelled the name of the place he came from, in the fords and on the plain. Gandaluz of Champagne and his men cried 'Provins!' and Jofreit of Senlis gave his battle-cry too. The Flemish cried 'Ypres!' and 'Arras!', and many a sword-blade resounded as the cries were uttered. Hot on the trail, men of Lorraine yelled 'Nancy!'

Many an eskelir who was unaccustomed to fleeing was driven to the ford with swords, over the sarcophagi in which lay the blessed dead who had found rest in heaven. The Admirat suffered ignominy at the hands of the imperial princes. As this tale tells us, no one swore by the grace of his kings from many lands. Many a heathen, overburdened with battle, parted from both lord and kinsmen without taking leave. The ships were tied up next to one another fully three miles long, transports, freighters, warships, small and large, with pennants flying. The pennants showed where the ship of a particular unit was anchored. Some men got to the wrong place when they fled through the fresh water of the river to the salty sea. Whoever got to a ship first did not wait for his brother. People still tell today how many an eskelir did not bother to ask for his seamen, and kings themselves had to cast off if they wanted to save their lives, some without raising sail. But true to his manly courage, the Admirat of all the heathens had turned to fight in front of his ships at the sea. I'll tell you who was holding out there: Sinagun and Ehmereiz, Pruanz and Utreiz, Iseret and Malatons, Marjadox and Malakrons.

Previously the trout had had red spots. Now the fish everywhere were red from the battle in the Larkant, and the land of the Provençals was all red in the tracks of many a fleeing group like the mountain Tahenmunt. Many a sorely wounded knight had fled there, pierced through his armour.

Rennewart came hastening on foot after them through the narrows, where he saw his old father with many units holding out with courage undismayed, like a young man. Meister Hildebrand's wife Uote did not wait with any firmer loyalty than did Terramer for many a troop of his men covered with blood.[91] The Protector of Baldac stood his ground bravely and boldly. Here a thrust, there a blow, whenever the onslaught of a new troop joined in the attack; that's the way the Christians came. I can claim that for the brave men, but I can tell you nothing about the cowards in this battle.

I'll tell you for sure about boldness, about how the Prince of the Provençals, Willehalm, the Marquis, and his allies gained renown. The Duke of Vermandois and Duke Bernart, his brother, came riding in pursuit, crying out with loud voices, and Buov, the doughty Landgrave of Commercey, and closest to him there raced the banner of old Heimrich. Now the path that the heathens had made with their hoof-beats was so wide that it was clearly visible. The banner of the King of Tandarnas was the very first of the Christians across the ford in pursuit of the heathens. Berhtram and Kibelin hewed out the first gaps in the ranks. Go to it! Charge closer! How many pennants and banners you could see on their tracks in pursuit! The six banners of the Christians, some tattered, some little more than a shred, were all across the ford now. You'll not hear in many years of such a stout defence, such a bitter attack, as was seen on both sides there from Terramer's warships. Many a knight was wounded as a result.

The Margrave let nothing stop him from pushing straight for the Admirat, for his heart compelled him to do that. Now he saw the god Kahun depicted riding on a griffon, just as Baligan had worn him at Roncesvalles in battle against the Emperor Charles, but Terramer's shield was even more splendid. Many a hero was wounded consequently when the Margrave saw the insignias under which Baligan and Malprimes, his son, had lost their lives. Their noble god Kahun had been depicted on their shields riding a griffon, and Terramer was fighting here under the same sign. That coat of arms was justly his, for he had inherited its wealth and power. Volatin was spurred on to where many swords clashed. Many kings of the heathen army were fighting to defend the Admirat, some his children and many his kinsmen. Many wounds were dealt out, here by thrusts, there by blows. The fit became infirm. There was little respite. The many charges caused close quarters on the broad plain.

Mounted on Brahane, Terramer moved toward the Margrave in an all-out attack. He smote him through the helmet even harder than Oukin had done previously. After that you could see that the hauberk from Jozerant was slashed to pieces. Kanabeus' son, the noble, high-born hero was wounded through the griffon and through Kahun. The edges of Schoiuse slashed him through all his armour, but the King of Lanzesardin charged between them and interrupted the duel. Kanliun showed that he did not like to see his father in such distress, but Rennewart came up to him and did not spare his brother. He slew Kanliun. Neither one had been able to tell the other who he was before it happened. Rennewart split King Gibue all the way to his sword belt, and he slew King Malakin, cutting through his chain-mail fastenings. The fourth victim was Kator, and Rennewart gave young King Tampaste a mortal wound too. His father had killed Vivianz in the first battle at Alischanz.

You ask how the retreat turned out? How the son parted from his father, and the father from his son? Just see how a strong wind scatters the dust back and forth. I cannot describe the results everywhere for you and name for you individually who lost his life there and who escaped on horse or aboard ship, but I will say that the Admirat, who had never been defeated, was laid sorely wounded on his warship. Hear who left the battle with him: Sinagun of Bailie and Bargis, Purrel's son, and his brother Tenebreiz. They were clothed in sweat. Many a good knight wore to the ships a coat of sweat checked with blood: such garments had been tailored there! They did not tarry longer, and the battle ended in flight. Noble Terramer lamented that for all his remaining days. Thus he who had often laid claim to Rome before the defeat took place departed from Roman soil.

Tedalun, rich in gold, and Poidjus of Vriende, the son of Terramer's daughter, each one relied so well on his hands during the retreat: even then many a Christian soldier exacted a toll in blood. The animal 'ezidemon'[92] was portrayed on Poidjus' banner. When Tedalun fled he did not want to carry the banner any more on his path of retreat. The expensive silk from Triant that Tedalun had been holding in his hand and the staff of lignum aloe, and the tip fashioned in Tasme struck Gandaluz with such force that his blood spilled all over the expensive silk. That joust was so powerful in its attacking force that it killed the Champagnois. Rennewart, the bold lad, offered Tedalun the same payment in return. Chasing after him swiftly on foot, he killed Tedalun, who had carried the banner of his sister's son bravely in the battle. Then Rennewart tried to get Poidjus to turn and fight with him, but he wouldn't. In that he showed good sense.

Rennewart saw the tremendous loss that had befallen them in the death of the renowned prince from Champagne and how his men were heaping lamentation upon lamentation for him. If there was ever grief equal to this, then it required many eyes for it and the stimulus of many hearts to provide much water for them and to renounce joy. And who would think of laughing where such a noble man lay dead? I wouldn't want to accuse anyone of such a thing. The Margrave had gained the victory with great losses and had burdened many a Christian heart with suffering. The Christian anguish was shared throughout his army. His men had come to the battlefield with many wounds still unhealed. All the men, the humble and the great, were heard sighing. If I had a lord who continually showed his disfavour towards me, and if I were in the battle in which he lost his life, I would have to call it hypocritical, if I were seen in mourning. But that did not happen on this occasion.

There were gains and losses there. Some had found joy, others a store of sorrow. That was the way it went then, here and there, all around in the army. Whoever Death had spared at least found himself alive, no matter how great his misery was otherwise. Everyone was looking for acquaintances on the battlefield and on the trail. Thus one man found his father in one place, while another his brother somewhere else – everyone was doing that – and the lord found his vassal. 'He who seeks, finds more than he who seeks not and does not budge through indolence.' If I were to turn my mind to telling you about all the booty, what wealth many a man acquired there, I would still be counting even today. Poor men became rich, those who wanted to take what they had a right to. Rich man, poor man, this one and that found more than his heart's desire. (I am not the one to count up separately for you what each one chose to take.)

Bernart of Brabant sounded a horn more loudly than Oliphant ever sounded at Roland's mouth in any place or at any time.[93] The Christian army rejoiced and lamented on the battlefield.

Now the sun had sunk very low that day, but many a Christian soul had mounted on high. Night began to fall.

You ask me who had provided the fine food for them at many a camp-site? The men from Samargone! The Christians found an amazing lot of food there from India and from Triant. There was much food from Alamansura, they found much food from Kanach, and much had been brought from Suntin. And then, of course, there was also much more food from Todjerne and from Arabi. If there had been three Roman emperors, each one with his own army, they would have found ample food there for their campaign. Much food from Orkeise, much food from Adramahut – many a battered hide was stuffed full with exotic food. (I could praise quarters where I found such supplies, if I wanted to.)

I can't name their foods individually, the game and the domestic meat, and the many kinds of fine drink, mulberry wine, white wine, red wine. The people of Cyprus and Philippolis do not have such good drink at their disposal as was found there in many different kinds. After the heat of the day many a man slaked his thirst so that his wisdom was not exactly equal to Solomon's. Night and day were quite different for the men as far as their tasks were concerned. One man drank to drown his sorrow in pleasure. There had to be an end to the lamenting about what the heathens had done to him in the battle. He thought that he had slain all of them and that all the heroes were cowards, save himself. The pain of his own wounds felt just like the dew in May. He felt no remorse for anyone any more, whether it be his father or some other kinsman. He did not care who lay dead there, nor did he care either who had remained alive. That's the way *he* strove for renown!

Most of those who participated in the feast had been bled from a vein or elsewhere on their bodies. If their speech was a little confused then, it was surely straightened out the next morning. Lord and vassal had so much that they lacked nothing. In German we would say they were 'comfortable'. In French, they had their *'aise'*. Here the *courtois*, there the uncourtly man, each gained plenty from the wealth that they found there. Some thought their gaping wounds no more than a bramble scratch. The heathens had had to pay a heavy tribute from their treasury. If the heathens' noble god Apolle and their Admirat were angry with them, the Christians at least did not have to worry about whether they had lost their favour or incurred their wrath. Mahmete, Tervigant and Kahun, whatever all the gods of heathendom were called, had few people under their command on the battlefield that night. As it is, they are still held in low esteem in Christian lands today. The Marquis did not serve them either.

Jesus with the Highest Hand had given him Giburc and that land in the battle that day. He maintained the reputation to his grave of never again being without victory since the day he lost Vivianz, his sister's son, on Alischanz and more of those who are still in God's presence throughout eternity. Mile, his sister's son, had been well avenged that day. Many tongues had much to lament in many different languages and much misfortune to relate at home.

Is it a sin to slaughter like cattle those who have never received baptism? I say it is a great sin, for they are all the creatures of God's Hand, and He maintains them, with their seventy-two languages. Terramer, the Admirat, with many mighty and splendid kings wanted to bring all the languages to Aachen, to the imperial throne, and then lead them to Rome. Those who opposed that were able to move them in a different direction with their swords and used up their bodies so totally that their souls are now illumined: they pay no heed to troubles.

The next morning, when day began to break, the pure Christians who had been so blessed that they had lost their lives in battle were carried together in many places. The noblemen were removed separately. The prince, the count, the baron, whoever had lost his life there for Heimrich's son, will never suffer anguish again in his soul. The poor men were buried on the spot, and the nobles were kept on biers, to be returned to their lands. What sorrow did those endure who had to see them so terribly mutilated! Whatever wounds could be seen were treated with balsam immediately. Costly plasters were prepared with musk and therabint, aromat and ambergris, but wherever no plaster lay, there was still a sweet smell. The balm did not allow them to decompose. If one treats a corpse that way, with flesh and skin and bones embalmed, after a thousand years it looks as if it had been lying just the one night. This is the effect of the process of embalming.

The princes and their high-born vassals took council and decided all together to head away from the field. They did not move out very fast, and their day's journey was not long, for many a wound forced some of them to ride away gently. Who would want to stay there any longer? They all had to leave. Indeed, so many heathens were lying where the battle had taken place that they had to make camp at a short distance away where the ground was not so wet with blood.

The Prince from the land of the Provençals lamented greatly that he did not find his friend Rennewart, and he was reluctant to leave. He said: 'I have still not heard where my right hand has got to. I mean the one who was acknowledged as outstanding by both sides, when the time had come, that day of fateful decision when I was victorious through him and through the Highest Hand. Now for the first time my sense of loss is greater than if I were in the city of Siglimessa and sold from there to Tasme. I am just as miserable here with my anguish.

'Alas, strong body, handsome youth, if I cannot serve you in your brave virtue, your sweet simplicity and your renown high and wide, then I am lost! Has death snatched you from me? Are you not to have my service and all that my hand can share? For you have won this land for me, and you have served my own life here and Giburc, my beautiful wife. Were it not for your exceptional bravery, my old father would be lost. But for you, each one of my supporters would be lost, all my kinsmen and brothers. You were the rudder for my ship, the favouring wind for my sails that has allowed Heimrich's sons to drop anchor on Roman soil. No man's renown has come soaring in such high nobility among all people living today. You freed my kinsmen, fighting on sea and on land. My loyalty would be disgraced, if my heart could not lament and my mouth tell of the loss of you. You brought back the army of the French that fled, to help me fight for God. Because of your bravery all Christians should mourn for you today and continue all the time that God will give the world to exist. You have earned renown for Christianity. For many years people will still relate how you fought on Alischanz. Mile and Vivianz, even when I lost you and all my army, I did not suffer such a great loss!

'O God, if You have pity, may all the angels in Your company recognize my loss! Let this be my purgatory, so that my soul shall receive no further pain, since my bodily joy is dead for ever more. Altissimus, since the heathens have given me such pain, keep me from losing You on Judgement Day and from the eternal lament that You do not turn aside! May Your mercy send me such consolation that my soul shall be freed from its bonds!

'People can see on my helmet that many a stout blow landed on me in the battle. Alas, that I was not slain by the Admirat's hand! When the Emperor and Bishop Turpin lost Roland to Marsilie's army and Olivier, who had fought well,[94] that loss was not as great as mine is. Have I inherited such a great loss from Charles? He was my liege-lord and not my kinsman. We were not of the same family. From whom have I inherited such destruction? What good is my princely name? My joy is dead, not just lame, and has disappeared from my heart. I am no longer respected by strangers and acquaintances since the strength of my high spirits has been diminished. Many a sad man burdened with troubles received joy from my hand here when I ruled in this land of the Provençals with great happiness. Indeed, the wretched man in trouble needed to turn no further than to me.

'You have reason to feel shame because of my loss, O Son of the Virgin, for I have offered my life and my possessions in Your name. The gaping hole that misery shot through my heart is still unclosed. If Your virtue stands unchangeably, You should not be changeable towards me now and should be mindful of my loss since it was Your Hand that ordained that man should have woman in his arms for love. Men of proper manly spirit serve for women's reward. I have heard many a spear break in the service of a woman, who now unfortunately cannot recompense me for this loss, but my heart still declares my love for her. Were it not for Your help and her consolation, I would be ever unrelieved of the bonds of misery. The hands of all kings with all their wealth could not relieve me of my suffering.'

When the tears raining from Willehalm's eyes became so numerous that they could not be counted, Bernart of Brabant came up, scolding him and diverting him from his great anguish. When the Duke saw the Margrave looking so despondent, he said to him: 'You are surely not Heimrich's son, if you are going to act like a woman. Great adversity demands courage. Misery will spread throughout this whole army because of you alone, if you are going to keep weeping just like a child for the breast. What we gain is sweet, and we have many sour losses. We have inherited no other lot. We seven strong brothers of manifestly noble lineage have to be rulers of our lands! Who ever yielded us land or its treasure without bloodshed and sword's point? You have Tibalt's land and his wife, and many a man will yet risk his life for that. You know that the Admirat of the heathens took six years to assemble his men, and they did not spare our bodies here. My heart and my eyes are in tears for your friend Rennewart, for he freed my son, the Count Palatine Berhtram, and the seven princes whom he released from the irons in which he found them locked.

'Rich man, poor man, everyone says we should not camp here. Let's go then and pitch our tents away from the battlefield. We'll have people search the hills and valleys for Rennewart, and we shall dismount on a nice field where there are not so many corpses lying around. We have won this victory, albeit with losses, against the superior forces of proud, noble heathendom. So have a manly mind! Then many a man who is now overcome with grief and is wrestling with his anguish will follow your example.

'Where has a princely peer of yours ever brought about such a great defeat? Since Adam's time no defeat of comparable dimensions has ever taken place until now. We saw the heathens fighting boldly as they fled. What if Rennewart has been taken captive while pursuing them? If that's what has happened, then we have good hostages to exchange for him, for the King of Skandinavia has been captured in the Larkant while defending himself stoutly. We have twenty or more noble kings and lofty princes, each one of whom is so valuable that Terramer will want him back, and we can exchange him for Rennewart. Now you should see to it – the time has come for this – that people hand over to you all the heathens who were captured on the field, in the ford and on the sea in all the ships. You should demand all such hostages as protection for your land. Tell them that you don't want their treasure. Every prince here will realize what necessity compels you to this step. Ride to all the camp-sites. Your father and your brothers shall be with you when you address the men. We have the larger part of the hostages anyway. Be happy now when your remember that God has honoured you here and increased your fame.'

Willehalm looked at Bernart and spoke to that duke, saying: 'God knows what He has done, but believe me, brave, experienced man that you are, if you are so perceptive, this victory has wrought a defeat in my heart since I have lost good friends, in whom all my happiness lay. Alas for the one day and now for the second day! On the one day I lost Vivianz and six other princes and all my men. I alone was able to escape by fighting. My best support perished there. That enormous loss drove me to seek your aid and that of many a man who cared to think of his loyalty and ventured to help me. Yesterday was that second day, and I can say this of both of them: any joy that my heart ever gained has been paid out to them in tribute.

'Nevertheless, I am in a position in which I have to act as if I were happy, which, alas, I am not. It is the duty of a leader to live boldly and give an example to his men. Ride with me throughout the army. I trust that the leader of every camp-site, wherever camp has been pitched, will not refuse to give me whatever heathens he has alive there.'

They rode and carried that out. All the high nobles from the heathen army who had been captured were brought to the meadow before Heimrich's tent. He kept guard over them for his son. Willehalm, the Marquis, could count it as a high honour to have in his power all the nobles from all the heathen lands who had been captured there. The King of Skandinavia was well known for his virtue. Nowhere in all the various heathen lands were there women who had ever given birth to such an excellent son since the time of Eve. Such was his reputation. The Margrave accepted his word of honour, but the others were quickly clapped in irons. Of them, twenty-five in number were lords of countries. After they had left

the battlefield they had been captured at the sea defending their
Admirat.

The Margrave spoke with propriety, saying: 'There is one thing I
know very well about you, King Matribleiz, and that is that you are
truly related to my wife. Because of that you shall be honoured here
by all of whom I request it. You have lived your life nobly and so
properly that there has never been known a crowned head over a
king's heart to which higher renown in such fullness could be
attributed. I can praise you in every respect for your courage and
loyalty, for your unstinting generosity and for your constancy that
knows no change. I shall tell you my intent and what I shall ask of
you, highly honoured man, and trust in you to carry it out. Take
some of these prisoners who can be trusted on their word and on their
chance for salvation to tell the truth and gather together from the
battlefield the kings who lie slain there and identify them properly by
name and country. They shall be lifted carefully from the ground and
kept so that they do not fall prey to wolves or ravens. We shall
preserve them in a more dignified way for the sake of her who is of
their race. Whatever kinsmen Giburc has lost here shall be embalmed
liberally with balsam and lie in state regally, as if he had died in his
own realm.'

Matribleiz immediately cast himself at Willehalm's feet, but he
was quickly lifted up again. He thanked the Marquis, saying that this
deed had set the seal upon all his renown and had showered his
loyalty with praise so that his fortune would ever blossom and his
much-proclaimed virtue too. And Matribleiz continued: 'Neither our
fighting nor our noble gods helped us to avoid suffering this great
defeat for all to see. It is burdensome for my heart to admit that we
fled. My noble god Kahun knows that his servant Matribleiz was
never born to flee. I was seen fighting indeed – the Christian army
will tell you that – but I was seized while fighting and forced into the
Larkant, not captured in flight. But praising myself does not help,
since I am a prisoner here. If we had all defended ourselves better,
more of the heathens would have escaped with their lives, and the
Admirat would have got away without losing his renown.'

The Margrave told him about a heartrending discovery that he
had made, saying: 'When the son of Kanabeus was defeated by the

sea, every Christian who wanted to take something with him did so. I found a tall, wide marquee of white velvet standing at Terramer's camp-site. A priest of the heathen faith was in charge there. I had been slashed through my helmet and came riding into the tent half-dead, not looking for any booty. I found twenty-three biers and an equal number of slain kings lying there with their crowns. Their names are not concealed, rather at the end of each bier there is an epitaph on a broad tablet of gold. I am sure that whoever provided the rich setting for them loved them. Each letter on the tablets was fashioned with jewels, and all the biers were beautifully decorated. You can read their names plainly and the realms from which each one stemmed and how he had lost his life. I was sorry that I was there, but I read some of them and asked the priest who had paid for all of that. He said it was the Admirat. My banner has been protecting that tent, for I had it placed in front of it and ordered my men to see to it that the priest should lose nothing that was there. My wound was responsible for my having found that. I saw many a cask of balsam there.

'Your Highness, I am telling you this so that the priest will give you some balsam if we need it, and I now release to you whatever else is in the tent. Carry the noble dead from Christian soil to where they will be buried properly, according to their own religion. First, let me supply you with strong mules to transport the kings who have been slain here, and the people to attend the biers on bridges, in fords and along the roads. If you need and desire more I shall grant it. No restrictions are to be placed on you here. Just ask, whatever is mine is at your disposal. You are hereby released from your word of honour.

'Your Highness, as I asked you to do before, ride out on to the battlefield and over the bloody traces. Whatever kings you find there bring them to Terramer, who launched his huge invasion through no fault of mine and whose grace and favour I would like to earn, if I dared seek it, in whatever way he might command, except for asking me to renounce Almighty God and to lose my Christian baptism and to give back my lovely wife. Indeed, I would sooner send many men to their deaths, as you have seen here. Your Highness, you may tell him when you get there that I am not sending the dead kings that are here out of fear. I am simply showing respect for his family, a sweet member of which it has been my pleasure to hold in my arms and who has often made me sad and happy since the day Tibalt attacked me. I could have handled him well enough, if the Admirat, who has now attacked me here, had wanted to stay in Baldac with the Baruc.

'I commend you, King Matribleiz, to Him who knows the number of the stars and who gave us the light of the moon. May you be in His care, and may He bring you to Gaheviez, for your heart has never abandoned virtue.'

The Margrave then gave safe conduct to that highly respected man and to the dead kings who had been found. Thus he left the land of the Provençals.

A SECOND
INTRODUCTION

WOLFRAM VON ESCHENBACH: HIS LIFE AND WORKS

Despite the fact that there is no historical evidence to document the life of Wolfram von Eschenbach, we probably know more about him than about any German poet of the High Middle Ages. Not only is he hailed by some contemporaries as the greatest poet, but he also speaks repeatedly about himself in his works, and his numerous asides give us insight into his personality. There is, of course, the possibility that he is concealing his real self behind the mask of a narrator, but if we take him at his word, a definite picture of Wolfram emerges. He was a man of extremely modest means, claiming that a mouse would find little to eat in his poor house. Through a reference to his daughter's doll we assume that he was a family man. We may also infer from his works that he valued the institution of marriage highly, marriage based on loving partnership of husband and wife.

We are less certain of his social standing. He does boast of being a fighting man, but whether he was a knight or even of the class of the *ministeriales*, we are not sure. He was surely dependent on a patron or patrons, if not for his livelihood, at least for the sources of his poetic works. We know he spent some time at the court of Landgrave Hermann I of Thuringia. Parts of *Parzival* were composed there, and in all likelihood Hermann commissioned *Willehalm*. Wolfram states that he obtained his source from Hermann, and it was probably at Hermann's court, a centre of literary activity of the day, that Wolfram became acquainted with the works of Heinrich von Veldeke, Hartmann von Aue, Gottfried von Strassburg, Walther von der Vogelweide and Neidhart von Reuenthal, to all of whom or to whose works he makes reference. Other works of literature with which he was acquainted include *Nibelungenlied, Rolandslied* and *Kaiserchronik.*

Despite all his knowledge of contemporary literature it is quite likely that Wolfram could neither read nor write. At least that appears to be his claim. In fact, he even seems proud of his analphabetism, yet he also delights in displaying his vast store of knowledge, however acquired. It is difficult for us, dependent as we are on the written word, to believe it possible for someone to have composed over 40,000 lines of poetry without being able to read or write, but in an age when only comparatively few possessed such skills, extensive compensation for the lack of them is, perhaps, not out of the question. Certainly there is no evidence in Wolfram's works of a formal (Latin) education, the only way he might have learned to read and write, and we note also that Wolfram always says 'I heard', when referring to his source, never 'I read', clearly indicating oral transmission of the material. Still, some scholars are extremely sceptical of the validity of Wolfram's statements and point out that his supposed inability to read and write could be a consciously adopted pose, that his method of composition is not that of oral-formulaic poetry but rather that of the literary author who maintains a critical distance between himself and his tale despite appearances to the contrary. They believe that his works may indeed have been intended for reading before a responsive audience – 'oral' transmission in that sense – but they are convinced that Wolfram intended a 'set' text that allowed for no variations and must have had a written basis. There are obviously strong arguments on both sides of the question, and the strangeness of medieval literature to the modern mind makes a definitive answer difficult, if not impossible. Be that as it may, Wolfram must have understood some French, whether he read it or it was read to him, but, by his own admission, he probably did not speak it very well. At any rate, he did not have the schooling of a cleric, and he is referred to as a layman by a contemporary, Wirnt von Gravenberg,[1] though he was obviously a man of deep religious feeling.

The small town of Eschenbach, renamed Wolframs-Eschenbach in 1917, in northern Bavaria is probably where Wolfram originated, but again there are no records to prove it. Nevertheless, because of references to places and people located in that area in Wolfram's works, it is reasonably certain. A von Eschenbach family is attested to there from 1268, probably well after Wolfram's death, but we lose track of it in the second half of the fourteenth century.

Wolfram's own dates and the dating of his works are even more uncertain. As we have said, there is no record of his birth or death. We are forced to rely on references to historical events in his works, and these, of course, are subject to various interpretations. However, a few dates are significant: in *Parzival* Book VII, Wolfram compares the battlefield outside the besieged city of Bearosche with the trampled vineyards around Erfurt, caused by the siege of that city, to which King Philipp of Swabia had fled in 1203–4. Wolfram comments that one can still see the traces of that siege. Therefore, we may conclude that at least *Parzival* Book VII could not have been composed before 1204. How old Wolfram may have been at that time we can only guess, but scholars set the beginning of work on *Parzival* between 1200 and 1210.

Willehalm followed *Parzival*. Wolfram names himself as the author in the prologue of *Willehalm* and identifies himself as the author of *Parzival*. We do not know how soon after the completion of *Parzival* he started work on *Willehalm*, but there are three historical events mentioned in *Willehalm* which may help. In 1212 a new siege weapon, the *drîboc*, or *trabucium* in Latin, a catapult, was first used in Germany, and Wolfram names the *drîboc* in a list of siege machines around Orange in *Willehalm* Book III. The only firm conclusion to be drawn from this is that Book III could not have been composed before 1212. That same year marked the coronation of Frederick II as Holy Roman Emperor in opposition to Otto IV. Otto had succeeded in getting himself crowned Emperor in Rome on 4 October 1209, but he had had to withdraw from the city in the face of an aroused populace. Wolfram makes a mocking reference to Otto's coronation in *Willehalm* (p. 194), something he could hardly have done before 1212.

Finally, Wolfram mentions his patron, Landgrave Hermann of Thuringia, in *Willehalm* Book VIII, in a way that seems to indicate that Hermann was already dead. If that interpretation of the passage is correct, then *Willehalm* Book VIII could not have been composed before 25 April 1217, the day of Hermann's death. Therefore, we can say that work on *Willehalm* began some time after 1212 and was concluded or stopped (see discussion of ending, p. 268ff) some time after 1217. This is obviously not very satisfactory, but it is the best we can do in dating *Willehalm*. The second decade of the thirteenth century seems most likely, but there are some scholars who believe in an even later dating.

In reviewing Wolfram's literary production, we have not yet mentioned his songs, nine in number, and the so-called *Titurel* fragments, which total some 170 stanzas in two groups. The majority of the songs ascribed to Wolfram are dawn-songs, or albas, which describe the parting of lovers at daybreak. Scholars have had little success in establishing a chronology, but the songs are generally assigned to Wolfram's early years, before *Parzival*. The *Titurel* fragments tell of the tragic love of Schionatulander and Sigune, two youthful lovers who figure in *Parzival*. Wolfram apparently planned an independent development of their story and for whatever reason never carried it to completion. The fragments are thought to have been composed after *Willehalm*, or at least after *Willehalm* Book VIII.

When and why Wolfram stopped work on *Willehalm* and/or the Schionatulander–Sigune tale is uncertain. Two possibilities spring immediately to mind: the death of Hermann of Thuringia in 1217 (or of his son Ludwig in 1227, if one accepts a later dating), resulting in the loss of Wolfram's patron; or Wolfram's own death. Ulrich von Türheim, who took it upon himself to compose a lengthy continuation of *Willehalm*, laments the death of Wolfram, but Ulrich's words may be more significant as a rhetorical device than for our chronology of Wolfram.[2] We are simply unable to answer such questions definitively.

'ALISCANS': WOLFRAM'S OLD FRENCH SOURCE

The source of Wolfram's *Willehalm* is readily identified as a version of the Old French *chanson de geste*, *La Bataille d'Aliscans*, one of a cycle of twenty-four poems of that genre which deal with the exploits of Guillaume d'Orange (Willehalm, William) and members of his family. The other *chanson de geste* cycles deal with the deeds (Old French *geste*, from Latin *res gestae*) of Charlemagne, most notably *Le Chanson de Roland*, and the stories of the rebel barons. These are heroic epics, full of combat and the feats of knights, imbued with a strong feeling of French nationalism. We know very little about the development of the *chansons*. Presumably they were composed during the course of the twelfth century in northern France by *jongleurs*, nameless minstrels who travelled from court to court or town to town, reciting their works to attentive audiences. Almost all the *chansons* have some basis in historical fact, but there are great variations, and the manuscripts themselves, even of the same poem, show wide divergences, so that it is difficult to establish what the original texts were, if indeed they were ever written down. The 'historical' events were already three hundred years or more old at the time the *chansons* were composed. Fact had ample time to become embellished and intermingled with fancy.

Guillaume, the central figure in *Aliscans*, bears some relation to the historical Count William of Toulouse. William was a grandson of Charles Martell, hence a cousin of Charlemagne, and attained his position under the latter and the latter's son, Louis, King of Aquitaine, who later became the Emperor Louis the Pious. Toulouse was one of the most important outposts of the realm in view of the hostility of the Basques and the Arabs in Spain, and William was able to maintain some semblance of order in that area. However, in 793, the Arabs invaded the Spanish March, captured Gerona, proceeded along the coast towards Narbonne, then headed inland towards Carcassone. They were met by William and a small number of Frankish nobles at a small river, the Orbieu. Here William distinguished himself by his brave feats of arms but was forced to withdraw because of severe losses to his command. Although they had defeated him, the Arabs turned back towards Spain, having also suffered heavy casualties. This is perhaps the most notable of William's exploits, but he did participate later in the siege and ultimate conquest of Barcelona in 801, the most important victory during Louis' reign in Aquitaine. In that campaign William had command of the rearguard and was honoured by Louis as *primus signifer*. After a threatening army attempting to relieve the beleaguered city had withdrawn without a fight, William and his men joined the actual siege.

William's renown is not based on his achievements as a knight alone. He was known perhaps even more for his work in the Church and for taking monastic vows himself in the last decade of his life. In 804 he established and endowed a monastery in the valley of Gellone – still in existence today as Saint-Guilhem-du-Désert – and in 806 renounced his worldly possessions and entered the monastery as a simple monk. Here he was noted for his strict observance of monastic regulations. He died on 28 May 813, and was canonized in 1066. He is venerated on 28 May.

If one compares this historical information about William with the events in *Aliscans*, it is obvious that a transformation has taken place. But we see only the beginning and the end of the process. There must have been many intermediate stages where imaginative minds were at work, where deeds of other men became identified with William, where something imperfectly understood or remembered was explained as something quite different, where other characters joined the emerging story, where new episodes were added or where the location of events was shifted. What remains constant is the figure of William, the courageous fighter against the Saracens, who is defeated in one battle in the face of overwhelming odds but who puts them to flight in a second encounter and who eventually enters a monastery and later becomes a saint.

We do know that popular songs circulated about William shortly after his death, and there is other evidence of the development of the material about William, but the earliest literary version that we have is the *Chançun de Willame*, composed in the early twelfth century.[3] Not much later a Latin *Vita Sancti Wilhelmi* was written, which, although nominally biographical, shows evidence of the influence of a poetic tradition.[4] We must look to the second half of the twelfth century for the composition of the *Aliscans* version that Wolfram must have known. This was a version of *Aliscans* similar to those extant today, a *chanson de geste* of over 8,000 lines.[5] We do not have the actual manuscript that Wolfram used, nor is any one of the extant manuscripts a copy of the one he must have had. Only one, the Arsenal manuscript (Paris), is possibly old enough, but it differs from what Wolfram's source must have been in several important respects and is clearly not in the tradition of his source.

Of the thirteen *Aliscans* manuscripts which we have, twelve are cyclical manuscripts: that is, they contain not only *Aliscans* but other *chansons* of the Guillaume-cycle, including some of the *geste Rainouart* which Wolfram probably did not know. The collecting of *chansons* of the same cycle in a single manuscript seems to have begun in the thirteenth century, for the oldest *chanson* texts of whatever cycle are not cyclical. It is likely that Wolfram's source was also not cyclical. This would lead us to believe that it might have been closer to the one extant non-cyclical manuscript of *Aliscans*, the St Mark's manuscript (Venice), but this is a fourteenth-century manuscript with many errors and omissions. However, it is very probable that Wolfram's source was in that manuscript tradition, that it differed from extant manuscripts but no more than they differ among themselves.

'WILLEHALM' AND 'ALISCANS': A COMPARISON

Even a superficial comparison of *Willehalm* and *Aliscans* assures us of one thing: Wolfram's work is anything but a translation of *Aliscans*. The very form of the two poems reveals a basic difference: *Aliscans* is composed in tirades, stanzas of a varying number of ten-syllabic, assonating lines. Each tirade, or *laisse*, has a certain individuality or independence, although closely related to the preceding and subsequent tirade. There seems to be a central idea in each *laisse*, such as a specific event in the general course of the action, a speech by one of the principals or an exchange of words among several. Each *laisse* usually begins with a few lines which recapitulate the content of the preceding *laisse*. Then the new subject matter of the *laisse* is presented and brought to a definite conclusion at the end. The concluding lines in turn frequently form the starting-point for the transitional introductory lines of the next tirade. Thus, a sort of building-block technique is characteristic of *Aliscans*. In *Willehalm*, on the other hand, the rhyming couplets of the courtly epic are used throughout, with four stresses per line. Wolfram does observe a kind of 'paragraph' of thirty lines which frequently begins with a new topic, but such sections or divisions of the text are clearly not stanzas, and new topics often begin in the middle of a 'paragraph' or elsewhere. There is a continuous, flowing narrative, at least within the conventional divisions into books. To be sure, there are instances where Wolfram appears to have translated rather closely, but such are the exception rather than the rule.

Willehalm is actually a reworking of *Aliscans*. While Wolfram sticks to the general outline of the action (that is, almost all the events in his source are narrated), he exhibits considerable independence in the precise sequence of the events. This is especially evident in the structure of the two battles. In *Aliscans*, one has the impression of a series of individual clashes between knights, whereas in *Willehalm* one can see how Wolfram has organized each battle so that the fighting develops organically, as wave after wave of heathens attack the Christians. Of course, individual duels are part of the whole picture, but they are sometimes rearranged to emphasize the progress of the battles and to become linked as part of the whole. In contrast to *Aliscans* where one event follows the other chronologically, Wolfram has changed the sequence to take into account the events that are happening simultaneously, a considerable advance in sophistication of narrative technique.

Along with rearrangement of the events there is also considerable expansion in the narration. Wolfram has almost doubled the number of lines of *Aliscans*. It is, of course, difficult to judge how much of this increase is due to inherent differences in the two languages, but there are several obvious reasons. *Aliscans* is characterized by its directness in presentation of the material. Description is kept to a minimum, and the events move with swiftness and vigour. *Willehalm*, as we have noted, is carefully organized. It has a gradual, slowly unfolding development, characterized by careful preparation. Wolfram likes to explain what is happening and to account for all loose ends in the strands of his narrative. He frequently provides motivation for events which occur without apparent reason in *Aliscans*, especially those which must have seemed unrealistic or unnatural to him, and he allows himself time to give his own personal views on what is transpiring in his tale.

One small example may serve for many. In *Aliscans* at the close of the first battle, Telamons is brought in quite abruptly (597f.). He is described as riding through reeds on his horse, Marcepiere, ahead of the others. Guillaume kills Telamons and seizes his horse, only to have it stolen away by the onrushing heathens (680ff.). In *Willehalm*, when the corresponding figure, Talimon, appears, we have already heard his name before. He had been mentioned as a member of King Josweiz' body-guard (p. 31). He joins the pursuit of Willehalm (p. 41) and a few lines later his horse, Marschibeiz, is mentioned. Willehalm kills Talimon and leads his horse away. Then, when Willehalm is attacked on all sides, Wolfram says: 'He [Willehalm] was forced to abandon the captured horse and killed it with a thrust behind its shoulders. He did not want to leave it for the heathens, as happens in fighting even now' (p. 41). We can readily see on a small scale the preparation, the realistic motivation and description and the author's personal observation. But that is not the end of Talimon! He is mentioned on several other occasions along with other fallen heathen noblemen (pp. 65, 109, 131, 171, 180), giving a greater sense of unity, cohesion and organization to the work. In *Aliscans* Telamons is not heard of again.

Another very important point of comparison is the attitude towards the heathens expressed in each work. This, too, has a bearing on the expansion in Wolfram's version. Put very briefly (but see the section on religion, p. 273ff.), *Aliscans* depicts the heathens as inhuman monsters, who deserve to be slaughtered by the Christians. Wolfram, on the other hand, sees them as courtly knights, every bit as chivalrous as the Christians. Exotic in appearance they may be (and Wolfram delights in describing them and their fabulously wealthy lands), but each one is brave and is fighting to gain the reward of a lovely lady. In the battle scenes in *Aliscans*, as a result, the narrative focus is entirely on the Christians, whereas in *Willehalm* the scenes are shaped more symmetrically, with a dual focus on the Christians and the heathens. Wolfram talks first about one side and then turns immediately to the other. The death of a noble heathen is balanced by the death of a Christian knight. In the case of

Mile, in the first battle, Wolfram seems to have introduced a figure not in his source, primarily to achieve such a balance: Willehalm kills the heathen Pinel, and Terramer slays Mile. Wolfram repeatedly stresses the losses and suffering on *both* sides, while *Aliscans* is concerned only with the Christians. Some scholars surmise that Wolfram's source may have been more kindly disposed towards the heathens than the extant versions of the text, but it seems unlikely that such a source would have had the well-developed, consistently applied dual focus of *Willehalm*. That is surely Wolfram's own design.

In contrast to *Aliscans*, Wolfram is quite skilful in maintaining a sense of proportion in his story. Willehalm is the central figure. About that there can be no doubt, but in *Aliscans*, in the first battle, Viviens is unquestionably the centre of attention and Guillaume is practically overlooked, at least until Viviens falls unconscious. Wolfram has kept the role of his Vivianz almost intact, but he has assigned a greater share of the spotlight to Willehalm. He brings Willehalm in repeatedly so that the audience never loses sight of him, while in *Aliscans*, after a brief mention at the beginning, Guillaume virtually disappears, as Viviens occupies centre-stage.

One of the major changes that Wolfram has made is in the treatment of Rennewart. Here, too, he seems to be seeking to maintain Willehalm as the central figure, for in *Aliscans* Rainouart virtually takes over the story in the second battle. The figure of Rainouart obviously captured the imagination of the *jongleurs* who narrated the poem. Almost from the entrance of Rainouart into the poem the manuscript tradition shows wide divergence, with numerous additions describing his exploits in detail. If one were to follow all the variants of *Aliscans*, one would have to believe that Rainouart won the second battle single-handed. Now it may be that the version of *Aliscans* that Wolfram used as his source did not have Rainouart perform quite so many feats of arms as in other versions, and some scholars believe this to be the case, but it is quite certain that Wolfram keeps Rennewart subordinate to Willehalm, even though it is still clear that Rennewart is a decisive factor in the second battle. Not only has Wolfram reduced the

share of attention which Rennewart receives, but he has also trans-
formed the character of Rennewart (see the section on Rennewart,
pp. 248–52).

We have concentrated our attention on sketching the general
differences between *Aliscans* and *Willehalm*. There are many more
specific ones that could be mentioned, such as things that would have
meant something only to a German audience: references to places
and events, to contemporaries and their literary works, to German
heroic poetry and mythology. Naturally, *Aliscans* has none of these,
but there are other things too, like the discussion of religion between
Giburc and her father, begun in Book III and concluded in Book V,
and the miraculous appearance of the sarcophagi for the fallen
Christian heroes of the first battle. These are not in extant versions of
Aliscans and again illustrate the considerable independence of his
source that Wolfram exercises. Still, the events of *Aliscans* are all
there by and large. They may be rearranged, added to, transformed,
expanded, diminished, commented upon or corrected, but Wolfram,
like all medieval poets, calls upon the authority of his source while
telling his tale and cannot stray too far from it, especially since
Aliscans was undoubtedly well known to his audience.

GIBURC AND WILLEHALM

Central to any interpretation of Wolfram's *Willehalm* must be the
human relationship which is at its core and the two people whose love
and marriage are linked, early in the work, with the suffering and
deaths of many men: 'Willehalm won the love of Arabel, and because
of this innocent people died' (p. 21). Inseparable from their love is
Arabel's baptism. As Wolfram has made clear in *Parzival*, in the
marriage of Feirefiz and Repanse de Schoye, and as Giburc herself
will explain later, human love and the love of God are totally
compatible forces. Just as Feirefiz seeks to be baptized when he
wishes to marry the Grail Bearer, so does Giburc seldom separate the
two motives: it is not that the one consistently comes first, but that the
two go hand in hand. Thus she declares to her father: 'I have accepted
baptism for the sake of Him who created all living things, water and

fire, as well as earth and air', but then she asks him: 'Shall I renounce Christ and the Margrave for the sake of Mahmete . . .?' (p. 114). Very shortly afterwards, in the same speech, she reverses the order, when, speaking of Willehalm, she says: 'It is for his sake that I have determined to observe poverty, and for the sake of Him who is the Highest.' Immediately after, however, she goes on to assert her allegiance to God the Creator, and this, one of the principal statements of the supreme power of Altissimus, can leave no doubt of the sincerity of her conviction. Later, in her speech to the assembly, she takes up the theme again: 'I serve the Hand of God the Artist in place of the heathen god Tervigant' (p. 157), and she denies the accusation that she has brought about this war for the sake of human love. She moves, in this speech, to an admission of guilt, assumed by herself alone, 'for the sake of the grace of Almighty God, and also to some extent for the sake of the Marquis'.

Such unambiguous linking of Giburc's love for Willehalm and her love of God in no way casts doubt upon her baptism. Indeed, the fervour of her faith is never in question. Nor is that of Willehalm, 'the knight who never forgot God', as Wolfram puts it in his opening prayer. The faith of both of them is firm, though it is sorely tested during the course of the events of which the poem tells. It has been said that, in this respect, *Willehalm* begins where *Parzival* left off, for *Parzival* had told of one man's struggle to achieve a firm faith and a true understanding of his relationship with God. Such struggle, if there has been one, is behind Giburc and Willehalm. Giburc never refers to any conflict which she may have faced when she had to leave her home, together with her husband and her children, in order to go away with Willehalm and become a Christian. Suffering there is, of course, in her present situation: 'God knows that I have laid up in my heart such a store of grief that my body is hardly able to bear it' (p. 155), she tells the men assembled for the second battle, but this is the suffering which she shares with Willehalm and all his kinsmen who have lost so much on the field of Alischanz, as well as the suffering which she alone must bear, in knowing herself to be the cause of the fighting and, as such, to bear the hatred of both sides. Her tears flow copiously as she recalls the loss of friends and relatives in the first battle; they flow again as she comes to the end of her great speech in Book VI: 'Indeed, my joy lies slain with them' (p. 157), she declares, and her grief is clear for all to see. Yet such demonstrations of grief are shown by Wolfram to be coupled with Giburc's capacity for love which lifts her grief out of despair and gives a new hope to the work. In the first case it is love for Willehalm, as the two of them lie together when he has returned to Orange; in the second, this intimate relationship has widened into love for all his kin and all her kin, and it finds expression in her appeal for mercy towards all the creatures of God. Aware as she is of hatred directed at her from both sides, she asks God to compensate them for their suffering and so she is able to turn her own suffering into a positive quality, transcending her own grief in order to look towards the mercy of the Father on all His creatures. These are the significant thoughts of the work, expressed most powerfully and originally by Wolfram, through a woman, and a woman who was once a heathen.

To Giburc Wolfram gives the designation 'saintly lady' in the brief address which opens Book IX. Giburc is not, of course, a saint of the Church. It is Wolfram who sees her in this light and balances his appeal to St Willehalm for salvation with this later appeal to the wife of Willehalm, beseeching her to grant that he may join her in the world to come (p. 199). These lines come in the middle of the second battle, cutting across the horror of the carnage and looking beyond the present events which have seemed to oppress the narrator so, towards the peace of his soul. The lines are telling, too, for the perspective which they put on those events: we are reminded suddenly that this is the account of a battle fought long ago and that Giburc and those who fought for her on the field of Alischanz are long since dead. Thus Wolfram, for all his involvement with his story, seems suddenly to be releasing himself from it. Though he returns straight away to his account, and is immediately plunged back into the grim descriptions of the fighting, these moments are important. Over the remainder of the poem there hangs the memory of this prayer, so that Willehalm's conversation with Matribleiz, his gesture in releasing him because he is a relative of Giburc and, more than that, in honouring the dead kings of the race of Terramer, out of love for her, and, finally, his commendation of Matribleiz to the Creator, can all be interpreted in the light of the sanctity of Giburc.

She it is who alone has raised her voice in an appeal for mercy for the heathens; only she has spoken of the kinship of all mankind through God the Father; and she alone has shown the capacity to answer hate with love. It must be these things which make her a saint in the eyes of Wolfram. She is above all a loving and suffering human being, while Giburc herself speaks significantly of her 'poverty'. She does not mean, first and foremost, material poverty, though, relatively speaking, she has made material sacrifices in leaving her heathen kingdom to become the wife of the Margrave. Her meaning becomes clear in her words to her father at the beginning of Book V. The poverty to which she refers is the whole way of life which she has assumed, and gladly assumed, along with the greatest spiritual wealth which she knows to be hers, both now and in the life to come. She desires only to 'observe poverty', and she appeals to her father: 'Let me live in poverty.' Poverty, then, that essential Christian concept, is central to the character of Wolfram's Giburc and, with charity, manifested in her all-embracing love for the creatures of God, it leads to his designation of her as 'saintly lady'.

Yet Giburc is no remote, unworldly figure – far from it. Her sanctity exists for Wolfram, it seems, in her capacity to live within the world, to suffer what the world has to offer her and to rise above that suffering in order to bear the message of the work. Thus we see her fully involved in the events of the poem. She defends Orange during the absence of Willehalm and is prepared to defend it with her sword; she lands on the ruse of setting up dead men on the battlements in order to deceive the enemy; she converses boldly and outspokenly with her father who is laying siege to Orange and threatening her personally with death. These are qualities of courage which Wolfram admires in her, but no less does he admire her gentler qualities, the traditional feminine attributes which she possesses to the full. She is delighted to dress in beautiful feminine garments when her husband returns and her duty becomes, not to defend the city in armour, but to give him the consolation which only she can give. The scenes of tender love-making, gently described by Wolfram yet leaving no doubt of the sensuous nature of this lovely woman, are as much a part of the total action as the scenes of war. Repeatedly Wolfram speaks, either himself or through Willehalm and Giburc, of the compensation which their deep mutual love affords them for the losses sustained.

We see Giburc, too, in her relationship with Rennewart, experiencing a shock of half-recognition and yet not venturing to express what she feels, except to her father-in-law Heimrich, with whom we see her in a special relationship of warmth and confidence. She concerns herself, of course, with the well-being of her wounded and weary husband, but, equally, with the provisions for the visitors. She betrays her entirely natural human fear when she begs Willehalm not to respond to the enticements of the ladies he may meet in France while he is away from her but to remain true to her and remember what she is enduring. It is his idea to convert this request into a solemn oath to know no joy until he has released her and to consume only bread and water. This oath, given to Giburc by Willehalm as he departs at the end of Book II, means that, during his ride to Laon and through so many momentous events, the memory of Giburc is firmly there, in the mind of Willehalm, and of Wolfram's audience. Again and again, when Willehalm declines fine nourishment, a comfortable bed, the kiss of greeting of his relatives, Wolfram recalls Giburc, left behind in peril in Orange. Moreover, the peril is a reality for us, for the beginning of Book III has seen the heathen forces preparing for a siege and the agony of Terramer, determined to avenge the shame inflicted upon his gods, even if it means the death of his daughter. As Willehalm and the forces he has amassed gallop towards Orange, they see the fiery glow in the sky which signifies the physical danger of Giburc. The opening of Book V shows Giburc in armour, physically defending the city, but, in this central conversation with Terramer, defending her faith with words too.

The time between the arrival of the forces in Orange and their assembly is filled with Giburc in her other roles, as wife and hostess, deeply concerned for the well-being of the visitors and moved by the strange young Saracen who has arrived with her husband's retinue. The famous speech to the assembly of noblemen can be seen as a continuation of her conversation with her father. She continues to uphold her faith and her decision to desert her heathen husband, but it is the impressive opening of her speech which presents the new and vital theme of mercy to God's creatures. As Giburc watches the departing troops from the windows, Wolfram places the outcome of the battle in the hands of God 'who takes care of everything' (p. 158). He seems to be reasserting the link between the men and the woman who is watching them: they go into battle with her words ringing in their ears.

No more is seen of Giburc and we are left to wonder if, indeed, Wolfram intended to bring her back into the poem, in a conclusion which told, perhaps, of the return of Rennewart and his reunion with his sister (see p. 270ff.). What we do have is still significant, for Willehalm's treatment of Matribleiz, and the words which accompany his gesture, can be interpreted as mercy: the husband acts now in accordance with the exhortation of his wife. The abstract thought of the work, so effectively placed in the mouth of Giburc, is given concrete expression by Willehalm.

It would seem, indeed, that, as far as Willehalm is concerned, sanctity lies for Wolfram in deeds. Already in the prologue, Wolfram is speaking of his hero as an exemplary knight who often wore armour and who knew the straps which bind the helmet to the head. Familiar as he is with danger, all knights in trouble can turn to him for help. It is this theme of 'help' which links the prayer to the Trinity with which the prologue opens with the address to St Willehalm. Hoping himself for the help of God, Wolfram can ask for help, too, from Willehalm, whom he twice refers to as 'helper', for Willehalm has often received the help of the Hand of the All Highest. This he has striven for by deeds of valour and by demonstrations of his purity and his humility.

Never again, however, does Wolfram refer to his hero as a saint, and the question of the sanctity of Willehalm is central to a consideration of his character. The Middle Ages regarded William of Gellone as a saint, and Wolfram's source presented him as such. Wolfram seems to have accepted this designation but the question remains of whether he has himself presented Willehalm the saint, or whether his address in the prologue anticipates a future state which lies beyond the framework of his poem. In other words: do the *deeds* to which Wolfram refers mean those performed by Willehalm the knight, or is he looking forward to the later stage of his life, in the monastery of Gellone which he founded and to which he withdrew after his career of chivalry? The latter alternative would suggest that Wolfram intended to pursue the account of the life of Willehalm and, in accordance with the cycle, to end it with the death of Willehalm the saint. This is pure surmise which lacks concrete support, for at no point in his poem does Wolfram betray such an intention. Perhaps, on the other hand, he was presuming in his audience the knowledge of the events in the life of St Willehalm which lie outside his immediate concern and not intending to present the Willehalm of his poem as a saint at all. Or perhaps, as a final alternative, he means us to see the achievement of sanctity in the Willehalm he does portray.

Such questions can hardly receive firm answers and the final possibility is bound up with another matter which has exercised critics. Are we witnessing the progress of a man towards the sanctity proclaimed in the prologue? Does Willehalm *develop* during the course of the work? On this point opinion is divided. Some scholars, though recognizing that Wolfram is much concerned in *Parzival* with the development of characters, reject the possibility in *Willehalm* which is based, not on a courtly romance, but on a *chanson de geste*, in which interest centres on events, not on characters. This somewhat misleading objection on the grounds of a technicality may in any case be disputed if one points to the nature of *Willehalm*: based on a *chanson de geste* it may be, but what has emerged is a unique work of no established genre (see the discussion of genre, p. 279ff.), which has more affinities with courtly than with heroic literature. Yet, given that one admits the possibility of character development, there remains the question of whether we do witness an actual development in *Willehalm*, or whether what seem like changes in his attitude and behaviour are simply the different reactions of a man to differing circumstances.

Scholars have seen, above all, a discrepancy between the behaviour of Willehalm after the first battle, when he slays Arofel, and his behaviour after the second battle, when he speaks with compassion and tolerance to Matribleiz and grants heathen burial to the heathen slain, and, finally, commends Matribleiz to the Creator of the Universe. This, for some, shows the achievement of a mature and humane state of mind, the culmination of a process. Willehalm is a different person at the 'end' of the work, raised by suffering and influenced by the stirring words of his wife and her example of all-embracing love. For others, however, no such change is reflected. The Willehalm who slays Arofel in cold blood and robs the corpse of its armour and steals the horse is a man under enormous pressure. He acts against all the accepted rules of chivalry, refusing to heed the pathetic plea for mercy from a terribly wounded and defenceless opponent, but he does so in sheer anger, recalling the death in his arms of his beloved Vivianz and determined to avenge it. When he wrenches the armour from the corpse he seems to be obsessed by the one thought of how best to escape through the enemy and he knows he can ride faster, too, on the superior horse Volatin, now that his own horse is tired and wounded. This is not incredible behaviour in a man who has lost all his troops and whose one thought must now be to return to his wife, who is herself in dire peril, and then turn to the task of seeking more help. When Wolfram allows Willehalm to add the shocking act of cutting off the head of the dead Arofel he shows us, by this brutal and unnecessary deed, how far Willehalm has been pressed by grief and strain. This is not the action of a man who is presented as an exemplary knight, but the desperate, irrational behaviour of an ordinary man blinded by fury.

When, at the site of the monastery, Willehalm speaks of the death of Arofel, it is not, as some have maintained, in a spirit of boasting. It may be that he would never give any account of the episode if he were not forced to some kind of defence when the King refers in deprecating fashion to the apparently frivolous decorations he wore in the grim situation of war. Far from boasting, Willehalm appears to be unburdening his conscience, when he speaks of the rich gifts which Arofel offered in exchange for his life, but all in vain. 'I beheaded the noble King' (p. 108), he tells his hearers, though refraining from saying that he did so only after he had slain him. Clearly, this transgression of knightly conduct is nothing to be proud of. As Wolfram did at the time, Willehalm links the death of Arofel with the death of Vivianz, but by now even this does not seem to justify the act, which Willehalm sees now as an attack on Love itself, since the noble Arofel, whose reputation he upholds, was fighting in the service of Love. Love, as Willehalm sees it, has taken the shield away from him in punishment for this deed. If Willehalm goes on to speak of the other kings whom he slew, he does so less to boast than because the episodes belong together, as part of what he has endured. This certainly would seem to be what Wolfram is implying when, at the end of the long account, he allows Willehalm to return to where he began, to the shield and the armour and the horse of Arofel, and when he comments of those who have been listening: 'Many of those who were sitting and standing there realized that he had suffered greatly, and this was why they did not take exception to his account . . .' (p. 109). This has been the account of enormous suffering, rather than the gratuitous bragging of a thoughtless man.

At the imperial court in Laon, we see Willehalm behaving in an uncontrolled manner, but, again, the situation prompts him to it. He has been ignored on his arrival; his sister has done her best to keep him out; her husband, the King, has appeared slow to acknowledge him, though he owes the imperial crown to Willehalm's support; and now the Queen has tried to prevent her husband from giving him material help. He behaves uncouthly, it is true, and violently, abusing the King with words and his sister physically. Again, one can argue that such behaviour, reprehensible though it undoubtedly is, is explicable in terms of what he has endured and what he believes to be the indifference of his relatives to a desperate predicament. Yet this is the same Willehalm who can move his listeners to tears with his account of the losses at Alischanz and it is the same Willehalm who responds instantly to the entrance of his lovely young niece Alize and seems to regret his uncouth behaviour the moment he sets eyes on her. This Willehalm, too, can respond with concern and kindness when he first sees Rennewart; he can inspire confidence and affection in the young man, who is quick to recognize his essential goodness. We see Willehalm reacting on several occasions in a kindly way to the boy: when his beard is singed, and when he forgets his club.

Such gentle concern does not surprise us either, for we have seen that Willehalm, the fighter, is capable of great tenderness: in conversation with his horse, for example, or, more importantly, in conversation with the dying Vivianz, and during the vigil over his body. There is nothing unmanly about Willehalm's grief at the death of his beloved nephew: Wolfram sees it as another facet of a full character, in which many responses may be resolved into a consistent whole.

Above all, of course, we see the gentle Willehalm in the moving scenes with Giburc. We see the battle-weary man return to his wife, and we have Wolfram's assurance that the love they give to one another is mutual compensation for the grief and losses sustained. When Willehalm rides to seek military support, he gives his wife the assurance of his love, and he keeps his promise to refrain from joy, symbolized in food and drink and all comfort, and in the kiss which he leaves behind him in Orange. The active knight and the loving husband are not two people but two sides of the same composite picture, and in this there is nothing which contradicts what Wolfram tells us elsewhere.

Whether the privation which he undertakes in his absence from Giburc, or his noble fight for the Christian Empire, can be seen to constitute a claim to sanctity is difficult to say with certainty. It may be that, for Wolfram, such aspects of his Willehalm, as well as his tremendous suffering, contribute to the picture of a man who will one day emerge as a saint.

The sufferings of Willehalm, very great after the first battle, reach their climax after the second. Expressing the irony which is basic to the work, and perhaps even to Wolfram's whole view of life, Willehalm, the great leader laid low by grief and suffering, observes: 'This victory has wrought a defeat in my heart' (p. 222). The immediate impetus to the lament is the loss of Rennewart, but this great personal loss is a part of a wider affliction, the many losses sustained in the two battles, and perhaps the sense of a hopeless conflict. He laments the two days which have claimed so dear a tribute from him. Yet the private sorrow of the man for the young nephew, so movingly and tenderly described in Book II, and indeed the tears which he has recently shed for his missing friend Rennewart, must give way to the call of duty: it is, after all, his duty as a leader to cheer his men and to put his own grief aside.

Thus Wolfram moves from the abyss of Willehalm's grief to what may be seen as his greatest moments. In conversation with Matribleiz, King of Skandinavia, he first refers to the relationship between his noble captive and Giburc: this, he explains, is why

Matribleiz is not to be held in chains but bound by his word of honour. Because of this kinship, and because of Matribleiz' reputation as a man of honour, Willehalm entrusts to him the task of collecting the slain heathen kings and having them embalmed in accordance with what he knows to be the heathen custom. Thanking him, Matribleiz refers to Willehalm's own 'much-proclaimed virtue' and goes on to speak of how he was taken prisoner at the River Larkant, he who was known for his courage in battle and would never have taken flight. One senses the despair of this illustrious king, as he tries to account for his presence among the captives and for the defeat which has befallen the heathen army. It may be that Willehalm senses this, too, as he goes on to confide in his royal prisoner, telling him of the chance which caused him to stumble, badly wounded, upon the white velvet tent in which he found twenty-three biers and twenty-three dead heathen kings embalmed upon them. The experience has moved him, for he says that he regretted being there, knowing as he must that some of the men had died at his hand and aware that he was intruding on a precious, though alien, rite. He learnt from the priest that Terramer himself had paid for this embalming and for the costly epitaphs and, already *before* the end of the hostilities, Willehalm had shown his respect for Giburc's relatives and a religious tradition not his own by placing his standard in front of the tent as protection.

What Willehalm now does is an extension of that action: he grants safe passage to Matribleiz to bear the heathen noblemen back home for burial according to their rites. He is prepared to place at his disposal whatever he needs for this process. To Matribleiz himself he gives a message, to be borne to Terramer: that this is not a gesture of fear, but a sign of his respect for his race, which is the race of Giburc.

The reference to Giburc, and to the joy and sadness which he has experienced through her, is important, for it implies the extent to which the thought of her is governing the action of Willehalm. When he, finally, commends Matribleiz to 'Him who knows the number of the stars and who gave us the light of the Moon' (p. 225), the echo of Giburc's words is clear. In different terms, at greater length, she had spoken in Book V of the Creator of all things, and this simpler statement of belief from the knight who only now speaks of the faith which motivates him shows the man united with the woman, Willehalm expressing in his words and in a significant gesture of respect and mercy his response to her appeal.

Whether this amounts to a development is not easy to say, and perhaps it is not that important to decide the question adamantly. It does seem, however, that Willehalm is working something out within his own mind during the course of his meeting with Matribleiz. He releases him from his oath of security, granting him complete freedom to perform what has evidently become a most important task. Earlier, his brother, Bernart of Brabant, had tried to console him for the absence of Rennewart and had offered him the hope that he might be a prisoner somewhere, in which case Matribleiz would be a valuable hostage (p. 221). Willehalm appears not to take up this possibility, or perhaps to allow what has became an issue of still greater concern to take precedence. As the conversation with Matribleiz proceeds, Willehalm is seen as a man moving towards a momentous gesture which arises from his experiences and in no way contradicts what he has done before. One may, of course, see this – and the entire portrayal of Willehalm – as 'development', or one may see it as a reflection of Wolfram's capacity to reveal human nature and human behaviour in the round, to show a complicated picture in which, in the end, the pieces fit.

RENNEWART

Wolfram's source, the Old French *Aliscans*, portrays Rainouart as an uncouth youngster of immense size, who, despite his origin as the son of the great heathen king Desramé, finds himself working at menial tasks in the kitchen of the court of King Louis. When Guillaume arrives there, Rainouart begs him to take him into battle with him. As his only weapon he carries a huge tree-trunk, his *tinel*. He behaves in a gross, insolent way, drinking too much and fighting with the cooks; he forgets his *tinel* repeatedly. He shows a complete lack of self-control, smashing a marble pillar with his *tinel*, hurling the chief cook on to the fire. In the actual battle, on the other hand, he excels himself, killing one heathen after another, motivated as he is not by Christian fervour at all but by a passionate and unexplained hatred for the Saracens. Rainouart, indeed, comes to dominate the battle with his strength and ruthless courage. Afterwards he returns to Orange, where Guibourc tells him for sure what he has long suspected: that she is his sister. He is baptized, and honoured by Guillaume with the position of seneschal. To set the seal on Rainouart's fame and happiness, he marries the Princess Aelis, the lovely young daughter of Louis.

This, then, is the material which Wolfram adapted for his purpose, and his treatment of his source in this respect, as in others, is indicative of his intentions with his work. Rennewart remains, in *Willehalm*, a central figure, yet he may not assume the position of all-importance which he occupied in the source. It is evident, from what we have seen of Wolfram's presentation of Willehalm and Giburc, that this must be so. Moreover, much of the portrayal of his Rennewart in the source must have been displeasing to Wolfram, who takes over only as much as is necessary for the progress of the narrative and, in general, softens the picture of Rennewart, providing explanations for his outbursts and showing him as a young man of considerable self-control, good breeding even, yet sometimes provoked beyond endurance. The burlesque qualities of Rainouart are largely removed and, although Wolfram has retained episodes and characteristics which must have been displeasing to him – Rennewart's roasting of the chef or, in the battle itself, his killing of his brother – the total picture is much gentler. We are presented with a Rennewart who is very much a victim of circumstances and in whom contradictory elements meet.

The very first appearance of Rennewart is already strangely contradictory, as he crosses the courtyard carrying a huge barrel of water (p. 101). He has the strength of six men and this burden is no more to him than a little pillow. Immediately Wolfram draws attention to the discrepancy between his appearance, grimy from his kitchen duties, and his true nature, as a child of high birth. Immediately, too, Wolfram employs three vivid images to describe him. He refers to the gold piece and the precious stone which, though they may become sullied, will yet emerge into their true radiance, and then he goes on to speak of the eagle which tests its young by holding them towards the sun and seeing which of them will have the courage to look straight into it. These powerful images remain to characterize Rennewart, the dirty young lad whose true appearance is disguised but who will emerge in due course, and the bold child who, like the eaglet, can choose when he leaves the nest and not be hurled from it like his lesser brothers. This picture, powerful and brilliant, does not bear close examination, it is true, for one will find oneself wondering whether, indeed, Rennewart *did* leave the nest voluntarily, since we are later told of how he was abducted by merchants. Nevertheless, the immediate effect is startling, and more particularly so when Wolfram follows with another surprising comparison, for Rennewart endures the bullying of the pages 'like a coy young girl' until, pressed beyond endurance, he reacts with the anger he has so far managed to suppress and picks up one of the pages and hurls him against a stone pillar. Wolfram does not even try to conceal the horror of this act, as he describes the page bursting open 'like an over-ripe fruit' (p. 102).

This is a powerful introduction to a character who will play a significant role in the rest of the work. In relatively few lines Wolfram has provided an insight into the contradictory figure who is clearly to occupy him very closely and perhaps even to present him with some problems, since, as will be seen, the question of the 'ending' of Wolfram's *Willehalm* is bound up with the presentation of Rennewart and his role in the poem (see pp. 270–73).

Although Wolfram's Rennewart is not the dominant figure that Rainouart is in *Aliscans*, a great deal of the central part of the work *is* devoted to him. We see his relationship with the Emperor, who is frustrated by the boy's refusal to be baptized. We learn gradually and gently of his love for Alize and hers for him, from the time she pleads with her father to allow Willehalm to adopt the boy and Rennewart's courteous leave-taking from the young princess, together with the kiss she plants on his smooth cheek and which, as he thinks, sows the young beard there, to Wolfram's own reference to Rennewart as the servant of Alize, fighting for her in the battle (p. 205). We witness the meeting between Rennewart and Giburc, and we follow the clues which are never fully taken up but which lead, we suspect, to the open recognition of brother and sister. Along with those peeping through a crack in the wall, we hear his long lament, prompted by the singeing of his whiskers but containing the history of his young life and ending with his declaration: 'After all, I *am* the child of Terramer' (p. 147).

Rennewart's indiscriminate hatred of the Saracens in the source is explained by Wolfram as the consequence of his belief that his relatives have let him down by not trying to find him, though Wolfram assures us that they have no idea where he might be. Rennewart declines to be baptized, not out of obstinacy, but because he believes that baptism is just not made for him. The comic episodes with the *tinel* are given a deeper significance by Wolfram, when he has Rennewart express his belief that God is testing him by allowing him to forget his club on *three* occasions and it is not far from this belief to Wolfram's own interpretation of the skirmish at Pitit Punt, when the French deserters believe that the Hand of God is striking them and meting out just punishment. When Rennewart then returns with the army and assumes command under the imperial flag, the idea is completed: Rennewart, the Saracen boy who has refused to be baptized, fights beneath the Cross and upholds the Christian faith in the coming battle. Moreover, Willehalm himself heartens the deserters by referring to the threefold temptation of St Peter.

Rennewart has risen from his role as kitchen-hand to his new role as leader of the forces supplied by the Roman King. His true nature is recognized, as Wolfram has implied in his images of the gold piece and the precious stone. As the battle proceeds, his uncourtly club is replaced by the knightly sword which he discovers to be very effective. If Wolfram were to take this idea to its natural conclusion, and if he were to complete his work in accordance with his source, Rennewart could become a knight, accept baptism and marry Alize. As it is, we are left in the dark about the fate of Rennewart, who disappears without trace after his decisive action in the second battle. For much of that battle Rennewart has dominated, until he gives way to Willehalm, and to Wolfram's concern with his vital message.

Wolfram follows his source in moving towards an encounter between Rennewart and Terramer. The son sees the father in front of him and we expect first the conversation and then the battle as related in *Aliscans*, but Wolfram does not wish, it seems, to relate that battle and instead, reminded of Hildebrand and the tragedy which would appear inevitable as the *Hildebrandslied* breaks off,[6] he makes a surprising and seemingly incongruous comparison of Terramer with Lady Uote, Hildebrand's wife, who waited patiently for his return. This abrupt turn of the narrative leaves us wondering. Deliberately, it seems, Wolfram has avoided the confrontation which he certainly would have found distressing and displeasing to relate, though he can hardly deny that it occurred, and Rennewart is gone, to appear again over ninety lines later. This time Wolfram does not flinch from telling of the combat between Rennewart and a close kinsman, yet his slaying of his brother Kanliun is quickly told (p. 215). Though Rennewart is mentioned twice more, once when he slays King Gibue and again, rather neutrally, as he watches the terrible conflict, he then vanishes.

It would seem that Wolfram has indeed subordinated Rennewart, in the end, to Willehalm, and what he meant to do further is a matter which cannot be divorced from the whole question of the 'ending' of *Willehalm* and of whether, in fact, Wolfram meant to conclude his poem where our text comes to an end.

VIVIANZ

In the case of Vivianz the situation is unambiguous. He is a martyr who dies in the first battle of Alischanz, fighting for the Christian faith. At his death there occurs a miracle by which God designates His elected one: a radiant light surrounds him and a fragrance is emitted from his body. Quite explicitly, Vivianz has been chosen by God and, as he rides away from the battlefield, where to the terrible wound he received at the hand of Noupatris has been added the fatal blow of Halzebier, he is directed by the angels to the River Larkant, where the Archangel Kerubin appears to him and promises that he will not die until his uncle has seen him again.

It is Wolfram's achievement to have elevated the hero of his source to the ranks of the saints and to ensure that the death of Vivianz in the first battle becomes the impetus to revenge in the second. The portrayal of Vivianz, the brilliant young knight full of promise, the

son of Willehalm's sister and beloved of Giburc and Willehalm,
culminates in his death-scene and in the conversation with his uncle.
Up to this time he has been seen as a noble knight, unconcerned for
his life as he engages time and again in combat with the heathens. His
name occurs in a list of names of those kinsmen of Willehalm who
fight for him in the first battle, but already it is linked with a lament
from Wolfram: 'Alas, that his tender years should have ended in
death before he had time to grow a beard!' (p. 23). The death of
Vivianz is already in the mind of the narrator, and the thought of
it must accompany him in the action which follows. We recall
Wolfram's words when Vivianz comes face to face with Noupatris,
like him a brilliant young knight and like him resolved to fight, if
necessary, to the death: 'Both men were duelling to the death'
(p. 27). Yet this combat, which brings death to Noupatris, is not yet
the fatal encounter for Vivianz, though his wound is a mortal one. In
agony he rides into further encounters and slays many heathens
until he meets Halzebier, the King of Falfunde, the nephew of
Terramer and, of course, of Arofel too. It is Halzebier who completes
the work of Noupatris, hurling Vivianz to the ground. The two
encounters are significant for the structure of the whole battle: the
victory over Noupatris marks a high point for the Christians who
begin by gaining the upper hand in the battle, while the thrust at
Vivianz from Halzebier is quickly succeeded by the defeat of the
Christians.

The death of Vivianz in the arms of his uncle is the first pause in
the narrative, when action gives way to lament and prayer. Yet,
equally, it marks the beginning of a new action, for Willehalm rides
from the River Larkant, after his vigil, and rides into battle with
fifteen kings (p. 49). His intense grief must be transcended if he is to
find his way from the battlefield and away to Orange. Yet this grief
and the anger which goes with it play a crucial role, as has been seen,
in his meeting with Arofel, whom he slays in revenge for Vivianz.
Halzebier, the son of Arofel's sister, has slain the son of the sister of
Willehalm, and for this Arofel must pay the price.[7]

This is, however, only the beginning of the revenge, for Vivianz
becomes the representative of all the Christians who died in the first
battle. His name is often coupled with the name of Mile, the other

nephew of Willehalm who perished early in the hostilities. Giburc asks Willehalm: 'Where is the radiant Vivianz? Where are Mile and Gwigrimanz?' (p. 58), and, at Laon, Willehalm singles out the two young knights to represent the many kinsmen slain at Alischanz. Many other names are mentioned, too, but it is these two which provoke the copious tears of his listeners (p. 84). Throughout his poem, Wolfram makes use of the rhyming of Vivianz and Alischanz to emphasize the link which he has established between the young representative of so many Christians and the second mighty battle. He does this as late as Willehalm's lament on the morning after the second battle, when Willehalm sees the two battles expressed for him in the loss of two dear friends (pp. 219–20).

Some critics have spoken, in fact, of Vivianz and Rennewart as parallel figures and as the two laments of Willehalm as parallel to one another too. Similarities there are, of course, in the two young men. In both cases, for example, Wolfram mentions a mere detail: that neither is old enough to have a proper beard. Both are much loved by Willehalm, and both are equipped for battle by Giburc. However, there are essential differences in the portrayal of the two young men, for Wolfram's purpose is different. It is the *death* of Vivianz which is all-important: there is no development of character here, for there is no time. This is the Christian knight fighting for his faith, not the young Saracen who only gradually learns about chivalry and moves towards his role as leader of the imperial army. It has been suggested that the pain of Willehalm at the loss of Rennewart is greater than that which he expressed at the death of Vivianz, that his lament is more bitter. This may be so, but – and this matter relates to the question of the 'development' of Willehalm (see p. 243ff.) – the circumstances are different. In Vivianz he lost a beloved nephew; in Rennewart he loses one whom he has come to regard as a friend and the 'right hand' who has gained the victory for him, though this victory in military terms is for him a true defeat, if it brings so much grief and loss with it. Vivianz died the death of a Christian saint, having made his confession and with the support of the sacred wafer. What has become of Rennewart is unclear, but, if he is dead, he has died without baptism. It is perhaps such considerations which lead to the bitterness of Willehalm and, in particular, to his blasphemous attack on the 'Son of the Virgin' (p. 220), who has inflicted upon him a wound which cannot heal. This is the lowest point of grief for Willehalm, who is yet able to transcend it, as he must, for the sake of his men, and as he does in deference to Giburc and her kin, and above all to the Creator of all men.

Willehalm's submission to the Will of God is apparent when he tells his brother: 'God knows what He has done' (p. 222). What God has done embraces, of course, the death of Vivianz, the loss of Rennewart, and, indeed, the defeat which this victory has wrought in the heart of Willehalm. If there was consolation for Willehalm in the fact that he was there beside Vivianz, to give him the wafer which would ensure the salvation of his soul, such consolation is absent now. Yet still Willehalm manages, in humility and complete recognition of the Will of God, to make his gesture to Matribleiz and so to all men. The saintly death of Vivianz remains a tender, self-contained episode, but, in the context of the whole poem, it is seen to have a special function. The orthodox standpoint of the Christian knight, reflected in the dying nephew and the grieving uncle, has widened into something much less orthodox and less easily defined, when a similar loss can prompt a great and magnanimous response from the man who has learnt to make his grief productive.

MINOR CHARACTERS

Wolfram's interest in ideas and his concern, in *Willehalm*, with broad issues of religion and politics, does not contradict his absorbing preoccupation with character; indeed, the two elements of his narrative are interdependent. At the centre of the conflict are the two people, Willehalm and Giburc, who have given rise to it. His picture of both of them is full and clear, despite its complexity, yet side by side with them are other important characters, together with other less obviously significant characters who emerge vividly, though in many cases not for long.

The two battles are full of such characters, memorable figures who dominate the scene and whose fate cannot be dismissed as negligible.

Some are remembered for their individual deeds: Noupatris, the noble King who wears a ruby crown on his helmet and has Amor and Amor's spear and salve-jar embroidered on his banner, and who dies at the hand of Vivianz in one of the earliest combats described, or Halzebier who actually deals the mortal blow to Vivianz and later, in the first battle, takes eight of Willehalm's relatives prisoner, only to die at their hands in the second battle. The ironic fate of this great King of Falfunde is fully appreciated by Wolfram, who devotes a relatively long passage to the account of the bold knight who had earlier so rejoiced to be selected as leader of the first battalion (p. 205ff.). The account of so much slaughter must strain the powers of the finest narrator, and Wolfram can hardly avoid repetition as he tells again and again of how a noble hero perished. Yet he has this capacity to bring to mind essential features of many individual men, and so the narrative avoids the monotony which might seem inevitable. Who can forget, for example, the mighty King Purrel with his extraordinary helmet made from the skin of the creature 'muntunzel', rainbow-coloured and impenetrable by shot or thrust or blow? This old warrior, who 'knew how to put up the stakes and collect them in such a game of chance' (p. 209), has to watch his sons being laid low, until he is himself struck down by Rennewart's club. The previous long description of his sturdy shield and armour, made from the dragon 'neitune', and of his helmet comes vividly to mind now as we learn that his limbs crack: they cannot be broken like any other man's and so, crushed and with blood running from his mouth, his ears and his nose, he is carried to the boat (p. 211).

Wolfram sometimes picks out distinctive features by which his characters are made memorable: the horny skin of Gorhant's men and their strange, inhuman voices (p. 32); the ship on the helmet of Kliboris, which, says Wolfram, is flooded with blood when he is slain (p. 202); the splendid, vivid cloak of Ehmereiz (p. 181). Sometimes he builds up the details, as he does in the case of Heimrich of Narbonne, for example: he is the old man, the wise old man, with a white beard; he is mentioned very early in the work, as the father who took the unusual step of making his godchild his heir and sending his own seven sons, disinherited, into the world to find their own ways. This Wolfram recalls when he implies that all the terrible events are attributable to this act: 'Alas that he [Willehalm] was not allowed to stay on his father's lands! If he should now come to grief, then the sin would be greater than the credit achieved by Heimrich for his charity towards his godchild. I think it does not balance properly' (p. 20). We see him comforting Giburc, acting in a kindly manner towards the embarrassed young Rennewart, and seating the guests at the banquet with obvious skill and pleasure. Above all, though, he evokes the attention of Wolfram during the second battle, when the full horror leads to an expression of intense compassion from the narrator, who speaks of the race of Heimrich as undergoing a new baptism, this time in blood (p. 200). Added together, these impressions, brief in themselves, constitute a full picture of a relatively minor character.

In some ways Wolfram's technique is similar in the case of Terramer, who is, of course, no minor character. The great heathen King is a complex figure. On the one hand he is the Admirat, the temporal leader of the Saracens, yet on the other he is the father of Giburc. The clash of roles gives rise to a tragic situation, which, though Wolfram does not develop it fully, nevertheless allows Terramer to emerge as a man tragically torn in his loyalties. It would have been easy enough for Wolfram to portray the heathen Emperor as the villain of the piece who has launched the tremendous invasion and is resolved to pursue it to the destruction of Christendom and in order that he may usurp the crown of Rome. This, indeed, is one very important aspect of his role: it must be, of course. Yet we are made to realize that his has been no easy decision and that he has been subject to pressures which he could not withstand. As he tells Giburc, he was reluctant to respond to Tibalt's request for support until he was forced to do so by the Baruc and his priests (p. 115). It was they who urged him to kill his daughter as penance for his sins, yet still he would prefer to persuade her by gentle means to return to her faith. Thus we see a man vacillating between extremes: 'Terramer behaved like this towards his dear daughter: beseeching her one day and threatening her the next' (p. 117). In his conversation with Giburc, too, he appears far from secure. He knows enough of Christian belief to be puzzled by it and to sense that his daughter would not have abandoned so much for trivial reasons. Mixed with the contempt which he expresses for Christianity is something very close to awe, so that his later reference to the 'sorcerer' Jesus who has strewn sarcophagi on the battlefield to hinder the heathen attack betrays the fear of a man who can find no other explanation (p. 177).

Wolfram expresses the tragic situation of Terramer in two moving lines: 'Thus the loyal heathen sat there on his couch lamenting bitterly' (p. 176). It is just before he enters the second battle. The mighty heathen ruler on his rich gold quilt is about to be equipped for combat, lavishly and with due regard for ceremony, by the many kings who serve him. Wolfram is deeply conscious of the discrepancy between such grandeur and the mood of the man, about to continue this war which, for all its political scope, he can still see in terms of the conflict between David and Absalom, the tragic clash of father and child. When, later, we see approaching the combat between Terramer and Rennewart, the potential personal tragedy is again made clear, though Wolfram declines to describe this encounter (see the section on Rennewart, pp. 248–52). When, on the other hand, he moves on to the description of the combat between Willehalm and Terramer, the less personal issues of the conflict are reasserted, as Wolfram recalls the famous battle between Charlemagne and Baligan (see the section on structure, p. 267). The heathen is terribly wounded, as is Willehalm himself, and, as Terramer is borne away to his ships, Wolfram lays stress on the significance of the defeat for the mighty King 'who had never been defeated' (p. 215), and he brings out its full irony when he tells us: 'Thus he who had often laid claim to Rome before the defeat took place departed from Roman soil' (p. 215).

A final piece remains of the complicated puzzle which is Wolfram's depiction of Terramer. It is he, Willehalm learns, who has paid for the costly embalming of the heathen kings in the white velvet tent and had gold tablets set at the ends of the biers to indicate their names. Such honouring of the slain goes beyond the duty of the ruler and betrays, again, the personal response of a man whom Wolfram refrains from actually criticizing but sees rather as a victim of circumstances. This discovery of Willehalm's contributes, as has been seen (see the section on Giburc and Willehalm, pp. 237–48), to his own gesture towards Matribleiz. With the ending of the text at this point, we cannot know for sure of the response of Terramer to the message which Willehalm sends, yet perhaps the total picture of the Admirat would lead to the expectation, the hope, that he may react with comparable magnanimity.

If the portrayal of Terramer emerges ultimately as positive rather than negative, this is characteristic of Wolfram, who not only appeals through Giburc for compassion but demonstrates his own compassion on many occasions. His is, indeed, a gentle nature, it would seem, and he rarely allows a negative judgement to prevail. Thus, at the other end of the scale, the Christian Emperor Louis is weak and vacillating, a man who is aware of his role yet unwilling to assume the responsibilities which attach to it, but he has his qualities: he is courteous and restrained in his reaction to Willehalm's behaviour, and eventually he does agree to give his material aid. This, of course, is no more than should be expected of him, since Willehalm is his vassal and has a right to his support in what has become the defence of the Empire. If Louis is weak rather than wicked, Wolfram can hardly admire him, but he is, frankly, not deeply concerned to present him as a more interesting character, though it is significant that, in referring to him, he denies him the title 'Emperor' and calls him 'King'. He is a man easily led, unworthy no doubt of the high office which he owes to the intervention of Willehalm himself, and it is all to the good for the present situation that he should abdicate to Willehalm the command of the army. Perhaps even less admirable is his treatment of Rennewart and his separation of Alize and Rennewart. Yet here again, if one is looking for a redeeming feature, he at least has the wit to permit Willehalm to adopt Rennewart when his daughter adds her pleas. .

When it comes to the wife of Louis, Wolfram possibly finds his tolerance towards human weakness stretched to the full. Even he cannot account for the unsisterly behaviour of a woman who has the doors closed on her brother and who does her best to persuade her husband not to help him. Little though we may condone the uncouth behaviour of Willehalm, we can see that, to some extent, the Queen receives her just deserts. Wolfram's displeasure is apparent. Though in the end there is a reconciliation between brother and sister, and although Wolfram does his best to compensate for the Queen's behaviour by showing her in copious tears at the news of the death of so many at Alischanz, he cannot really obliterate the original impression. His failure to give her a name is very unusual indeed, and it almost certainly signifies his disapproval of her.

One wonders that two people who are at the best negative could have produced a daughter as remarkable as the Princess Alize, who is undoubtedly a favourite with Wolfram. He stresses her purity and her beauty, and he gives to her quite extraordinary powers of reconciliation, which he compares to the healing of a wound (p. 85). The tough knight Willehalm reacts instantaneously to her entrance, regretting his behaviour and wishing that he could go back on it. She calms his rage and subsequently even succeeds in persuading her frightened mother to come out of hiding and join the rest of the family. Above all, however, though the two aspects of her role are connected, Alize is seen in her relationship with Rennewart, as the sweet confidante whose obvious loyalty prompts him to reveal his secret to her. Her feeling for him is betrayed, though without stress, when she begs her father to let him go with Willehalm, and only in retrospect does the scene of leave-taking, as she sits beneath the tree, take on its true significance, when Rennewart attributes so much importance to the kiss which she gave to him (p. 146). This kiss and the love which goes with it accompany Rennewart in the battle in which he fights as the 'servant of Alize', and we are left to wonder at the outcome of the young love which Wolfram presents with characteristic sensitivity, and at the fate of a unique figure.

The delicacy of the portrayal of Alize contrasts sharply with Wolfram's picture of her grandmother, the resolute old Countess Irmschart. Above all, we recall her for two actions at the Court in Laon: her swift intervention to prevent Willehalm's actually killing his sister (p. 82) and her firm offer of help to Willehalm. She cuts through the wrangling with her simple question: 'What am I good for after all, old woman that I am?' (p. 88). The old lady is a match for her knightly sons, determined, like them, to help Willehalm with her material aid but, more than that, to put on armour if need be and to wield a sword. Somehow one believes that she would be capable of doing this and in a poem which sees its principal female character defending a city with her own strength, it is certainly not incongruous.

The work is peopled with extremely vivid characters, rarely conforming to types, though obviously certain groups of society must dominate. One class has a particularly individualized representative in Wimar, the merchant who treats Willehalm with kindness and hospitality when the Court, and his own kinsmen, are excluding him. Though a merchant, he is, we are told, of knightly origins. It would be too much to speak of him as a comic character, yet there is perhaps a touch of humour here, in this man who behaves in a very human way and clearly earns the approval of Wolfram. There is, for example, the brief argument about who should ride the horse (pp. 75–6) and, on the next day, there is the picture of Wimar sitting at the imperial table and receiving full reward for his treatment of Willehalm: 'This was the experience of a lifetime for Wimar', says Wolfram (p. 95).

THE STRUCTURE OF THE POEM

It is obvious that the structure of Wolfram's *Willehalm* corresponds in broad outline to that of *Aliscans*, yet there are significant differences. *Aliscans*, for example, begins *in medias res*, while *Willehalm* begins with a prayer to the Holy Trinity, a gradual introduction of the author, source and patron, and a brief account of Willehalm's earlier life, leading then to the first battle at Alischanz. There seems little point in dwelling on the specific differences here, but since Wolfram has so precisely and consciously organized the material of the *chanson*, a discussion of the structure of *Willehalm* itself seems in order.

Lachmann established the division of the poem into books in the first edition (1833), based in part on the large initials in the Saint Gall manuscript, and we shall follow his pattern when referring to the major divisions of *Willehalm*, as we have in our translation. However, some scholars have attempted to discern smaller structural units based on groups of lines or groups of thirty-line sections. We feel that such groupings depend for their validity too much on who does the counting and what *he* perceives to be a unit, since there has been little unanimity. We prefer, therefore, a less arbitrary approach and shall consider the structure of *Willehalm* from three angles: time, place and events.

The chronological structure of the poem is readily discernible because Wolfram usually marks the passing of time clearly with references to daybreak, nightfall and other times of day. One needs only to be alert to his references to be able to calculate the time periods rather easily. Without going into too much detail, we can develop a brief summary of the chronology.

The first day begins on the day of the first battle and ends as Willehalm holds watch over the slain Vivianz all night in the middle of Book II, and the second day ends as Willehalm slips out of Orange at night to ride off for help at the end of Book II, ending a precise time-series of two days.

The narrative then proceeds in Book III on two time levels: Orange-time and Willehalm-time. It is a period of indefinite time, and Wolfram switches back and forth between Giburc and Willehalm, giving the impression of events occurring simultaneously. He underlines the indefiniteness of the time by stating that he does not know how many days it took Willehalm to journey to Orleans (p. 67). Willehalm spends the night there and resumes his journey the next morning.

With that, a new period of definite time begins. Willehalm has his encounter with the magistrate and his brother, Arnalt, continues on to spend the first night at a monastery, leaving his shield there when he departs the next (second) day for Laon. After he is snubbed by the Court at Laon, he spends the night at the house of Wimar, returning to the Court the next (third) day for the King's celebration. The dramatic events of that day occupy the last third of Book III and about half of Book IV. Although the end of that day is not indicated, that concludes another definite time sequence (three days).

The King had ordered his men to assemble at Laon in ten days for the campaign to relieve Orange and rescue Giburc. There is therefore an interval of eight days (counting the third day of the previous series as the first of the ten and the last day as the day of assembly) during which Willehalm stays at Laon and Rennewart is introduced into the narrative.

With the assembly of the forces a new three-day definite time-sequence begins. During this period the army spends the first night in Laon, the second at the monastery and the third in Orleans, where Louis hands over command of the army to Willehalm. No specific ending for the third day is given, but presumably the army sets out for Orange on the next day.

Again a period of indefinite time occurs during which the army approaches Orange. Book IV ends with expressions of great anxiety for Giburc by Willehalm and with a distant glimpse of the fire at Orange, the result of the heathens' last assault. But that assault has not yet taken place, for as Book V begins we are back in Orange-time, at some indefinite point in that time, but one that must have preceded the fire mentioned in the last lines of Book IV. The narrative covers the discussion of religion between Giburc and Terramer during an earlier armistice and the last assault on Orange at night. When the Marquis and his men, having ridden all night, arrive at daybreak, Orange-time and Willehalm-time come together, and we leave the indefinite time-interval during which Wolfram has again switched back and forth.

A final definite time-sequence of four days has begun. The arrival and entertainment of the nobles fills Book V and carries over into Book VI, completing the first day. On the second day the council of war is held, culminating in Giburc's appeal for mercy for the heathens. Book VI ends with the army moving out. The third day begins early in Book VII after the army has camped for the night. Both the Christian and heathen armies are organized into battalions, and the battle commences. It rages all day, through the whole of Book VIII and well into Book IX, ending at dusk with the victory of the Christians. Willehalm's long lament for the missing Rennewart begins the fourth day, and the poem 'ends' before the day is over.

The poem, or the fragment of it that we have (see discussion of ending, p. 268ff.), shows a remarkable symmetry in its time-structure, except for the very last time-segment with its four days, and we can add to that a geographical symmetry which corresponds to the chronology. The geographical structure should be apparent from our discussion of the time-relationships, but the following outlines may make the structure of both time and place more evident:

Time:

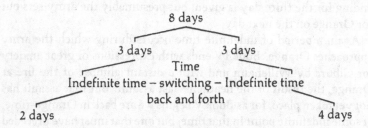

Place:

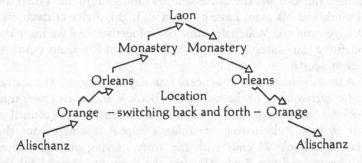

Such symmetry would not appear to be chance, and it has frequently been introduced to argue that *Willehalm* is really a finished work. Be that as it may, we must not forget that Wolfram is only following the basically symmetrical course charted by his source in the parts that correspond, but the striking aspect is the precision and consistency that he has employed in making his audience aware of it. Wolfram must have been very conscious of time-relationships in his works. His frequent references to time are invariably accurate, as, for example, when Arnalt tells Willehalm about the approaching celebration at court in Laon in three days. Furthermore, our attention is drawn repeatedly to the connection of the second part to the first; for instance, upon Willehalm's return to Orleans, we are reminded of his first visit there when Wolfram says: 'This time the Margrave was able to ride through Orleans without paying a toll, for no one detained him for it now' (p. 110), and most notably, the connection of the second battle to the first through repeated reference to the fallen heroes of the first battle on *both* sides.

As we have seen, the time-symmetry is not quite perfect, with the first time-sequence of two days not really balanced by the four days at the end. This is a matter involving the problem of the ending (see p. 268ff.). If the poem does indeed end approximately as we have it, then one might find the chronological imbalance at the ending quite fitting, but if, on the other hand, the poem is unfinished, then we might view this imperfection as evidence that this is so. In fact, an unfinished *Willehalm* could call all our observations on time-symmetry (and place-symmetry, too) into question, because we have no way of knowing how Wolfram would have developed his narrative further.

Our third category, the structure of events or action in *Willehalm*, is less readily adaptable to graphic representation, but several aspects should be mentioned. It has been pointed out that the composition of *Willehalm* seems to be building towards a peak at the end, as opposed to the building-block, add-on style of *Aliscans*. In addition, a transformation and an intensification of the events themselves have been observed. We should like to use these ideas in describing the structure of the action.

Basically the structure of *Willehalm* rests on the two battles on the field of Alischanz, the defeat of the Christians in the first and their ultimate victory in the second. The middle part bridges the two and looks both ways: back in lament for the fallen heroes and ahead towards the revenge that must inevitably come. All the while there is an anxiety for Giburc. As a result, the composition of the events appears to have a symmetry too, but it is not a static symmetry since the action is *aimed at* and *moves toward* the second battle. It does culminate in the defeat of the Saracens, and this fact has been adduced as evidence that *Willehalm* is not a fragment. However, this disregards the fate of Rennewart, whose appearance in Book IV initiates a strand of action that is never satisfactorily tied up in the poem as we have it.

Close attention to the text reveals that Wolfram also develops the course of events ideologically through transformation and intensification of the action. The prime cause of the conflict is Willehalm's winning of Arabel–Giburc from the heathens. Her husband, Tibalt, sets out to get her back and to have revenge. His father-in-law, Terramer, reluctantly agrees to support him. Initially the conflict is presented as a family matter, and Wolfram voices his disapproval. At this stage Willehalm is called simply the 'Margrave' and both Tibalt and Terramer are referred to as 'King'.

When the first battle begins we see that it is not just a family feud, but it is rather a religious war, an ideological struggle. Giburc, we are informed, had converted to Christianity, the death of the Christians is that of martyrs, the heathens appeal to their gods for assistance, Willehalm exhorts his men to defend their faith and Terramer appeals to his men to avenge their gods for Giburc's apostasy. It is a difficult situation for Wolfram, for what should have been a praiseworthy act, Giburc's conversion to Christianity, has become the cause of great suffering on both sides. The idea of a crusade is introduced in the middle of the first battle when Wolfram notes that the Christians are wearing crosses on their clothes, and at the height of the battle the fate of those killed on both sides is emphasized: the Christians are destined for eternal salvation, the heathens for eternal damnation. Vivianz' death has all the characteristics of the death of a saint.

At the end of the first battle Willehalm is utterly defeated. He must seek help, and only now do we learn of his relationship to the Roman King, his brother-in-law. This is the first step towards the second battle, which Wolfram develops gradually into a confrontation bet. een East and West, between the Holy Roman Empire and the Saracen world, between Willehalm as representative of the Emperor and Terramer, who not only intends to retrieve his daughter but also expresses a political intention: to occupy Aachen and Rome and to crush Christianity. We cannot follow all the details here, but the parallels on both sides are developed quite clearly:

Louis, the secular Protector with the Pope as religious head for the West, versus Terramer, the secular Protector with the Baruc of Baldac as religious head for the East. Christianity and heathendom, God and the forces of evil are contending, just as they had previously when Charlemagne and Baligan, to whom, incidentally, according to Wolfram, Louis and Terramer are related respectively, had clashed. At the height of the second battle, in describing the action, Wolfram uses imagery that evokes cataclysmic events, the Flood and Judgement Day, saying: 'If someone dammed up the Rhine and the Rhône for a fortnight and then suddenly removed the dam, it would not have produced as great a flood as Terramer's forces did, for he literally swamped the whole Christian army. Yet the Christians kept fighting so valiantly that there will be enough to tell of their deeds on Judgement Day and in all the years between, so great were the heathen losses' (pp. 199–200). The transformation and intensification of the action have been achieved. In the end, of course, Christianity and the Empire must triumph, for that is the side of Altissimus.

Our consideration of the structure of the action from the point of view of its ideology has left out at least one important element, one that does not seem to fit in with the rest: Giburc's impassioned plea to the Christians before the second battle to spare the lives of the heathens, if possible. The idea of mercy towards an adversary in combat is, as we have seen, foreign to the heroic world of *Aliscans*, but it is not to the ethical world of the courtly knight. This is Wolfram's world, we believe. At least he introduces the idea of the brotherhood of man independently of his source, and his aversion to killing in any form can be well documented not only here, but also in *Parzival*. To be sure, *after* the battle Willehalm is magnanimous in victory and arranges for the embalming and the transport home of the heathen kings for proper burial, but during the battle immense slaughter *has* taken place, precisely what Giburc had hoped to avoid. As in the case of Rennewart's ultimate fate, we are presented with a structural problem which we cannot solve without resorting to speculation. We can only take note of it. Is the 'ending' as we have it the only possible resolution of the ideological conflict? Or did Wolfram, by introducing the idea of the brotherhood of man, envisage a different resolution which was never concluded?

THE 'ENDING' OF THE WORK

Wolfram's *Willehalm* is a complex work which presents many problems of interpretation and provokes contrasting viewpoints. Central to critical discussion is the question of the 'ending' of the work, of whether or not it is complete as the manuscripts have it and as we have presented it here. Although authoritative opinion among scholars is weighted now towards the belief that the poem breaks off before the conclusion which Wolfram intended, there are arguments on the other side. It must even be admitted that the present two translators, though agreed on most other matters, are divided on this point.

We therefore present here the principal arguments relating to this question and must leave it to the reader to make up his mind, or, if not to do that, then at least to be aware of this vital further dimension to the interpretation of a work already difficult.

Recent important research has listed a very large number of manuscripts of Wolfram's *Willehalm*, a factor which implies the popularity of the work in the Middle Ages, but of over seventy manuscripts only twelve are complete.[8] Of these twelve only one dates from the thirteenth century: all the others belong to the fourteenth and fifteenth centuries. This oldest and very beautiful manuscript, which can be seen in the Stiftsbibliothek in Saint Gall, in Switzerland, is believed to have been copied around 1250, probably earlier rather than later than that date. It was on this manuscript that the scholar Karl Lachmann based his edition of Wolfram's works which appeared first in 1833 and laid the foundations for subsequent editions.

Of the twelve complete manuscripts, ten conclude at the point where our translation ends: 'Thus he left the land of the Provençals' is the final line. In the Saint Gall manuscript, however, the final page, which must have contained the last four lines of our text, is missing, and these four lines, together with fifteen further lines, have been added in the lower margin of what is now the last page. Karl Lachmann, who saw this addition as the work of another scribe, rejected the lines as authentic Wolfram, despite their reappearance in another, later manuscript, but Albert Leitzmann, in his edition which dates from the first decade of the twentieth century and is regarded by some as more reliable, includes the fifteen lines and thus demonstrates emphatically his own belief that the poem is not completed. The lines are also included in Schröder's new edition (1978).

Preferring to leave this question open, we present our translation of these lines here and add them to the evidence which must be weighed up in the consideration of the poem as a whole:

> Away from the army, away from the flower-strewn grass, he was accompanied by many a sorely wounded knight. Now he was informed where he should go.
> It was only then that the Margrave increased his lamenting. It was the third day after the attack had been endured. The Margrave only now really went for all the stakes in his game of anguish. Gibert, wise man that he was, said: 'Someone to whom God has granted an army that he should console has no need to behave like this . . .' . . .

Although some critics agree with Lachmann in rejecting the lines as Wolfram's own, others find in them characteristic features of his style, while others, more cautiously, decline to be emphatic where the evidence is so slight.

It is justly maintained that, if someone felt prompted to continue the poem at the point where Wolfram broke off, it is strange that he did so for only fifteen lines. It has also been pointed out that, if indeed Wolfram did compose these fifteen lines, subsequent scribes might have felt it appropriate to cease their copying at a point which had at least some ring of finality.

If some scribe felt the need to try his hand at continuing the work, he was not alone. Ulrich von Türheim, a Swabian poet of limited talent, was surely expressing the feeling of his contemporaries when he sought to complete Wolfram's work in his enormously long *Rennewart*, just as he had endeavoured to complete Gottfried's *Tristan*. In neither case is he successful: that much must be admitted, for how could this undistinguished poet take over from artists of such quality? Yet *Rennewart* raises a number of points of interest in the present consideration, though it provides no conclusive answers to our questions.

Early in his work, Ulrich von Türheim speaks of his temerity in taking on the task of completing the work which Wolfram had, as he implies, *chosen* to leave unfinished (160–168). He quotes as the final line *'sus rûmt er Provenzâlen lant'* ('Thus he left the land of the Provençals'), and emphasizes the grief of Willehalm at the uncertainty surrounding the absence of Rennewart (176–9), thus expressing, one suspects, the question which must have dominated in the minds of all who heard Wolfram's narrative. Later he speaks of the disappointment at Wolfram's failure to continue the work, and that at a point when it was at its best (10262). If later he refers to Wolfram as dead (21713), this is still no proof that his death prevented the completion of *Willehalm*. We can be sure of nothing, except that Ulrich von Türheim, and no doubt many others, were conscious of a sense of frustration at being deprived of the ending of a much appreciated story and that Ulrich, equally conscious of his limitations as a poet, felt that he would be doing a service in supplying the missing conclusion.

As has been said, the majority of critics believe that *Willehalm* is a fragment and base this opinion on the inconclusive nature of the present 'ending' and in particular on the fact that the fate of Rennewart is left untold. It seems inconceivable that Wolfram, having been so interested in Rennewart himself, should drop him so abruptly, and just as inconceivable that he should have thought that his audience would be satisfied with such an abrupt ending. There is ample evidence in *Parzival* that Wolfram dislikes leaving ends untied and makes every effort to account for even small details. Yet, in *Willehalm*, there are a number of loose ends. Is Rennewart dead? (This seems unlikely since he was still alive at a very late stage of the battle.) Is he a captive? (The suggestion by Bernart is not taken up.) Wolfram has laid stress on the love between Rennewart and Alize, speaking of its developing and enduring (p. 145), but never, in fact, saying that it ended in marriage. He has spoken of the fame which Rennewart will achieve (p. 145), but the poem 'ends' without his achieving any widespread or formal recognition. The horse which Wolfram has said he will gain (p. 206) is not mentioned again. Apart from Alize, no other character in the work knows for sure of the relationship between Rennewart and Giburc, though Giburc has a feeling, an intuition, which will not be confirmed, says Wolfram, until much later (p. 148). This seems to indicate some kind of recognition scene, which does not, of course, materialize.

Those who maintain that *Willehalm* is complete as it stands point to the tragic quality of the poem and maintain that Wolfram has put an entirely new meaning into the substance of his source. To complete the poem in accordance with the source, with the conversion of Rennewart, his knighting and the marriage of Rennewart and Alize, would be to detract from this new emphasis and distort the inner form of the poem. It has become irrelevant to Wolfram, they say, to relate the continuation of the Rennewart story.

Not all those who consider that *Willehalm* is a fragment are thinking in terms of a 'happy ending' for the Rennewart action, as contained in the source. Even if by now the rather facile rounding-off of events in a marriage celebration would be aesthetically inappropriate, Wolfram's audience would expect to learn what had happened to Rennewart. Wolfram could, then, have gone against his source, unlikely though that seems in view of the relationship between the medieval poet and his acknowledged source, and ended the work with a sombre, tragic conclusion to the Rennewart story. Alternatively, and more likely, he could have brought his poem to a rather swift conclusion, telling of the fate of Rennewart and Alize, of Giburc and Willehalm, rather in the way he concludes his *Parzival*. Those who favour this possibility often think in terms of a tenth book, beginning at 451, 1 (p. 218, 'The next morning, when day began to break . . .'), telling of the events following the battle and providing, not least, an epilogue, however brief, to balance the prologue.

If *Willehalm is* incomplete, then there are three possible explanations: that Wolfram died before he could complete it; that his patron Hermann von Thüringen died and he was unable to complete it under his successor; that he came to find the end of the narrative offered by his source unacceptable to him. Most critics favour one or other of the first two possibilities, but there are also those who point to

Wolfram's gradual movement away from his source and his increasing preoccupation with his new emphasis.

At the end of Book VIII Wolfram seems to be threatening to abandon his work and wishing that someone else might take over. It may be that he is oppressed by the account of carnage which he has lamented on three occasions towards the end of this book (p. 196f.) culminating in his final cry: 'Alas for the murderous slaughter which occurred there on both sides . . . !' Equally, he could be aware of his own approaching death or dissatisfied with his position after the death of his patron. Just as easily, however, this could be Wolfram, not uncharacteristically, teasing his audience with the suggestion of his inadequacy to the task in hand when he knows that he is at the height of his powers, about to rise again to the fine address to Giburc which opens Book IX.

If, however, Wolfram did indeed feel ill at ease with his tale, for whatever reason, he might have wished to complete it quickly, if necessary abandoning his source and his original conception of his own material. Such thinking is behind a theory which has been put forward by some who seek to reconcile what seems like the finality of the Matribleiz scene with the admittedly unfinished Rennewart action. This is described as the 'emergency conclusion' (the *Notdach* theory), but it is still not a satisfactory explanation, for one would expect a specially designed conclusion to supply the answers to the many questions left unsolved, even if it did so in a cursory way. One would expect a conclusive ending, even if it remained unsatisfactory. Moreover, there has been preparation for the Matribleiz scene: as early as p. 132 Giburc herself praises King Matribleiz for his loyalty and constancy, when she is explaining Terramer's offer of peace to the Christians and his choice of Matribleiz as the supervisor of the terms. This reference would seem to suggest that Wolfram already has in mind the role which Matribleiz is to play later, when Willehalm himself attributes to him the same qualities of loyalty and constancy.

The question of the 'ending' of *Willehalm* cannot, it seems, be decided with absolute certainty, though the arguments may be put forward with conviction. Problems remain, whichever opinion one may favour, for this is perhaps one of the most difficult problems arising from medieval German literature. Much of the evidence within the work itself, together with one's acquaintance with medieval literature, points to the unacceptability of a story which left in the dark the fate of a principal, and no doubt popular, character. Yet the nature of this work, the fact that it is so clearly the product of a great mind who is himself grappling with one of the central problems of existence, leads to the suggestion that this 'ending' is not inappropriate: a more conventional, tidier conclusion might have detracted from the theme which has become, or indeed may always have been, his principal concern.

The darkness which dominates as the poem comes to its close is not the gloom of Willehalm at the loss of his friend: that, though it is a part of his mood, would be too limited. Rather are we aware, as Matribleiz leaves the land of Provence, that the struggle between men of different faiths cannot be solved by the generous gesture. The problem remains, much as one may admire the words and the action of Willehalm, and acknowledge the enlightened nature of Wolfram himself. For those who accept that Wolfram meant to go no further, this is as it should be. Yet there is the contrasting viewpoint, based now not on the Rennewart action at all, but on the nature of the poem and Wolfram's own view of life. Joy and sorrow belong together, he tells us, so is it inconceivable that he may have intended an ending happier than this one, if not *the* happy ending which one may reject as inappropriate to his new conception of the material? A conclusion which told of St Willehalm's entering a monastery would mean that the work ended on a note of reconciliation, with joy and sorrow balanced. Here would be no solution to a problem which Wolfram rightly conceived as insoluble save in limited, personal terms, but it would be a step towards a hopeful future.

RELIGION IN 'WILLEHALM'

In the absence of the kind of conventional conclusion which might justifiably be expected of such a narrative, and of a formal epilogue to match the prologue which opens the poem, one is faced with problems of interpretation which might have been solved within the substance of another work. Yet, on the basis of Wolfram's treatment of his source and by examining those elements and the emphasis in *Willehalm* which are peculiarly his own, we may arrive at some fairly firm decisions about his purpose.

From the prologue on we can be in no doubt about the religious standpoint represented here. The prayer to the Trinity proclaims the narrator in his allegiance to the Christian God and expresses his humility in the face of the task before him: it asks for divine guidance in telling the story of the knight who was himself the servant of God. This is a statement of a deeply felt personal relationship of one man with God, but at the same time it defines God as the Creator of all things. It ranges, then, between the sense of an intimate relationship, as of the child with the Father, and the awareness of the Omniscient Power which directs the Universe.

The religious tone of the prologue is undeniable and if, during the course of the poem, other, more secular considerations take over, this is rarely for long. When humour intervenes, this serves to bring into relief the dominant mood of seriousness to which, again and again, the work returns as its keynote. 'There is not much joy in this tale,' Wolfram admits (p. 143): 'I should need to be very clever to discover any joy in it . . .' Sorrow, he tells us, is an essential ingredient of human life, 'for sorrow is our beginning, and with sorrow we come into the grave'. What he calls the 'dual companionship' of joy and sorrow cannot be avoided by mankind, he declares, in one of his brief interruptions of the flow of his narrative (p. 143), and the story which he has to tell gives ample proof of the truth of what he says.

In *Parzival*, too, he had spoken of the ups and downs of human fortune ('But such is the way of the world: joy today and grief tomorrow'),[9] but in that earlier work, the optimistic view had prevailed. Parzival found the Grail, as was his destiny; he was reunited with his beloved wife; Anfortas was healed. In the marriage of Feirefiz and Repanse de Schoye, Wolfram had seen the hope of the union of East and West and had actually spoken of how Feirefiz had the message of Christianity proclaimed throughout the land of India. The last lines of *Parzival* had contained a simple message of faith: 'When a man's life ends in such a way that God is not robbed of his soul because of the body's sinning and who nevertheless succeeds in keeping his fellows' good will and respect, this is useful toil.'

The situation in *Willehalm* is much more complex. Not for a moment does Wolfram question the validity of the Christian faith which is seen as the primary motivating force of the Christian knights and, indeed, as the foundation of the marriage of Willehalm and Giburc. Yet there remains the problem of the heathens who have, after all, their own beliefs and, sharing as they do in the common humanity which is the gift of the Creator of all things, have the right to the compassion and, if the circumstances arise, the mercy of the Christians.

It is Giburc, the woman doubly named, Arabel–Giburc, who stands between the Christians and the heathens, who expresses this right in her central plea to the assembled forces before the second battle of Alischanz: 'Spare the creatures of God's Hand,' she appeals to them (p. 155), and Wolfram himself echoes her words at the end of the battle (p. 218): 'They are all God's creatures,' he says, and those who slaughter the heathens are committing a grave sin. In sparing the heathens, he makes clear in Giburc's speech, the Christians will be acting in accordance with their own faith and honouring their own God. Through the powerful arguments of Giburc, who points out that all men begin life as heathens and speaks of heathens who have been saved by the mercy of the all-merciful Father (p. 155–6), Wolfram expresses his own concern for the heathens and his hope that the mercy of the loving God will preserve them still (p. 156). Yet this hope may not be seen as a more definite prospect, and elsewhere he is emphatic in seeing the heathens as damned (p. 33f.). The Christians, on the other hand, prompt the angels to rejoice when, in death, they rise to heaven (pp. 24, 31, 33). When she speaks to her father, Giburc herself refers to the damnation of the heathens, led astray by their gods (p. 67). Her motive on this occasion is clear and it does not contradict what she says elsewhere, nor detract from Wolfram's own sadness at what he fears may be the fate of the splendid knights: 'It grieves me to think that their god Tervigant may have destined them for hell' (p. 26).

The convinced Christian poet cannot compromise when it comes to matters of faith but he can, and does, express sympathy for those who do not have the good fortune to share his religion. That is why the attitude which Wolfram advocates through Giburc is one, not of tolerance, but of mercy. The Christian faith in *Willehalm*, as in *Parzival*, is supreme but its validity will be asserted most emphatically if its exponents act in accordance with their overriding identity as the children of a loving God, 'the true Lover', as Wolfram puts it in *Parzival*.

Thus Willehalm, in his gesture to Matribleiz as the poem comes to its 'end', shows that, though he cannot accept for himself the rites of burial which the heathens practise, he can accept that these rites exist and that they have a significance for the heathens. His moving account of how he chanced upon the beautiful white tent with the dead kings laid out inside has shown already that he was impressed by the evidence of a tradition alien to his own yet sincerely upheld. Building upon this experience, Willehalm now asks Matribleiz to see to it that those heathen slain who lie upon the battlefield should be accorded burial 'properly, according to their own religion' (p. 224). Such respect for Saracen rites is clearly admirable to Wolfram, who succeeds here in raising his Willehalm above the conflict which has raged for so much of his work but who, already in *Parzival*, has shown a similar magnanimity in the Baruc, the heathen ruler, who arranged that Gahmuret should be buried in accordance with Christian custom, and lavishly, at his expense. The supreme gesture had surely been the Baruc's erection on the grave of a precious emerald cross, the symbol of the death of Christ, and the importance which Wolfram attaches to the Baruc's generosity seems to be confirmed by his reference to it again in *Willehalm* (p. 50).

Thus Willehalm, in speaking to Matribleiz, acknowledges the distinct tradition of heathendom and honours the race of his beloved Giburc, but his parting words to Matribleiz reiterate one of the major themes of the poem. He transcends the differences between them and seems to ignore the fact that Matribleiz, in common with his comrades alive and dead, has fought in the name of his gods and has waged war, not least in order to wrench Giburc from the bonds of her baptism and restore her to her former faith. Instead he commends the heathen king to Him 'who knows the number of the stars and who gave us the light of the moon' (p. 225). This is the Creator to whom the prologue is addressed. This is the Divinity whom Giburc twice called 'Altissimus' (p. 62; p. 114) though Wolfram and then Willehalm both take up the term (p. 212; p. 220). In her central conversation with her father, between the prologue and the closing commendation of Matribleiz by Willehalm, Giburc has spoken of the God 'who prescribed the course of *polus antarcticus* and the other stars, who set the firmament in motion and ordered the seven planets to compete against the swiftness of the heavens' (p. 114). The religious thought of the work is thus perfectly balanced, totally consistent.

It would be naive to suggest, that, even with the closing passages, Wolfram is within sight of a reconciliation of Christians and heathens, although this *has* been suggested. The poem is too profound for that and its problems are still largely unresolved. Willehalm's gesture is magnanimous in the man for whom this victory has wrought defeat in his heart, but it is limited in scope. It does not represent anything approaching a final settlement between the opposing forces, and we are left in the dark, of course, about how Terramer will receive the gesture from the enemy. There is no sign at all of Rennewart, still less any indication that he will, as in Wolfram's source, accept baptism. On the contrary, he has told Willehalm that baptism just does not suit his nature (p. 103) and seems to be expressing another important, if unorthodox view of Wolfram's, that baptism is not the only means to salvation. Certainly such a view seems to be present in *Parzival*, where Wolfram says of the heathen Queen Belakane that her purity was a pure baptism, as well as the tears which she shed in grief for her dead lover, Isenhart.[10]

For, in many respects, Wolfram von Eschenbach *is* unorthodox, though not so much in his attitude to the doctrines of the Church as in his capacity to stand out against the dominant views of his day. Who else, after all, raised his voice to lay claim to any rights for the heathens? Against the background of the crusades, and with the example of the *Rolandslied* and the *Aliscans* before him, Wolfram's original mind rose above the obvious, to express some new and entirely characteristic views.

He treats the heathens and the Christians with remarkable equality. Again and again, in describing the heathen knights, he accords them attributes comparable to those of their Christian foes. Splendidly equipped, courageous and powerfully motivated, the heathens emerge as noble opponents, many of them highly individualized and deserving the attention which Wolfram devotes to them. Divided as the Christians and heathens are in their religion, they are nevertheless united in their pursuit of chivalry: in this respect there is nothing to choose between them, and Wolfram is generous in his praise of men on both sides. Individuals are picked out for his particular attention: thus the miracle which occurs at the death of Vivianz is repeated when Tesereiz dies, for that heathen is a martyr too, though the word is not actually used to describe him, as it is for Vivianz. Love sent him to the battlefield: he is the Lover *par excellence* among the knights – 'the Garland of Love' (p. 55) – and he dies in the struggle for Love's sake. When the Christian God is the True Lover and in a work where human love and love for God are seen to be closely related, the knight who dies nobly in the service of Love warrants the praise which he receives in full measure. When it comes to the choice between remaining with the gods and going to the aid of his father, Kanliun does not hesitate: his duty as a knight and a son takes precedence over his obligation to the gods which have been placed in his care, and for Wolfram this is only right (p. 199).

As far as actual knowledge of the heathen religion is concerned, Wolfram is decidedly hazy. According to him, the Saracens have four gods – Apolle, Mahmete, Tervigant and Kahun – but he implies a certain vagueness – or is it perhaps more like indifference? – when, having named them all, he adds 'whatever all the gods of heathendom were called' (p. 218). These gods are idols, as Wolfram envisages them, and he emphasizes that they are set up on waggons and brought along with the army, on to the battlefield. Early in the work, too, he explains that the gods receive sacrificial gifts from their devotees (p. 21). Apart from these superficial features, Wolfram attributes little positive identity to the gods, nor to the religion they are supposed to represent. His own ignorance would seem to be the most likely explanation for his reticence, or he may simply be following literary tradition, but the effect is not unsatisfactory, for heathendom emerges as a negative force, though a force it certainly is, which sets itself on the destruction of Christianity. In contrast,

Wolfram is explicit in his interpretation of the Christian faith, with the Trinity as its focus and the death of Christ on the Cross as the expression of the Love which is its central feature. This is a thoroughly orthodox belief, of course, but Wolfram's originality is shown in the fact that he allows a woman, and a woman of heathen origin at that, to expound the teaching of the Christian faith. Giburc's famous speech to the assembly constitutes the core of the religious thought of the work, but elsewhere, particularly in her conversation with her father, Wolfram allows her to speak of her own baptism and of the God to whom she is now totally committed. The mystery of the Crucifixion, so precious to Christians, is too much for Terramer, who betrays in his questions to his daughter both his contempt and his fear: the heathen ruler knows enough about the Christian faith to realize that it is a power to be reckoned with.

THE PROBLEM OF GENRE

It has been pointed out recently that one reads *Willehalm* with different eyes depending on what one believes its genre to be. If one expects a courtly romance, one's expectations are quite different from those one might have if one thinks of it as an heroic epic. In our discussions we have consciously avoided assigning any specific genre to it other than 'courtly epic'. The Old French source, *Aliscans*, is a *chanson de geste*, clearly heroic poetry, in which the deeds of heroes are the important things. Action is paramount and characterization plays a much smaller part. The heroes are painted with bold strokes, either black or white, and we listen attentively as they perform their feats of arms. Their problems are relatively clear-cut, too: loyalty to one's king, keeping one's word, courage in the face of danger, steadfastness in battle.

In a courtly romance, on the other hand, there is not as much emphasis on the events themselves as there is on the people who perform them. Characterization becomes quite differentiated, and one might even speak of a kind of development in the leading figures, whether this be from a lower to a higher moral plane or whether it be the gradual unfolding of inherent qualities. The problems encountered are likewise less simple to solve. Complex obligations often conflict, and above all there are the problems of Love, how to acquire it, how to keep it. People make mistakes, suffer the consequences but eventually learn how to achieve that balance of ideal courtly life best represented by King Arthur and his knights, and everything ends happily.

Another genre is the medieval legend, the saint's life, in which the holy hero falls prey to, or doggedly resists, temptation, endures suffering and torture for his faith, perhaps dies a martyr's death or is aided by a miracle – the variations are many. At any rate, the main emphasis is on the ultimate beatification of the hero. The Divine Hand is always involved.

There are other medieval genres, of course, but these three are the ones that have been applied to *Willehalm* most frequently. Certainly, *Willehalm* contains elements of each. It would appear easily possible to eliminate the genre of legend. To be sure, Willehalm did become a saint eventually, and Wolfram does speak of him in the prologue as a saint, an intercessor for knights: 'Let every knight who calls for his aid in time of trouble be assured that . . . Guillaume will declare that same distress before God . . . That doughty, noble intercessor knows every sorrow which can befall a knight' (p. 18). Furthermore, the Hand of God is very much in evidence in the ultimate victory of the Christians (for instance, the sarcophagi of the fallen heroes of the first battle impede the heathens' charge in the second; Rennewart is the unwitting agent of God in forcing the French to return to fight). But most such elements are part and parcel of the source, and that is anything but a legend. Nor does it seem that Wolfram is trying to remodel it into a saint's life. The thrust of the narrative is towards the victory of the Christians, not specifically to glorify the life of a saint, saint though he may have become.

Neither of the other alternatives seems to fit exclusively either, although there are certainly elements of both in *Willehalm*. There is action, but mostly only in the battles, and even here it is more generalized than the largely individual heroic combat of the source. It is not action for its own sake. In fact, Wolfram repeatedly deplores the killing, whereas *Aliscans* delights in every heathen death. Scholars may not be of one mind regarding the question of 'development' in *Willehalm*, but surely all would agree that Wolfram has given his characters considerable depth, and the difficulties they face are not the simple ones of the *chanson*. The people themselves are much more like those of the courtly romance in their attitudes towards one another, in their sense of propriety, even though propriety may be violated occasionally, and in the elaborate *courtoisie* of their celebrations and entertainments, not to mention the great emphasis laid on Love and the service of ladies. Despite its 'ending' Willehalm seems much more akin to the courtly romance than to the heroic epic.

The recasting of heroic material into a courtly mould must have presented Wolfram with many problems, but they had been recently faced by the poet of the *Nibelungenlied*, who had fused the heroic Nibelungen material with the Kriemhild romance. A version of this was undoubtedly known to Wolfram. Like that poet, Wolfram created a 'courtly' epic based on heroic sources, but *not* a true courtly romance. *Willehalm* is a work that does not fall into conventional categories. The term 'tragic romance' has been suggested for this unique work, and we are inclined to agree that it is quite appropriate, regardless of our differences of opinion about the ending.

NOTES

INTRODUCTION

1. An excellent new English translation by A. T. Hatto is available in this series.
2. Also available in English translation by A. T. Hatto in this series. We take our quotations from *Tristan* and *Parzival* from Professor Hatto's translations.

TEXT

1. The Old French author of the *Couronnement de Louis* tells how Guillaume lost the tip of his nose in his encounter with the Saracen giant Corsolt, whom he killed. Later in *Willehalm* Giburc uses this distinctive feature to identify her husband (p. 58).
2. We use this spelling throughout, to distinguish the Count Palatine from his uncle, Willehalm's brother Bertram.
3. 'Soldier': not to be confused with modern English usage. A 'soldier' in the Middle Ages was simply a knight fighting in the pay of someone else, an honourable way of gaining wealth and renown. The term has none of the negative connotations of 'mercenary', hence we have retained the original. Similarly, in the case of the designations of various heathen ranks and titles such as 'amazur', 'emeral' and 'eskelir', where modern equivalents are difficult to find or are not readily understood, we have left them in their original forms.
4. In his *Eneit* (= *Aeneid*) Heinrich von Veldeke refers to a figure of Amor in the temple holding a salve-jar in one hand and two

spears in the other. One spear is of gold, signifying love; the other is of lead, signifying indifference or even hate. Wolfram is obviously referring to the golden spear here and to the salve-jar which represents the healing power of requited love, overcoming the yearning and anguish caused by a wound from Amor's golden spear.

5. The name of Korsaz seems to be an alternative form of Korsant, which Wolfram uses elsewhere to denote this king.

6. In Wolfram's *Parzival* Feirefiz is the half-brother of Parzival. The child of the heathen queen Belakane and Gahmuret, later to be the father of Parzival, Feirefiz is characterized by his distinctive colouring, 'black and white like a page of parchment'. He is famed also for his power as a king and always associated with enormous wealth.

7. The Baruc is the spiritual leader of the heathens, as opposed to Terramer, who is the secular leader, the Admirat.

8. Sekundille, beloved of Parzival's half-brother Feirefiz, is a heathen queen always associated with great wealth. In *Parzival* Book XV it is she who inspires Feirefiz in his fateful battle with Parzival.

9. Wolfram addresses the spirit of his story, here personified as Lady Adventure.

10. In the source Vivien momentarily forgets his oath never to flee from the Saracens but Wolfram does not relate such an episode. The reference here to cowardice thus has no foundation and adds poignancy to the confession of this sinless boy.

11. Medieval legend had it that the soldier who pierced the side of Christ (John 19:34) was a blind man whose sight was restored to him by the blood of Christ when it ran down his spear and on to his hand, which he then raised to his eyes. Wolfram refers to this familiar legend again (p. 154). The apocryphal Gospel of Nicodemus calls the soldier Longinus.

12. Dismas is the name given by the Gospel of Nicodemus to the second of the two malefactors crucified along with Christ. Luke 23:42–3 relates that 'he said unto Jesus, Lord, remember me when thou comest into thy kingdom. And Jesus said unto him, Verily I say unto thee, Today shalt thou be with me in paradise.'

13. Traditionally the death of a martyr was accompanied by a radiant light and a mysterious fragrance.

14. Book II of *Parzival* tells of the costly funeral arranged for Parzival's father Gahmuret by the Baruc, who accorded him Christian burial when he died in his service. The grave-stone was a ruby surmounted by an emerald cross.

15. Heinrich von Veldeke, whose *Eneit* was composed in the last quarter of the twelfth century, was much admired by Wolfram and his contemporaries and acknowledged as the master, but this reference to the older poet's ability to write better is not necessarily to be taken at its face value: Wolfram is capable of such expressions of humility when he knows it to be ill-founded (cf. end of Book VIII and p. 272).

16. Wolfram uses the term 'Roman King' for Louis the Pious throughout the poem. He speaks also of Charlemagne, Louis' father, as 'Emperor' and of the office of 'Roman Emperor', of what later became known as the 'Holy Roman Empire', but strangely enough does not accord Louis that title, even though Louis is quite clearly seen as the head of the 'Empire'. We have followed Wolfram's practice.

17. All manner of remedies are used in an effort to cure the terrible wound of Anfortas, the King of the Grail in *Parzival*.

18. The circumstances which led to the death of Baligan at the hand of Charlemagne would be familiar to Wolfram's audience from the *Rolandslied*.

19. Wolfram's dismissive reference to Chrétien de Troyes resembles his criticism late in *Parzival*, when he maintains that Chrétien had not told the story properly, but there seems to be no reasonable explanation of why he should suddenly refer to Chrétien as his source here.

20. One explanation is that this refers to the Gates (Pillars) of Hercules, the ancient mythological name for the promontories at the eastern entrance to the Straits of Gibraltar.

21. 'Liver sea' translates the German *Lebermeer*, in the Middle Ages the designation for a fabulous, dangerous coagulated sea in which ships could become hopelessly mired. It was thought to lie in the north-west.

22. Wolfram leaves his audience in no doubt about the way in which Willehalm insults his sister, but he does not actually use the abusive words of his source and explains that he refrains from doing so out of consideration for his courtly listeners.
23. *Not* the modern English 'pub-keeper' but rather a member of the heretical Manichaean sect of the Paulicians (Old French *popelicant*). The spelling and meaning may have been confused with the biblical 'publicans' (Latin *publicani*), the Jews who collected taxes for the Romans.
24. Books V and XVI of *Parzival* describe the anguish of the Grail King against the background of the sumptuous Grail Castle.
25. The precise nature of this pastime is unclear. It is apparently Old French *joer as barres*, which had been recently introduced into Germany and involved leaping over hurdles.
26. The Middle Ages considered Plato a prophet, an idea that goes back to the early Alexandrine Church Fathers. The sibyls as prophetesses from classical antiquity were also incorporated into Christian tradition at an early stage and their prophecies interpreted from the Christian point of view. Wolfram seems to have regarded Sibyl as a proper name. In *Parzival* Book IX, too, he links Sibyl and Plato as authorities on the sin of mankind and, there, as prophets of redemption.
27. We have changed Wolfram's form Helias (Elias) to the form Elijah in accordance with the Authorized Version. The Bible does not link the names of Elijah and Enoch as Wolfram does both here and in Book VI (p. 155) but it does state that each was taken up to heaven (2 Kings 2:11; Hebrews 11:5). Giburc's assertion, both here and in Book VI, that Elijah and Enoch, though heathen, were not condemned to perdition, is based on orthodox teaching, as is her statement that all the other children of Adam were destined for hell until Christ burst open the gates and released them.
28. In the *Chanson de Roland* Marsilie died of grief and disappointment *after* the battle in which he had lost his right hand at the sword of Roland. It is Wolfram's idea, too, to make Tibalt the nephew of Marsilie and Terramer the cousin of Baligan.
29. See pp. 67 and 229.

30. In *La Prise d'Orange* Guillaume entered the city of Orange peaceably when he gained his bride.

31. We understand Giburc's words here as an implied threat.

32. The reference is to the *Eneit* of Heinrich von Veldeke, which Wolfram could assume to be known to his audience.

33. The notion of a celestial hierarchy stems from Colossians 1:16 and was known to the Middle Ages in the formulation of nine choirs, divided into three groups according to their proximity to God. The nine choirs are

I	1. Seraphim	II	4. Dominions	III	7. Virtues
	2. Cherubim		5. Principalities		8. Archangels
	3. Thrones		6. Powers		9. Angels

The tenth choir was reserved for those fallen angels who had joined Lucifer in his rebellion.

34. Wolfram shows some considerable confusion about this character, whom he adopted from his source. The French source *Aliscans* called him *li caitis* ('the captive'), because he had been imprisoned as a boy in Spain, but Wolfram, not knowing this or misunderstanding the word, translates it as 'poor', knowing at least that the young man had no possessions, though for this *Aliscans* had supplied the explanation: he had renounced possessions in order to be unencumbered in his pursuit of the Saracens. Wolfram calls him consistently *the* Schetis, translates it as 'the Poor' and adds to the confusion with the adjective *pauvre* (see just below in the text). In the original list of the sons of Heimrich of Narbonne (p. 20) he is named fourth, but Wolfram later insists that he is the youngest of the brothers (p. 129).

35. Parzival's father, as the younger of two brothers, had found himself without inheritance on the death of his father. Gahmuret, like the sons of Heimrich of Narbonne, had made his way in the world through chivalry.

36. The miraculous burial of the Christians in sarcophagi is not mentioned in Wolfram's source. However, there is an old Roman cemetery near Arles with numerous sarcophagi that may be seen even today. Wolfram must have known of the existence of such a cemetery (though it is impossible to say with any

certainty how he knew it), and incorporated it into his tale. The stone coffins constitute an important feature in *Willehalm*, here, where the Christian slain are believed to have been buried by no human hand, and later, when Terramer interprets the field strewn with stone coffins as evidence of the intervention of the 'sorcerer' Jesus, who has supplied an impediment to the heathen onslaught (p. 177).

37. The language which Wolfram uses to describe Rennewart is in general colourful and exaggerated, and he associates with him a number of vivid images.

38. The reference is to Book III of *Parzival*, where the young hero encounters a group of knights on horseback and, brought up in ignorance of chivalry, takes them for gods, having heard from his mother that God is 'brighter than the day'. The leader of the knights is Karnahkarnanz who is greatly impressed by young Parzival's radiant beauty and from whose lips Parzival first hears the word 'knight'.

39. This vivid statement has the ring of a proverb of some kind.

40. Legend had it that the remains of St James the Elder were buried in Compostela which became in the Middle Ages a popular place of pilgrimage. St James of Compostela (Santiago) is the patron saint of Spain.

41. The reference is almost certainly to the custom of sending dainties to one's fellow-guests at table.

42. Anfortas, King of the Grail, transgressed the law of the Grail by serving Orgeluse who was not his elected queen. He received the terrible wound as punishment and his whole kingdom was cast with him into desolation. *Parzival* also tells of the relationship between Anfortas and the heathen Queen Sekundille, later the beloved of Feirefiz. Among the gifts which she bestowed on him was her servant Cundrie who then became the messenger of the Grail. Here, as elsewhere, Wolfram refers to Sekundille in order to give his audience a familiar point of comparison in his description of great wealth (cf. pp. 40, 73, 128). This whole paragraph represents our attempt to handle an extremely complex piece of Wolfram's syntax.

43. *Parzival* Book XVI describes how the Grail King was restored to

youthful radiance when Parzival released him from his agony by his question 'Uncle, what ails you?'

44. Wolfram is thinking of a political poem in which Walther von der Vogelweide spoke of the Crusaders as 'cooks' carving up the roast of the Byzantine Empire (a reference to the seizing of Constantinople in 1203). Walther had said that the roasts thus carved were too thin and so did not last, and Wolfram links this allusion with the love poems of Walther and arrives at a macabre joke about the death of the cook.

45. It is a great honour for Rennewart to be allowed to sit next to Giburc, who shows her kindness towards him in the protective gesture of tucking part of her cloak round him.

46. Wolfram's audience would readily respond to this allusion to Nördlingen, a town in a rich agricultural area in Bavaria.

47. There is no mention of such atrocities in Wolfram's source, and this is the only place in *Willehalm* where such unchivalrous behaviour is reported, in sharp contrast to Wolfram's normal attitude to the heathens (see p. 235ff.). However, reports of atrocities by the heathens are not unknown in other *chansons de geste* and in the German *Rolandslied*.

48. *Le Charroi de Nîmes* tells of this conquest and the reference here demonstrates Wolfram's acquaintance with the wider details of the cycle.

49. Investiture took place in two different ways in the Middle Ages: an object which the lord kept (e.g. a sceptre) was used to transfer power symbolically to the vassal, or an object (e.g. a flag) was actually given by the lord to the vassal to symbolize the transfer.

50. See p. 47 and note 11.

51. See p. 115 and note 27.

52. Giburc's statements relate to the theological controversy which surrounded the fate of children who died without baptism. In general it was held that salvation was impossible without baptism, though Wolfram is clearly putting forward the opposite point of view (see also p. 277).

53. The tenth choir was reserved for those fallen angels who had joined Lucifer in his rebellion (see p. 120 and note 33).

54. Greek, four alphabet letters, referring to the four Hebrew con-

sonants JHVH (Yahveh or Jehovah), the name for God that the ancient Hebrews considered too holy to pronounce.

55. The allusion is presumably to Wolfram's younger contemporary, the poet Neidhart von Reuental, though the actual reference is obscure. Neidhart evolved a new genre of poetry which has been described as 'courtly village poetry' Though sometimes less than tasteful, the poems were popular and would doubtless have been known to Wolfram's listeners.

56. Rennewart is almost certainly alluding rather mysteriously to his hopes of winning the hand of Alize.

57. The 'secret' was that Jesus was the Messiah; cf. Matthew 16: 13–20; Mark 8: 27–30; Luke 9: 18–21.

58. cf. Matthew 26: 69–75; Mark 14: 66–72; Luke 22: 56–62; John 18: 17, 25–7.

59. cf. John 18: 10, where the defender is identified as Peter – also Matthew 26: 51; Mark 14: 47; Luke 22: 50–51.

60. cf. 2 Samuel 18: 33.

61. The opening of Book VI of *Parzival* finds King Arthur encamped with all his splendid knights on the Plain of Plimizoel and ready to send for Parzival to join his company.

62. In *Parzival* Trebuchet the smith made the sword of Anfortas which was given to Parzival at the Grail Castle. The sword had special properties, withstanding the first blow but breaking at the second and then capable of being rendered whole if held under the spring of Lac before daybreak.

63. One of the four rivers flowing from Paradise, cf. Genesis 2: 10ff.

64. Wolfram here allows himself a rare jibe at the heathen faith.

65. Wolfram's form of Old French 'bofu', a costly material.

66. The Middle Ages knew two traditions about the ostrich, either of which might be applicable here: (1) the ostrich buries its eggs in the sand and leaves them until the sun hatches them. The brilliance of the 'pofuz' might do the same here. (2) The ostrich stares at its eggs for three days, causing them to hatch in the brilliance of his gaze. Likewise the 'pofuz' here.

67. This is the same castellan of Kler who had been a lookout for Terramer (p. 167f.). Wolfram now gives his name.

68. The concept of a material, white and proof against fire, is one

which Wolfram uses also in *Parzival*, where we are told that salamander worms (a confusion with silk-worms perhaps?) had woven in fire the material from which the surcoat of Feirefiz is made. That surcoat, Feirefiz explains, protected him in his joust against a fiery knight.

69. The distance between Wissant, the port on the French coast to the south-west of Calais, and Steiermark in Austria would no doubt impress Wolfram's audience, for whom both places would be realities.

70. Wolfram uses the word *tumbrel*, which we translate as 'carts', but an alternative translation would be 'scales'. The latter alternative has the recommendation that it leads on to the next sentence where there is no ambiguity, but our preference is based on our belief that Wolfram would have been more likely to vary his image. It is not, of course, impossible that the original contained a deliberate ambiguity.

71. Lignum aloe was the firewood burned in the Grail Castle in *Parzival* Book V. Its fragrance when burned was used to fumigate Anfortas' festering wound (*Parzival* Book IX). Wolfram locates a whole forest of this exotic aromatic wood in the Orient. See also p. 48.

72. The idea of gold from Kaukasas scratched out by griffons' claws is also mentioned in *Parzival* Book II and may be traced back to the Greek historian Herodotus. Precisely what Wolfram intended with this passage is unclear. Since Tedalun was a 'forester' we have used the term 'cutting rights' for his rights to the gold of Kaukasas. We assume that his right to a 'tithe in many a desolate harbour' also refers to the gold coming from Kaukasas, which Wolfram obviously considered to be extremely remote from any civilization.

73. The word occurs also in *Parzival*, where Wolfram adds the explanation that the stone is called 'carbuncle' in the West. A carbuncle is a red stone (a ruby or perhaps a garnet).

74. The wooded hills of the Spessart in Franconia would again be familiar to Wolfram's audience and so constitute a real comparison with the vast resources of Poidjus.

75. *Parzival* again supplies a clue to the identity of the fabulous beast

used as an emblem both by Feirefiz and by Poidjus: Wolfram tells us that even poisonous snakes are doomed once 'ezidemon' has caught their scent.

76. Wolfram's sarcasm is undisguised in this reference to the conflict between the two Welfs of Bavaria and Hugo III, Count Palatine of Tübingen. Welf 'VII' was defeated at Tübingen in 1164.

77. Another (see note 63) of the four rivers flowing from Paradise; cf. Genesis 2: 13.

78. Etzel, Ermenrich, Witege: Wolfram goes to Germanic legend for the names of heroes whose exploits, even so, cannot rival those of his own heroes. The adventure attributed to Witege is perhaps to be construed as a light-hearted aside invented by Wolfram for the occasion.

79. Presumably the town of Kitzingen on the Main, not far from Wolfram's Eschenbach.

80. They intended to launch straight into the fighting with their swords.

81. Possibly the great forest known as *Herecynia silva* to the north of the Roman road which extends from the Rhineland to the Danube, or, more likely, the forest surrounding the monastery of Ellwangen, not far from Nördlingen and thus very much within the neighbourhood of Wolfram's audience.

82. Otto IV was crowned on 4 October 1209. If, as has been suggested, the remark is sarcastic, it is not unreasonable to suggest that Wolfram might not have ventured such a remark until after Otto's death in 1218. Another argument – and one which is equally difficult to support with any certainty – is that Wolfram had experienced only the coronation of 1209, not that of Friedrich II in 1220. Neither argument speaks against a dating of *Willehalm* in the late 1210s. See p. 229ff.

83. Beratzhausen on the Laber, north-west of Regensburg, seems the most likely of the possibilities here. The reference to hats remains obscure.

84. See p. 272.

85. In his *Parzival* Wolfram had told of the perilous adventures of Gawan in the Castle of Wonders, which contained the Bed of

Wonders. When Gawan leapt upon the bed it started rolling and lurching around with the effect of an earthquake.

86. The three-armed cross (*crux comissa*) as opposed to the four-armed cross (*crux immissa*) was known as the 'Antonius-cross' after the Egyptian hermit Antonius who used that sign for protection and healing. It was also the cross adopted by the Hospitaller order, which flourished at the end of the twelfth and the beginning of the thirteenth centuries. Members wore a blue three-armed cross on their black clothing. The vulgate Bible confuses the Hebrew word *tav* ('sign') with the Greek letter *tau*(T), in Ezekiel 9: 4 (*Transi per mediam Ierusalem et signa Thau in fronte virorum gementium et dolentium*). This mark became associated with the marks placed on the doorposts by the Jews in Egypt at the first Passover (Exodus 12: 17ff.). Both of these stood as prefigurations of the cross of Christ, even though they were never considered identical. Apparently Wolfram thought they were.

87. i.e. Baligan, in the *Rolandslied*, mentioned here as Terramer's uncle (see p. 267).

88. Another of the references to the secret love of the pair.

89. A precious green silk interwoven with gold thread. The Grail is carried on a piece of *achmardi* in *Parzival*, where Wolfram tells us several times that the material is made in Arabi.

90. An area in Nuremberg where the work-shops of armour-makers could be found.

91. See p. 251f. and note 6 below.

92. See p. 187 and note 75.

93. A reference to the *Rolandslied*: Oliphant is the name of Roland's horn.

94. Another reference to the events of the *Rolandslied*.

A SECOND INTRODUCTION

1. In his *Wigalois* I. 6346.

2. *Rennewart* I. 21711: 'Alas, skilful Wolfram! Would that God had found it fitting to grant me his artistry when he [Wolfram]

was not to live any longer: then I would be completely unconcerned [about my ability as a poet].'

3. Edited by D. McMillan, Paris, 1949–50 (2 vols.).

4. Published in *Acta Sanctorum ordinis Sancti Benedicti*, saec. iv, vol. 1, p. 72, and in *Acta Sanctorum Bollandiana*, vol. vi, p. 798.

5. Edited by E. Wienbeck, W. Hartnacke and P. Rasch, Halle a. d. S., 1903.

6. The *Hildebrandslied*, or *Lay of Hildebrand*, is the oldest extant piece of German heroic poetry, dating from the early ninth century. In it Hildebrand, having been away for many years, returns home to an armed confrontation with his son, who has grown to manhood and refuses to recognize his father, believing him to be dead and suspecting a trick on Hildebrand's part. At this point the poetic fragment breaks off, but in all probability the ending was tragic with Hildebrand forced to kill his son.

7. The relationship of the uncle and the sister's son was, of course, traditionally a very special one, and it is one which Wolfram stresses throughout.

8. A complete, up-to-date listing is given in Schröder's edition, pp. xxi–lxv (see Introduction, p. 14).

9. We again take our quotations from A. T. Hatto's translation, p. 62.

10. *Parzival*, p. 27, translated by A. T. Hatto.

INDEX OF NAMES
IN
'WILLEHALM'

We have compiled two lists of names in *Willehalm*, in the hope that they will be of help to our readers in making their way through the mass of names in the work. The first is a list of characters, together with an indication of the first appearance or mention, and a further indication of significant features, relationships or function. In this list we have included the names of the heathen gods, of swords and horses, since these play an active role in the poem. The second list is of place names and of the associations of places. We have made no attempt to identify the places which Wolfram names, but we would draw the attention of interested readers to the work of Charles Passage and of Werner Schröder (see p. 310 and p. 14).

CHARACTERS

AKERIN (1) (p. 36), otherwise referred to as the Baruc (p. 50), the spiritual leader of the heathens (the Caliph of Bagdad), as opposed to the Admirat (Terramer), who is their political leader. His seat is in Baldac. First mentioned as a man of widespread reputation, he is later mentioned in connection with his magnanimous burial of Gahmuret (p. 50).

AKERIN (2) (p. 50), King of Marroch and of the race of the Baruc; one of the fifteen kings who attack Willehalm (p. 50); before Terramer enters the second battle, Akerin brings him his ruby quiver and his bow (p. 177); he fights to the right of Terramer.

ALEXANDER (p. 209), one of the sons of Purrel.

ALIZE (p. 85), daughter of the King of France, beloved of Rennewart and his inspiration in the second battle. Her beauty is described at length (p. 85ff.); she helps to reconcile Willehalm and his

BUOV of Commercey, (p. 20), first mentioned as one of the sons of Heimrich of Narbonne, Willehalm's brother; with Scherins and Alize, he persuades the Queen to rejoin the company after the quarrel with Willehalm (p. 90).

BUR (p. 50), King of Siglimessa, one of the kings who attack Willehalm.

EHMEREIZ (p. 29), King of Todjerne, son of Giburc and Tibalt; one of the fifteen kings who attack Willehalm but Willehalm refuses to fight with him (p. 50); characterized by his beautiful cloak, made of *pofuz* (p. 181).

EKTOR (p. 175), King of Salenie, leader of second battalion in the second battle, standard-bearer of Terramer (p. 175), slain by Bernart of Brabant (p. 211).

EMBRONS (p. 50), King of Alimec, one of the fifteen kings who attack Willehalm, and slain by Willehalm (p. 51).

ESKELABON (p. 28), King of Seres, brother of Galafre, killed by Vivianz (p. 37).

ESSERE (p. 52), emeral who gave his sword to Arofel, in Halzebier's army; slain by Rennewart (p. 205).

FABORS (p. 31), King of Mecka, one of the sons of Terramer.

FABUR (p. 178), a king whose land is across the Fison, fights to the left of Terramer and is slain by Rennewart (p. 203).

FAUSSABRE (p. 29), King of Alamansura, Terramer's sister's son, dies in the first battle (p. 131).

FRABEL (p. 50), King of Korasen, one of the fifteen kings who attack Willehalm, and slain by him.

GALAFRE (p. 29), King of Kanach, 'whiter than a swan' (p. 29), brother of Eskelabon, slain by Vivianz (p. 37).

GANDALUZ (p. 182), Count of Champagne, slain by Tedalun in the second battle (p. 216).

GASTABLE (p. 50), King of Komis, one of the fifteen kings who attack Willehalm, and slain by him.

GAUDIERS (p. 24), of Toulouse, one of the eight Christians taken captive by Halzebier (p. 37), but not among those listed as freed by Rennewart (p. 204); his fate remains obscure.

GAUDIN (p. 24), 'with the brown hair', one of the eight taken captive by Halzebier and freed by Rennewart.

GERART (p. 23), of Blayes, brother of Samson and Witschart, one of the eight taken captive by Halzebier and freed by Rennewart (p. 204).

GIBERT (p. 20), brother of Willehalm, with Bertram of Berbester, joint leader of fourth battalion in second battle.

GIBOEZ (p. 168), the Castellan of Kler, Tibalt's standard-bearer (p. 181), the look-out (p. 167), wounded by Rennewart (p. 211).

GIBUE (p. 215), a heathen king slain by Rennewart.

GIBURC (p. 21), Arabel, the heathen wife of Tibalt, took the name of Giburc when she was baptized and became the wife of Willehalm.

GIFLEIZ (p. 183), a count from the land of Arnalt, jousts with Sinagun.

GIRANT (p. 209), of Bordeaux, slain by Purrel.

GLORJAX (p. 31), one of the sons of Terramer.

GLORION (1) (p. 29), a heathen king, slain by Vivianz.

GLORION (2) (p. 174), King of Ascalon, fights in the sixth battalion in the second battle, under Aropatin.

GOLIAM (p. 211), King of Belestigweiz, slain by Rennewart.

GORHANT (p. 32), king who accompanies King Margot, has his land near the Ganjas (p. 32), his men have horny skins and low like cows (p. 32), in the ninth battalion in the second battle.

GORIAX (p. 50), King of Kordubin, one of the fifteen kings who attack Willehalm; he escapes.

GROHIER (p. 176), King of Nomadjentesin, responsible for Terramer's chain-mail leg-coverings (p. 176), fights to the right of Terramer (p. 177).

GWIGRIMANZ (p. 23), 'the Burgundian', fights together with Vivianz in the first battle (p. 58), not clear what happens to him; he probably dies.

HALZEBIER (p. 21), King of Falfunde, relative of Terramer and Giburc; takes eight Christians captive in first battle (p. 37) and is himself slain by the surviving seven in the second battle (p. 205f.); deals the mortal wound to Vivianz (p. 37); opens the action of the second battle (p. 170), slays Hunas of Saintes (p. 205).

HAROPIN (p. 178), 'the old Tananarkois' (p. 208), father of Kliboris, fights to the left of Terramer in the second battle (p. 178).

HASTE (p. 50), King of Alligues, one of the fifteen kings who attack Willehalm, and slain by him.

HAUKAUUS (p. 50), King of Nubia; one of the fifteen kings who attack Willehalm, he escapes.

HEIMRICH of Narbonne (p. 19), father of seven sons, including Willehalm; husband of Irmschart; a brave old man with a white beard; sits at table with Giburc (p. 135), leads the second battalion in the second battle.

HEIMRICH (p. 20), 'the Schetis' (see p. 286 note 34), Willehalm's brother, leads the fifth battalion in the second battle, together with King Schilbert of Tandarnas, slays Poidwiz (p. 202).

HUC of Lunzel (p. 209), killed by Purrel (p. 209); father of Anselm of Poitou.

HUNAS of Saintes (p. 24), one of the eight taken captive by Halzebier and freed by Rennewart, but then slain by Halzebier (p. 205).

HUWES of Milan (p. 24), taken captive in the first battle though not in the list at the time, he replaces Samson in Giburc's list (p. 58) and Gaudiers at the time of his release (p. 204).

IRMSCHART of Pavia (p. 71), old countess, wife of Heimrich of Narbonne, mother of Willehalm, to whom she offers her aid (p. 88).

ISERET (p. 213), a heathen king.

IWAN (p. 208), count from Rouen in Normandy who bears the imperial standard.

JOFREIT (p. 213), from Senlis, a leader in the second battle.

JOSWE (p. 50), King of Alahoz, one of the fifteen kings who attack Willehalm, and slain by him.

JOSWEIZ (p. 29), King of Amatiste, ruler of Hippipotiticun, son of Matusales and a Moorish woman, coloured like the swan (p. 190), leader of the seventh battalion in the second battle.

JOZERANZ (p. 24), Willehalm's kinsman, not clear whether he dies or is taken prisoner in the first battle.

LIGNMAREDI (p. 206), name of the horse belonging to King Poidwiz but appropriated by Rennewart (p. 206).

LOUIS (p. 63), King of France, son of Charlemagne, husband of the daughter of Heimrich of Narbonne, thus brother-in-law to Willehalm; father of Alize.

MAHMETE (p. 21), one of the heathen gods, 'favourite god' of Terramer (p. 21).

MALAKIN (p. 215), heathen king slain by Rennewart.

MALAKRONS (p. 213), a heathen king.

MALARZ (p. 31), one of the sons of Terramer.

MALATONS (p. 213), a heathen king.

MALATRAS (p. 31), one of the sons of Terramer.

MARGOT (p. 32), King of Pozzidant and of Orkeise, which lies close to the edge of the earth (p. 32); in ninth battalion, under Marlanz of Jerikop (p. 175).

MARJADOX (p. 213), heathen king.

MARLANZ (p. 174), King of Jerikop, leader of the ninth battalion in the second battle.

MARSCHIBEIZ (p. 41), name of the horse of King Talimon, taken by Willehalm and killed by him (p. 41). (See p. 235).

MARSILJE (p. 116), King of Saragossa, uncle of Tibalt.

MATREIZ (p. 31), one of the sons of Terramer.

MATRIBLEIZ (p. 61), King of Skandinavia, Gruonlant and Gaheviez, highly esteemed and a kinsman of Giburc; he was to have supervised the terms of the truce (p. 132) and at the 'end' of the work he is released from captivity by Willehalm so that he may arrange fitting burial for the heathen slain and bear Willehalm's message back to Terramer (p. 223, see p. 276ff.).

MATTAHEL (p. 50), King of Tafar, one of the fifteen kings who attack Willehalm, and slain by him.

MATUSALES (p. 31), King of Amatiste, brother-in-law of Terramer, father of Josweiz whom he sent out from his land of Hippipotiticun (p. 174) to fight on the side of Terramer; known for his power and wealth (p. 190).

MERABJAX (p. 31), one of the sons of Terramer.

MILE (p. 23), Willehalm's sister's son, slain by Terramer (p. 26),

second battle; bears the beast *ezidemon* in his banner which is carried by Tedalun. The last we hear of him is that he refuses to answer the challenge of Rennewart (p. 216).

POIDWIZ (1) (p. 174), King of Rabes, son of Oukin, slain by Heimrich the Schetis (p. 202); his horse runs empty-saddled alongside his old father and prompts his poignant lament (p. 206).

POIDWIZ (2) (p. 33), son of Anki, in the company of Poidjus and Tesereiz, fights in the second battle in the ninth battalion under Marlanz of Jerikop.

POUFAMEIZ (p. 29), King of Ingulie, dies at the hand of Willehalm in the first battle (p. 41).

PRÉCIEUSE (p. 202), name of the sword of Bernart of Brabant, gained by Charlemagne from the heathen king Baligan.

PRUANZ (p. 213), a heathen king.

PURREL (p. 178), King of Nubiant, husband of Baligan's daughter; in the second battle he fights together with his fourteen sons in Terramer's army, to his left; he wears marvellous armour, bright green and as hard as a diamond, made from the skin of the dragon *neitune* (p. 208); his helmet is rainbow-coloured, made of the skin of the dragon *muntunzel*, impermeable to thrust or blow; the club of Rennewart breaks on it and the blow crushes him and renders him senseless; his men bear him away to a ship (p. 211).

PUTEGAN (p. 176), King of Ormalereiz, responsible for sounding the horn of Terramer (p. 176).

PUZZAT (p. 33), the name of Willehalm's horse in the first battle, replaced by Arofel's Volatin (p. 53f.); conversation of Willehalm with Puzzat (p. 43).

REMON (p. 209), baron from Anjou, slain by Purrel (p. 209).

RENNEWART (p. 101), son of Terramer, brother of Giburc, employed in the kitchen of King Louis; beloved of Alize; fights as the 'right hand' of Willehalm in the second battle and is instrumental in securing victory for the Christians; he is missing as the work 'ends' (see p. 268ff.).

RUBIUN (p. 29), heathen King of Azagouc, slain by Vivianz (p. 37).

RUBUAL (p. 31), heathen king in the retinue of Josweiz, fights in the seventh battalion under Josweiz in the second battle.

TAMPASTE (1) (p. 29), King of Naroklin, who dies at the hands of Vivianz (p. 37), and is remembered (p. 215); father of Tampaste (2).

TAMPASTE (2) (p. 50), young King of Tabrasten, son of Tampaste (1), one of the fifteen kings who attack Willehalm, he escapes and is slain by Rennewart (p. 215).

TEDALUN (p. 186), chief forester of Lignaloe, Burgrave of Tasme, standard-bearer of Poidjus, slain by Rennewart (p. 216).

TENEBREIZ (p. 215), one of the sons of Purrel, leaves battle with Terramer (p. 215).

TENEBRUNS (p. 51), King of Liwes Nugruns, whom Willehalm slays just before he slays Arofel (p. 51).

TERRAMER (p. 21), the Admirat, secular ruler of the heathens, the father of Giburc, son of Kanabeus, ruler of nine kingdoms, King of Kordes, Gorgozane, Happe, Lumpin, Muntespir, Poye, Semblie, Suntin, Tenabri; ruler of Baldac. Severely wounded by Willehalm in the second battle and borne away by sea (p. 215).

TERVIGANT (p. 22), one of the heathen gods.

TESEREIZ (p. 32), King of Collone, 'the proud Latrisetan' (p. 187), praised particularly for his service to Love, slain by Willehalm in the first battle (p. 56).

TIBALT (p. 21), first husband of Giburc, 'the Arabois' (p. 85), King of Arabi and Todjerne, Kler and Sibilje; described as kind and gentle, courtly and courageous (p. 176), commands second battalion in the second battle with his son Ehmereiz (p. 171).

TROHAZZABE (p. 181), Duke of Karkassun, standard-bearer of Ehmereiz.

TURKANT (p. 29), King of Turkanie, brother of Arfiklant, slain by Willehalm in the first battle (p. 41).

TURPIUN (p. 29), King of Falturmie, dies at the hand of Willehalm (p. 41).

UTREIZ (p. 31), one of the sons of Terramer.

VERMANDOIS, the Duke of, (p. 214).

VIVIANZ (p. 23), nephew of Willehalm, brought up by Giburc; dies a saintly death (p. 48) and becomes a major impetus to the second battle (see pp. 252ff.).

VOLATIN (p. 53) name of the horse of Arofel, appropriated after his death by Willehalm.

WILLEHALM (p. 20), the Margrave, the Marquis, Willehalm *au court nez*, husband of Giburc, eldest son of Heimrich of Narbonne (see pp. 231ff. and 242ff.).

WIMAR (p. 75), a merchant who, alone at the French Court, pays attention to Willehalm and gives him hospitality for the night (p. 75ff.); later Wimar is entertained at table with Willehalm and his kinsmen (p. 95).

WITSCHART (p. 23), brother of Gerart and Samson of Blayes; taken prisoner by Halzebier (p. 37), released by Rennewart (p. 204).

ZERNUBILE (p. 178), heathen King of Amirafel, responsible for the drums and trumpets (p. 178), slain by Heimrich of Narbonne (p. 201).

PLACES

The following is not a complete list of place names in *Willehalm*, but it includes the most important names in the poem.

ADRAMAHUT (p. 73), place of origin of fine silks.

AGREMUNTIN (p. 174), kingdom of Josweiz.

AHSIM (p. 80), kingdom of Pinel.

ALAHOZ (p. 50), land of Joswe.

ALAMANSURA (p. 80), place of origin of fine silks; a distant land known for its hot climate.

ALIMEC (p. 50), land of King Embrons.

ALLIGUES (p. 50), kingdom of Haste.

AMATISTE (p. 29), kingdom of Josweiz.

AMIRAFEL (p. 178), land of King Zernubile.

ANJOU (p. 209), place of origin of Baron Remon.

ARABI (p. 29), city of Tibalt; place of origin of fine silks.

ARABIE (p. 63), land of King Tibalt.

ASCALON (p. 174), kingdom of Glorion.

ASSIGARZJUNDE (p. 177), place of origin of Terramer's helmet.

AZAGOUC (p. 174), kingdom of Rubiun; place of origin of silks and precious stones.

BAILIE (p. 172), kingdom of Sinagun.

BALDAC (p. 50), seat of the Baruc and place of burial of Parzival's father Gahmuret (p. 50); Terramer is designated the Protector of Baldac.

BARBERIE (p. 50), kingdom of Kursaus.

BEATERRE (p. 178), land of King Samirant.

BELESTIGWEIZ (p. 207), land of King Goliam.

BERBESTER (p. 154), city of Bertram, and his battle-cry.

BLAYES (p. 23), place of origin of the brothers Gerart, Samson and Witschart.

BOCTAN (p. 41), land of King Talimon (1).

BOITENDROIT (p. 177), kingdom of Samirant.

BRABANT (p. 92), land of Duke Bernart, and his battle-cry.

COLLONE (p. 33), kingdom of Tesereiz.

COMMERCEY (p. 58), city of Buov.

DANJATA (p. 50), land of King Korsuble.

ETNISE (p. 174), kingdom of Pohereiz.

FALFUNDE (p. 25), land of Halzebier.

FALTURMIE (p. 29), kingdom of Turpiun.

GAHEVIEZ (p. 174), kingdom of Matribleiz.

GANFASSASCHE (p. 45), kingdom of Aropatin.

GANJAS (p. 32), kingdom of Gorhant.

GIRONDE (p. 70), land of Count Arnalt.

GLORJET (p. 117), palace of Willehalm in Orange.

GORGOZANE (p. 32), one of the lands of Terramer.

GRIFFANE (p. 32), part of the realm of Poidjus.

GRIKULANE (p. 33), part of the territory of Tesereiz.

GRUONLANT (p. 174), one of the lands of King Matribleiz.

HAPPE (p. 32), one of the lands of Terramer.

HIPPIPOTITICUN (p. 174), part of the territory of Josweiz.

IMANZIE (p. 177), land of King Oukidant.

INDIA (p. 21), land of Sekundille, and Feirefiz.

INGULIE (p. 40), land of Poufameiz.

JANFUSE (p. 174), land of Korsant.

JAZERANZ (p. 177), place of origin of hauberks.

JERIKOP (p. 174), kingdom of Marlanz.

JETAKRANC (p. 190), place of origin of mother of King Josweiz.

PAVIA (p. 80), place of origin of the Countess Irmschart.

PERSIA (p. 30), land of Arofel.

POINZAKLINS (p. 188), river which borders territory of Aropatin.

POITOU (p. 209), land of Count Anselm.

PONTARLIER (p. 88), land of Count Scherins.

POYE (p. 32), one of the lands of Terramer.

POZZIDANT (p. 32), kingdom of Margot.

RABES (p. 174), land of King Oukin and his son Poidwiz.

RANKULAT (p. 59), kingdom of Libilun.

SAIGASTIN (p. 50), kingdom of Korsude.

SAINTES (p. 24), place of origin of Hunas.

SALENIE (p. 175), kingdom of Ektor.

SAMARGONE (p. 73), capital of Persia, seat of Arofel, battle-cry of Arofel's army in the second battle.

SCHIPELPUNTE (p. 177), kingdom of Bohedan.

SEMBLI (p. 32), one of the lands of Terramer.

SERES (p. 28), kingdom of Eskelabon.

SIBILJE (p. 116), city of Marsilie, to which Tibalt lays claim.

SIGLIMESSA (p. 50), city of King Bur, a centre of commerce.

SKANDINAVIA (p. 80), kingdom of Matribleiz.

SOTIERS (p. 33), one of the lands of Tesereiz.

SUNTIN (p. 32), one of the lands of Terramer.

TABRASTEN (p. 50), kingdom of Tampaste (2).

TAFAR (p. 50), kingdom of Mattahel.

TAHENMUNT (p. 213), mountain of uncertain location.

TANANARKE (p. 178), kingdom of Kliboris.

TANDARNAS (p. 125), kingdom of Schilbert, battle-cry of the fifth battalion in the second battle.

TASME (p. 45), city of Poidjus, place of origin of precious silks; Tedalun is the Burgrave of Tasme.

TENABRI (p. 32), one of the lands of Terramer.

TERMIS (p. 35), palace of Willehalm where Vivianz was brought up and made a knight.

TODJERNE (p. 29), land of Ehmereiz who assumed its possession when Giburc left; previously she had worn the crown there (p. 116).

TOTEL (p. 33), place of origin of Willehalm's helmet.

SUGGESTIONS
FOR
FURTHER READING

As we have said in the Introduction (p. 14), we have confined ourselves to works in English and have omitted reference to articles in journals, though there are many illuminating articles which we could have mentioned: for further more detailed study we would refer the reader to the bibliographical works which follow our list.

Bacon S. A. *The Source of Wolfram's Willehalm* (*Sprache und Dichtung* 4), Tübingen 1910.

Gibbs M. E. *Wiplîchez wîbes reht. A Study of the Women Characters in the Works of Wolfram von Eschenbach.* Duquesne Studies, Philological Series 15, 1972.

Gibbs M. E. *Narrative Art in Wolfram's 'Willehalm'*, Göppinger Arbeiten zur Germanistik 159, 1976.

Green D. H. and Johnson L. P. *Approaches to Wolfram von Eschenbach*, Mikrokosmos 5, Bern–Frankfurt-am-Main–Las Vegas, 1978.

Hatto A. T. *Wolfram von Eschenbach: Parzival*, Penguin 1980.

Lofmark C. J. *Rennewart in Wolfram's 'Willehalm'*, Cambridge 1972.

Poag J. F. *Wolfram von Eschenbach* (Twayne's World Authors Series TWAS 233), New York 1972.

Richey M. F. *Studies of Wolfram von Eschenbach*, London 1957.

Walshe M. O'C. *Medieval German Literature*, London 1962 (especially pp. 156–75).

Translations of *Willehalm*

Kartschoke D. *Willehalm. Urtext und Übersetzung*, Berlin 1968.
Passage C. E. *The Middle High German Poem of Willehalm by Wolfram von Eschenbach*, translated into English prose, New York 1977.
Unger O. *Wolfram von Eschenbach, Willehalm*, Göppinger Arbeiten zur Germanistik, 100, 1973. (A translation into modern German verse.)

Bibliographical Works

Bumke J. *Wolfram von Eschenbach Forschung seit 1945*, Bericht und Bibliographie, Munich 1970.
Bumke J. *Wolfram von Eschenbach*, Sammlung Metzler 36, Stuttgart 1976, 4th revised edition.
Pretzel U. and Bachofer W. *Bibliographie zu Wolfram von Eschenbach*, Berlin 1968.

FOR THE BEST IN PAPERBACKS, LOOK FOR THE

In every corner of the world, on every subject under the sun, Penguin represents quality and variety – the very best in publishing today.

For complete information about books available from Penguin – including Puffins, Penguin Classics and Arkana – and how to order them, write to us at the appropriate address below. Please note that for copyright reasons the selection of books varies from country to country.

In the United Kingdom: Please write to *Dept E.P., Penguin Books Ltd, Harmondsworth, Middlesex, UB7 0DA.*

If you have any difficulty in obtaining a title, please send your order with the correct money, plus ten per cent for postage and packaging, to *PO Box No 11, West Drayton, Middlesex*

In the United States: Please write to *Dept BA, Penguin, 299 Murray Hill Parkway, East Rutherford, New Jersey 07073*

In Canada: Please write to *Penguin Books Canada Ltd, 2801 John Street, Markham, Ontario L3R 1B4*

In Australia: Please write to the *Marketing Department, Penguin Books Australia Ltd, P.O. Box 257, Ringwood, Victoria 3134*

In New Zealand: Please write to the *Marketing Department, Penguin Books (NZ) Ltd, Private Bag, Takapuna, Auckland 9*

In India: Please write to *Penguin Overseas Ltd, 706 Eros Apartments, 56 Nehru Place, New Delhi, 110019*

In the Netherlands: Please write to *Penguin Books Netherlands B.V., Postbus 3507, 1001 AH, Amsterdam*

In West Germany: Please write to *Penguin Books Ltd, Friedrichstrasse 10–12, D–6000 Frankfurt/Main 1*

In Spain: Please write to *Alhambra Longman S.A., Fernandez de la Hoz 9, E–28010 Madrid*

In Italy: Please write to *Penguin Italia s.r.l., Via Como 4, I-20096 Pioltello (Milano)*

In France: Please write to *Penguin Books Ltd, 39 Rue de Montmorency, F-75003 Paris*

In Japan: Please write to *Longman Penguin Japan Co Ltd, Yamaguchi Building, 2–12–9 Kanda Jimbocho, Chiyoda-Ku, Tokyo 101*

Hesiod/Theognis	**Theogony** and **Works and Days/Elegies**
Hippocrates	**Hippocratic Writings**
Homer	**The Iliad**
	The Odyssey
Horace	**Complete Odes and Epodes**
Horace/Persius	**Satires** and **Epistles**
Juvenal	**Sixteen Satires**
Livy	**The Early History of Rome**
	Rome and Italy
	Rome and the Mediterranean
	The War with Hannibal
Lucretius	**On the Nature of the Universe**
Marcus Aurelius	**Meditations**
Martial	**Epigrams**
Ovid	**The Erotic Poems**
	Heroides
	The Metamorphoses
Pausanias	**Guide to Greece** (in two volumes)
Petronius/Seneca	**The Satyricon/The Apocolocyntosis**
Pindar	**The Odes**
Plato	**Early Socratic Dialogues**
	Gorgias
	The Last Days of Socrates (Euthyphro/ The Apology/Crito/Phaedo)
	The Laws
	Phaedrus and **Letters VII and VIII**
	Philebus
	Protagoras and **Meno**
	The Republic
	The Symposium
	Theaetetus
	Timaeus and **Critias**

Plautus	**The Pot of Gold/The Prisoners/ The Brothers Menaechmus/ The Swaggering Soldier/Pseudolus**
	The Rope/Amphitryo/The Ghost/ A Three-Dollar Day
Pliny	**The Letters of the Younger Pliny**
Plutarch	**The Age of Alexander** (Nine Greek Lives)
	The Fall of the Roman Republic (Six Lives)
	The Makers of Rome (Nine Lives)
	The Rise and Fall of Athens (Nine Greek Lives)
	Plutarch on Sparta
Polybius	**The Rise of the Roman Empire**
Procopius	**The Secret History**
Propertius	**The Poems**
Quintus Curtius Rufus	**The History of Alexander**
Sallust	**The Jugurthine War** and **The Conspiracy of Cataline**
Seneca	**Four Tragedies** and **Octavia**
	Letters from a Stoic
Sophocles	**Electra/Women of Trachis/Philoctetes/Ajax**
	The Theban Plays (King Oedipus/Oedipus at Colonus/Antigone)
Suetonius	**The Twelve Caesars**
Tacitus	**The Agricola** and **The Germania**
	The Annals of Imperial Rome
	The Histories
Terence	**The Comedies** (The Girl from Andros/The Self-Tormentor/The Eunuch/Phormio/The Mother-in-Law/The Brothers)
Thucydides	**The History of the Peloponnesian War**
Virgil	**The Aeneid**
	The Eclogues
	The Georgics
Xenophon	**Conversations of Socrates**
	A History of My Times
	The Persian Expedition

FOR THE BEST IN PAPERBACKS, LOOK FOR THE 🐧

PENGUIN CLASSICS

Saint Anselm	**The Prayers and Meditations**
Saint Augustine	**The Confessions**
Bede	**A History of the English Church and People**
Chaucer	**The Canterbury Tales**
	Love Visions
	Troilus and Criseyde
Froissart	**The Chronicles**
Geoffrey of Monmouth	**The History of the Kings of Britain**
Gerald of Wales	**History and Topography of Ireland**
	The Journey through Wales and **The Description of Wales**
Gregory of Tours	**The History of the Franks**
Henryson	**The Testament of Cresseid and Other Poems**
Walter Hilton	**The Ladder of Perfection**
Julian of Norwich	**Revelations of Divine Love**
Thomas à Kempis	**The Imitation of Christ**
William Langland	**Piers the Ploughman**
Sir John Mandeville	**The Travels of Sir John Mandeville**
Marguerite de Navarre	**The Heptameron**
Christine de Pisan	**The Treasure of the City of Ladies**
Marco Polo	**The Travels**
Richard Rolle	**The Fire of Love**
François Villon	**Selected Poems**

FOR THE BEST IN PAPERBACKS, LOOK FOR THE (penguin)

PENGUIN CLASSICS

ANTHOLOGIES AND ANONYMOUS WORKS

The Age of Bede
Alfred the Great
Beowulf
A Celtic Miscellany
The Cloud of Unknowing and Other Works
The Death of King Arthur
The Earliest English Poems
Early Christian Writings
Early Irish Myths and Sagas
Egil's Saga
King Arthur's Death
The Letters of Abelard and Heloise
Medieval English Verse
Njal's Saga
Seven Viking Romances
Sir Gawain and the Green Knight
The Song of Roland

PO #: 4500387424